MASTER OF SHADOWS

In fifteenth-century Constantinople, Prince Constantine saves the life of a broken-hearted girl. But the price of his valour is high. John Grant is a young man on the edge of the world. His unique abilities carry him from his home in Scotland to the heart of the Byzantine Empire in search of a girl and the chance to fulfil a death-bed promise. Lẽna has remained hidden from the men who have been searching for her for many years. The fates of these three will intertwine. As the Siege of Constantinople reaches its climax, each must make a choice between head and heart, duty and destiny.

MASTER OF SHADOWS

MASTER OF SHADOWS

by

Neil Oliver

Magna Large Print Books
Long Preston, North Yorkshire,
BD23 4ND, England.

British Library Cataloguing in Publication Data.

Oliver, Neil
   Master of shadows.

   A catalogue record of this book is
   available from the British Library

   ISBN   978-0-7505-4297-5

First published in Great Britain in 2015 by Orion Books
an imprint of The Orion Publishing Group Ltd.

Cover illustration © Vaida Abdul by arrangement with
Arcangel Images

Published in Large Print 2016 by arrangement with
The Orion Publishing Group Ltd.

Magna Large Print is an imprint of Library Magna Books Ltd.

Printed and bound in Great Britain by
T.J. (International) Ltd., Cornwall, PL28 8RW

For Trudi, Evie, Archie and Teddy, my fellow travellers.
All my love, always.

ACKNOWLEDGEMENTS

I have never been more worried about releasing a book into the wild. Non-fiction feels like it can take care of itself, but a novel seems strangely vulnerable. For that reason, I have depended a great deal on the confidence and encouragement of others. I owe an enormous debt to Eugenie Furniss, my literary agent at Furniss Lawton. A thousand thank yous for all manner of support and help, but most of all for persuading me this was the right time (and for laughing along with me as nervous hysteria ran its course). The whole team at Orion got behind the project with invaluable energy. Editing is such a marvellous skill – indeed an elegant one – and I have been fortunate in finding myself in the hands of masters. Special thanks to Jon Wood and Jemima Forrester for having faith from the very beginning, for all the reading and re-reading, the vital comments and suggestions and above all the assurance that this was an idea worth sticking with. Thanks also to Graeme Williams, Angela McMahon and Julia Pidduck, and to Jane Selley for a beautiful job of copy-editing. Huge gratitude to Factual Management, to my agent Sophie Laurimore who always looks after me and listens patiently while I fret and grumble, and to

Mark Johnson and Jamie Slattery – without your daily attention, I would be forever in the wrong place, at the wrong time and without a clue. Special thanks as well to Mum and Dad, avid readers both, for raising me in a home that was always full of books. And finally, a limitless thank you to Trudi, my wife and the mother of the three best babies in the whole wide world. I love you.

For more than eleven hundred years the Byzantine Empire controlled much of Europe, as well as that part of Asia known once as Anatolia.

Its capital city was Constantinople, founded by and named after the Roman Emperor Constantine in AD 330. In the centuries that followed it became a centre of Christian learning, art and theology as well as an architectural wonder – a man-made heaven on earth.

During its long life Constantinople was besieged more than twenty times – by Arabs and Avars; Bulgarians and Persians; Slavs and Vikings and more besides. In 1204 the city fell to the Christian soldiers of the Fourth Crusade. The city was raped, sacked and torn to pieces – left in tatters until 1261, when the Byzantines took it back.

Then in 1453 the twenty-one-year-old Ottoman Sultan Mehmet II brought a truly massive army before the ancient walls of the place they called the Great City.

Standing in defiance of the young sultan's ambitions was Emperor Constantine XI. He was more than twice the age of the sultan and had inherited an empire that was unravelling and failing before his eyes.

In the years and months before the siege began, he had asked for help from throughout Christendom. But the four-centuries-old Great Schism – between the Catholic Church of Rome and the Orthodox Church of Constantinople – meant that even the Pope turned his back on the Christians of the East, and they were *left alone, to stand or fall.*

When the Ottomans arrived outside his gates, Emperor Constantine had no more than eight thousand soldiers at his command, ranged against a force of perhaps a quarter of a million men.

Among the city's defenders was a man cloaked in shadow. He is mentioned in accounts of the siege, but only in a few lines here and there.

Some writers described him as a German, but in fact he was a Scot, and his name was John Grant.

PROLOGUE

Like a loved one, the darkness took him in her arms. The ghost of the torch flame, extinguished moments before, drifted in front of him, fading to yellow and then blue. He waited until there was nothing before his eyes but steady blackness.

It was the silence that sometimes felt overwhelming underground. He held his breath, straining with the effort of listening. The silence pressed against him from all sides and leaned down from above. He was a threat to its dominion – likely to make a sound and tear apart the quiet. Only the darkness held him safe.

He reached out to the side with his right hand until his fingertips brushed against the cool wall of the tunnel. Crouching, bent over like a half-shut knife, he took a step forward into the cramped space, then another and another, and then stopped.

Instead of rock, his fingers felt empty space. He had reached a corner – a twist away towards the right. He moved sideways again until his fingers regained contact with the wall and began inching silently forward once more. Sometimes his hair brushed the roughly hewn roof of the tunnel and he flinched from it like a child ducking a blow.

In his left hand, his good hand, he clutched a knife, its blade curved like a tiger's claw. Experience had taught him that a sword was unwieldy in the tunnels, an encumbrance. He made no noise as he drifted into the darkness, all but floating over the ground as he felt for each step. His breath trailed noiselessly from his open mouth. With his eyes closed he summoned his consciousness and sent it out ahead of him, further into the void.

He had covered a dozen yards beyond the corner when, on an impulse, he stopped. He trusted his impulses, however slight. The texture of the darkness had altered. Where before it had been smooth and still, now it was disturbed, ruffled. Ripples, like waves from a pebble dropped into water, pulsed against his face and chest. Beats from an anxious heart.

There was someone else there, someone else trying to be silent but disturbing the peace just the same by being alive. He smiled. With his knife held low he reached out swiftly with his right hand, straight in front. He touched a man's face, felt stubble on the chin, and cold sweat. A gasp broke the silence – split it in two.

He stepped forward into the space created there, smelt the sour gust of the exhaled breath. His knife hand moved of its own accord.

A lammergeier draws lazy shapes in the sky above the city of Constantinople. Columns of warm air rise from white limestone buildings seared by summer heat, and the bird rides the updraughts in ever-widening loops. Always watchful of movement below, he tracks his shadow, a tiny black cross, as it flickers across the rooftops.

A thousand feet beneath his breast lies the Church of St Sophia, like a mother hen surrounded by needy chicks.

Seemingly attracted by the shape of the dome, he begins a spiralling descent, and as he comes closer to the church, so do we.

Beneath the dome, inside the church, a broken-hearted girl climbs over the balustrade surrounding the first-floor gallery. Fingers of sunlight through tall windows illuminate her slight form so that she seems to glow. A shadow – her own, and twice her size – rises on the wall behind her. Her long brown hair gleams like the kernel of a horse chestnut, and two tears trace shining paths over high cheekbones.

Her name is Yaminah – meaning *suitable, proper* – and she is twelve years old. Beyond the plinth are two stone steps, leading downwards. On the lower step is a second balustrade, this one of carved wood and four feet high. Carefully, slowly, she climbs up on to its top rail, only four inches wide. With both arms spread for balance, she straightens until she is looking out across the void beneath her feet. While she steadies herself she lets her gaze drift down to the bowed heads of the mourners gathered a hundred feet below for the funeral of her mother.

Unaware that she is doing so, she smoothes the heavy material of her dress with both hands. After all, a princess has to look her best.

Yaminah is an orphan, but soon – in just a few moments, in fact – she will be reunited with the person she loves more than anyone else in the world. One brave step will be all that is required to bring them together again.

Well-schooled in the Christian faith though she

17

is, suicide seems like no sin at all to a girl wishing only to be with her mother once more, to hear her voice and smell the clean scent of her long fair hair...

But when it came to it – when Yaminah focused properly upon the reality of the long fall towards the floor below – she changed her mind. Her heart and head were still filled with a smothering fog of sadness, but a pinprick of light had appeared amid the gloom. She could not – did not – identify it in that moment, but it was a flicker of understanding. Yaminah had realised that while she wanted her mother to be alive once more, truly she herself did not want to die – no more than her mother had wanted to die and leave her only child alone in the world.

All at once she knew that although her grief had near overwhelmed her, the need to avoid a long drop towards the flagstones so many tens of feet beneath her was stronger still. With her gaze fixed on the gallery directly opposite, she let out a long, slow whistling breath.

And so, as it happened, it was the scream of a woman that stole Yaminah's balance away and had her topple from her perch. The sound of that one relieved exhalation from high above – so out of place – had caught the ear of a lady mourner. Looking up, she saw the child balanced precariously in all her finery – and yelped, hand to mouth.

Snapped back from their thoughts by the unexpected sound, the faithful looked around at the lady who had made it, then up towards the point where she was staring. Thus when Yaminah fell out into space with her arms spinning like a penny whirligig, she had their full attention.

Prince Constantine had noticed her some little while before the mourner cried out at the sight. He had been watching motes of dust drifting through shafts of sunlight – anything to distract him from the misery of the occasion (misery that was not his, but misery just the same) – when an unexpected movement on the gallery high above caught his eye.

He was standing at one end of a row of mourners and she had appeared above him, although a little to his right. The strangeness of her actions meant he said and did nothing while she clambered hesitantly on to the balustrade. Like a scene from a dream, it all seemed beyond his control.

But while the lady mourner's cry made Yaminah fall, it also pulled Constantine firmly back into the active world.

Rather than toppling forwards, the girl seemed only to hop in fright, so that she was bolt upright as she began her descent towards the shining marble floor. A collective gasp was tugged from the lungs of the congregation as they watched her flutter into space. A broad beam of sunlight caught the moment so that the silvered fabric of her gown shimmered. All below were transfixed. Hundreds of pairs of eyes opened wide, stretching the fragment of a second into ages.

All were rooted to the spot – all save Constantine. Without any conscious decision, he had begun to drift away from the rest, pulled into a position directly below the girl. Her arms spun and her head was thrown backwards. Her hair stood straight up like fronds of weed in the clearest sea; the folds of her dress billowed with the force so that her skirts ballooned outwards. Her long, skinny legs, exposed for all to see, were cycling too, searching fruitlessly for purchase – for some or other friction to slow her descent.

They called it a miracle ever after, said Our Lady herself had reached out a hand to spare the child. Perhaps her billowing dress performed some part of it as well, taking just enough speed out of the drop. In the end, though, it was to Prince Constantine that she owed her life.

Without a thought for the consequences, he had placed himself squarely between the girl and the pitiless slabs of the floor of the church. The sun shone, the dress shimmered, the faithful held their breath, and a teenage prince of the Byzantine Empire thrust out his slender arms.

None of those who witnessed the moment would ever forget it (most would struggle to believe they had even seen it with their own eyes). But there it was – a shining angel fell to earth and a callow boy reached out for her, caught her, and crumpled beneath the impact like a bag of washing.

PART ONE

Badr

1

Scotland, 1444

John Grant had disappeared, as was his intention. Lying on his back among the long grass and flowers of the meadow, he was invisible to all but the birds. He watched the slow circles of one black shape against the blue. Flower heads on long stalks, yellow and pink, nodded in and out of the frame at the whim of the breeze, as though passing the time of day. The bird changed tack and passed from his sight, leaving him gazing into infinite sky. With nothing left to focus on, he let go instead, letting the emptiness rush towards him.

There have always been those who feel the spinning of the earth and the momentum of her orbit around the sun. While most people are tricked by the illusion – of a world fixed in place – a handful sense reality. John Grant felt the rush as the planet turned her face from left to right across the sky, sensed too her flight into the limitless dark. When he lay in bed at night he listened to the rumble and hum of the great ball as it turned and turned on its axis.

Given the nature of Earth's journey it is a wonder the sensitives are so few, while the many are blissfully unaware. Earth pirouettes at a thousand miles an hour, faster than a bullet fired from a gun. To circle the sun in just three hundred and sixty-five days (give or take) she hurtles through the void at sixty-seven thousand miles an hour. The solar system of which she is an infinitesimal part, clings to the rim of a great spinning vortex called a galaxy. Once around the glowing centre takes two hundred and twenty-five million years and since the world began, five billion years ago, the great odyssey has been completed fewer than twenty times.

On that day in the year 1444, John Grant had been alive for a few weeks more than twelve years – a fraction of a fraction of time in terms of the voyage of the earth, but a long time for a boy alive to the speed of it all, to the hell-for-leather gallop across time and space.

He was tall for his age, and lean. His mother despaired that for all he ate, which was as much as she had to give him, he stayed thin as a whip. She would have liked him sturdier, with more flesh between him and the world.

As well as tall, he was sandy-haired and hazel-eyed. More than hazel, they were flecked with gold, so that sometimes they seemed to sparkle with tiny suns. He was pleasing to look upon. He was quick, too – of mind as well as of hand and foot. Some noticed that when he walked, his footsteps made no sound.

The lightness touched his mother's heart. At times he seemed to her a will-o'-the-wisp – something too slight for the world that might disappear, for no reason, at any moment. If he had been a pot of soup she would have stirred in flour, to thicken him. By day she watched his grace and mistook it for frailty. By night she lay awake wondering how she had kept him safe so far and dreaded the nameless threats posed by the days, weeks and years to come. Always she feared that the next gust of wind might snatch him away like a seed from a dandelion clock.

Had she known his secret, that he could feel rushing infinity plucking at his clothes, seeking purchase like a wind ruffling the topmost leaves of a tree, she might never have slept again. But John Grant lacked the words to share what he knew and so left the truth unsaid. Perhaps he understood, anyway, that what he had to tell was too much for others to hear.

Young John Grant knew nothing of planets, suns and galaxies, of course – and even less of bullets and miles an hour. How could he? He had no way to make sense of what he felt and no one alive in 1444 had yet learned the truth of it anyway. Earth would have to hurl around the sun another one hundred times and more before Nicolaus Copernicus, of Royal Prussia, would explain it – that we are in thrall to the sun and she to the universe.

Although John Grant had noted the bird's sudden change of heart, he had not allowed it to matter. But when a flight of half a dozen more sped across his line of sight, all in the same direction as the first, he began to pay attention. Pulled back, forced to ignore the falling into space, he sat up and looked around. Before there had been the sound of birdsong from a stand of trees some hundreds of yards away to his right. Now they were silent. Those that had not taken flight listened as well.

From the sun-hardened ground beneath him

there came the faintest suggestion of a disturbance. It wasn't a vibration just yet – more a ringing in his ears – but it was there. He stood up. He was not alarmed as such but his senses were heightened. Instinctively he turned until he could see his home, a long, low cottage built of dry stone and roofed with turf. A curl of white smoke rose languidly from the chimney. It should have been a reassuring sight. But given the tightness building in his chest, it worried him instead. Rather than a source of comfort, the house seemed ... asleep, unaware, and therefore vulnerable.

But vulnerable to what? He did not know. He felt the ever-present sensation he called (to himself and only to himself) the *push*, accompanied by the faint taste of iron in his mouth. Doubt and fear might be unsettling – a pricking of the skin – but the push brought only certainty and had him set off downhill towards the house at a steady dog trot. After a hundred yards he stopped. The vibration beneath his feet was unmistakable now, and its source lay behind him, somewhere off beyond the trees and the silent birds. He was between its cause and his home – a barrier, however flimsy, and therefore a grain of comfort. He picked up the pace.

2

Hawkshaw

His companions called him Bear. Badr (which means full moon) felt unfamiliar in their mouths and so they had exchanged it for something that made more sense to them. He was huge, after all – well over six feet tall and broad like the door of a castle's keep. He was darker than those he lived among now, his skin like a tanned hide. His hair and beard, both long and unruly, were black as the night sky. His eyes were black as well, like a bird's, so that no light escaped them. Across his cheekbones and around his eyes were clusters of darker pigment, larger than freckles. Around his head was wound a black scarf that kept his hair from falling into his eyes.

He had appeared among them weeks before. He had ridden along the rutted track to the Jardine stronghold on a warhorse black as his hair. The saddle and other tack were of a style unfamiliar to the Scots, but it was the man who was strangest of all. Folk in the fields stopped what they were doing and straightened aching backs, the better to examine him as he passed by and to remember the moment ever after. Though he knew he was stared at, still he kept his gaze straight ahead. It was not disdain, rather the air of a man with other things to think about. The long curved sword on one hip

27

attracted fascinated glances.

Man and horse were still hundreds of yards short of the palisade encircling the tower house when there came the sound of iron bolts yanked free from their catches. Heavy wooden gates were pushed outwards. Three men, mounted on shaggy ponies, emerged from inside the stockade, fell naturally into an arrowhead formation and set off at a canter.

Badr had watched their approach with detachment. The lead rider pulled up some little way in front of him while his companions drew wide and passed either side. They spurred their mounts around and took up flanking positions to the rear of the intruder. Their leader stood up in his stirrups in an effort to gain a height advantage, but in vain. It seemed to him that even the stranger's horse, an expensive destrier by the look of it, gazed down at him.

'What do you want here?' he asked.

The black horse stopped, apparently of its own accord, and Badr fixed his gaze upon the man who addressed him.

'I have come a long way,' he said. 'They say this house is home to a powerful lord. I would like to offer him my service.'

The Scot smiled, glancing at his companions. They nodded in return. They were younger, less experienced and keen to be reassured that all was well, but their leader remained guarded, suspicious.

'My name is Armstrong,' he said. 'I'll take you to him. But you must give up your sword. You are welcome, but my master's guests must surrender their arms.'

Armstrong placed his right hand on the pommel of his own sword. He was no match for the new-comer in terms of physical size, but he stood his ground just the same. His eyes were green, almost startlingly so, and unblinking despite the fact that the sun was behind the Moor and shone straight into Armstrong's face. The visitor was certainly big, powerfully built and armed for battle. He carried himself well, with the confidence of experience hard won. He was a threat to any and all. Something in his bearing, however, exuded calm as well. Everything – from the tone of his voice to the way he sat in the saddle – suggested he felt no need to prove himself. Armstrong, a man-at-arms and a leader among his own kind, had lived long enough to gauge a situation. He had survived his share of tense encounters and in so doing had learned some of the tricks of reading men. For the time being the giant meant no harm – and he could be a powerful ally to any who secured his loyalty. His lairdship would surely be pleased to make his acquaintance at least.

Badr Khassan nodded and dismounted. His movements were smooth and quick, made perfect by hard muscle and taut sinew unencumbered by superfluous bulk. He landed on the track with hardly a sound. With one hand he reached back, like a girl, to free long hair from inside the collar of his cloak.

He walked towards Armstrong, unbuckling his sword belt. By the time he reached the mounted man he had wound the leather strapping around the crescent-shaped scabbard. He passed it over casually, as though giving it away for good and without regret.

'Your master is a sensible man,' he said, his face breaking into a smile that revealed teeth startlingly white. 'For as long as I take shelter under his roof, my sword is his to command.'

'So be it,' said the Scot.

Taking the scimitar, heavy as a child, and placing it across his garron's neck, Armstrong pulled on the reins so that the beast wheeled around towards the entrance of the palisade. With neither word nor backward glance he set off for home. Badr followed, leading his own horse and trailed at a respectful distance by the others. He considered the manner of the man who had spoken to him. He had read confidence in his demeanour, and something more besides. The Moor was long enough in the tooth to know the effect his appearance had on most people, men and women alike, and yet this Armstrong had met his gaze and addressed him plainly, and with the authority of one certain of his own abilities as well as of his station in life. Whoever commanded such a man – even just one such man – was a warlord Badr Khassan looked forward to meeting.

The stronghold had been called Hawkshaw for longer than anyone could remember. It had been home to the Jardine family for four generations. The first of them had been a Frenchman, Guillaume du Jardon of Normandy, and it was his great-grandson, Sir Robert, who held it now – and who had ordered and overseen the building of the gloomy three-storey pile that dominated the surrounding land from its perch on a rocky outcrop overlooking a bend of the River Tweed.

Clustered around the outside of the palisade were the homes of some of Sir Robert's followers, low dwellings of timber and turf. Thin tendrils of smoke trailed skywards from fires within. Women, small and skinny as whippets, emerged from some of the doorways, stooping low beneath stone lintels and followed by scrawny tykes. They peered at the new arrival as he and his minders wound their way up the pathway to the tower house.

While careful to maintain his leisurely air, Badr glanced around him, reading the story of Hawkshaw. The bleak, square house at its heart lacked panache, but was an imposing structure nonetheless. Everything about it, from the thickness of the walls to the miserly proportions of the few windows and arrow slits, spoke of a preoccupation with defence. There was no door-way on the ground floor – instead a heavy wooden ladder descended from a narrow portal a dozen feet up on the left-hand wall. If attackers breached the palisade and threatened the house itself, the ladder could be pulled inside, making it all but impossible for any unwelcome guests to gain access. Best of all, the house squatted upon a natural high point – a shelf of pale grey stone that, as well as giving the advantage of height, had likely provided most of the building material.

'Leave your horse with Donny there,' said Armstrong, glancing over his shoulder to Badr and gesturing to the younger of the pair bringing up the rear. 'Follow me up to the house and we'll see if his lairdship has time for you.'

Leaving the stranger trailing behind him,

31

Armstrong dug both heels into his horse's flanks and trotted up the last tens of yards to the foot of the ladder. Badr watched the Scotsman as he jumped lightly down from the saddle and walked to the base of the tower.

'Jamie!' he called up, one hand cupped by the side of his mouth.

Seconds later a sandy head appeared at the doorway.

'What can I do for you, sir?' said the head. It was unclear whether the use of 'sir' had been a genuine acknowledgement of seniority or something light-hearted between men of equal rank.

Armstrong climbed a few rungs up the ladder and began talking, too quietly for Badr to hear. After a couple of exchanges the one called Jamie disappeared back inside. Badr sniffed the air of the place – horses, and the hot, new-baked smell of an iron forge at work. He breathed deep of it.

Armstrong stayed on the ladder, glancing occasionally at the newcomer. Badr heard the sound of a man clearing his throat and spun slowly around on his heels. The one called Donny, a short, weedy man with a weak-looking chin and watery blue eyes beneath a head of alarming red hair, had evidently delivered the horses into the care of a stable lad out of sight of where they stood, and had now returned. Badr found it hard to guess the ages of the men and women he encountered in these lowlands of Scotland. Many seemed so physically worn out – weakened by some or other hardship and the always unforgiving climate – that their adulthoods appeared like an extended old age. This one's manner suggested some residue of youth, but his face was a mask of weariness.

Silent by his side was the third of Badr's guardians, a taller, heavier individual with dark hair and a face dominated by a scar that looped around his right eye and down his cheek, like a question mark. Both were keeping a respectful distance, hands on hips and feet shoulder-width apart. Their downcast eyes, however, made a lie of the seeming confidence of their stances. Beyond standing by, they seemed uncertain. Had Badr decided to move against them, it appeared unlikely they would have done much about it.

Badr would have been content to remain silent but Donny gave in to temptation.

'Whaur are ye fae anyway, big man?' he asked, rocking forward and upwards on to his toes in desperate search of more height.

Badr was at a loss. During his travels through the long island, he had mastered much of the tongue spoken by the English, but the variant form that prevailed here in the land of the Scots was often beyond him. By way of a reply he shook his head slowly, a carefully quizzical expression on his face to convey, he hoped, friendliness as well as a lack of understanding.

Donny tutted and glanced at his companion, eyebrows raised in exasperation, before trying again.

'Whaur ... are ... you' – he pointed at Badr with one bony finger, and nodded for emphasis – 'from?'

Badr smiled, none the wiser. Mercifully, he heard a shout from the direction of the tower house and, grateful for the distraction, turned once more towards the ladder and Armstrong.

'Sir Robert is heading out now for a ride,' called the Scotsman. 'He will see you when he comes down.'

'An' who the fuck's this, then?'

The words escaped him, but Badr understood their sentiment just the same. He turned back again to see who had growled and found he was looking into a new face – and for once, it was more or less level with his own.

'Well?' it said.

Another question, as aggressive as the first and seemingly addressed to all three men, rather than to Badr alone.

'Just turned up out of the blue, Will,' said Donny. His tone was cheerful, placatory – born of experience of dealing with this bristling, aggressive individual. 'Spotted him on the road outside and brought him in. Armstrong knows all about it, he's up at the house.'

'Is he indeed,' said Will, looking not at Donny but at Badr. 'And what about the big ugly bastard? Does he speak for himself or does he just stand about casting shadows?'

Donny laughed nervously, as did his comrade with the scarred, questioning face.

The Moor ignored the tone as well as the insult.

'My name is Badr Khassan,' he said. 'I have been travelling but I am tired. I would stay here a while – a few days, a week or two maybe, if your master permits.'

Will nodded elaborately, sarcastic to the core.

'Good for you,' he said.

There was a smell of drink about him too, and alcohol never brought out Will Kennedy's good side (if Will Kennedy had a good side, he had kept it safely hidden all these years).

More or less as tall as Badr, the newcomer had none of the width. He was skinny as a rail, with a chest that was almost concave. Years of stooping – the better to get his bullying face as close as possible to the noses of his intended victims – had made him round-shouldered as well. For all the cruelty in his countenance, his long, thin face was handsome, with pale blue eyes. He was bearded, the dark hair shot with grey.

As soon as Badr laid eyes on the man, the word 'snake' sprang instantly to mind. There was a hint of wiry strength coiled in that mean frame, like meat that had dried tough, as well as the suggestion of a viper's speed.

He wondered again at the nature of this environment that had produced his oldest friend, Patrick, and that was home still to his woman and his child. The discovery of predators such as this Will, topped to the brim with venom, reminded him of the innumerable dangers that lurked in the undergrowth wherever he travelled. Though he had not yet laid eyes upon Patrick's family far less spent time with them, still he felt a protective reflex in his chest, a need to find them and to see to their well-being.

Tension crackled in the air, but not for Badr. The charge passed between the Scotsmen as they waited to see who would move first, who would speak.

It was while Badr and Will were still eyeing one

another's potential, gauging intent, that the laird of the house stepped unobserved on to the top rung of the ladder. Looking down at Armstrong, Sir Robert noticed that his man was intent on observing something happening off down the slope beneath the tower. Following his gaze, the laird drew a breath when he spotted the stranger. Even from a distance Badr was a striking figure, built altogether differently from those around him. And of course he recognised Will Kennedy – malcontent and bully, but fearless and quick with knife and sword. Faced off against each other, the foreigner and Kennedy reminded Sir Robert of a full moon and a crescent. Hearing the gasp, Armstrong looked up, though Sir Robert was in no doubt that his man had already sensed his presence.

'Bloody Kennedy,' Armstrong said, but the seeming exasperation was more for show than anything sincerely felt. 'If there's no trouble available he'll make his own. I should get down there.'

'Wait a moment,' said Sir Robert. 'Might as well see what our visitor makes of the locals.'

Unaware of the audience on the ladder, Will Kennedy continued with his posturing. He was wearing a woollen cloak over woollen trousers and an ancient and heavily stained leather jack, a garment packed tight with wool and worn in hope of taking some of the hurt out of blows from swords and dirks. It was tied shut across his narrow front with four leather loops around four wooden toggles. As he stepped closer to the bigger man, within arm's reach, he delicately pulled back the left-hand side of his cloak with the fingertips of his left hand. Hanging by his side was a cruel-looking long-bladed knife, the handle angled forwards so it might be easily and speedily drawn with the right. Will glanced down at the weapon theatrically, as though surprised to find it there at his side, and then up again into Badr's face.

'Careful now,' said Badr softly.

'Careful?' said Kennedy, his blue eyes narrowing, and letting his cloak fall back into place so that the knife was concealed from view.

Without another word Badr took half a step towards his antagonist. For the briefest of moments the two men were touching, chest to chest, before Badr stepped back again. The move had looked for all the world – and to Armstrong and Sir Robert – like the first steps of a dance. It had lasted no longer than a heartbeat, and the expression on Will's face when it was over was one of shock. No one – not even women – invaded his personal space so completely and so calmly without his consent. He looked as though he had been slapped across the face.

In fact it was a gasp from the red-headed and suddenly red-faced Donny that broke the spell. Will Kennedy snapped his head around at the sound and, realising that Donny was pointing witlessly at the ground, looked down between his own heavily booted feet. Four wooden toggles lay on the hard-baked mud, along with their looped fastenings. Reflexively he raised both hands to his jacket and found that it was hanging limply open. Where the toggles had once been there were just four stumps of leather, cut through so cleanly the fresh ends shone bright white.

'Knives are dangerous,' said Badr. 'Best avoided.'

If Badr Khassan had a blade of his own – and it appeared he did – no one glimpsed it that day, nor on any day thereafter.

3

Badr was as close to the fire as he could get without actually sitting among the flames. For all that he had found to admire and even enjoy in this northern land, the enervating cold was an affront. Weeks had passed since his arrival at the gates of the Jardine stronghold, and one way or another he had enjoyed (or endured) a complete round of the seasons in the countries of England and Scotland. For one grown to manhood in a sun-baked land far away to the south, the rain and wind that presided over so many days, not to mention the toll exacted by the gloom and gnawing cold of winter, had been hard to take. It was summer now – late summer admittedly, but summer just the same – and already the chill of evening was deeper than he would have liked.

His nightly devotion to the fireplace in the great hall had become a source of amusement to the rest. At mealtimes he made sure always to occupy the last place on the bench, right beside the hearth. He then switched from side to side of the trestle table during the course of the evening to ensure that both sides of his body received an even toasting. At least as important to him as the food was the chance to bake his sorry hide in the searing heat of the flames curling around pine logs heaped and hissing.

Angus Armstrong, the man who had first confronted Badr on his approach to Hawkshaw, sat apart on a dark wooden chair so worn and polished with years it shone like the surface of deep water. He flexed his legs so as to rock back and forth, allowing the back of his head to brush against the wall in the deep shadow cast by the fire. He watched the big man, saw a gleam in the eyes he interpreted not as malice but mischief. He waited.

'Is it good red blood in your veins, old Bear?' shouted Jamie Douglas from the opposite end of the table. 'Or maybe water – cold water, at that!'

The taunt was good-natured and Badr knew it, but he adopted the body language of one struck by insult and rebuke. He had been among these lowland Scots long enough to learn the nature of their humour. Among the men at least it was all about teasing and challenging one another in hope of scoring points, and he knew how much the castle's inhabitants enjoyed the possibility of seeing him finally, and for once, flex his muscles. If you were ever to be allowed to give it out, you had first to prove you could take it. His size and obvious strength had marked him as a slumbering giant, and the chance that he might one day be provoked into action made him a prime target.

He froze, head down over a plate of venison stew (the climate might not have been to his liking, but he had to admit the food available hereabouts made up for some of the discomfort).

39

All at once he seemed like a figure carved from seasoned wood. He had even stopped chewing. Undaunted, Jamie's voice came again.

'You're like a big old hound, steaming there by the hearth!' he shouted, nudging the men to his left and right as he leaned forward to look down the length of the table toward Badr's hulking form, silhouetted against snapping flames.

Here was bravery indeed from a young blade. Badr was twice Jamie's age and twice his size. Any physical clash seemed certain to end in disaster for the slighter man.

'Mind these teeth then, boy,' said Badr evenly, his gaze fixed on his food. And then he growled. It was a trick he had learned in boyhood and perfected since. It was the first time he had used it among these folk, however, and the effect was instantaneous. It was a primal sound, animal – and for as long as it lasted, Badr's humanity seemed far away, buried deep, or gone. Every spine around the table felt icy fingernails traced lightning fast from waist to neck and back again. Every hair rose on every square inch of skin and not a soul moved. Every spine and hair, that is, save those of Angus Armstrong, who read the signs for what they really had to say and remained on his perch, calmly rocking. For everyone else around the table, the air seemed sucked from the room and replaced by fear. The sound came from low down, and it tugged like a cold hand at the curled tail of monkey brain that waited tensely in the dark cave of every man's imagination.

Without moving, without even raising his head, Badr growled a second time, louder and more menacingly than before. After a handful of seconds he began to rise from his seat, pushing himself back with so much power that the whole bench, with half a dozen full-grown men upon it, swung slowly away from the table with a squeal of wood on stone. Once he had room to move, he stepped clear of the bench and turned to face the younger man, still seated between his comrades. None of them had the nerve to meet Badr's eye; instead, each waited, motionless, praying that the coming storm would pass them by. He growled a third time and kept his stance low, careful not to straighten to his full height, the better to increase his width. Every other fellow seemed turned to stone. Most forgot to breathe. It was finally happening. Badr began to advance, slowly. A bear right enough.

Jamie found his voice. He stayed on his bench, small now and getting smaller, recoiling inside his own frame. His face suddenly grey, he offered only:

'Come on, Bear ... just playing you... No offence meant...'

It was almost the voice of a child.

Badr's lip curled and at once the growling stopped. Silent seconds passed, and time dripped from the rafters high above like cold water.

'NONE TAKEN!' he bellowed, so that every man around the table jumped, and now other ears and eyes paid attention. 'Got you there, boy!' he shouted, and roared with easy laughter.

All the while Badr had dominated the space, time had seemed to stand still, but at once the world jolted back into motion. The noise of the

41

Bear's laughter and the accompanying release of tension were so abrupt that a few of the men let out helpless yelps of relief. Then it was all about slapping the table and regaining lost ground by laughing along with the friendly giant in their midst – desperate to appear party to the joke.

Still low, weight on the balls of his feet, Badr launched himself at Jamie, grabbed him in a steely hug where he sat, and scooped him into the air like a little boy. He set him down on his two feet, roughly, so that the younger man almost fell backwards, and then ruffled his sandy hair with one hand. Jamie breathed out heavily, his relief still huge and making him grin gormlessly in his happiness at finding himself alive and unharmed. Armstrong only watched, eyes alight with reflected flames, as he let the front legs of his chair come to rest upon the floor.

If the air in the room had been crushed, as though by a storm cloud that had loomed and lowered, it was clear once more. Food and drink appealed as before and the men in Badr's company breathed deeply of life as they turned their attentions back to the meals in front of them.

The knowledge of a happening at the men's table spread rapidly around the hall. From the raised dais, Sir Robert Jardine, master of the house and uncle and guardian to young Jamie, saw only his charge being hoisted high. Satisfied that it was nothing more than horseplay, he said nothing. Though his motivations remained hard to fathom, the big man had been something of an asset. His presence among the armed patrols that checked the borders of Sir Robert's lands had added weight to Jardine authority hereabouts. His calm confidence steadied the younger men, and their air of self-possession while on duty meant that nowadays their job was half done without the need for word or action.

Turning to address the man on his right, Sir Robert said: 'I would not be without ... remind me, what name is it they use for Khassan nowadays? He's practically a war band all on his own.'

'Bear,' muttered the cadaverous figure, hunched over his plate like a crow. 'They call him the Bear, sire.'

As he said the nickname the second time, he nodded his head from side to side, loftily, adding mocking emphasis to the word. He took a moment to consider his master's face and glimpsed the shadow of the handsome man of years before, now all but consumed.

'You don't care for our guest, Davey?' said Sir Robert, his thin lips twisting into a smile.

'You don't need me to like him – or any of the men, sire,' he replied. 'I'm wary of strangers – especially strangers dark as Badr Khassan, or as massive. Allowing something that size indoors is like giving house room to a bull ... if you ask me.'

'I care less about the colour of his skin than the strength of his sword arm,' said Sir Robert. 'As for a bull, he has the manners of a gentleman. I've heard not a bad word about him in all the time he's been among us. They say he hasn't so much as raised his voice in anger to man or woman.'

While Sir Robert spoke, he kept his eyes on the room and on the men and women enjoying his hospitality. His gaze was tireless. A borderer by birth and inclination, he lived by little wars – either raiding or fending off his neighbours. Scottish, English – their nationality was of no significance and no concern to a Reiver such as he. His holdings were his world, jealously guarded and set apart from all other obligations. He lived as he saw fit, and neither listened to nor tolerated any authority but his own. Here, where the kingdom of the Scots rubbed together with that of the English, were all the unhealed wounds and jagged ends of broken bones left by uncounted years of feuding. No distant monarch held sway here, and those folk that made their homes along the disputed borderlands understood they were beyond the help or care of kings. It was therefore to local strongmen – men like Sir Robert Jardine – that they looked for any kind of security, never mind the maintenance of law and order.

'Nine weeks,' said Davey carefully. 'Nine weeks he's been here, and anyway, that's the thing about animals: bonny enough outdoors and from a distance but less appealing squatting by a man's own fireside.'

'My fireside, Davey,' said Sir Robert. 'Mine.'

Davey Kennedy, master of Sir Robert Jardine's stables and elder brother of Will – Will of the sheathed knife and the severed toggles – turned his attention back to his food.

'And no word of Grant?' said Sir Robert, wiping up the remnants of his meal with a last lump of bread. He licked his lips and remembered the taste of sweeter flesh.

It was a statement of fact rather than a question, but Davey heard his master's dissatisfaction coiled around each syllable.

'It's been years since there was more than rumour of him hereabouts,' he said. 'I doubt he's even in the country. There's no safe bed for him within a hundred miles of Hawkshaw – nor will there ever be again. He has accepted that. Patrick Grant is gone, and will stay gone.'

Sir Robert chewed his food. He took up his cup and drank long and slow of the finest wine his folk could find. He tasted only blood and bile.

'Why the troubles on my land, then?' he asked. 'Who torments my tenants? Who burns their homes and takes their beasts?'

He turned to look at Kennedy and his gaze seemed to burn the other man's face so that he squirmed.

'His bitch is here, and his brat,' said Sir Robert, running his tongue back and forth over his teeth to clear them of the scum of half-chewed food. 'He'll be back for them one day. If not, then he'll send for them sooner or later.'

'More likely he's dead in a ditch,' said Davey Kennedy. 'And there's an end of it.'

'That,' said Sir Robert, 'would be more disappointment than I could bear. If I don't stretch Patrick Grant's neck myself, I won't rest easy in my own grave.'

He took another gulp of wine before continuing.

'Keep watch over his family,' he said. 'They are the key to it, bait in the trap. The day will come when I'll see all of them swinging on the gibbet. Mark me, now – they will all hang for what he did to me.'

4

Given all that was to happen that day, it started quietly enough for the folk of Hawkshaw. There had been reports through the night of trouble on the southern marches – cattle taken, homes raided and set ablaze. A patrol was to ride out, assess the damage and set others to work to put things right.

Sir Robert Jardine considered himself beholden to none and policed his own lands as he saw fit. The men he gathered around him to those ends were bound either by blood or by the silver coins in his purse, but he placed the full weight of his trust in none of them, not even close family. He reviewed his situation every day and made whatever adjustments he felt necessary.

Before he'd finally retired to his bedchamber on the uppermost floor of the tower house, he'd given Davey Kennedy the task of leading whatever force he deemed necessary to the site of the trouble. A little after dawn, with a watery sun rising, the master of the stables was at the head of a dozen mounted men trotting out through the gateway of Hawkshaw's palisade. There was little in the way of conversation. Each man remained withdrawn, maintaining as much distance as possible from the rest and from the chill of the morning.

Davey Kennedy was fuming. The task of leading such a routine patrol was a long way beneath his

46

dignity, as he saw it. It was, however, in keeping with his master's way of doing things. If challenged (and who would have dared?), Sir Robert would have said it was important his senior men remained battle ready at all times, and vital that they had up-to-date, first-hand ex-perience of the people and the lie of the land.

What use to the household and the estate was any who had grown distanced from the day-to-day realities of the fight and the need for restless vigi-lance? Sir Robert therefore insisted (and a grudg-ing part of Davey Kennedy both understood and even approved of the strategy, in principle at least) that rank was no bar to service. Even the laird himself was no stranger to the drudgery of riding the marches, maintaining the boundaries of his own lands and underlining his authority through the simple tactic of remaining visible at all times.

But early morning was early morning, and Davey, a man who liked his bed more and more with every passing year, was in a foul temper. It had given him some little satisfaction, therefore, to insist that his quarrelsome brother join the party, and he looked back over his shoulder to the end of the line of horsemen where Will, as silent and morose as Davey himself, trailed some half a dozen horse lengths behind the others. Davey kept watching his brother until he made eye contact. With a jerk of his head he signalled that Will should join him at the head of the troop. Once they were trotting side by side, he slowly looked his brother up and down.

'Like what you see, do you?' said Will, without lifting his gaze from his garron's mane.

'Aye, you're a pleasure to be around, brother,' said Davey. 'No chance anyone will ever mistake you for a ray of sunshine.'

'If you've nothing worth saying, I'd prefer the quiet,' said Will, eyes now fixed straight in front of him.

They rode in silence for several minutes.

'I'll go on ahead, Davey,' said Will at last. 'See what's to see.'

'For what reason, when we're all going anyway?' said Davey, meeting his brother's gaze. 'Not like you to put yourself out on behalf of others.'

'It suits me to be by myself,' said Will, his face expressionless. Then he smiled, dripping sarcasm. 'It might make me happy.'

'This ride out is for no one's pleasure,' said Davey. 'The point is to be seen. To let it be known we will respond to any and every breach of our lands.'

'Oh, it's *our* lands, is it now?' said Will.

He dug his spurs into his horse's flanks. The beast reared in pain and surprise and plunged away from the line.

By the time Davey Kennedy and the rest of the riders reached the Henderson farm, the focus for the trouble during the night just past, there were no signs of life. There was a chaotic mess, sure enough. While the thatched roofing of the main cottage was largely intact, there were clear signs of burning. The whole lot of it was sodden, evidence of efforts to douse a fire, but it looked as though the flames had never fully caught. In any event, much of the thatch had slumped into the interior under its own weight. Some of the poor

48

belongings of the Henderson family, tenant farmers who paid Sir Robert rent for the privilege of their miserable existence, were strewn around the doorway. Smashed pottery, clothing, bits and pieces of broken furniture were testament to a raid. But for all the signs of destruction, there was not a soul to be seen or heard. The cattle were gone too – driven off by whoever had descended upon the place in the night. No doubt the Hendersons had sought comfort and shelter with some or other neighbours.

'Will!' shouted Davey Kennedy. 'Show yourself!'

Nothing. Not a reply, not a murmur.

'Look inside,' he ordered, gesturing to Jamie Douglas and another of the troopers, Donny Weir. The pair jumped down from their horses and sauntered over to the doorway. The lintel was low, no more than five feet off the ground, and both had to duck awkwardly to pass beneath and into the darkened interior.

Seconds later Donny re-emerged, his usually ruddy cheeks white as a fish's belly. He said nothing, but looked straight at Davey Kennedy for a long moment, and then away again.

Kennedy dismounted and ran to the doorway. Misjudging the height in his haste, he bumped his head on the lintel hard enough for the men to hear, and to wince in sympathy.

When his eyes adjusted to the gloom inside, he spotted Jamie crouched by his brother's side. Will Kennedy was slumped in one corner of the ransacked cottage, eyes wide and his throat laid open from ear to ear. His dead face was discoloured with bruises, evidence of a heavy beating administered before the fatal wound.

Davey said nothing at all, just walked slowly over to his brother's corpse. Hearing his approach, Jamie turned to look at him. He was holding Will's cold right hand.

'Look,' he said, holding it up for Davey to see. The knuckles were split and bloodied. 'Put up a fight.'

'Aye,' Davey replied. 'I'm sure, for all the good it did him.'

Back outside, the word had spread, courtesy of a whispered account from Donny Weir.

'I'd like to meet the man that bested Will Kennedy,' said one man. And then, after a pause: 'Or maybe I wouldn't.'

Davey emerged from the cottage, followed by Jamie Douglas, who was wiping his hand hard on his trousers.

'Donny Weir,' he said, 'and you, Jamie: you found him – take word of my brother's death back to Hawkshaw. The rest of you mount up.'

He spat on the ground, then walked smartly to his horse and climbed back into the saddle. Donny Weir and Jamie Douglas made ready to depart. Silently, the rest got back on their mounts. Davey Kennedy set off first. There would be time later for the business of seeing that his brother's body was properly taken care of. For now, his time would be best spent elsewhere, and he nudged his beast towards the rutted track they had followed to reach the Henderson place. The troopers, heads down and stealing glances at one another, followed suit. When they reached the track, Kennedy kicked his garron into a gallop.

5

John Grant felt the vibrations of the galloping horses before he heard them. Even as he ran full tilt towards home, he could detect them through the soles of his bare feet as they pounded on the grass.

The push was hard upon him now, insistent as a scolding parent. The cottage was seconds away, but still he felt compelled to stop and look back towards the rise and the trees beyond. Now that he was standing still, his heart thumping, the tremors threading up from the ground and agitating his skin like needles were unmistakable. By paying attention to the push he was able to orientate himself so as to face, and therefore pinpoint, the source of the staccato pulse. He was facing in precisely the right direction when he finally heard the sound of their approach, just seconds before a band of mounted men appeared on top of the rise and spilled downhill towards him. They were perhaps a quarter of a mile away. At the sight of him, the leader of the group seemed to begin urging his mount even harder. Seeing this, reading it as more bad news, John Grant turned to complete his dash for home.

'Mother!' he cried as he covered the last ten yards. 'Men are coming!'

He charged through the doorway of the cottage and knew exactly where to look to find his

51

mother's face. She was tending the fire in the hearth, coaxing enough heat to boil water, but at the sound of his voice, and his sudden appearance in her domain, she dropped the blackened stick she had been holding and turned to face him. Jessie Grant was tall and long-limbed, like her son. Her face was handsome rather than beautiful, so that it was the way she held herself, her balance and poise, that turned men's heads.

She saw the alarm on his sweat-slicked face and straightened.

'Why so fearful, son?' she said, but his manner told her all she needed to know. If he was afraid, then he had good reason. She ran to meet him, taking him briefly in her arms, and then, pushing him behind her, she ducked her head and stepped out into the daylight.

John Grant followed her and moved around his mother so as to stand by her side, close enough that they were touching. The horsemen had slowed to a trot, and as they arrived in front of mother and son, the leader pulled up his mount and climbed down from his saddle.

'Good afternoon, Mr Kennedy,' said Jessie. 'What brings you to my door ... and with so many friends?'

Her pretence at nonchalance and warmth was convincing enough – perhaps enough to fool the larger part of the audience – but John Grant felt the fine hairs on her arm, the arm touching his own, standing on end. Though her hand was tucked out of sight in her apron, the taut tendons of her forearm told him it was balled into a fist.

Davey Kennedy smiled but said nothing as he

closed the distance between them.

In the end he came much too close – close enough to place a heavy hand on John Grant's shoulder and pull him away from his mother.

'Still no father for the boy?' he asked.

Davey Kennedy was a head and shoulders taller than John Grant, but the boy took care to thrust out his chin and look the man straight in the eyes.

Davey cupped John Grant's chin and turned the boy's head first one way and then the other, as though considering his worth.

'He's growing up pretty, is he not?' As he said it, he turned to the men. They understood the joke and laughed accordingly.

John Grant freed himself from the man's grasp and stepped back to his mother's side.

Everything about Davey Kennedy's physical presence radiated threat, like a static charge in the air before a storm. John Grant found the force of it nauseating, and unconsciously he took some steps backwards away from the man, as though to escape a bad smell.

Davey Kennedy turned fully towards the men and took a few paces towards them.

'Thomas Henderson's farm was raided last night, Mrs Grant,' he said, addressing the words over the men's heads before spinning around on his heel to face mother and son once more.

'Why are you telling me?' said Jessie.

'Well ... something of what we saw reminded me of some of your husband's handiwork, back in the day,' he said, now strolling back towards the pair.

Jessie sighed and looked down at the ground between her feet for a few seconds before replying.

Whatever his failings, and they were numerous, Patrick Grant had been no bully and no thief.

The wife of an absentee husband did not have her troubles to seek, however. She had been both mother and father to the boy for most of his years. For almost all of the time he felt like the blessing he was and she thanked God for him. But at moments such as these she longed to stand behind the protection of a man, and she silently cursed the name of Patrick Grant, wherever he was.

In the pause while no one spoke, John Grant felt the presence of another, suddenly filling the silence. The hackles on his neck rose and sent a crackling tingle through his body, as though a cold fingernail was trailing up and down his skin. Whoever it was, they could not be in the cottage – he had seen that his mother was alone. If not inside the building, then whoever it was had to be behind it. He felt the push and it turned his head. Still he saw nothing and no one. There was someone there, just the same. He knew it.

'As you well know, Davey Kennedy, my husband has been gone for years – almost all the boy's life,' she said. 'Why you seek to blame him for trouble on the Jardine estate is beyond my reasoning.'

Jessie smiled at her son. For as long as her fond gaze lasted, John Grant felt like it was just the two of them. His whirling senses were briefly calmed, pacified like troubled water anointed with oil.

Davey Kennedy strode towards Jessie and punched her on the side of her head with all of his strength. She dropped like a felled tree – still conscious but utterly befuddled, a roaring in her ears.

John Grant hurled himself at his mother's attacker, even managed to land a substantial punch
that brought a gout of blood from the man's nose.
Davey Kennedy lashed out reflexively and caught
the boy across the face with a sweeping blow from
the back of one hand, before using it to wipe the
crimson from his own face.

'Take the bitch back to her fireside and do what
you will,' he said, standing over his victims. 'And
if she still can't remember where that bastard
husband of hers has been hiding, do it all again
until she does.'

The mounted men leapt from their horses.
Suddenly offered unexpected entertainment,
they were on the ground and over to Jessie in
seconds. Their own Will Kennedy was dead, after
all – and who were they to question his grieving
brother's tactics for finding the killer.

Leaving the boy where he lay, they picked Jessie
up between them and carried her clumsily but
swiftly into the cottage. Their hands were hauling
at her clothes, pushing her skirts up around her
hips. There was a burst of oafish laughter from
one of them and a groan from the semi-conscious woman.

John Grant rolled over on to his front and was
trying to get up on to his hands and knees, still
stunned, when Davey Kennedy kicked him in the
stomach. It wasn't the hardest blow, but was
designed instead to humiliate and subdue. The
wind was knocked from the boy's lungs just the
same, and he stayed down.

He was still alert enough to see the giant
shadow that rushed from behind one gable end

of the cottage and grabbed his tormentor by the neck, lifting him easily off the ground.

The sound that escaped the bully's compressed throat was muffled and weak, but still discernible.

'You...'

The cracking sound that silenced Davey for ever was louder than his last word. His neck broken, he dropped to the ground like the innards of a butchered beast.

Wordlessly, still uselessly winded, John saw the great shape cross to the doorway of the cottage. Before the man stepped inside, he drew a long, curved sword from his belt. It was already stained with drying blood, from work done earlier in the day. And then, finally, John Grant knew no more.

6

Donny Weir would have howled the news of Will Kennedy's demise for the last mile back to Hawkshaw. Like every whipped dog, he knew how to yelp. The whip hand had often been Will Kennedy's, and the urge to share the astounding knowledge of the messy death of his oft-times bully bubbled in Donny's breast like a rising spring. They had ridden at full gallop and their horses were wide-eyed and flecked with sweat by the time they reached the gates of Hawkshaw's palisade. The sentry had watched their frantic approach and the way was made open for them.

'Hold your tongue now, Donny. We must tell it

first to Sir Robert,' said Jamie Douglas, the younger head but certainly the wiser. He had been giving the same counsel for most of the ride back and was now repeating it over and over like a prayer. 'There will be an awful price for this,' he hissed as they swept beneath the lintel at full speed. 'You make Sir Robert the last to know now, and you'll likely end up paying a portion of it yourself.

'Where is my uncle?' he shouted towards a group of troopers standing near the base of the fortress. He and Donny brought their mounts to a clattering halt and fairly leapt from their saddles. Before any could answer, Donny spotted Sir Robert climbing down from the single, heavily defended entrance to the tower. He thumped Jamie on the shoulder and pointed.

Jamie reached out and lowered Donny's clumsy paw, making eye contact with Sir Robert as he did so. Apparently sensing trouble, the master of the house jerked his chin upwards, questioningly, towards the breathless new arrivals.

'Well – where's Kennedy and the rest?' he asked, his face dark like a sky bearing storm clouds.

'Mr Kennedy sent us ahead, sir,' said Jamie, keeping his eyes fixed on Sir Robert's, though the urge to look at the ground between his feet was all but overwhelming. Uncle or not, Sir Robert Jardine was a hard man to please and the wrong sort to trouble. 'Will is dead, sir,' he said. 'Murdered.'

Sir Robert blinked but gave no sign of emotion. Jamie knew his uncle well enough to know that the lack of an outward show of feelings meant nothing at all.

'Tell me,' said Sir Robert, stepping closer to his nephew while the rest of the men looked on silently, careful not to move and draw any attention upon themselves at such a time.

'Mr Kennedy sent Will on ahead of us this morning – to the Henderson place,' said Jamie. He cleared his throat and swallowed before continuing. 'When we got there ourselves, there was no sign of ... of life. The place was a mess, the house put to the torch, belongings scattered all around.'

'And Will Kennedy?' asked Sir Robert.

'There was no sign of Will at first,' said Jamie. 'Davey told us...' He glanced over at Donny. 'Mr Kennedy told Donny and me to check inside the house. So we did. And we found Will alone in the place – dead. His throat was cut ... his head was all but severed.'

At the addition of such marvellous and gory detail, Donny Weir made an involuntary tutting noise with his tongue and shook his head, as though disapproving. Jamie glared at him and Sir Robert made a half-turn of his head that brought Donny swiftly back into the here and now. He rushed a cupped hand to his mouth to reinforce his sudden, mindful silence.

Sir Robert remained quiet for a few more seconds and then turned away from his nephew to face Donny and the rest of the men who had been listening. More of them had drifted over, keen to hear what was going on but sensing the need to keep their mouths shut.

'Mount up,' said Sir Robert, his voice clear and strong. 'Our Will Kennedy is dead, slain by someone who has chosen to make himself my enemy.'

The undoubted force of the laird's intent seemed to blow across the courtyard like a gust of wind. Men turned to look at one another, exchanging short sentences that mixed together into a murmur of disquiet.

A black bird on the highest masonry of the tower house gave out a rasping cry before spreading its wings and taking to the air, as though intent on carrying the news further afield. Before it had time to beat its wings a second time it was pierced through by a long, thin shaft of ash wood, tipped with shining steel and fletched with grey goose feathers. Someone gasped in surprise and all looked up in time to see the crow transformed from a creature of the sky into what looked like a bundle of black rags on the end of a stick. The lifeless heap of it landed a few feet from the bottom of the tower house and a scruffy dog trotted over to inspect the windfall.

All eyes, Sir Robert's included, turned then to focus on the archer, though every man in Hawkshaw knew instinctively who it was that must have loosed the arrow – who alone among them had such casual mastery of the art. It was Angus Armstrong. He walked towards them, his longbow of the good red yew held loosely in his left hand.

'Are we going hunting?' he said, to no one in particular, though all waited for Sir Robert to respond.

'Aye, hunting it is, Mr Armstrong,' he said. 'We will ride out to find the rest of the patrol. I tell you all now: I will know the whole story by nightfall.'

There were shouted orders then as men came to their senses and set about the business of preparing to leave, and on a war footing. Violent death was hardly a rarity in these debatable lands, but Sir Robert Jardine of Hawkshaw was known to be unusually vengeful – even by the standards of the day. He interpreted any abuse of his men as an attack upon his own person. And then there was the matter of the victim. Will Kennedy was feared at best by most of the community around Hawkshaw, but none had expected to live to see the day when any gained the upper hand in a fight with the man.

'Where is the Moor?' shouted Sir Robert, as he strode towards the stables. Angus Armstrong had recovered his arrow from the crow's carcass. He and Jamie Douglas and several more of the men trotted over to his lairdship and kept pace with him.

None of them had offered any immediate reply to Sir Robert's enquiry.

'Khassan – Badr Khassan? Where is he?' asked Sir Robert a second time, a note of impatience rising in his throat like gall.

'He's not here,' said Armstrong.

He it was that had been first of all the Hawkshaw men to meet the giant stranger upon his arrival on the road in front of the fortress more than two months before. Having brought him inside the palisade, Armstrong had felt a responsibility for the stranger's presence ever since. Though he had grown to respect, even to like the man they called the Bear, still he had bothered to keep an eye on the stranger's comings and goings.

Sir Robert stopped and turned to face Armstrong, a man he valued above all others and found it worth paying attention to – in times of strife, most of all.

'He's not here, my lord,' said Armstrong again. 'I have not seen him since yesterday, in fact, and I am confident of saying he did not spend last night at Hawkshaw.'

Badr Khassan had been in the habit of leaving Hawkshaw on his own. If anyone asked him about it, he always put it down to curiosity.

'I am a stranger in a strange land,' he would say. 'There is much to see and to know.'

Sir Robert had been informed of Badr Khassan's habits and had been content to leave him on a long leash. As far as he was concerned, if people saw the Moor on Jardine land, then he served as a visible symbol of his own ever-present authority in these parts.

It burned Armstrong to have to admit that he had no idea concerning Khassan's whereabouts. He did not make mistakes, and yet ... and yet it seemed to him that the Bear's absence at such a time was more than a coincidence. For the first time in a long time he felt he had been – now what was the word ... outmanoeuvred. He would not let the same thing happen twice in one day.

Sir Robert remained stationary, and for a moment Armstrong knew he read thoughts similar to his own on his master's face.

Saying nothing, Sir Robert turned and strode faster still, down towards the stable block. A groom had his horse ready, as always – a tall and broad-chested destrier, a warhorse – and he almost leapt into the saddle in his haste to be away. The beast was briefly startled and reared

61

slightly in protest, but Sir Robert brought it quickly and easily under control before wheeling it around and making for the gates of the palisade at a canter.

Casting his mind back to the evening before, to his conversation with Davey Kennedy, he stumbled suddenly across memories of Patrick Grant. Along with thoughts of Grant came memories of a woman. Those images were worn and stained, like portraits hung on a wall exposed to too much daylight. Before mounting his horse he had had not an idea in his head of where in his demesne to begin the search for the foe. Now, without knowing quite why, he shouted out their destination. They would head first of all to the sometime home of the man who had wronged him and all his heirs, leaving them with so little when they might have had so much.

7

John Grant dreamed he was flying high in the sky, or perhaps swimming in deep water. In any event, he was weightless and graceful as he soared, twisted and dived through an element that offered no resistance. He loved it. And then he hated it. All at once there was an awful dizziness as the world, or at least the world inside his head, began to spin, faster and faster. He felt the contents of his stomach pitch and roll. He closed his eyes as the sensation, so briefly perfect and wonderful, turned into a lurching fall. He was sinking deep or plummeting to earth and he opened his mouth to cry out, or to vomit, or both...

He returned to consciousness then, helpless and weak like a drowning man dragged from rapids. He lay on his back, his head supported, mercifully, by something soft. The world still spun for him – not the familiar grinding turn of the planet on its axis that he lived by, but a hideously tight rotation. When he opened his eyes he saw not his mother, nor even an empty heaven above, but a huge black face that seemed to be in high-speed orbit around his own sorrowful skull.

He breathed in sharply and felt the spinning start to slow. He tried to rise, pushing with his elbows, but a crushing pain in his head made him clench his eyes shut and collapse back on to the grass. Strong hands held his shoulders then, and when he opened his eyes a second time, just slits, the huge black face was almost stationary and beginning to speak.

'Stay down for now,' it said, the voice gentle.

'My mother?' said John Grant, remembering all of it at once. 'Where...?'

'She will be well. She sleeps. That's best for now.'

'Did they... Was she...?'

'They did not touch her,' said Badr Khassan. 'She rests now on her bed. The blow to her head was a heavy one, I think.'

John Grant raised a hand to his face, felt a crust of dried blood.

'Where are they?' he asked.

'They are at peace too,' said Badr. 'Though a deeper peace than that presently enjoyed by your mother.'

'You...?'

'Yes, little master,' said the Moor. 'I have sent them ahead to face judgment.'

'You killed them?' asked John Grant.

Badr shrugged, made light of the deed. He limited his reply to the practicalities of the work.

'Small spaces like the inside of your cottage make it easier for one man to deal with many – keeps the targets bunched together, no?' He reached behind his back for his scimitar, unsheathed it and held it in front of John Grant's face. 'And my good friend was with me, so all was well.' He allowed himself a grim smile.

Stunned as he was, head spinning and with a still-sickening ache in his middle, John Grant was suddenly aware of his mother. Turning to look at the cottage, he saw her standing in the doorway, leaning heavily against the woodwork. Seeing her son lying on the ground, and with a huge stranger kneeling over him, she cried out.

'Get away from him!'

She lunged towards them, but after no more than a couple of strides her legs gave way beneath her and she toppled headlong.

Badr Khassan was by her side in an instant.

'I am a friend,' he said, reaching for her as she struggled to rise once more, only making it to her knees.

Jessie lashed out blindly with both fists, but while the blows connected, they seemed as ineffectual as raindrops. Badr crouched beside her, easily pinning her arms by her sides. She looked into his face then and his calm expression slowly made her relax. The tension went out of her arms and she allowed him to help her rise to her feet.

John Grant was standing too now, unsteadily, and he stumbled towards his mother with his arms outstretched. They came together, all of them, and made an unlikely trio. Badr backed away from mother and child while the pair embraced.

'Who are you?' asked Jessie, defeated, still holding her son and with her back to the giant stranger.

'I am all the trouble in the world,' replied Badr, his eyes towards the ground at his feet. 'But I came to settle a debt.'

Jessie turned to face him, an unspoken question on her face.

'You are the wife of Patrick Grant?' he asked. 'And the boy is his son?'

'Patrick? You have news of Patrick?' she said, eyes widening in disbelief.

Badr was silent for long enough to let finely pointed roots of fear grow down into Jessie's chest.

'Patrick Grant is dead,' he said, taking care now to look her in the eyes.

Jessie took a single step backwards, stumbling. For a moment Badr thought she might fall once more, but she rallied, steadied herself, and reached out instead for her son. Failing to feel him with her outstretched hand, she turned to look for him. But John Grant was nowhere to be seen.

'John!' she called out, her mind reeling, knocked in all directions at once. There was a sound in her head like rushing water, and she thought she might faint. 'John!'

From behind the cottage there came a single cry. Jessie turned towards the sound, but Badr Khassan was quicker. He passed her in two great strides and was ducking around the low gable end before she was even under way. Picking up her skirts with both hands, she followed the giant unsteadily, and as she rounded the building she almost ran into his great broad back. Beyond him stood John Grant, stiff as a post, arms by his sides, staring at a row of dead men laid out neatly on the ground, their heads against the back wall of the cottage, like so much firewood.

'We cannot stay here,' said Badr.

His voice reached her across a yawning chasm – the distance between the familiar past and the uncertain future.

'They would have had you – all of them,' he said.

She could not stop looking at the bloodied corpses of Davey Kennedy and the rest. It was already impossible to think that these empty, broken shells had ever lived. The absence of life, plucked from them so recently, made it seem they had always been dead. John Grant had seen enough, however, and turned to bury his face in her chest.

'And when they were done with you, they would have killed you,' Badr added. 'The boy too, I don't doubt.'

'My father is dead,' said John Grant, quietly. It was a statement rather than a question.

'Patrick Grant saved my life,' said Badr. 'I would do the same for his family. You must come with me, both of you.'

Jessie looked at him over one shoulder.

'Where can we go?' she asked.

'As far away from here as we can get,' he said.

8

It seemed to John Grant that sleep wanted nothing whatsoever to do with him. Lying on his back and looking up into a sky stirred thick with stars, he felt he would never sleep again. It was hard even to close his eyes. He tried to summon his father's image but found he was able only to visualise an outline, almost a shadow.

He had always felt sure he knew what his father looked like – that he would have recognised him at once if he appeared before them now – but the features of the face, let alone any expressions, like a smile or a frown, eluded him. He knew he ought to be mourning the loss, crying. But all he felt was anxiety – a nagging emptiness that made him feel he had forgotten something important. Somewhere there as well was the truth of it all – that his mental image of his father was made not of his own memories, but those of his mother.

Patrick Grant had been in his life for only fragments of time, and all of those when he was too young to remember. The picture that came to his mind at the mention of his father was made of snatches of detail his mother had given him, though she had few enough of her own. He did not properly remember his father at all. His memories were hand-me-downs and borrowings; leftovers and scraps from meals enjoyed by others while he was left hungry, but treasured just the same.

The night was a warm one, but still as a tomb – as if the universe itself waited, breath bated, to see what might happen next. He slowly turned his head until he could make out the shape of Badr Khassan, a seated silhouette a shade darker even than the night, leaning against a solitary tree some little way from where John Grant lay close by his mother. He looked at her next, curled into an S and with her back to him. There was no way of telling if sleep eluded her too, but she seemed peaceful.

Badr had forced them onwards, southwards, for hours, long after darkness fell. He had allowed them mere minutes back at the cottage to gather together a few belongings – clothes, some food – before selecting a garron for each of them from among those of the dead troopers. The rest of the beasts he had driven away, with shouts and claps and a slap to the hindquarters of the one nearest. The animals had scattered, together with the remnants of the life John Grant had known before the coming of the Moor.

Khassan had almost thrown him into his mount's saddle before being slightly gentler with his mother. For many hours thereafter they had kept up a punishing pace – a ride made all the harder by the big man's insistence on staying far from any roads or even trackways.

'They will be after us soon enough,' he said as they started out. 'Distance from this place must be our only friend now – the more miles the better.'

He had led them into the high country then,

from where it was possible to see in all directions and so ensure they kept away from any who might observe their flight and speak of it to others.

'The fewer folk catch sight of us for the first few days, the better it will be for us,' he said.

John Grant had nodded his assent to whatever Badr said. Jessie, however, devoted all her efforts to watching the landscape around them. Her expression seemed as desolate as the hills they passed over, and since leaving their home she had remained all but silent.

It was while John Grant was a little ahead and just out of earshot that Badr took the opportunity to speak to Jessie.

'I know about the boy,' he said.

Jessie kept her eyes on the track ahead.

'What about him?' she asked.

'I was close to Patrick,' he said. 'For many years. We talked together and I knew him well.'

It was no answer to her question, but Jessie guessed at his meaning just the same.

'He is all I have,' she said.

'And you are all he has, I know,' said Badr. 'I wish only to tell you that I will do all I can for you both. I had hoped to find you well. If I am honest, I had thought you might be ... better looked after.'

'By another man, you mean?' She did not ask the question harshly – if anything, there was a smile in her voice, for the first time. 'I think not.'

She turned to look at Badr, and he felt sudden embarrassment and turned away.

'I had not expected to find you both in danger,' he said. 'And now it is clear that my presence here, and my actions, has done more harm than good. I came only to see that you were safe and well – as Patrick had hoped – but I have brought trouble with me instead.'

Jessie nodded.

'We have been alone until now,' she said. 'Jardine and his men have hung over us like a shadow all the while. Trouble of one sort or another would have come our way eventually. I am glad you are here … to share it.'

He stole a glance at her profile and saw the proud set of her jaw.

'I must tell you that I had not prepared a rescue mission,' he said. 'Beyond finding shelter tonight, and putting more distance between us and Jardine tomorrow … I have no plan.'

Jessie Grant said no more and instead kicked her horse into a trot that put her alongside her son.

The sky was cloudless and the moon, not quite full, seemed to shrug one hunched shoulder at them. The long dusk of summer had given time for their eyes to adjust to the fading of the day, and now a million stars added lustre to the curtain of night.

As they dropped down below a ridge of high ground and on to a wide terrace, the way ahead had seemed blocked by huge figures. Badr had pulled up his great black warhorse in alarm, and while his eyes struggled to make sense of the scene before them, it had been John Grant who was first to recognise the ambush for what it was: a circle of standing stones. The push would have told him if there was life up here and it had not done so.

'I have seen the like of this before,' said Badr, after John Grant had explained. 'Stones stood on end by the ancients, for some or other magical purpose, or so I was told.'

'I am told my father said the people who lived here before us felt the need to track the journeys of the stars, and also of the sun and the moon,' said John Grant.

'Astronomers,' murmured Badr, nodding.

'Ast...?' said John Grant, failing to catch the whole of the word.

'Astronomers,' said Badr carefully. 'Astronomy is the study of the arrangement of the stars.' He looked at the boy then, searching his face for understanding and finding none.

'These are Greek words,' he said.

'Greeks?' asked John Grant. At least this time he had been able to repeat the word the Moor had spoken.

'Having saved your skin, now I must save your soul, I see,' said Badr. 'Your education begins now. It will pass the time for both of us.'

Badr had them settle by the stones, almost in their shadows. It would be as good a place as any to pass the night, he said, and perhaps the spirits of the ancients would watch over them through the remaining hours of darkness. Though he said nothing, John Grant was pleased by the choice of campsite. He knew, even if the Moor did not, that standing stones like these were regarded with suspicion by most folk hereabouts. It was said they had witnessed wickedness long ago, scenes of human sacrifice and witchcraft and the like, and none but the brave and the foolhardy risked spending time among them. They would be safe, he thought.

71

Lying in the darkness, his thoughts whirling like a gin, he stretched his arms out beyond the edge of his blanket until he could place his hands, palms downwards, on the cool grass. He spread his fingers and waited. There it was – the rumbling vibration of the spinning of the world. He could hear it too, deeper than the deepest bass note beneath the rise and fall of his own breathing and the beating of his heart, like wind in distant tree-tops. It was a comfort, a reminder that far beneath his cares, the world was turning, spinning forwards into the dark, as it should and always would. He let go and gave himself up entirely to the fall towards the stars, a movement so enveloping and so vast that all other considerations were swept away like dead leaves.

It was his mother's voice that brought him back.

'Why *did* Davey Kennedy and the rest turn up at my door?' she asked.

Badr considered the question for a few moments.

'You would have had to ask his brother,' he said.

'Will Kennedy,' she said. 'That snake. What was he up to this time?'

Badr nodded approvingly at the use of the word.

'I spent enough time at Hawkshaw to learn the truth of that,' he said. 'He, and a few others in thrall to him ... encouraged tenants like Thomas Henderson to part with an extra coin or two each month. If they did so, then their homes and children were left alone.'

'Folk have little enough as it is,' she said. 'Why are there always men like Kennedy ready with ideas to make life harder still?'

'Will Kennedy has nothing at all now,' said Badr. 'It was his gang who burned out the Hendersons the night before last. Drove them off for holding back what they owed him.'

'And you?' asked Jessie.

'I found him there yesterday morning,' he said. 'Perhaps he meant to cover his tracks – or maybe he was drawn back there by his own ill will. Whatever – he did not expect to encounter me there. We had words.'

'Well ... good,' she said.

'I expect there was no particular reason for Davey to lead his troopers to your door,' he said. 'You and your son were just–'

She interrupted him before he could finish.

'We were just somewhere he could bring his anger,' she said. 'Jardine and his cronies have needed little excuse to make trouble for me and mine.'

There was a silence then, and John Grant gave himself completely to the planet's spin, relishing the freedom from thought.

'What happened to my husband?' asked Jessie, and the boy drew back from the void.

Badr moved in the darkness, turned to face the place where she lay.

'Your husband saved my life,' he said. 'Men came to kill me – and would have succeeded.' He coughed to clear his throat and rubbed his hands over his face.

'I was asleep, laid low with a fever. They locked the door of my bedchamber from the outside and set the house ablaze. They used some infernal mixture, I think, to make the flames take hold fast and fiercely. The smoke befuddled me, made my sleep all the deeper.'

'And Patrick?' she asked.

'Unknown to my enemies, he was in the attic room above me. He broke through the boards of his floor – my ceiling. He was able to rouse me. When I awoke, my clothes were on fire and he was beating out the flames. Together we jumped for our lives from a window – to a lower balcony of a building next door.'

'So what happened to Patrick?' asked Jessie, her voice empty of emotion. 'Why is it that you are here while he is not?'

'Your husband had me jump first. It was the push he gave me that made all the difference, I am sure,' said Badr. 'But I landed badly, heavily. What with the burns and the fever and all, I ... I lost consciousness.'

John Grant heard the scratching, rustling sound of restless hands once more.

'When I came to, Patrick Grant was not with me. I was alone on the balcony and the fire was all around, spreading between the buildings. I heard people crying, men shouting. I got to my feet, calling for him.'

He paused and then stared down at his hands.

'I looked down into the alleyway below, and ... and he was lying there. He did not manage the leap, or missed his grasp. Something.'

He shrugged hopelessly.

There was a long pause then, a silence none felt able to break.

'I was not there for him as he had been for me,'

said Badr. 'Either to send him on his way or to catch him as he fell.'

'He was dead,' said Jessie. John Grant listened for any sound of loss, and heard none. It had been a plain statement of fact.

'He wasn't dead,' said Badr. 'Not then. Not quite. I made it down to him and found him still alive.'

'Did you take him to where others might have helped him?' asked John Grant.

He felt Badr and his mother turn to look at him, as though just that moment remembering he was with them.

'Did you get help?' he asked once more.

'There was nothing to be done,' said Badr quietly. 'He lived only long enough to tell me where to find you.'

John Grant felt his face flush with hot blood.

'He told me where to find you,' Badr said to the boy. 'And asked that I might seek you out. If needs be, keep you safe.'

'Did he make me part of the debt as well?' asked Jessie.

'He did,' said Badr. He paused.

'Why was Patrick with you?' asked Jessie.

'He is my friend,' said Badr. 'He was my friend.'

John Grant detected a smile in the voice, alongside the sadness.

'Where did it happen?' asked Jessie after another silence. 'All of this.'

'The Eternal City,' said Badr, as though the answer should have been obvious, or known to her at least.

'In London?' asked Jessie, confused.

'London – that sewer,' he said. 'The only thing everlasting about that shit pile is the stench. Spare me the thought.'

Neither mother nor son spoke a word; only waited for their guardian to stop speaking in riddles and make himself clear.

'*A'udhu Billah*,' muttered the Moor. 'My refuge is in Allah. Truly Patrick Grant kept his people in ignorance. You have my sympathy, mistress, and you too, little master.

'Patrick Grant and I were together in the Eternal City of Rome,' he said. 'Home of your Holy Father.'

Before Jessie had time to consider how much remained to be explained about her late husband's last adventure, her son threw back his thin covering and sat upright in the dark. Hearing the movement and sensing the boy's sudden change of mood, Badr stood up and took a few silent strides in his direction.

'Someone's out there,' said John Grant, his skin pricking beneath his clothes, almost painfully, like a bout of chilblains.

'Where?' whispered Badr, and hairs rose on the boy's neck at the soft sighing sound of the great curved sword being slid from within its fur-lined sheath.

'Not sure,' said the boy. 'Still some way off. More than one person, though – and horses.'

Badr was crouching by John Grant's side and there was more than enough moonlight for him to see which way the boy was facing. Taking that direction as his cue, he set off downhill. The big man's sudden absence made mother and son feel suddenly and terribly alone and helpless. They huddled together – she straining to persuade her senses to let her hear or see anything useful, he reassured by the way his own senses told him there was nothing and no one to fear. He clung to her just the same, savouring the closeness and enjoying the warmth of her breath against his cheek. Agonising minutes drew out. Neither spoke.

He felt a movement in the otherwise still air, but detected no threat from it. He breathed out a long, steady sigh of relief. The return of their guardian some little while later almost made Jessie cry out. He came to them as fast and lithe as a deer and had one hand cupped gently over her mouth before she had a chance to make a sound.

'You were right, boy,' he said quietly, his voice betraying admiration, or disbelief. Badr was a trained and battle-hardened survivor. He relied on his senses more than his sword, or his horse, and yet he had noticed nothing at all before this callow boy had quietly warned of the presence, albeit distant, of a threat to their safety. 'Half a mile downslope from us and moving south, on the same line as ourselves but across a terrace below the plateau where we are now. Sir Robert Jardine and around a score of men. Their horses' tack makes no noise. They must have the metalwork wrapped in rags to muffle any sound. I came close enough to the last of them to hear their talk.'

'And what were they saying?' asked Jessie.

Badr said nothing for a moment or two before continuing, almost reluctantly.

'Let us just say they have visited your cottage,' he said. And found their comrades. I knew they would set out in pursuit but I did not expect them to follow us into the night.'

He placed a heavy hand on the boy's shoulder.

'How did you know Sir Robert and the rest of them were out there?' he asked. 'What gave them away to you?'

John Grant was quiet, looking down at his fingers interlaced on his lap.

'Well?' asked Badr once more.

'I just ... I knew,' he said finally. 'I always know people are there before I see them.'

'You did it before,' said Badr. His tone was light and John Grant looked up at the dim outline of the Moor's face, the eyes flecked with starlight. 'While I waited at your cottage yesterday for the right moment to deal with your attackers. I could see you and your mother, though you both had your backs to me. I made no move, no sound at all, I know it – and yet you turned towards where I was crouching. If I hadn't ducked back behind the building then, you would have looked me straight in the eye.'

John Grant felt the Moor's face crease into a smile and more starlight flashed along the edges of great white teeth.

'How did you do it?'

His hands balled involuntarily into fists before he answered. No one had noticed before, far less asked questions. Not even his mother. The moment, and this man, seemed right nonetheless.

'The push told me,' he said.

'The *push?*' said his mother, her voice rising into the first show of real feeling since they had set out. 'The push ... *told* you? What in the name of Almighty God are you talking about? What is the push?'

He felt the colour rise into his cheeks. He hated his mother's disapproval more than any rebuke. Worse still, her tone carried a note of hurt – that here was a secret he had kept from her.

Badr said nothing and instead allowed the weight of a mother's interrogation of a dutiful son to do its work.

'It's what I call it when I ... know something that I ... well, that I can't see, or hear,' he said, almost sadly.

'The *push?*' she asked again, apparently no further forward in her attempt to take in what she was hearing.

'That's how it feels, like the air gets, I don't know ... thicker maybe ... and moves in my direction,' he managed. 'It feels like I'm being pushed ... from the direction of whatever it is I can't see...'

'Or hear.' It was Badr who finished the sentence.

Whatever had moved John Grant to reveal some of his view of the world, the shocks of the day – the beating, the fear, the sight of all the bodies – left him then. He had said enough. He would leave out any mention of the turning of the planet, the feel and the sound of it.

'Well it's all surprises today!' said Jessie, louder than she intended, and all three of them flinched at the sound. She went on, standing now and turning on the spot, giving vent to pent-up emotion, hissing like a kettle come to the boil. 'My long-absent husband is dead – in Rome and half a world away,' she spat. 'I've come within a sweaty

79

finger's breadth of being raped in my own home. Now I'm on the run with my child and a giant who has just killed, on my behalf, more men than I've ever had round my table at one time.'

She sat down, hard, upon the ground and buried her head in her arms. She mumbled the rest of it into her skirts, so that they hardly heard what she said.

'And now my son says he has the power of witchcraft ... that he *feels people*.'

'I don't feel people,' John Grant said. He regretted having revealed any of it. 'I said I feel the push of them.'

All three were quiet then, briefly lost in their own thoughts. Somewhere out in the night a dog fox barked and received no answering call.

'Why now?' asked Jessie. 'My son and I have been alone for most of the years of his life. Why do you come among us now?'

Badr sighed. 'I feel time catching up with me,' he said.

Jessie Grant snorted, nodding her head.

'I have seen a great deal of the world. I have done many things, but...'

'But?' she asked.

'But I have been selfish.'

'How so?' she asked.

'All the battles I have fought, all the lives I have cut short...' He stopped, hesitated. 'All of it has been for myself,' he said, feeling for a pathway through jumbled thoughts. 'I have neglected the needs of others. Others I should have helped, cared for. I have kept my back to them. Or at least I have never done enough that was right.'

He fell into silence and Jessie Grant let him be. More silent minutes passed before her son whispered into the dark:

'I feel it again – from beyond the stones.'

John Grant was briefly angry with himself. All the while his elders had spoken, his skin had fairly jangled with the presence of figures unseen. His earlier confession of his ability had made him feel ashamed, furtive, and for the first and only time he had sought to ignore the warning.

The Moor placed a finger to his mouth, demanding silence. His other hand he held palm outwards, towards Jessie. He rose into a low crouch and crept across the grass until he was behind one of the great monoliths. Painfully slowly he moved his head around one edge until he could peer across the interior of the circle, a space illuminated by moon- and starlight, and empty.

In spite of herself, and in spite of Badr's signal to remain motionless, Jessie got to her feet and began closing the gap separating her from her son. Hearing the movement, the rustle of clothing, Badr turned towards them. The action caused him to lose balance momentarily, and he stumbled forward into the gap between two stones. Sensing sudden danger, more intense than the push, John Grant leapt to his feet and reached out for his mother.

All three were therefore exposed to harm's way when Angus Armstrong, archer and would-be assassin, released the stored power of his bowstring.

9

'I could not have loved you more,' said Jessie Grant.

Her eyes were closed and her words barely audible, so that he felt he was reading them on the cracked, dry parchment of her lips. John Grant, down on his knees, bent and pressed his face against her cheek. Her skin was cold and clammy to the touch, and matched the silvery blue cast applied to her complexion by the moonlight. Much worse, he found he was struggling to recognise her through the veil of injury and pain that separated them now.

The three of them – Jessie and John Grant, and Badr Khassan – were together in the burial chamber of an ancient tomb. Armstrong's arrow had found Jessie, piercing her from side to side just above her hipbones. Fast as thought, Badr had spotted the source of the missile – a man standing beyond the far side of the stone circle. Without apparent concern for his own safety, the Moor had begun sprinting towards the archer, and the archer had turned and disappeared into the shadows.

Badr had returned a minute later, anger and frustration rising from him like a charge of static electricity. He found the boy kneeling, cradling his mother's head in his lap. He had known at once there was no saving her, but he could hardly have expected the boy to leave her where she fell.

Against his better judgement, then, they had carried her away from the circle of stones in search of shelter, a more private place. Only by luck had they chanced upon the tomb. Badr's attention had been drawn first of all by what he took to be a stand of gorse bushes, a low, dark hump barely discernible in the gloom and close by the place where Jessie had been felled. The Moor fancied there might be some cover there, perhaps a protective hollow in which to crouch out of sight and wait for the woman to die.

There had been gorse right enough, but the thorny bushes had taken root, in their hundreds, around the entrance to a megalithic tomb. Carefully placed upright stones and lintels made a passage leading to a roughly square chamber that was more than large enough to shelter the three of them. The roof was formed by a pair of colossal stone slabs that had once been placed neatly together. The millennia that had passed since the long-dead farmers had completed their self-appointed task had seen the slabs slump apart, however, so that the chamber was partly open to the night sky and flooded with moonlight. Badr had crawled into the passageway first and then turned to haul Jessie in behind him by her shoulders. John Grant had struggled forward on hands and knees, doing his best to support her legs. Despite their efforts, she had groaned as their manoeuvrings caused the arrow shaft to twist and turn inside her body.

The roof of the chamber was higher than that of the passage, but still low. They had laid Jessie out between them and then knelt either side.

John Grant had busied himself for a minute or two by smoothing her clothes, making sure her legs were together and decently covered. Content that at least her dignity was intact, he had then fussed over her hair, tidying stray strands from her face and forehead.

It was as he was finishing the job that she spoke to him.

'I could not have loved you more,' she said.

'I love you too, Mum,' he said, his face buried in the space between her neck and her shoulder. 'I need you... I...' He broke off and rolled on to his heels so that he could look at her face. He rocked back and forth, like a penitent at prayer.

'Don't leave me. Please...' he said.

Badr Khassan, giant and warrior, more used to causing harm than coping with its consequences, reached out with one uncertain hand. Unsure at first where best to lay it, he left it hovering for a moment before deciding to place it gently on the boy's shoulder. He was so slight, even fragile, and Badr winced at the thought that this boy would soon be alone in the world. John Grant tore his gaze from his mother's face and looked at him. Badr looked back and saw fear. Worse, he saw a wordless cry for help.

'Leave her be, son,' he said. 'Her wounds are beyond what little skill I possess. I am quite sure they are beyond any help.'

Badr watched as the boy slumped, collapsing into himself and seeming to diminish. For all his anguish, though, he apparently understood that he was being told the truth.

Badr reached for a bag at his belt. After rummaging inside it for a moment, he produced a small glass bottle wrapped in leather. He removed its stopper and, cradling Jessie's head in one hand, helped her take a few sips from it.

'It tastes bad – bitter,' he said to her. 'But it will help the pain.'

He settled her down and watched as she licked her lips, seeking every trace.

'I could not have loved you more,' said Jessie again, her voice near as quiet as a thought.

Both of them looked down at her. Badr felt like an intruder. He was certain, however, that Armstrong would shortly return with the rest of the troopers. His concern that all of them must remain in the chamber, out of sight, kept him from absenting himself from the scene. Jessie's eyes were open and she looked more like herself. John Grant laid his hand gently upon one of her hip bones, as close to the arrow as he dared. He could feel her battling to reassemble herself, the self he had always known. She knew it was slipping from her like worn-out clothes, but by a force of will that passed through his fingers and into his body, he detected her efforts to rally, if only for a little while.

'I know that, Mum,' he said. He felt the need to swallow, and would have sworn a handful of jagged gorse was lodged in his throat. He reached for one of her hands and clasped it tightly in his own, like a drowning man.

'Stay with me,' he said. 'Please stay with me.'

She turned her head so that she was looking straight at him. Her eyes were all darkness, the pupils dilated, and he felt them draw him forward with their own gravity. She tried to raise her head from the dry earthen floor of the chamber, but the effort was beyond her. She blinked hard, swallowing her agony.

'My son,' she said. Her hand had been limp within his own, and frighteningly cold, but now he felt her fingers squeezing back as though willing him to understand something she lacked the strength to say.

'I know, Mum,' he said. He needed her to know he felt loved by her, had always and only felt loved by her, and he pulled her hand towards him and buried his face in her palm. The smell of her skin, so familiar, seemed like the scent of his life, of his world.

'Mum... Mum,' he said, hungry for the feel and the sound of the word. 'I could not have been more loved.'

Her hand relaxed and felt suddenly heavy. He placed it gently by her side, and when he looked into her eyes, he knew that she was gone. It was the very instant of her dying, and as he watched, a shimmer like smoke, or perhaps the heat haze from a flame, rose from her body, hung in the air for a moment, and disappeared.

He gasped and looked at the Moor.

'Did you see?' he asked, his eyes suddenly blinded by tears, his voice broken into brittle shards. 'Did you *see?*'

Badr shrugged helplessly and shook his head, uncomprehending.

'See what?' he asked.

John Grant understood that he and he alone had been vouchsafed the vision. He turned back to his mother and found he was looking only at some form resembling the mother he loved. He gasped and raised his hand to his mouth, stunned by the change and by the sudden absence. Her scent was still on his skin, had somehow outlived her, and he breathed deeply, a great jagged gulp of a breath that he hoped to hold inside his chest for ever.

The tears overwhelmed him then and he dropped his chin on to his chest, his whole body racked with sobs. Badr, a novice in the art of comforting broken-hearted boys, shuffled over to him on his knees, his hair brushing against one of the roof slabs of the chamber so that he felt like a clumsy bear in a cave right enough. For all his years, for all the wisdom he possessed, he found he had nothing to say, nothing of value to offer. He thought about taking the boy in his arms, but did not. He waited helplessly while the waves of John Grant's grief broke around them both.

Suddenly the boy stopped crying, a breath hitched in his throat. He tensed, and Badr felt the change in his posture.

'They're coming back,' said John Grant.

Badr held one finger against his own lips. Slowly and silently he crawled to the passage and down the length of it. Part of the stone circle was visible from the mouth of the tomb, was in fact aligned upon it, and at first the Moor saw no one. The stone sentinels were alone in the moonlight but he knew better than to doubt the boy's instincts. He heard a scuffling behind him and looked round to see John Grant scuttling towards him down the passage. He stopped just behind him and to one side, and Badr reached out a hand, to make sure he went no further, and placed it on his knee.

Well balanced though he was, squatted down on his hunkers, the big man reeled and almost fell backwards into the passage. He kept his hand on the boy's leg, desperate to regain his equilibrium, but a tide of force was pushing against his whole body. There was more besides. Where before the world had been steady beneath his feet, now he felt a horribly disorientating sense of falling, and turning. It was like trying to maintain his balance while standing on a floating log. Overwhelmed and dizzy, as though a sudden earthquake had taken hold of the land, he took his hand from the boy's knee and spread both arms out so that he might brace himself against the passage walls.

As soon as his hand left the boy, the sensations were gone – the world fixed in place once more and his stance upon it secure. He stared at John Grant, aghast. The boy looked back at him, and nodded once, almost in sympathy, before turning and crawling back down the passage.

After a few moments, his senses still rattled, Badr heard, or rather felt, the approach of galloping horses. Seconds later they appeared from the low ground below. With Sir Robert Jardine and Angus Armstrong at their head, they made a circuit of the stones before riding into the centre and gathering there. Badr listened to Jardine's shouted instructions, and while he could not, at such a distance, make out the words, the intent was clear. The horsemen scattered in all directions and began searching the surrounding area. Wider and wider they moved, holding on to their horses' reins while they rode, and leaning outwards and down, scanning the ground for evidence of disturbance.

There was a shout, from a voice Badr recognised at once, and then Jamie Douglas returned to the stones leading three horses – Badr's stallion and the two beasts he had selected for Jessie and John Grant.

Badr had hoped to find the horses again at daybreak, but if only their mounts were seized this night, he and the boy would have to count themselves lucky. Once or twice a mounted man passed close by the gorse bushes. One of them even took the trouble to dismount and strike at a few jagged branches with his sword – but neither he nor anyone else spotted the earthen mound, and the stone chamber within it, squatting in the midst of the thorns.

Armstrong cantered over to Jamie and the pair exchanged a few words. They would be encouraged no end by the find of the horses, thought Badr, and grimaced. As well as their means of transport, the horses carried on their backs the only food and supplies they had in the world. The fugitives were on foot now, and equipped with only their clothes and Badr's weapons.

Armstrong put two fingers to his mouth and gave a short, sharp whistle. The mounted men quickly gathered to him, and after a few more words and gestures, the hunting party spread out, with Armstrong and Jardine at the centre of a wide front, and headed off downhill into the night.

'They think they have us on the run,' Badr whispered to himself, as he crawled back into the chamber.

John Grant was lying by his mother's side, his head touching hers, one arm slung across her chest. When he heard Badr return, he sat up quickly, embarrassed despite his grief.

'Can we take the arrow out?' he asked.

Badr did not reply, but crawled over to Jessie and touched the steel arrowhead with one hand. John Grant watched him closely but nonetheless missed the moment when the knife appeared in the big man's hand. He glimpsed the flash of metal and then it was gone again, and Badr was holding the arrowhead, the ash shaft neatly cut away. He looked at it for a second or two, considering its shape, then tossed it aside. Gently he pulled on the feathered end of the shaft, turning it as he did so, until the whole length of it was clear.

John Grant sighed heavily, apparently relieved to see the thing removed from his mother's body, dead as she was. Content that the operation was complete, the defilement undone, he settled down by her side again. His need to touch her overwhelmed any care that the Moor might be watching him, and he began gently to stroke the hair over her ear with the back of his hand.

Badr crawled into the darkness against one side of the chamber. He settled down with his back against the wall, his legs straight out in front of him. From there he could keep an eye and not be seen, and he watched as the boy curled into a sleeping position, his face back in the space between his mother's neck and shoulder. John Grant opened one eye and, despite the shadow, fixed his stare on Badr's face. For a moment the Moor felt the hairs rise on the back of his neck.

'Now you know what it's like,' said the boy. 'What it's like to be me.'

Badr said nothing and only nodded, remembering the dizzying, sickening disorientation he had felt in the passageway for as long as his hand had been in contact with the boy. He was unsure whether or not John Grant was able to see his features there in the shadows.

'I have never let anyone close before – while I could feel the push. I did not know what would happen if anyone touched me while it was upon me. You're the first to … to share it.'

Badr nodded in the dark and closed his eyes.

He had not expected to sleep, but he awoke to find the silvery-blue light of the moon replaced by that of early morning. The boy was still sleeping; in fact he appeared not to have moved. Rather than crawling down the passage, Badr risked raising his head through the gap between the roof slabs. As he had expected, there were no signs of life. Armstrong and his men would surely be searching fruitlessly elsewhere, hopefully many miles away.

It was when he ducked down into the chamber once more that he spotted the bones. Scattered on the ground around the walls were long bones, ribs and, here and there, fragments the Moor easily recognised as parts of skulls.

Disturbed by Badr's movements, John Grant awoke. For an instant he was unaware of all that had happened, still befuddled by sleep, but when he looked at his mother's body, the truth of it all rushed around him like flood water. He turned to look at Badr and saw that the big man was holding, balanced on the palm of one large hand, a human jawbone, the teeth shining like misshapen pearls. He gasped, horrified, and then as his eyes grew accustomed to the light he spotted the rest, scattered around the four walls of the chamber like bleached driftwood. Feeling suddenly unclean, he stood up, brushing at his clothes, and it was only by luck that his head found the gap between the slabs rather than a skull-cracking collision. Realising that he was visible to any lurking predators, he ducked back down again.

'They are long gone,' said Badr. 'Hopefully many miles from here. Perhaps back at Hawkshaw licking their wounds.'

John Grant slumped down on to the floor, his sorry head between his upraised knees and his momentary revulsion at the sight of the desiccated human remains replaced by overwhelming sadness.

Aware of the need to get moving, and to keep moving, Badr gently ruffled the boy's hair.

'Let us take care of her now,' he said.

The thought of leaving his mother in such a lonely place, surrounded by the scattered remains of ancient dead, brought a horrified protest from the boy at first – until Badr suggested that perhaps there was no better place to lie than among friends.

'These are the bones of people like your own,' he said. 'They lived and died long ago, that much is true, but no doubt they farmed the land around here just like you ... just like your mother.'

Without another word, John Grant silently set about tending to his mother's remains.

'She didn't sleep like that,' he said. 'Never on

her back.'

With great tenderness they rolled Jessie on to her left side. Only a few hours had passed since her death and the stiffness of rigor mortis had not yet set in, so that John Grant was able to move her arms and legs until her body formed a familiar S shape. He placed her hands together beneath her chin, and arranged her long hair so that it seemed to flow over her shoulder and down towards her waist.

They went outside then, and Badr used his scimitar to collect swathes of gorse branches, still covered in delicate yellow flowers shaped like tiny silk slippers. It was a laborious and painful process to get the greenery back inside the tomb, but when it was all in position, Badr withdrew from the chamber, back into the passage, so that mother and son might be alone.

John Grant knelt down by his mother's side. For an instant it seemed to him that he was the adult and she the child, and that he was a father come only to see that his daughter was safely asleep. The moment was brief, however, and quickly replaced by cold reality. He stooped and placed the gentlest of kisses on her cheek, and then another, and a third.

'You will always be with me, Mum,' he said. 'I promise.'

He began gently to place the gorse, layer by layer, over her body. Badr helped, and soon there was not a trace of her left visible. By the time they had finished, the chamber was all but filled with the fragrant, thorny harvest, and they turned and left her there.

'No one will disturb her,' said Badr. 'The thorns will deter even the most determined of passers-by.'

John Grant nodded, his face expressionless.

'Come,' said Badr. 'We must make a move. The sun has risen already, and by the time it sets, I swear we shall have put this place far behind us.'

'I would stay here for ever,' said John Grant.

Badr turned to face the boy and found him gazing back at the entrance to the tomb, his mother's tomb.

'She lived her life protecting you,' said Badr. 'That duty is mine now. I will not fail her in death … as I did in life.'

John Grant was silent.

'Come,' said Badr again. 'Now. Our first task is to get down off this desolate hillside and find two horses. I plan to take you far from here, and walking is not in my nature.'

Without looking again at the boy, he began striding downhill. He counted a hundred paces before he allowed himself a glance over his shoulder. He saw John Grant raise one hand to his mouth, kiss the fingertips, and hold them palm outwards towards the entrance of the tomb. Then he turned and ran towards the Moor without looking back.

10

For the rest of the day that followed, John Grant said not a single word. Badr Khassan, still unnerved by his momentary brush with the push, was content to let him be. As the last of the light was leaving the sky, they descended a steep slope that led on to a wide and level plain. A river, black and smooth as oil, ran parallel to the base of the slope, murmuring softly. Set back from the river, cut into a sheer wall of rock, was the low entrance to a cave. Badr judged they would find no better shelter.

'We can allow ourselves a fire tonight,' he said. 'See if there's wood to be gathered. Dry wood, mind.'

For the next hour they occupied themselves making a camp – setting and lighting a fire, clearing stones from the spot within the cave where Badr proposed they might sleep, gathering piles of bracken and other foliage for bedding. They had no provisions, and the thought that tomorrow's priority had to be finding food weighed heavily on the Moor's mind. A look at the boy, however, reminded him that there were empty spaces in the world that required more than meat and drink to fill them.

The cave was shallow, little more than a rock shelter, and as the darkness deepened so the stars revealed themselves once more.

Doubting the boy was in the mood for answering questions, and in hopes of distracting them both from a grief so dark and heavy it was palpable, Badr began to speak.

'There is more than one kind of light in the sky,' he said.

John Grant said nothing, but Badr sensed the boy was paying attention. He was seated cross-legged by the fire and gazing into the flames.

'Long ago, Greek astronomers observed that while most of the stars remained in place, a few were ceaselessly on the move across the heavens. They called them planets, a word that means *wanderers.*'

He paused to add more wood to the fire, and sparks danced high like living things.

'Some people have seen patterns among the stars – the word for such shapes and forms is constellations – and there are many stories to explain their presence there ... stories of animals, and hunters, and gods.'

'My mother told me the righteous dead cut their way through the curtain of night on their way into heaven,' said John Grant. 'The pinpricks of light are glimpses of the glory of heaven, seen through the holes left behind.'

Badr was taken unawares by the boy's little speech – and found it was he who was suddenly lost for words. John Grant continued to look deep into the fire.

'Do you think my mother made it through?' he asked. 'To heaven, I mean.'

Badr took a deep breath before answering.

'I hope so, John Grant,' he said. 'If your mother

was undeserving of heaven, then there's precious little hope for the rest of us.'

'So there ought to be another star in the sky tonight,' said John Grant, looking beyond the flames and out into the night.

'There ought to be,' said Badr. 'There surely ought to be.'

The morning that followed was bright and clear. Badr awoke lying curled on his side against the rear of the cave. He glanced at the boy, lying on his back close by the smoking remains of the fire. He was quite still, but his eyes were open. Badr wondered if any sleep had been had there, and then, noting the blue of a cloudless sky, resolved to try and raise his own spirits, if not those of the boy. A fresh start was in order and he stood and stretched, feeling the years in his muscles and bones. He slowly rolled his head around on his shoulders, his beard brushing his chest, and then stretched back until he was looking at the roof of the cave. He repeated the move over and over, first in one direction and then the other, listening all the while to a crunching sound deep in his neck like a wooden wheel grinding upon gravel. He stopped and rubbed his face with both hands. Feeling suddenly unclean, aware of his own heavy scent, he strode down to the river and began removing his clothes.

Still immobile, disinclined to move as much as a finger, John Grant watched the Moor strip off. He could not recall ever having seen a man's naked body before, far less the body of a black man. Dark though the skin of Badr's back and legs was, still John Grant could make out distinct

97

shiny patches – some on the shoulders and others on the man's lower legs. They were clearly burn scars, healed well enough but with a texture that looked tight, less flexible than the surrounding flesh. He thought about what Badr had said about the circumstances leading to his father's death – how Patrick Grant had rescued him from a burning bed in a burning house.

The Moor waded out until the dark water was up to his armpits before leaning forward and beginning to swim. He kicked his legs up behind him and his strokes were powerful and sure. John Grant watched as he struck out for the opposite bank, some tens of yards away. The current carried him downstream, but his confident poise in the water made it clear he was unconcerned. Reaching shallow water once more, he turned and began swimming back. Before he made it, the flow of the river had carried him out of sight, and John Grant wondered vaguely what would happen if he never saw his guardian again. After a few minutes he heard the sound of heavy breathing and Badr appeared beside the pile of clothes he had left behind. He picked up his cloak and dried himself roughly with it before dressing once more.

He returned to the cave and crouched by the smouldering embers of the fire, gauging whether it might be brought back to life. Seeing glowing flecks of red among the greys and blacks, he stooped and brought his face close to them, before blowing softly. John Grant watched, still as a corpse, until there was a soft whoosh and the Moor's efforts were rewarded with a bright orange tongue of flame that curled upwards from the remains. Carefully Badr placed small twigs around the flames, coaxing them with more of his own soft breaths.

'I have heard it said that no one who has been loved is ever truly lost,' he said, attending to the fire rather than looking at the boy. 'That if those who loved them breathe on the embers now and then, their memory returns to warm the living.'

'How is it you know so much about every-thing?' asked John Grant.

Badr smiled and shook his head, in the manner of a big dog, so that droplets of water were flung in all directions.

'I had the benefit of an education, my boy,' he said.

'I am not your boy.'

Badr kept tending to the fire, slowly adding larger pieces of wood. There was already warmth to be had from it, and he rubbed his hands together over the flames.

'No indeed, and I do not forget it,' he said. 'It is nonetheless my duty to take care of you. I gave my word. You are not mine – but you are my responsibility.'

John Grant roused himself at last, stood up and walked away from the fire.

Minutes passed while Badr allowed his thoughts to be absorbed and consumed by the flames, and John Grant stared out at the eddies and whorls winding and unwinding on the black slick of the river's surface.

'You felt the push, didn't you?' the boy asked at last. 'When you touched me ... just before the horsemen came back ... you felt it, didn't you?'

Badr looked up, but the boy still had his back turned to him.

'I felt ... drunk,' he answered. He was struggling to find the words to describe the sensation. 'Or as though I was falling. And there was pressure ... like the force of that river I just swam in. I felt I might have been swept away.'

'What you said last night about the stars that move across the sky...?' John Grant turned to look at him. 'The wandering planets?'

Badr nodded.

'Well I think there's another planet – and that we live our lives upon it.'

'My teachers said only the heavens moved,' said Badr. 'That we alone are fixed in place and all else moves around us.'

'Well I tell you we are on the move as well,' said John Grant. 'I feel it – and now you have felt it too.'

Badr turned back to the fire, poked at the flames with a stick and watched as the end blackened and charred in the heat.

'Are you hungry?' he asked.

John Grant shrugged his shoulders.

'Well I am,' said Badr. 'And now you have a decision to make.'

John Grant looked at him squarely.

'I am going in search of food,' said Badr, standing up straight. 'And when I leave, I shall not return. I have had my fill of this place. There is a fire here, and shelter of a sort. If you want to stay, I will not force you to leave.'

The boy looked at him sullenly.

'I would prefer that you accompany me,' said Badr. 'You have seen something of the world as it

100

is – perhaps too much for one so young. I would ask that you come with me, so that I might keep my word to your father.'

John Grant walked past Badr, into the cave, and hunkered down with his back against the wall.

Without another word, Badr strode down to the riverbank and turned to follow its course. He counted a hundred paces before he allowed himself a look back over his shoulder. The boy was coming, and at a run. He caught up easily, and the Moor was impressed by the turn of speed. For all that he had fairly sprinted over the ground, his footfalls on the hard-packed earth along the riverbank had made hardly a sound.

'You are quick on your feet, I'll give you that,' he said.

John Grant said nothing, but Badr noticed he was not winded, and breathing quite easily, so the sudden burst of exercise had had no apparent effect on him.

'Maybe it would help you to know that I lost my mother too – and when I was younger than you are now.'

They kept walking in silence for a few more minutes before the boy replied.

'Did she die?' he asked.

'No,' said Badr. 'But she was taken from me just the same – or rather I was taken from her. I never saw her again, and I have no idea whether she lives or not.'

John Grant weighed the information carefully.

'What happened?'

Badr snorted, almost a laugh.

'Where to begin?' he said, more to himself than

to the boy. 'My father said our family came once upon a time from a place called al-Maghrib al-Aqsa.'

He smiled when he said this, savouring the words, and his white teeth flashed. He glanced at the boy and laughed at the look of complete incomprehension he found there.

'I am not surprised to find you know nothing of this world below,' he said. 'One such as you...' He looked up into the sky and raised his hands in an attitude of prayer. 'One such as you who has all of the heavens to worry about!

'In your tongue, al-Maghrib al-Aqsa, the land of my forefathers, might be translated as *the farthest west.*'

Again he looked at the boy's face but found little that could be called understanding. At least he glimpsed curiosity, the root of intelligence, and he pressed ahead.

'Some of your people – those who have had an education at least – might recognise the name Morocco,' he said. 'And so that is the name I will ask you to remember. Repeat it, please.'

John Grant cleared his throat, but said nothing.

'Morocco,' said Badr a second time.

'Morocco,' said John Grant, enjoying the feel of the word in spite of himself.

'Good,' said Badr. 'And so now your education begins again.'

'But your mother?' asked John Grant.

'I am coming to that, I promise,' said Badr. 'My father said our people came long ago from...?'

'From Morocco.'

'Quite so. Good. My people came from

Morocco, *the farthest west,* but had made a new home for themselves far to the east. Perhaps my ancestors were merchants ... perhaps they were sailors, or warriors. That much has been forgotten.

'You should know that you live on the edge of the world, John Grant,' said Badr. 'There is much else to see – and I would show you. And you might learn that at the *centre* of the world there is a powerful pull – and people are drawn there from everywhere else. People like me, like you, all else besides. All in a muddle.'

'And your mother?' asked John Grant once more.

'I lived with my mother and father, and my three little sisters, in a village in a land named Macedonia.'

'Macedonia,' said John Grant.

'In Macedonia – yes, good,' said Badr. 'We were Christians – like you – but in a land within reach of another faith. A powerful and hungry faith.'

'What do you mean?' asked John Grant. 'Hungry?'

'Your people follow Jesus and his mother Mary,' said Badr. 'But there are other kinds of people in the world. My people were within reach of followers of another man, named Muhammad, who lived and died eight hundred years ago.

'They are Muslims and they follow their Muhammad all the way to God and paradise.'

'But you said they were hungry,' said John Grant.

'Hungry for land ... and people,' said Badr. 'It is the custom of the followers of that faith – which is called Islam, which means *submission to*

God – to steal the children of Christians and make Muslims of them, and also warriors to fight their battles for them.'

John Grant was listening in the same way he had once listened to his mother's stories at bedtime.

'Muslim warriors came to my village one day and took me – took me from my father's arms,' said Badr. 'They took all the young boys of my village and tied us to a long rope and led us away from our lives of before.'

'And they taught you to fight? Made you a warrior?'

'They taught me everything. But they made me a Muslim first – made me promise on my life to follow only Muhammad. They gave me to another family and I was raised as their son.'

'And you never went home?'

'Not until I was a grown man – and a warrior. They called me a janissary then.'

'Janissary?'

'Which means *new soldier*. They called us janissaries and had us fight their wars.'

'And when you went home?'

'And when I went home, my village was gone. Just ruins.'

'What about your mother ... and your father ... and your sisters?'

Badr shook his head.

'Gone,' he said, and shrugged. 'Just gone.'

They walked on in silence, the only sound the whisper of the river surging alongside.

'I would like to be a janissary,' said John Grant. 'I would like to be a janissary and kill the man who killed my mother.'

'I can teach you to make war,' said the Moor. 'But first...'

He looked at the boy and smiled, and pointed ahead of them.

'First?' asked John Grant.

'First we eat.'

They were approaching a sweeping bend in the river. Beyond it, a few minutes ahead and shielded by a stand of sycamore trees, a curl of white smoke rose into the cloudless sky.

'Your people have been hospitable to me before,' said Badr. 'Let us see if they will be so again.'

With that, he broke into an easy, loping run. John Grant followed him, effortlessly.

11

In the East, 1448

The urgency was gone from John Grant so completely it might never have existed. In place of any desire to stay pressed tight against her, inside her, he obeyed his present need and rolled off her and away. They were different people than they had been; at least she was to him. And soon, he knew, his seeming indifference would bring about the change for her as well.

He lay on his back, eyes open and taking in the details of the little room for the first time. Moments before – and for hours before that – his mind had been filled only with thoughts of finding a woman. He had found one, found her, and pursued her then with all the energy with which he had been taught to make war. Everything about her had been all that mattered. Now, while the sweat of her was still wet upon his skin, his thoughts were all and only fixed on everything else *besides* her.

His weapons were by the bed, along with his clothes and his purse. He reached down towards the floorboards with his left hand and found the little leather bag tied with a cord. He was pleased by the weight of coins there. As a skilled and practised mercenary, he was well paid, and in recent years John Grant and Badr Khassan had struck a rich vein.

The walls of her room were roughly plastered and painted white. There were bits and pieces of furniture. Two chairs with woven hemp seats were set side by side against one wall. A table that had been fine once, but many meals and years ago, took up too much of the remaining space. He imagined it had been better suited to the tavern below.

The bed upon which they were lying was comfortable enough, the mattress feather-filled and as pleasantly plump as the woman beside him. The moonlight, spilling limply through the one arched window, was helped by the glow from a fire in a corner of the room. There was a pile of chopped logs beside it, and he thought about getting up and adding one or two of them to the failing flames, then decided against giving any signal that might be interpreted as a desire to linger long.

He chanced a look at his erstwhile lover, from

the corner of his eye. For a few moments she lay as he had left her, breathing heavily, arms by her sides, heels planted wide apart, each spread knee only inches from the mattress. Without his humping body on top of her, she seemed incomplete and faintly preposterous. The dance was over but she did not yet care that her partner had moved on. The act itself – or at least the need of it, the same that had drawn him to her – mystified him now, and with an equal and opposite force. Her breasts, so enthralling mere moments before, seemed intent on departing too, somehow deflated and each of them making for a separate armpit. She was a pretty one just the same, and still young enough to carry her weight with aplomb.

It had been her smile anyway that drew his attention first of all, while she bustled between the tables of the tavern below the room where they lay. She had been busy topping up cups and glasses with wine and beer, swapping banter with the customers. The fact that her pretty face was bobbing atop a shapely frame, all curves and good length of bone, had only served to seal the deal – like finding that a finely appointed house was blessed too with a plentiful garden.

He was sorry – for it and for her, and maybe for himself. That he had ever wanted her so hungrily seemed incredible now. She giggled as she closed her legs and reached down to pull a coverlet over both their naked bodies. She had sensed a sudden chill and seemed determined to retain some warmth. He said nothing, but when she cosied over to him and placed her tousled head upon his chest, he wrapped an arm around her shoulder.

He had liked her before and he liked her still. He had no wish to hurt her feelings, but the need for intimacy was gone.

'What's good to eat here?' he had asked her, emboldened by an afternoon's worth of rough red wine on an empty stomach. She had her back to him – indeed he had been staring at her rolling hips and buttocks when the words escaped his lips. She stopped. And turned. For her own part she had already noticed him – knew what she was going to see before her gaze fell upon him once more. Pretty – that was the word that had come to her at her first sight of him, and it was the word that came to her while she considered her reply.

'Everything,' she said, hand on one full hip. 'Anything and everything you fancy. It's all good here, and plenty of it.'

She turned away again, to continue her round of the busy and battered tables that filled the place.

Pretty, she thought again, and smiled a crooked smile.

She was hardly the first to see it – woman or man. Some women found his appearance effeminate and moved on quickly in search of something more overtly male. Those that approved of his looks – looks that mirrored or complemented something of their own appeal – often found they could not get enough of him (though he got enough of them, and soon enough).

Badr Khassan slapped the young man's thigh beneath the table, then kept his huge hand there and pinched hard just above the knee – so that John Grant's leg flinched and snapped straight out in front of him like a length of knotted rope. His knee banged off the underside of the table hard enough to unbalance his freshly refilled glass. The whole lot of it toppled into his lap, soaking him through to the skin in an instant, so that he gasped and then groaned. The empty glass smashed on to the floor.

Hearing the breakage, she turned to find its source and that pretty face all in the same place. He shook his head at her wide-eyed, and held up his hands in a gesture of apology. She might have smiled at him, but took the trouble to glare instead before marching quickly in his direction.

John Grant looked hard at Badr, but the Moor was already apparently deep in conversation with the man seated to his right. She was beside him by then and he noticed the smell of her – hot, and with an underlying tang of salt. She smelled, it seemed to him, like a sea breeze, and as inviting. He felt a heaviness between his legs, defying the clinging cold of the spilled wine. She looked down into his lap and he moved his hands quickly to cover himself, lest she see the bulge.

'Nothing there to worry about,' she said.

Badr guffawed beside him, understanding the joke before he did. He wanted her then, and desperately. Everything about her – every line and swollen curve, the hot scent of her and the lopsided smile on her pretty face...

Hours had passed and much strong drink had been taken. Confidences exchanged and lingering looks. Unnecessary touching when they brushed past one another between tables as the evening wore on. He had taken her wine and taken her too.

But that was then. Now his fingertips brushed

against her breast and he glanced down to see a fan of stretch marks etched darkly, the colour of aubergine. She placed one leg over his and he felt, for the first time, the sharp rasp of bristled hairs on her shins. Evidently she took as much care of her appearance as circumstances allowed, but in the aftermath of their coupling the imperfections registered more clearly, demanding the attention he had previously paid only to the curves of her behind and the rise and fall of her breasts as she breathed and laughed.

Rather than the sea, it seemed to him now that her skin smelled of sweat, yesterday's as well as today's. Her curls, so beguiling in the candlelit tavern and so intoxicating while he had buried his face in her neck as he ground his hips against her, smelled of cooking fat. Her panting breath against his chest was stale wine. She made a soft, warm sound of contentment and his body stiffened slightly, involuntarily, in response to her easy comfort, her familiarity with him – all but a stranger.

'Quick ... but not too quick,' she murmured, and giggled again.

It was true and he knew it. He almost blushed but took the second half of her sentence, and the fondness behind the laugh, as proof that she had taken something for herself from the encounter.

Although he was already beyond her, making a memory of her, still he cared what she thought. In spite of himself and his reservations, he tightened his arm around her and pressed his face against the top of her head. Just a girl – just a girl, and he planted a kiss among her curls.

He realised his lips had moved, and wondered

for a moment if he had spoken out loud. She made no sign of it and he relaxed. He cared what all of them thought, but never enough to ask or to stay. He would leave when she fell asleep or when the fire went out – whichever came first.

All unbidden, the memory of his mother came to mind – settled down where it chose, by his side like a faithful hound. He thought of the tomb and the gorse flowers, and about the arrow and Angus Armstrong. The months and the years had passed since her death there in the moonlight, but the archer had not forgotten them. John Grant had turned from boy to man and Badr Khassan had guided him as best he could, and yet neither time nor distance had kept their foe at bay.

The girl was dozing now, her consciousness drifting like a skiff that had slipped its mooring. He listened to her breathing, deep and peaceful, and wished he might let go and join her there.

It was thoughts of Angus Armstrong that pre-occupied him then. John Grant imagined him out there in the night and prayed for a day, and soon, when his hands might be warm with the archer's freshly spilled entrails.

Not for the first time it struck him how far he had landed from the life he had once expected. He was like a seed plucked by the wind from among the branches of a tall tree and carried out of sight. He glanced at the sleeping girl and then up into the rafters of the room above a tavern in a land that was foreign to him, and shook his head in disbelief.

He was a farmer's son, and still little more than a boy. He ought to have been destined for a life of quiet hardship on the land. He looked at his hands, spread the fingers and thought how their skin should have been stained dark by now – ingrained like the hands that had once cared for him and loved him.

He considered his fingernails, ragged and short, and recalled the sight of stubborn crescents beneath other nails that had once untangled his unruly hair or picked at careless traces of food left dried upon his cheeks.

He remembered casual contact from two hands moved by love of an altogether different sort – that he had not known for years. He struggled to recall that touch that had once seemed more familiar than his own, and for a moment he ached to have those careworn hands upon him one more time, ruffling his hair or laid upon his shoulders in the preface to a mother's kiss.

Once it would have seemed to him unthinkable to find himself an hour's walk from his mother's cottage – and yet here he was, a warrior with blood-soaked hands, half a world away from that home and from the jagged darkness that now cradled Jessie's bones.

Instead of tending crops and husbanding beasts – the stuff of life – he was a bringer of death. By Badr's side his tools had been the sword and the knife, and the man and the boy had earned their living harvesting souls ranged against them in wars not of their making. They were mercenaries – killers for hire and masters of the trade. A mere boy he might be, but his was a precocious talent that enthralled his guardian and mentor as much as anyone else.

This night – the girl and the red wine – was only a distraction on the way to yet another fight in which their only concern would be the potential for profit. They were far from any home; flotsam carried this way and that by one conflict or another across the bloody face of the continent.

Soon enough they would stand alongside Christian soldiers in the army of John Hunyadi of Hungary. The grand plan, about which they cared not at all, was to drive off the Ottoman Sultan Murad II. Good luck to their employer if the objective might be met, but they would still fill their purses with silver and gold along the way.

He might have wept then for a life unlived and another cut short. But his eyes stayed dry as though cured by smoke from the fire.

12

Kosovo Poljo, Pristina; one month later

John Grant had known what had to happen as soon as his eyes met those of the beautiful stranger. Hubbub all around, and yet something in the other's expression made it plain. A connection – mutual understanding reached in a heartbeat.

His heart, already working hard, reached for a new height, goaded by anticipation. Separated by the crowd though they were, each had all but ceased to notice the rest of the participants in the busy market square. Most had already paired off (let them dance their own dances). Those left alone and slumped in corners or collapsed on the floor were, anyway, beyond anyone's concern.

For John Grant it was as though they came together through deep water; movements slow, sounds muted and distant, echoing and strange. It was a striking, haunting face that came towards him: angular lines but softened and made perfect by dark oval eyes. There was light and life aplenty there, but something else as well, hard and selfish, cruelty perhaps. Those were the faces and eyes that John Grant liked best of all, and there had been more than a few along the way.

Moment by moment and step by step the rhythms of the dance brought them closer together. Each had eyes only for the other.

Caught in his own moment, Badr Khassan could only watch the courtship unfolding in front of him. He was impressed in part by John Grant's prowess, but also disapproving, and more and more so as the years passed. He had raised him as a son and, like any good father, had revelled in the youngster's achievements; gasped, in fact, at the speed of his maturing. Just as often nowadays, however, Badr wondered if all was well. He had set out to make a warrior of the lad, and he had succeeded. But John Grant was a killer too, which was different. Badr Khassan was not in the business of caring for souls, but still he wondered if enough had survived of the gentle young man he had taken into his care.

The boy he had met had been sensitive to every tide and current in life's ocean. But as the years passed, a space had opened up in the youngster's heart – had been torn open long ago, in truth.

Those who met the boy, and then the young man, were impressed by his charm. Men envied his talents but women noticed something more, something else. For all the seeming tenderness in John Grant's eyes, there was an absence as well. The most sensitive understood what was amiss. For the best of them, the kindest, there was no mistaking it. If he opened up at all, it was to reveal a room made strange not by what it contained but by what it lacked.

The space he had to offer might seem welcoming at first, but something played upon the visitor's mind. Here and there were marks on the wall, from paintings taken down; the shapes of missing furniture, windows filled in and painted over. Something was gone, a view made unwanted and unbearable.

It was something John Grant had lost while still too young. There was a grate in the room, but no fire; candles on their sconces, but no warming light. Since she was gone, because she was gone, he hunted high and low. But he would not find her.

The boy, the man, was motherless.

Badr felt the loss of Jessie Grant, but he grieved most for the boy. Some of the resultant hardness had served him well – served them both well.

John Grant's awareness of everything and everyone around him remained astonishingly heightened, and at first Badr had wondered how the lad might cope beyond the cottage and a life shared only with his mother. But in her absence, steel had grown inside, and some other hard shell outside.

Having no other trade to teach, the Bear had made his cub into a soldier like himself. Since neither felt loyalty to a flag or to any man but each other, they fought for money. Skilled as Badr was – and exceptional as John Grant became – they had lived hard but well. Winning most and losing a few, they had made every venture pay, one way or another. But nowadays it was neither for money nor for reputation that Badr's heart ached.

Distracted as he was now by his own affairs, still he found time to look out for his charge. In the moments he could dedicate to the other's craft, he felt himself moved as always by the elegance and flair of it all.

The distance between John Grant and the fresh focus of his attention was closing now, and Badr finally looked away – in part to give them privacy and also to pay proper attention where it was more urgently required.

The perfect face had made its intentions clear. Sinuous movements promised much; too much as it turned out. John Grant's ploy was always the same and always worked. He seemed so defence-less – his heart exposed. Any onlooker would have said he was bound to get hurt. His expression was as open as his hands, giving it all away.

Both felt the need, the hunger to come close, but it was John Grant who stopped, suddenly still. It was anyone's guess whether those big brown eyes that gazed upon him then burned with lust or love, but they burned brightest of all close up.

John Grant felt the charge of the other's life force jangling on his face and upon the exposed skin of his hands and arms. Only his eyes moved then, taking in the shape and the form as well as the intent; deciding where first to lay his hands.

And then finally the agony of anticipation was over and they came together lightly, so lightly. A statue no longer, John Grant returned to life and shifted his weight, minutely, on to his right foot. His partner seemed all at once confused and certainly unbalanced. Had there been a mistake, signals misread and only shame and embarrassment ahead?

All at once the silence ended for John Grant, and the tumult of the combat in the dying moments of the battle rushed over him. The fighting had spilled away from the battlefield and into a nearby town, the lanes and alleys, the streets and houses and here in the market square. Swords danced where there was room, but in the press of the final moments it was about knives and fists and teeth as well.

The karambit was a knife shaped to resemble a tiger's claw. Curved so that it described an arc, it was carried close to the body, hidden, and brought into the light only when the intention was to draw blood. It came from Asia, where the ways and wiles of the tiger were well known. The index finger of the good hand was inserted into a hoop at the base of the knife, the fist clamped tight around the handle. In action it was used when two bodies were close enough to touch, and most blows came from below, delivered with an upwards slashing motion like that of the cat.

John Grant savoured the heat of the embrace as he took his latest enemy in his arms. His left hand, bearing the cruel blade, was now tightly between them, but so sharp there was little effort involved in sliding it free. The fine edge parted clothing, skin and muscle with ease. The soldier's face, handsome and bright, was against his own, hot skin and a slick of eager sweat. John Grant drew softly back from him, the better to read the expression there, and as he pulled away, he reached up with the knife and ran an inch of shining silver across the taut, exposed skin of the neck. The agony of the wound to the abdomen had made the man throw his head back anyway. He lacked the breath to scream, however, and only crimson gushed from an ever-widening slit that ran from ear to ear.

Badr had finished his own man with his scimitar, and as the lifeless body hit the paved floor of the square, he took a moment to steal another glance at the more elegant display of artistry. There, amid the ugliness of bitter hand-to-hand combat, as defeated Christians struggled to hold off their Muslim opponents, he witnessed the final act of something as beautiful as it was cruel.

John Grant stepped away from his man and Badr would have sworn the lad performed a little bow. Certainly his head snapped forward an inch as the dying man fell to his knees and toppled sideways. Satisfied but not sated, he turned lightly in search of more and Badr closed his eyes.

When he opened them once more, he saw John Grant running towards him.

'There's nothing more for us here,' the young man shouted as he reached his friend. 'The day is theirs. We would do best if we left now.'

Badr clapped him on the shoulder and pulled

him to his chest. He embraced him then, like a father, before leading the way into an alleyway off the square. John Grant did not notice the Moor's tears.

'You are right,' said Badr, rubbing one hand across his face. 'These Ottomans are on the up and up, I tell you. Hunyadi and his Hungarians have given all they have, and more than once – and all to no avail. Murad's Muslims are too many and too keen.

'Their exploits might make us rich. I believe, lad, that the time has come to switch sides.'

John Grant laughed a bitter laugh while they ran, jumping corpses and dodging shattered doors and the remnants of makeshift barricades.

'God ... Allah – what's in a name for two such as we?' he said.

13

Somewhere in Turkia, six months later

The fighting had begun soon after dawn, and the Moor looked around him at a heap of slain. Not all were his own handiwork but he had sent more than a few of them on their way, right enough. The air was thick with the stink of it – with the iron-laden reek of spilled blood and the putrid exhalations from split and punctured bodies.

For Badr Khassan and John Grant, everything had changed, and also nothing. Upon an ebbing tide – ebbing at least from the forces and soldiers of Christ – they had allowed themselves to float into the service of the Ottomans.

It had been easily accomplished. Badr spoke the Moorish tongue, and everything about him – from the colour of his skin to the style of his clothing – advertised him as one most likely to fight for the Turks. That his companion was smaller by far, and fairer, mattered not at all once their would-be employers had witnessed the younger man's handling of the karambit.

The sun was held low in the sky by the weight of morning, but the air shimmered with summer heat. No more than an hour had passed, but already the matter was decided. The Christian emperor's forces were broken. Discipline was all but lost, and those men still fit for flight were leaving the field in disorder, pursued by the victors. Here and there the determination of individual captains maintained pockets of resistance, and it was in the face of one such knot of desperate souls that Badr and John Grant now found themselves.

Badr had briefly lost track of the younger man in the fray, and in a momentary lull he surveyed the scene and spotted his erstwhile student. There he was – student no longer and locked in single combat with a bull-shouldered armoured giant apparently bent on splitting his foe into multiple parts. Taller and heavier by far than John Grant, the huge crusader was wielding a double-handed broadsword in the manner of a butcher's cleaver.

Despite his size advantage, however, he was winded and all but spent, and the smaller man evaded the clumsy blows with ease. Finally

120

broken, the bull dropped his head and lowered his weapon, resting the cutting edge on the ground as a support.

John Grant stepped lightly forward and used his own momentum to put more weight behind his own weapon as he sliced the giant's head cleanly from the stooped shoulders. The head spun high and the massive body fell forward. For a moment its descent was stopped, comically, by the prop of the broadsword – its point digging into the sand, the pommel trapped against the giant's belly and briefly taking its owner's dead weight. Then slowly and sadly the whole mass toppled sideways, landing with a soft thump. The severed head, having hit the ground first, rolled around in a circle before coming to a halt close by the dead man's knees.

Badr realised he had not been the only man observing the contest. The sight of the felling of a champion had drained his fellows of any dregs of spirit. Christian soldiers had grown familiar with defeat in the East, and judging that there was nothing more to be achieved among their dead and dying comrades, the remaining handfuls turned to leave the field.

Some kept their weapons, while others dropped theirs in hopes of a speedier exit. The general withdrawal, messy though it was, might soon become a rout, and each man assessed his own chances of survival and acted accordingly. It was as Badr watched the last of them turn and flee, pursued by the Sultan's forces, that he caught sight of the bird.

A lammergeier was easy to spot – ten feet of

wings and a long, narrow tail making a distinctive silhouette against the blue – and he gave himself over to the sight of it. He remembered that his own people called them *huma,* and chose to believe that such birds never touched the ground. Badr, however, had seem them land many times, especially upon battlefields heaped with gore. Rather than flesh, it was the bones they favoured, tearing them free from muscles and tendons and flying high into the sky from where they might drop them on to rocks to smash them. Then came a spiralling descent as the birds flew down to gorge upon the bloody marrow and even upon the milk-white shards.

Badr had no time for any nonsense about flight without end, but he did cling superstitiously to another of his people's legends: that whomsoever was touched by the shadow of the *huma* would one day sit upon a throne as king.

And so when he saw the bird begin to drop, not in the expected corkscrew but in a vertical stoop like that of a falcon eyeing prey, he was transfixed. Like a thunderbolt from heaven itself the raptor plummeted towards the earth, its pointed wings swept neatly back, its great talons extended. As it dropped, its colours became clearer – blue-grey wings and tail, tawny breast and head, eyes ringed with crimson.

Just as it seemed it must surely hit the ground, driving itself into the sandy soil of the plain like a feathered meteorite, the bird extended its wings, folded away its feet and swept across the landscape in a graceful arc just a few yards above the battlefield.

At the very moment when its trajectory began to rise once more, the lammergeier pulled backwards and upwards with its wings, so that for a moment it seemed frozen in space.

It was an instant so brief that only the Moor was gifted the sight of it, the bird's shadow cloaking John Grant's back like a black mantle, and he gasped, the air knocked out of his lungs by the impact of the vision. Badr Khassan and only Badr Khassan saw his adoptive son draped with the shadow of a cross.

A lump, hot and jagged, rose in his throat and two tears burned molten at the corners of his eyes. Every hair on his neck and arms stood on end and he wondered if lightning had followed the thunderbolt.

He would have sworn the air thrummed and jangled, and it was while he drew in his breath to shout the name of John Grant across the sand, to tell him what he had seen, that he felt a blow to his back. He exhaled, heard the whistling of his own breath and looked down to see a broad arrowhead protruding from his front, down on his right side close by his hip, on the end of its long thin shaft.

There was no pain. Instead he was filled from the top of his head to the tips of his toes with an overwhelming rush of love for John Grant. Filling his lungs with life-giving breath once more, and never taking his eyes from his charge, he bellowed the young man's name with the roar of a wounded bear.

John Grant's head snapped around, as did some of those of the retreating crusaders. None but John Grant cared what they saw, however, and he was running towards his friend before he noticed the arrow.

Badr sank to his knees, and regained his balance there. He placed one hand lightly on the arrow shaft and felt a vibration from it, likely stirred by his own breathing. He was pleased he was still thinking clearly. John Grant reached him, dropping down in front of him and catching sight of the arrow for the first time. He reached for the head of the thing, but before he could touch it, a movement behind his wounded friend captured his full attention. Looking beyond Badr, he saw a face he had seen too many times before.

Angus Armstrong was running towards them at full tilt. As he came on, he sought to nock another arrow on to the string of his longbow, but before he could do so he stumbled, one foot catching on a rock.

He went down heavily, at full length. One hand, his right, partially broke his fall, but the other still gripped his bow. His head narrowly missed connecting with another boulder, all but buried in the sandy soil to his left, but while he avoided injury, one end of his bow snagged neatly in a cleft in the same stone.

As he hit the ground he was aware of a cracking sound and thought at first it was one of his own bones – which would have been worse. As it was, he realised it was the sound of his longbow snapping neatly in two.

Even before Armstrong stumbled, John Grant had been on his feet and sprinting towards their foe – the man who had hunted and haunted them over the years.

He had known that his life, both of their lives, depended upon him closing the distance before the archer had time to loose another arrow. Now the predator was downed, sprawling in the dirt, and Armstrong had not been the only man to register the sound of the snapping bow.

John Grant increased his pace, seeing at last a crucial advantage, but before he could come to grips, the fallen man had pulled himself up on to all fours. John Grant, still running at full speed, aimed a kick at his enemy's face, but rather than connecting with flesh and bone, his foot met only fresh air.

Armstrong was always dangerous, always fast, and in the fractions of a second available to him before a booted foot sent him into oblivion, he rolled to his right, clear of the blow.

John Grant clawed at the air in his desperation to slow down, but the momentum of his failed kick kept him travelling forward and beyond his target. Armstrong was able to stand, and by the time John Grant had turned to face him, the archer held a knife in his right hand and a lethally tipped arrow in his left.

Here now was a contest John Grant might relish. Badr had taught him to fight with the sword and the axe, as well as with the knife, but it was with the hook-bladed karambit that he naturally excelled.

The Moor had wondered what so appealed to the boy about such a meagre weapon, and had concluded it was the intimacy of the act. Killing should leave a good man with feelings of taint, of having been made unclean. If the opponent was to be deprived of life, robbed of everything and every moment, then for some it seemed only right to commit the act while close enough to touch. Badr Khassan, himself a master, had been amazed by his student's aptitude, and by now, after years of practice and hundreds of encounters, not even he would have willingly faced down the Scot.

John Grant walked forward with a swagger. His back was straight, his arms loose by his sides. When it was over, he knew, he would have no memory of drawing his knife; it would appear in his left hand when the moment required it. The key was in never letting the foe catch so much as a glimpse of the thing. He must only feel it, Badr had said.

He was circling the archer now, taking his time and listening to his heartbeat, allowing his breathing to slow down, when Badr called his name for a second time. Hearing something new in the wounded man's tone – something as desperate as it was insistent – John Grant turned from the fight and towards his friend.

14

The opium had dulled Badr's pain, and now he listened to the sound of his own breathing. He was lying on his side in the half-dark of a cave. In front of him a shaft of sunlight split the darkness and pooled on to the floor. He raised one arm, felt a stab of pain that made him grunt. Determined, however, in spite of the discomfort, he reached his hand forward until it was bathed in the light.

'Keep still, Badr,' said John Grant.

The younger man had returned from the mouth of the cave, where he had stood for a minute or so to content himself they were alone – that none of the crusaders had chosen to follow. Already the battlefield was busy with scavengers, birds of prey, dogs and other scurrying, scuttling forms.

It had taken an agonising effort to move Badr from where he had fallen. At first, in spite of the arrow thrusting from his abdomen, he had been able to walk, slowly and leaning heavily on his companion. John Grant had seen many wounds in his short life, caused by all manner of weapons and projectiles. He had seen faces cloven in two from crown to chin and heads hacked from necks; chests and bellies laid open and their contents spilled upon the ground; the brittle ends of snapped bones protruding from ragged wounds in arms and legs.

He had inflicted all of these himself over the years, and more besides. But the sight of the arrow piercing Badr's Khassan's body from back to front gave rise to feelings of horror he had not felt since that day long ago, at the cottage, when he had first beheld the corpses of the slain troopers. Those dead had seemed unreal, like broken toys, but the blood and the gore of their wounds had stayed with him for weeks. Glimpses of the scene had featured in his dreams and he had awakened cold and nauseated.

Those days were far behind him now, however; his profession had hardened him. But Badr's pain

127

unmanned him.

They had made their way towards a cliff face that bordered one side of the plain. The enemy had appeared upon its heights in the prelude to the fighting and John Grant had noted caves and shallow rock shelters there. The sunlight had added to Badr's misery and the priority had been to get him somewhere shaded and cool. After a few tens of yards of treacle-slow progress, stumbling over the broken, rock-strewn terrain that lay between them and the cliff, Badr had suddenly slumped to his knees as though his legs had transformed into strings. The shock of the impact jarred the arrow and he bit down on a rasping cry. The pain braided through the sound reached deep into John Grant's own body and pulled hard on something there, so that he almost retched.

The position of the arrow meant Badr could only lie on his side, and John Grant felt him slowly twisting towards the ground in search of rest.

'No, Badr,' he said, stepping around to his back, reaching his hands into the big man's armpits and using all of his strength to pull him backwards over the ground. 'We can't stop here.'

If their progress had been slow before, it deteriorated then almost to a standstill. John Grant could manage only a few yards of hauling at a time. Whenever he stopped, he had no option but to support Badr's almost unconscious weight on his knees and shins, the feathered end of the arrow protruding insolently from between his lower legs. A snail's trail of blood stretched darkly across the rocks and dust, evidence of the severity of the wound and of the meagre distance covered.

The sun was high in the sky by the time they reached the blessed shadow of the cliff. The closest cave entrance was narrow, like a mean mouth, but widened into a large chamber beyond. A stream of water flowed sluggishly from somewhere high in the roof and then gathered in a shallow depression before snaking towards the entrance and beyond. As John Grant pulled Badr inside, his blood mingled with the water and flowed rosy pink over the pale bedrock.

It mattered to get properly out of sight, away from prying eyes, but when John Grant stopped, thankfully, and lowered Badr down on to his side by the stream, the Moor spoke for the first time in the hour it had taken to cover the ground.

'Not the dark – don't have me lie in the dark,' he said. 'I want to see you while we speak.'

At the rear of the cave a narrow blade of sunlight cut a golden scar on to the floor. A crack in the roof reached all the way to the clifftop high above them, and it was through this that the water seeped, filling its pool before spilling into the shallow channel that led to the cave mouth.

John Grant set about moving Badr further into the cave and to a point where he might benefit both from cool shade and the light of day. The presence of water made the shelter ideal, and John Grant wished with all his heart they had been settling down only to make a meal and spend the night.

Badr wanted to lie on his right side with his face close to the sunlight. Once he was in position, John Grant made him as comfortable as was possible – raising his head slightly on a folded cloak and positioning the big man's arms and legs in an attitude of rest.

More than anything he wanted to deal with the arrow, but experience of such wounds had taught him there were terrible dangers. Removal of the shaft might increase the flow of blood, doing more damage. The thought, the realisation indeed, that the wound was a fatal one, circled like a vulture and he failed to drive it off. For the time being, and until he could think of how or even if help might be obtained, the Bear would have to lie there in the cave.

Misery radiated from him like heat from a fire, and John Grant reeled before it, his vision blurred and swimming in sympathy with his friend's suffering.

From a bag on his hip he took a glass bottle, sheathed in leather decorated with worn and tattered stitching. There in the cave it was more precious than gold or diamonds, and John Grant removed its stopper with a care that bordered on reverence. The soft popping sound brought a sigh from Badr.

'*Af-yon,*' he said, returning in his misery to the tongue of the Muslim.

John Grant crawled over to Badr on his knees and stooped to raise the great dark head. Holding the bottle, which contained a tincture of opium, he allowed a little of the dark liquid to pour into the Moor's mouth. Content that he had given him as much as was appropriate, he settled Badr once more and took up a position close by, close enough that he might gently caress the big man's shoulder from time to time, hear his breathing.

All at once, and for the first time, John Grant took in the sight of his friend lying helpless, perhaps beyond help. The enormity of it broke over him, threatening to wash him away. The memory of a night long ago, back in the land of his birth, was suddenly before his eyes. Badr's shape disappeared and it was Jessie, his mother, that he saw, her face lit not by a shaft of sun but by silver-blue moonlight.

It was then that he had risen quickly to his feet and made for the cave mouth and fresh air.

After a few minutes spent staring at the blue through a mist of tears, he had allowed his gaze to settle upon the birds and dogs busying themselves among the dead and nearly dead.

How many more, before day's end? he wondered.

He scanned the landscape around him with all possible concentration. Once more he reprimanded himself for breaking off from dealing with Angus Armstrong. Never before had their tormentor been so exposed and vulnerable. The moment had finally come, and then ... and then the sound of Badr's anguished cry had made him turn from his quarry.

The need to help his friend had overwhelmed the opportunity finally to dispatch the man who had caused so much pain. He must surely be out there now somewhere. Perhaps he was far away, licking his wounds and plotting; maybe he was watching from some hidey-hole and weighing his chances.

Without his bow John Grant doubted Armstrong would come close, far less seek to tackle them. At close quarters Armstrong was likely dangerous enough, but not as lethal as he. The archer, his wing clipped, had wisely chosen to flee from the scene, and now they were well hidden.

Over the years, John Grant had begun to suspect Armstrong wanted something other than their deaths – that his objective after all was to create a situation where one or other of them was left alive and at his mercy. He clenched his fists until the bones in his knuckles shone white, and then turned back into the cave.

Badr's breathing had grown deeper, easier. The rasp of it – and the pain that caused it – had been smoothed by the drug, jagged edges turned to ridges and creases. John Grant watched as the Moor turned his hand in the shaft of light, considering first the back and then the palm. Aware of the younger man's return, Badr lifted his eyes and looked at him.

'Did I ever tell you how *af-yon* came into the hands of men?' he asked.

John Grant shook his head and sat down cross-legged, close enough that his back was almost touching the Moor's chest. It was easier to listen to him, and be with him, if he did not have to see the discomfort etched into his face. Badr's relief, however temporary, crossed the gap between them and seeped into him. He would have no need to feel for a pulse, since he could feel the irregular tempo of the big man's heart as vibrations on his own skin.

'Once, long ago, when the world was younger, a saintly holy man lived on the banks of a great and holy river, far away in the east,' said Badr.

John Grant would have been happier if Badr had been content to rest rather than using his energy for the business of storytelling – but he made no protest.

'The holy man shared his little hut of reeds and grass with a tiny brown mouse. The mouse was quick, very quick, and mischievous, always on the move and on the lookout for crumbs. As is always the case, the mouse was also much troubled by larger creatures that wanted to eat her, and one day she asked the holy man to transform her into a cat. The holy man smiled and thought about it, and then did as the mouse had asked. Instead of a mouse crouched before him on its hind legs, attending to its whiskers as before, there was now a sleek white cat.

All was well for a few days until the cat realised she now faced the attentions of the dogs that prowled the land around the holy man's house from time to time, always on the lookout for food. Since the holy man ate next to nothing, the pickings were meagre indeed, but still the dogs came. If there were no scraps to be had, then perhaps they might kill and eat the white cat.'

Badr broke off from his storytelling to smile at his charge. John Grant was looking down at his hands, folded in his lap. As he listened to his own words, Badr could not be sure he had not told the story before, perhaps more than once. The rhythm of the telling was soothing, however, and he kept going for his own sake as well as that of John Grant.

'So the cat asked to be transformed into a dog, the better to fight off her latest foes, and the holy man obliged. When the novelty of a canine existence wore off, she had the holy man make of her a wild boar, and then a mighty elephant. All too soon thereafter, and no longer content with life on the ground and all its many travails, she asked for the form of a monkey.

'Each time the holy man granted the wish and each time she found reasons to change again.

'Finally she asked to be transformed into a beautiful maiden so that she might find a rich man and marry him. Once more the holy man granted her wish, and in no time at all the maiden, who was named Postomoni, had found herself a king, who fell in love with her at once and married her and made her his queen.

'All was well until the day when Postomoni, who had never retained any form long enough to master the intricacies of its being, stumbled while crossing the palace courtyard and fell into a well and drowned. The king was broken-hearted and sought out the holy man.

'"Grieve not," he said, when the king had broken the news and finished weeping. "Postomoni began life as a mouse. I made her into a cat, and then a dog, and then a boar, and then an elephant and finally a monkey before at last I made her into the beautiful maiden who became your wife and queen. Now I shall make her immortal.

'"Let her body stay where it lies. Fill the well to the top with earth and in time a plant will grow there, from her flesh and bones. This plant shall be called *posto* – the poppy – and from within its flower buds you will harvest a thick sap."

'The king dabbed at his tears with the cuff of

his robe and asked what use the sap might be to him. The holy man explained that all men would come to taste it. Once tasted, they would hunger for it, just as the king hungered for Postomoni.

'"Each man who eats or drinks the sap, which is called *af-yon*, will find within himself the characters of all the animals. He shall be fast and mischievous as the mouse; he shall lap milk like the cat and fight like the dog. He shall be savage like the boar, mighty as the elephant and filthy in his habits like the monkey. Finally he shall be lofty and imperious as a queen."'

The telling of the tale had sapped Badr's strength, his energy drawn from him just as opium was drawn from poppy heads.

'*Af-yon*,' he said once more, and John Grant brought him the bottle.

'Why now, Badr?' he asked. 'Why do you tell me this now, in this place?'

The Moor was silent for a while, letting the dark and bitter liquid flow down his throat.

'I was thinking on the women I have known.'

John Grant moved restlessly, easing muscles and joints that had stiffened while he sat listening to the story.

'And...?' he asked.

'I had a child once,' said Badr. 'A daughter.'

John Grant's eyes opened wide with astonishment. He wondered first of all if the big man might be dreaming, or hallucinating.

'Then where is she?' he asked.

Badr did not answer right away. His eyes were open to the shaft of sunlight and he was smiling at whatever he saw there.

'Your father made me your guardian,' he said. 'And I count myself the luckiest of men. I would ask that you take care of my daughter if needs be – see to it that she is safe.'

'Where would I find her?' asked John Grant. He felt as though he was playing along with a game of make-believe.

'At the centre of the world,' said Badr, his voice as dry as autumn leaves. 'In the Great City of Constantinople. May God forgive me ... I do not even know her name, but her mother was Isabella ... Isabella Kritovoulos ... Izzi.'

Badr seemed at peace, and John Grant studied him, committing the details to memory.

A daughter? A lost love? Another life – other lives? He felt time slipping away from him, sands through the narrows of an hourglass – and with those moments would go the truth of it.

'Why have you spent these years with me?' he asked. 'Why are you here, at war, and not at home?'

There was yet another pause, and Badr winced as he shifted his position in search of more drops of peace before continuing. The drug began to reach his brain like a rising tide of warmth.

'Constantinople was never my home,' he said. 'No more than this cave.' He wanted to laugh, but the sound that left his lips was more of a growl.

'But what of your child?' asked John Grant. 'And what of Isabella?'

Badr pulled in a long, slow breath.

'She was not mine either,' he said at last. 'I wanted her... I wanted them...'

'And so why have you lived without them?' asked John Grant. 'How ... how have you lived without ... without your flesh and blood?'

'However long we love them, however much we love them, we can never truly know them – not completely,' Badr said.

'What do you mean?' asked John Grant.

Badr drifted, his consciousness weightless as a boat upon an ocean. 'I was thinking about your mother,' he said at last.

'How so?' asked John Grant.

He wanted more of Izzi and the girl, but Badr's words were leading them both on a dance, his thoughts flickering like spectral lights in northern skies so that there was nothing to be done but follow wherever they might lead.

'I mean that there was more to Jessie Grant than met the eye,' said Badr.

He felt another tide of warmth rising beyond his chest, past his chin, until it filled his head and washed out his next thought unformed and unfinished. Then the wave broke and receded, giving him back his senses. It had been a matter of seconds, but the world had moved on for him, as though an hour had passed between breaths.

John Grant paid attention once more to the faint percussion of heartbeats pulsing against his cheekbones and fingertips. They were coming faster, harder than before. In his anxiety, he failed to realise they were not the irregular beats of one, troubled heart, but the mingling of two.

15

'Jessie Grant was your mother, but she was more besides,' said Badr Khassan. 'She was the woman who loved your father. She was the woman who loved you and raised you.'

'I know all of that,' said John Grant. He felt uncertainty prickling upon his skin, a sense of impending doom or of foundations shifting beneath him. For the first time in a long time he felt the tilt of the earth and almost gave in to it.

'She loved you and raised you,' said Badr. 'But she did not bear you.'

John Grant was silent, feeling the spinning of the world and his place upon it.

'It was not Jessie Grant who gave you life,' said Badr. 'That was the work of another...'

Angus Armstrong lay upon the clifftop, as close as he dared to the fissure through which sunlight and water entered the cave. If he remained still and kept his breathing shallow, he could just hear the voices of John Grant and Badr Khassan, strangely altered by their passage through the rock.

He had been baffled and bored by the Bear's talk of mice and monkeys and maidens, but his attention had certainly been piqued by mention of a long-lost daughter. Carefully he tucked away the sparkling nugget, safe among the store of information that kept him always close on his quarry's trail. If he was honest with himself, he had to admit it was the chase, the pursuit through months and years, that pleased him.

Killing was the work of a moment, but hunting might last him a lifetime.

Better yet was the talk of Jessie Grant. Not for the first time he remembered the night years before when an arrow meant for the Moor had found the woman instead. It had been the last in his quiver, and if it had struck Badr Khassan, as he had intended, he might have taken his time with the woman and her son.

As it was, the Moor had sighted back along the trajectory taken by the arrow and spied his location beyond the circle of stones. Low and menacing, the giant had set out in his direction with a burst of speed that was quite unexpected (and deeply upsetting) in one so large.

Armstrong had taken the only course open to him then and had turned and fled. Finding his horse where he had left it, tethered to a solitary tree silhouetted against the night sky, he had mounted the beast with a great leap and galloped ahead to rejoin his fellows.

He smiled at the memory, amused by the thought of his panic in the face of the Bear. Now the old monster lay in a cave below him, mortally wounded.

When Armstrong and the hunting party had returned to the stones that night, they found nothing and no one, not even the woman's body. Clearly the Bear and the boy had taken Jessie Grant with them, and Armstrong wondered again, as he had many times, just how they had managed to disappear so quickly and so completely.

He was brought back from his musings by the sound of John Grant's voice.

'Of course Jessie was my mother, Bear,' he said. 'It's just the opium … giving you dreams.'

Many feet below the spot where Armstrong lay, John Grant placed the palms of both hands on the smooth rock of the cave floor by his sides. The vibration was faint, but unmistakable – the low rumbling of the world turning on its axis. He drew strength from the force of it while he waited for Badr to speak again.

The Moor was growing weaker and his consciousness moved back and forth, swaying like a reed, but in a river made of opium.

'She was your mother,' he said. 'Of course that is true. Mothering is the work of years, an occupation without an end.'

'What are you saying, then?' asked John Grant. He was not looking at Badr – instead his gaze was directed into the darkness while the world beneath him hurtled into the void at an impossible speed.

'You did not grow in the womb of Jessie Grant,' said Badr. 'You were born from another. One who gave you up before you were even weaned.'

John Grant said nothing.

'Compared to a lifetime of love, the work of giving birth is the lesser task,' said Badr. 'Vital, I grant you, but lesser.'

He rode upon the river, rising and falling, while John Grant remained silent.

'Don't you remember?' asked Badr. 'Don't you remember what she said to you the night she died?'

140

'I could not have loved you more,' said John Grant at last. He had listened to the words in his head a thousand times.

'I could not have loved you more,' said Badr Khassan.

Suddenly they sounded different to John Grant, and he blushed. Had she meant, after all, 'I could not have loved you more ... *if you had been my own*'?

The thought, the apparent truth of it, ran around his innards like a rat, so that he felt hollow.

'Who then?' he asked. 'Who gave me life?'

'The woman who gave you life was ... your father's great love,' said Badr. 'I am sorry to say it, but you should know. A woman he saved from death just as he once saved me.'

'But who was she?' asked John Grant. 'Where is she?'

'My bag,' said Badr, gesturing weakly to his belongings, heaped by his side. The scimitar was sheathed, beside his cloak and a bag of leather.

John Grant crawled over on hands and knees and reached for the bag.

'Look inside.'

In all the years, John Grant had never had cause to inspect Badr's few belongings. The act felt intimate now, as he unfastened the ties and lifted the flap.

'Wrapped in blue,' said Badr.

John Grant reached inside. Alongside a few little books bound in dark leather, some bundles of dark cotton wrapped variously around clinking coins or ampoules of some or other liquid, he saw a square package of pale blue.

141

'Gently,' said Badr. 'It would be a shame to break it now.'

The fabric was fine, perhaps silk, thought John Grant, and as he began to unwrap it, he saw it was a scarf, fine and for a woman. He looked at Badr, mystified, as he unwound the layers. Inside he found a large shell, as big as his hand.

'Do you know what that is?' asked Badr.

John Grant turned it over and over reverently, as though handling a sacred relic.

'It is a scallop shell,' he said, more loudly than he intended. The strangeness, the unexpectedness of it left him almost disappointed.

'It was your mother's,' said Badr. 'Not Jessie's – but the one who bore you.'

John Grant felt empty, as though he was looking into a void, and the void was inside himself.

'Why do you have it?' he asked.

'Your father wanted me to keep it for you,' said Badr. 'And so I did. He never told me when I should give it to you. But now seems the time.'

He coughed and shuddered at the pain of it.

High above, where the sun shone and water flowed, Angus Armstrong had been pressing ever closer to the fissure. The words of the Moor and John Grant were on the outer limit of his hearing, and he was holding his breath while he strained to gather in the information rising towards him, fleeting as minnows in dappled shallows.

At the mention of the scallop shell, however – such a telltale possession, evidently treasured by Patrick Grant and loaded with import – all thoughts of concealment disappeared.

Then the revelation that it came from her, from

the woman...

In his desperation to hear more easily, to catch every last little fish, he reached too far forward and for a moment allowed his head and upper body to block the opening.

The effect in the cave beneath was instantaneous. While Badr breathed low and slowly and John Grant struggled with what he was being told, the shaft of sunlight between them was abruptly broken. The shadow stayed in place for no more than a fraction of a second, but it informed the younger man of another matter of great import. They were not alone.

He hissed in anger and frustration as he leapt to his feet. Surely it was Armstrong. Who else? Gifted the knowledge that their tormentor had sought them out yet again, that he was somewhere above them, John Grant finally made sense of the arrhythmic percussion of the heartbeats he had felt – and could still feel – against his face.

There was Badr's – slow and deep as always. But there was another besides. He understood it now and cursed himself for his mistake. What he had interpreted as one troubled, wounded heart was in fact the beats of two, woven into one messy plait.

Despite his wound, Badr's reflexes had him try to rise as well, to accompany his ward as always. A desperate gasp escaped him as his strength failed him utterly and he slumped down once more. John Grant shot him an anxious glance, but decided his most urgent business lay elsewhere.

Laying aside the shell and its wrapping, he sprinted for the cave's narrow entrance, his footfalls making scant impact on the bedrock so that he fairly seemed to fly. Back in the daylight he blinked and grimaced. He turned to look up at the sheer face of the cliff rising above him. All at once a black shape appeared at the top, no more than a shadow against the dazzling blue, but he knew it for what it was – who it was.

Angus Armstrong right enough – drawn to them always, as though attached by an unbreakable thread.

Suddenly the shadow changed shape. Armstrong had moved something, or rather rolled something off the edge of the precipice, and with only a sliver of a moment to spare, John Grant realised that a boulder as big around as a cartwheel was hurtling towards him out of the sunlight. He flinched and ducked to his right and the missile impacted deafeningly but harmlessly on the ground, splitting into many pieces. By the time he had collected himself and looked up once more, the silhouette was gone.

It was a hopeless situation and he knew it. There was no sense in risking abandoning Badr long enough to circle around the cliff face in search of a gentle approach to the top. Even less appealing was the thought of scaling the cliff itself, vulnerable every inch of the way to attack from above. He breathed deeply, in search of calm and the clearer thinking that might accompany it. Stepping back into the comparative safety of the cave's mouth, he weighed his options. As the minutes passed, he found his way back to his original assessment of the situation: denied the advantage conferred by his longbow, Angus Armstrong would surely avoid coming face to face with him in combat.

High above, the archer was already on his way – away from the cliff and the cave, and away from John Grant. There were no doubts in Armstrong's mind and no uncertainty. He had his destination and the promise of his prize – *the* prize.

Sir Robert would be pleased, well pleased.

Back in the cave, Badr floated on a river of opium and memory. His eyes were open and the shaft of sunlight from the cave's roof shimmered and shone before him like a waterfall of burnished gold, twisted like a girl's braided hair, or billowing like a ship's sail. Within it, against it, he saw the seasons of his life. Along with much else, he was losing his sense of time, or time was losing track of him as it let him go. Moments lengthened so that seconds gave space for whole sequences of events...

'You are a fool, Badr,' said Patrick Grant, from across the years.

Badr smiled at his old friend's passion, anxious as always to guard and to protect. For the first time he noticed how closely the son resembled the father. Hazel eyes flecked with gold.

'If you stay with her, you will die,' said Patrick. 'It is that simple, Badr. Her father will see to it.'

A wave of regret washed over him. He saw that it was in his own foolhardiness, his own stubbornness, that the seeds of Patrick's death had been sown.

'And if you won't give a thought to your own safety, then think of hers,' said Patrick. 'Isabella will live, but her life will be ruined. In her family's eyes, *she* will be ruined.'

Patrick turned his back on his friend, his shoulders shaking with frustration.

Badr remembered how his pet name for her – Izzi – had been too ... light for his friend's taste. She was royalty, after all, he said, or as good as. The girl could claim descent – distant and on her mother's side, but real enough – from emperors past.

Her father, the schemer, was a minister of the imperial court. Some said he might soon be made *mesazon* – most senior of the emperor's ministers and the most trusted, called upon night and day.

To Patrick, *Izzi* seemed too slight a word for one such as she.

From the cave's mouth, John Grant heard a mumbled word and queried it.

'My son?' he asked. 'Did you say *my son?*'

'*Mesazon,*' corrected Badr. 'The go-between.'

Back in his past, the Moor heard his old friend's voice again.

'Their sort are all about bloodlines and breeding. No one will want a pup from a bitch that's been had by the wrong dog.'

He turned to face Badr.

'And you, my friend, are the wrong dog.'

Patrick had pulled his chin towards his chest and half closed his eyes, as though in expectation of a blow. But Badr had laughed instead, a great roaring sound that made the other man jump with surprise...

Lying on his side on the cold stone of the cave, Badr laughed again at the memory – laughed at his friend's nerve as well as at his determination to make his case.

'What is it, Badr?' said John Grant. He had returned from the cave mouth and now took up a
position seated by his old friend, his back to him
and one hand on the big man's shoulder.

'He was brave,' said Badr. 'Braver than me.'

He seemed to have altogether forgotten the
events of just moments before – the younger man's
flight from the cave, the explosive impact of the
boulder pushed off the cliff by Armstrong, all of it.

'Who?' asked John Grant.

'Your father. He feared no one. And nothing.'

John Grant gently patted Badr's shoulder.

'I wish he had been afraid,' he said.

'You think that would have saved him?' said
Badr. 'I am not so sure.'

'Maybe if he had feared someone, or something, he would have come home to my mother,
and to me.'

Badr offered no answer, just gazed ahead into
the golden light, hypnotised by the way it seemed
to pulse and breathe.

'Tell me about his woman,' said John Grant.
'Tell me about my mother.'

Badr did not see John Grant, but Patrick
instead...

It was another place for the Moor, and another
time.

Patrick Grant was seated on the harbour wall at
Corunna, Galicia's port town on the Atlantic, his
feet dangling over the water. In his hands he held
a scallop shell, wrapped in its sky-blue scarf.

'I do not think I will ever see her again,' he said,
turning the package over and over, stroking the

fabric with his fingertips.

Badr was seated beside him and fairly towering over him, so that to an onlooker they might have seemed more like father and son. They were so close together that their bodies were almost touching, and Badr gave Patrick a nudge with his elbow that caused the smaller man to overbalance. He almost dropped the shell into the harbour.

'Careful, you big lump,' said Patrick.

'Sorry, sorry,' said Badr, holding up both hands in abject apology. 'I forget my own strength – especially around the little people.'

For all his sadness, Patrick had to smile.

'I'll give you little people,' he said, and pushed back, ineffectually, with his shoulder. It was like leaning against a bolted door.

Badr frowned. He had mastered the English tongue long ago, but the Scotsman's turns of phrase often left him baffled.

It was the springtime of 1432, and Patrick Grant was preparing to board a ship bound for Scotland, and home.

They were an unlikely pair in more ways than one. As well as the difference in their sizes, there was the child – in fact a baby boy just three months old and lying swaddled in a basket.

'Talking of little people,' said Badr, nodding towards the infant. 'How exactly do you propose to get him home?'

'There's a family aboard – merchants, trading Scottish wool for olive oil,' said Patrick. 'The wife is nursing one of her own, born a month early. She has agreed to lend a hand, or rather a tit.'

Badr laughed and shook his head at his friend's

predicament. Patrick saw the look and pressed on.

'I'll be paying her for her trouble,' he said. 'If we have to disembark and find another wet nurse along the way, then we will. It is time that I have, and a mother for the boy that I lack. And anyway, the crew has goats aboard – one way or another he'll not starve. He'll suck on a milk-soaked rag if he's hungry enough.'

Badr patted him heavily on the back.

'Changed days, eh?' he said. 'From fighter to father.'

Patrick reached out to the basket and rocked it gently.

'He's the fighter,' he said.

'He will have to be,' said Badr. 'Without a mother.'

'He has me,' said Patrick. 'And I will give him a mother, in time.'

'How could his own mother send him away?' asked Badr. 'What woman turns her back on her own young?'

There was movement in the basket and the baby cried out, a high, reedy sound that made both men wince.

Patrick reached in, dropped the scarf and shell among the blankets and picked up the baby, brought him in to his chest.

'He'll be hungry, no doubt,' said Badr.

He stood up and held out his hands for the baby. Patrick passed him over. In the big man's arms the infant looked pathetically small. Now standing upright himself, Patrick reached out for his son and Badr handed him back. The crying had stopped and the baby was calm, comforted by the movement and the change of position.

'Her heart is broken,' said Patrick. 'It was broken before I got to her. I thought I could put it right. As God is my judge, I let her be. I left her alone when I could, and went to her only when my heart demanded it.

'And then I thought ... well, I thought our baby would put it right.'

'But it did not,' said Badr.

'It did not,' said Patrick. '*He* did not. I think she feels ... no – I tell you she *believes* she has no right.'

'No right to what?' asked Badr.

'To much of anything now. To happiness ... to love ... to a life,' said Patrick. 'She's the only person I've ever met who feels that her own life does not belong to her.'

'I wish I had been there for you,' said Badr. 'In France, and against those English.'

Patrick Grant nodded, and breathed out through his nose so that the sound was close to a rueful laugh.

'I have not always needed to have you holding my hand,' he said.

'I might have steered you clear of ... all of this,' said Badr.

'I am sure you would have put yourself in harm's way for me, Badr – but I doubt even you could have shielded me from...'

'From what?' asked Badr.

Patrick looked him in the eye before answering.

'From love,' he said.

They were not in the habit of discussing such things, and the spoken truth of it sat between them like an uncomfortable stranger.

Badr grunted, to fill the silence.

'I loved her,' said Patrick. 'I doubt even your skill on the battlefield would have spared me such wounds.'

Badr sighed and clapped a big hand on his friend's shoulder.

'But if she believes, as you say she does, in a loving God, why does she think he would want her to be unhappy and alone?' he asked. 'How could she believe he would want her own flesh and blood to grow up without a mother's love?'

Patrick Grant began walking towards a gang-plank leading up to the side of a ship moored alongside the harbour wall, the boy-child cradled in one arm. The ship, a three-masted and lateen-rigged carrack bearing the name *Fuwalda*, creaked and groaned like a tethered beast. Among other people on the deck, a young woman, plump and with strawberry-blonde hair, stood by the base of the mizzenmast, her face turned towards Patrick and his son. Badr stooped and picked up the baby's basket before following.

'He will not grow up without a mother,' said Patrick. 'I promise you that. I promise *him* that, here and now...'

Back in the cave once more, the vision ended, Badr looked away from the shaft of sunlight and up at John Grant's profile.

'Tell me about my mother,' said John Grant a second time – for to him, only a moment had passed while Badr had breathed twice and mumbled once.

'She was a lost soul, I think,' said Badr, struggling to hold on to the present.

John Grant looked down at his friend. His need to press him for more, to know more, was almost overwhelming. But he saw the man was drifting like a ship that had slipped its mooring. From moment to moment he came close, then floated out of reach once more, pulled by a dark tide.

He was lying in a slick of blood that seeped slowly from his wounds, a slow but enervating flow that John Grant was powerless to staunch.

'I am thirsty,' he said.

John Grant reached for a water bottle by his side. The rivulet that entered the cave from above and pooled in a shallow dish of rock before spilling forwards and on towards the daylight was perfectly drinkable. He cradled the Moor's head as he held the opened bottle to his lips and let a trickle of water into his mouth. Badr was able to swallow without coughing or choking and John Grant let him have a little more.

'Not too much, Bear,' he said, pulling the bottle back from the big man's lips.

'What difference will it make?' whispered Badr, and John Grant returned it, and let him have a few more sips.

This time, there was a tightening in Badr's chest and he was convulsed with coughing. John Grant held him, turning his head towards the floor for fear he might choke. He spat to clear his mouth and there was dark blood mixed with the water. He gazed at the gobbet and his eyes lost focus.

'Proclaim: in the name of thy Lord who created...' he said, 'who created man from a blood clot.'

'What?' asked John Grant, gently stroking his long dark hair, but the Moor, at peace once more, had drifted beyond his reach...

Badr was a little boy again and seated with others like him at a wooden table covered with books. They were learning the literal word of God, as was their duty as Muslim converts. They were learning the Quran (which meant *recitation*) by rote, and in Arabic.

A bearded man, his head wound around with a long white cloth, was reciting the verses one by one, and Badr and the rest of the boys repeated them, for fear of punishment.

'Proclaim! And thy Lord is the most generous, who teaches by the pen,' he said, his voice still unbroken, the voice of a child. 'Teaches man what he knew not.'

Young Badr kept his head down, careful to avoid the teacher's gaze.

When he raised it once more, it was into Izzi's face that he looked. She was telling him that she loved him.

'So kiss me,' she said. Her hair, long and dark blonde, like honey, was loose around her shoulders. He stepped towards her and ran his fingers into that waterfall of thick tresses. He held her head and felt how fragile she was, like a figure made of blown glass. How was he to keep her safe when the touch of his own hands might break her?

'Kiss me,' she said again, and closed her eyes. Her lips were soft and slightly parted. He glimpsed the tips of white teeth. And he kissed her and reached his arms around her and pulled her to him as though to make her part of him.

When he opened his eyes he was looking only at the clot of blood, suspended in the gobbet of water and mucus he had coughed on to the floor of the cave.

'The scallop shell,' he said. His words were faint, ghostly.

John Grant had forgotten all about the keepsake and looked around for it. It lay upon his own folded cloak, where he had placed it before rushing out in search of Angus Armstrong. He reached over and picked it up, along with the scarf. Sitting down by Badr, he ran one finger around the edge of the shell. It felt old and dry and brittle.

'Do you know what it means?' asked Badr.

'Means?' asked John Grant. 'No.'

Badr coughed again – but out of frustration rather than pain.

'I never did think I would have time to educate you properly,' he said. 'And it seems certain I was right.'

He looked at the young man and was struck again by how much he was his father's son.

'The scallop shell is the symbol...' he paused for breath, 'of the Great Shrine of St James in Galicia. Pilgrims carry the shells as mementoes of their journey.'

'And this was my mother's?' asked John Grant.

'That's where your father took her,' said Badr. 'After he saved her life, he took her to the shrine in hopes she would be safe there. Out of sight.'

'Out of sight of what?' asked John Grant. 'Of who?'

Badr looked into the young man's eyes and smiled.

154

'Out of sight of the world,' he said. 'Out of sight of Robert Jardine and Angus Armstrong and the rest of them. I would prefer you to hear it all from her one day.'

'How do they know about her?' asked John Grant. 'What is she to them? Why do you leave it until now to tell me these things?'

Badr sighed, and then coughed long and hard.

'I thought I would have more time,' he said at last.

He breathed in deeply, a rattling draught that filled John Grant with fear.

Badr was walking hand in hand with Izzi. He did not need to look at her to know it was she. The touch of her hand was enough. They were walking towards a setting sun, and skipping along in front of them was a boy of about eight or nine years. Badr did not need to see his face, either, to know that it was John Grant.

It was a time that had never been, in a place he had never known. A dream of a might-have-been. He felt tears stinging his eyes and blinked to clear his vision.

'My son,' he said.

John Grant reached for him once more, positioned himself so that Badr's head was cradled in his lap. He brushed tears from Badr's face and leaned back, closing his eyes against his own grief.

Blindly he reached for the scarf and began running the fabric through his fingers.

He felt something solid knock against the heel of one hand. Looking down, he saw that one end of the scarf had been pulled through a little gold ring, and knotted. He worked at the knot until it came loose, and the ring fell into the palm of his hand. It was small, wrought for a woman's finger rather than a man's.

'It is one of a kind,' said Badr. 'Like the woman it was made for.'

John Grant looked at him through the circle of gold.

'Your father had it made as a gift for your mother,' Badr said. 'A keepsake.'

John Grant rolled it between thumb and index finger and then held it closer to his eye. It had been fashioned to look like a little belt, but with the buckle undone in a gesture of submission. On the inner circumference was an inscription – words he could read but not understand.

'*No tengo mas que darte,*' he said.

'I have nothing more to give thee,' said Badr.

PART TWO

Lẽna

16

Galicia, 1452

'Lẽna... Lẽna...'

The sound of her name, repeated over and over, drifted up from a courtyard in the valley below.

'Lẽna... Lẽna...'

Like smoke, the word reached her through the leaves and branches of the forest, dispersed and diminished, but unmistakable. It was the nuns' name for her and also the local word for firewood. Since it was she who provided the kindling and logs for their fires, it was appropriate, and the thought of it always made her smile.

She was seated on the stump of a large pine tree she had felled years before, at the centre of a clearing that was altogether the result of her own labour. Her axe was at her feet, and as she looked at it, listening to the girl's voice calling her name, she realised she had rested long enough to get cold. The chill of the dying of the day had raised goose bumps on the exposed skin of her arms. She rubbed them with both hands and stood to get the blood moving, stamping her feet to speed the process.

A stranger happening upon her there and then might have mistaken her for a man. Her hair was dark, almost black, and though silver threads were plentiful now, it was thick and unruly as always, soft sleek curls like the fleece of a newborn lamb.

She always cut her hair herself, short all over. Whenever anyone questioned the style – and those occasions were rare – she either gave no reply or explained that long hair was only a hindrance to one who spent her days working in the woods with axes, hammers and wedges.

She was tall for a woman, and while her build was slim and light, years of hard work had toned her muscles and broadened her back. Veins stood proud on the backs of both hands and on her forearms, and taut tendons and hard muscles defined her upper arms and shoulders.

Her movements too belied her gender. Years of practice with the axe and hammer had given her a physical confidence more suggestive of a male than a female. Her ease with the tools of her trade was impressive too, allowing the weight of the steel and the length of the axe shaft to do most of the work, so that to an observer it seemed effortless.

More than anything, from a distance at least, it was her clothing that was most masculine. Always she had favoured trousers over skirts, and her tunics and cloaks of rough linen and wool were of a sort normally worn by men. Her trousers were tucked into knee-high leather boots tipped with steel plates at heel and toe, much worn but well cared for like all of her few possessions.

Despite the effect the years of woodcutting had had on her body, up close there was no mistaking the truth of her. Now forty years old, she was still an arresting sight, even more so than in her youth.

When she smiled or laughed, it seemed every other year had passed her by. Her complexion was dark, in part from years spent outdoors in all weathers, making her pale blue eyes all the more startling. The skin of her hands and arms was tanned too, so that when she stripped to bathe, the contrast with the milk-white paleness of her narrow-waisted torso and long legs made her wince. There was white too in the many scars that marked the skin of her hands and arms, and that took no colour from the sun.

'Lẽna!'

They often called to her rather than trek up the steep hill into the woods to find her, but now she noticed something unfamiliar in the tone. There was urgency in the cry. The feeling of cold was gone from her body now. She turned to face in the direction of the call and reached down for her axe with her right hand. Not once in all the years in the woods had she felt the need of a weapon, but her actions were without conscious thought. Instead it was reflex that moved her arms and legs.

She was walking towards the sound of her name, and as she did so she passed the axe to her left hand, her good hand. If needs be it would be wielded by both, but it was her left that ran the show, and she raised the tool so that the weight of the head made the shaft slip easily downwards, through her fingers, until the cold steel rested against her thumb and index finger. The heft, the hardness and certainty of the metal, brought comfort as she weighed the situation.

Whoever had been calling for her – and it had sounded like Osana, one of the young initiates –

was silent now.

The forest too was silent, unnaturally so. No birdsong, no insects. A breath held.

It was a small sound, a misplaced step close behind her, that opened a door into the memories stored like wisdom in her muscles and had her drop and turn and swing her axe in a long arc parallel to the ground. It was only at the moment that the carefully sharpened edge of the axe head met the steel of a sword blade that she caught sight of her enemy for the first time. For a fraction of a heartbeat she reproached herself – how had he got so close?

A look of astonishment flashed across the man's features as he realised that his sword – held in front of him as he advanced through the trees towards her – was now out of his hand and spinning away to his left. It landed heavily, disappearing into the brown pine needles that thickly carpeted the forest floor.

Not that she could have known it, but he had not meant to harm the woman. Their job was only to find her and take her captive – indeed, any permanent damage inflicted upon their target would likely be followed by their own deaths at the hands of their master – but suddenly the task had taken on an unexpected air of physical danger. He looked into her eyes as he backed smartly away, arms stretched out in front of him in a gesture of submission.

'Who are you?' she said evenly, her pale eyes unblinking as she crabbed sideways in the first steps of a wide circle around him. 'What do you want?'

Whatever he wanted and whoever he was, he

162

stayed quiet. His silence was not his undoing. Rather it was a glance beyond her, over her left shoulder, that betrayed his companion. He realised his mistake at once and bared his teeth in a grimace as she turned to locate whoever was behind her.

It was a second man, older and bigger than the first but quieter over the ground. He was perhaps a dozen paces away, but as soon as she spied him he stopped his approach – apparently no more keen than his accomplice to come within reach of the axe.

There was a moment of perfect stillness then, while no one breathed or blinked or flexed so much as a finger. And then the world turned and a breeze blew through the treetops and she smiled an ancient smile as she shifted both hands to the base of her axe shaft, reached way back over her head with it and pulled forward to send it whirling towards the younger man.

He had the reactions of youth sure enough, but they were not enough, not by a long chalk. In the moment she had raised her weapon she read his body, saw him flinch towards his left and made a minute adjustment to her aim so that the heavy blade, lethally sharp, struck him on the side of his head just in front of his right ear. Two pounds of steel sent on their way by practised muscles and backed by the momentum provided by nearly four feet of spinning ash shaft ensured his skull was split open like a watermelon. The impact smacked him off his feet and he was dead before he hit the ground.

Certain of where the axe's journey would end,

even before she let go of it, she had turned from the throw to face the second man, stooping low as she did so and slipping both hands into the loose tops of her boots. When she straightened, still moving towards her target, she had a long-bladed knife in each hand. She could smell him now as well, an animal stink that spoke of weeks and months in the same clothes, and perhaps fresh fear.

The older man, after a startled glance in the direction of his felled companion, returned his attention to his erstwhile prey. They had been told she was no stranger to the fight, but none of it had prepared him for this last handful of moments among the trees. She crouched low then and moved towards him like a hunting dog, without any visible trace of hesitation, far less the fear to which his trade in the pursuit of hostages had made him more accustomed. He backed away quickly, sword raised in his right hand and with his left outstretched for balance.

If the third man had played fair she would have allowed for him too – even dealt with him, given a few more seconds. But while his companions were usually effective enough in their own, direct way, he was an ambush predator. As the others advanced upon her, he had buried himself beneath a mound of undergrowth at the base of a towering pine tree. So well concealed was he, so still, that when he leapt to his feet the woman was already past him and wholly focused on the only other person she knew to be in her territory.

Even so, she registered his appearance and was turning her face towards him as he brought the lead-weighted cosh down towards her temple. In the heartbeat of time before the blow landed, she flexed her left arm backwards and down.

She was conscious just long enough to feel her blade penetrate his right leg, above the knee. The lights were out in those unforgettable eyes, however, before she could be rewarded with the sound of his squeal.

17

It was dark when she regained consciousness. She was lying on her side, wrists and ankles bound behind her back with what felt like leather ties. She had no idea where she was, and while she allowed her thoughts to reassemble, she gazed into the campfire that burned some yards in front of her.

While her face and front were warmed by the flames, her back was chilled and stiff. Worse than any other discomfort, however, was the sickening pain in her head. She remembered the blow that had dropped her, and all at once the events of the attack returned. She played them through calmly, assessing her movements and mistakes. The dancing flames became her focus, allowing her mind to work freely.

'How is it?'

A man's voice, speaking in a language she had forgotten she knew.

'Bad enough,' came the reply. 'Bitch got me a

good one.'

'Still bleeding?'

'No ... no, that's stopped, thank God. But the wound needs tighter binding.'

'And riding?'

'I'll ride all right – even if it kills me. He said to keep to the trail the pilgrims follow, but heading east. I don't know how you feel, but I'd rather die on the road than fail to meet him.'

While the conversation went on, her eyes grew accustomed to the dark. The man she had seen – and the other she had not – was on the other side of the fire, tending to three horses tethered to the same pine tree. It was not just the language that had taken her by surprise – though English was rarely heard in Galicia, even this close to Santiago de Compostela, where pilgrims from around the world were commonplace.

What had struck her most forcefully was the accent. Her captors were Scottish. Slowly, so as not to alert them to the fact that she was awake, she arched her aching back and reached downwards with her arms, towards her heels. At the same time she flexed her legs, risking cramp in her calves as she sought to form herself into an O, with hands and feet touching behind her back.

'We should have buried Tom.'

'And how would we have done that? The ground's hard as iron. Did you mean to dig a grave with your sword?'

'Ach, I know. But come on – it's our Tom we're talking about, my own sister's child. I should've seen to him myself. Laid him out and covered him at least.'

'We should've made *her* do it. Forget it now. We had to leave him. Did you want to wait while folk – men, maybe – came looking for us ... after they'd found the women and girls – nuns, mark you?'

There was no reply, just a sound, perhaps the scraping of feet.

'If I was you, I'd worry less about poor dead Tom and more about your everlasting soul!'

He laughed, a cruel laugh that turned into a coughing fit. After hacking for a few moments, he spat thickly.

'Have you ever seen the like of it – her, I mean ... the way she handled that axe?'

It was their first mention of her existence, and her body stiffened.

The other snorted in an attempt at derision, but it convinced neither him nor his companion.

'Come on!' he hissed. 'And when she went for the knives ... Jesus Christ, if you hadn't skelped the living daylights out of her when you did ... well, I don't know what...'

'She'd have butchered you like a spring lamb, is what.'

'Aye, she might well,' said the other. 'I'll not deny it.'

There was silence then for a few moments and she closed her eyes, willing the pain in her head to recede.

'Who is she, anyway?'

'Stop asking me that! No one ever said. All I know – and all you need to know – is that she belongs to Sir Robert Jardine. I'll tell you this – he's welcome to her.'

Her eyes were open again, and wide. A chill ran

the length of her as though the fire had suddenly been extinguished and replaced by a blast from Brother North Wind.

Jardine. Sir Robert Jardine. She remembered the last time she had lain bound hand and foot, his prisoner. His face came back to her, clear as though he were here now, lying on top of her and pressing his face into her own so that his foul breath enveloped her, filling her nose and seeming to cling to her skin and hair. The years peeled away like wind-blown paper.

Long ago he had made of her a gaming piece, to be moved upon the board and exchanged for all the stuff of his dreams. Robert Jardine ... and if he had *her,* what of Patrick Grant? She had escaped – *they* had escaped – and she had turned her back on all of it. She blushed red hot with the truth that she had lived half a life, denied herself everything, in order to be safe. All at once the sacrifice, the price paid, seemed meaningless and obscene. She had surrendered all in hopes of disappearing from the world – and now the world was back, and she was back, and all that she had given up counted for nothing. These men had torn a gash in the thin curtain separating then from now, and she was Jardine's prisoner all over again. It might as well always have been so.

She exhaled softly as finally her tethered, booted feet made contact with her fingertips. With a final effort she forced the heels of her hands apart just enough to enable the rough edge of one steel toe cap to make contact with the tight bonds of leather. Her muscles and joints burned white hot with the strain of the posture and she ground her teeth for a few seconds, to retain her focus. With minuscule movements, she rubbed leather against steel.

'Simon ergo Petrus habens gladium eduxit eum: et percussit pontificis servum, et abscidit auriculam ejus dexteram. Erat autem nomen servo Malchus.'

Her voice cut deep into the night, louder than she had intended, but she was sure she heard the sound of both men turning towards her from where they stood beyond the flames.

While one remained with the horses, the other, the man who had felled her with his cosh, slowly circled the fire. She had heard the soft whisper of his sword blade as he drew it from its hide-lined scabbard, and he used it now like a walking stick while he limped heavily towards her. He was almost on top of her before he stopped.

'What did you say?' he asked, so close that the toes of his feet were almost touching her stomach.

With her eyes fixed not on her captor but on the flames, she repeated the verse, in Latin, from the Gospel according to St John:

'Simon ergo Petrus habens gladium eduxit eum: et percussit pontificis servum, et abscidit auriculam ejus dexteram. Erat autem nomen servo Malchus.'

He poked at her chest with the toe of one boot. 'Eh? What's that?'

She sighed, before continuing in English: 'Then Simon Peter having a sword drew it, and smote the high priest's servant, and cut off his right ear. The servant's name was Malchus.'

He grunted at her, lost for words.

'What was his name?' she asked. 'The dolt whose skull I laid open to the sky?'

169

Suddenly comprehending – realising she was making fun of him and his dead companion – he spat his venom at the woman at his feet.

'Fuck you!' he roared, taking his weight on his sword and drawing back his left leg a second time, intending, in his rage, to kick her hard enough to lift her into the air.

But as his clumsy left foot, unbalanced by pain and weakness in his right, lunged forward, she whipped both her hands from behind her back. The severed ends of the cut ties of her bindings hung loose from each wrist. Cramp and cold made her slower than she might have wished, but still she had time to parry the kick from where she lay.

While he gasped and stumbled, she sprang to her feet. Her ankles were still tightly bound, but she kept her balance. Her captor straightened too as best he could, given his wound. He was still holding his sword, but as he turned to face her, she struck him in the throat with her open left hand. Her arm had been as fast and sinuous as a striking snake, and she felt his Adam's apple collapse beneath the taut webbing of flesh between her thumb and index finger. He dropped heavily to the ground, his throat crushed, the airway blocked.

The few seconds of the fight had given the other man time to collect his thoughts. He had been frozen, stunned by the lopsided sequence of events. He let out a cry – fury and alarm in equal measures – and leapt towards her through the flames of the campfire. The ends of his long hair sparked alight, along with the fraying threads of his jacket. Before he could reach her, she squatted down, picked up the sword and used it to free her ankles. With both hands tight on the handle, she brought the sword upright and straight in front of her in time to catch her would-be assailant on the point of it. His own weight and momentum ensured he was punctured front and back, sliding down the length of the thing before coming to a rest against its hilt. His face, wide-eyed and dying, brushed against her own for a moment or two, so that she felt the stubble on his chin, before she dropped him and the sword down to her right. He slid from its length and flopped lifeless on to the ground like a stillborn calf.

'My, my,' said a man's voice from behind her. 'You're a handful and no mistake.'

She pirouetted on the spot, elegant as a dancer, until she had the sword pointed at the latest arrival. He looked to be roughly the same age as her, and handsome, with eyes of green. His head was as cleanly shaven as his chin, and she noticed the light of the campfire's flames dancing upon his polished pate.

Flames reach us wherever we are, she thought.

But for all she had taken in, in a heartbeat, about the man's appearance, it was his arrow's cruel steel point that preoccupied her most of all. It was just four long strides away, pointed straight at the end of her nose and backed by all the awful power of a fully drawn war bow of the good red yew.

'Drop the sword please, mistress,' he said. 'I'm running short of arrows, and broadheads like this one are for downing heavy horses. They're the very devil to dig out of dead faces. From this range, though, it'll likely pass straight through

171

and disappear into the trees. Either way, I'd just as soon spare myself the effort.'

She did as she was told, first lowering and then dropping the heavy sword. Three more men, all of them younger than the first, appeared out of the darkness either side of her.

One crept forward gingerly and stooped quickly to collect the surrendered weapon before withdrawing to a respectful distance. None of these Scotsmen had felt the need to fear a woman before (at least not since they'd grown old enough to disregard their mothers' wrath), and the experience was unsettling for all.

She was looking the archer straight in the eye as he finally eased the tension in his bow and lowered it in front of him, though she noticed he kept it in a state of readiness, the nock at the shaft's end still engaged upon the string.

'I am no one's mistress,' she said.

18

From a distance, the little caravan of horses and riders might have seemed like any other party of pilgrims heading east and away from the shrine of St James. In the common speech of Galicia they talked about *O Camino de Santiago*, the Way of St James. Any number of routes led to the shrine, as symbolised by the grooves in the scallop shell that was the symbol of the pilgrims' path – many ways, but all of them leading to the same destination.

On closer inspection, however, an observer might have noticed that the reins of the horse occupying the central position in the line of five were not controlled by its rider. Instead they were fastened to a rope held by the man immediately behind. Furthermore, the rider on the tethered horse, a woman, had her hands tied behind her back.

She was unconcerned about the discomfort, oblivious even. Lẽna's mind was wholly occupied processing what scraps of information she had gleaned from her captors' conversations.

The name Robert Jardine was one she had not heard spoken out loud for half a lifetime, and had hoped never to hear again. The thought of the man was unpleasant enough, but the way they had described her as his property made her sick to her stomach. It was a notion that stripped away her womanhood to leave her feeling like a child.

Then there was the manner of the men's approach, their tactics for handling her: all of it made plain they had been well instructed on the subject of her abilities. None of them had so far given any hint that they either knew, or suspected, the details of her past.

Three of her captors posed a negligible threat. In any one of several scenarios she had rehearsed in her head, they amounted to little more than static obstacles, inconveniences. The fourth, however, the man holding the reins of her horse, was different. Though she had not encountered the like in twenty years, she had recognised his manner at once. His intelligence was innate, his self-confidence the product of experience. The way he moved, his demeanour, reminded her of herself. Added to that – the quality that made all the difference – was the way he addressed her and treated her. There was no hint of malice or spite, no seeming need on his part to exercise dominance or inflict suffering.

In every way that mattered he had treated her with courtesy. Evidently he felt he had nothing to prove, no point to make. And so he was to be feared.

In spite of herself, in spite of her predicament, Lẽna found it pleased her to hear Scottish accents again. There was warmth in the sound that sharpened her thoughts of Patrick Grant, made him seem close by. She was surprised to find she was pleased by the memory of him.

The ebb and flow of the conversation wafting around her might have sounded like an argument, so combative and aggressive was the tone of much of it. Lẽna knew from experience, however, that she was listening to Scotsmen playing a game with one another, teasing and mocking by turns.

Nonetheless she kept her gaze fixed straight ahead, over her horse's head, and feigned disinterest. A burst of laughter rose and then fell, like a wave.

'Where will we meet his lordship anyway?' It was the voice of one of the younger men, in front of her in the line. As far as she could tell, his name was Jamie and his voice, more than any of the others, reminded her of Patrick.

'Never you mind,' said the leader, from somewhere behind. 'Just keep thinking about what needs to be done today.'

'Ach, he's always like this,' said another of the young voices. 'You've no idea what it's like riding with this man. It's just question after question after question. It's like being out with a nosy bairn.'

There was a snorted laugh from the fourth member of the group. He was the rider tasked with bringing up the rear of the party, and he said little. Lẽna suspected there was intelligence somewhere inside him, or at least a careful listener.

The little caravan continued on its way in silence for a while. They were keeping up a brisk pace and it was obvious they were making for their destination with all haste. The leader, the one holding the reins of Lẽna's horse on long lines, broke out of step with the rest and urged his own mount to speed up until he was alongside her.

This had been his practice from the moment they had set out. He watched her, tried to coax her to talk. Always he was attentive, as though her presence fascinated him. He said nothing for a minute or two, but Lẽna was aware of him looking at her yet again.

She had spent the time assessing him as well. That process had begun the moment she first encountered him, staring at her down the shaft of an arrow pointed at her nose. Lẽna was yet to hear his name. None of the men ever used it and she suspected they were under orders to keep him nameless – at least in her hearing. She wondered why.

'A lonely life you picked for yourself,' he said.

She did not reply, and kept looking ahead with what she hoped was an open and unconcerned expression. She had been guarded at all times so far.

'Someone so ... capable,' he said.

She gave no hint she was even paying attention to him, but she processed the question just the same. *Capable,* he had said. It was a leading word, suggestive.

'Surely there was more you might have done,' he said.

She felt his gaze upon her, intent.

She exhaled slowly, and the sigh itself was an answer of sorts.

'I miss the rain,' she said.

In spite of himself, he made a small, surprised sound, almost a gasp. He had attempted conversations with her for the last three days, always without success. This sudden statement caught him unawares.

'The rain?' he asked.

'On the island,' she said, still looking ahead and not at him.

The words, the language, felt strange in her mouth. She seldom talked to anyone, and then always in the Galician tongue, and so she spoke slowly, as though remembering a taste from childhood.

'It seemed like it rained every day. I hated it at first, but after a while I liked it. It does not rain so often here, and I miss it.'

She waited to see if her remarks made any sense to him, or perhaps confirmed what he already knew, if anything.

'Islay,' he said. It was a statement, not a question, and she sighed again.

He might have asked her something else but she did not hear it. Instead she kept looking straight ahead, just as before, between her horse's ears. With the rise and fall of the trot she let the years slip away like dead leaves until she looked not at the real world around her, but with the eye of memory at her twelve-year-old self, at the grand and stately home of Alexander Mac-Donald, Lord of the Isles...

They had arrived at Finlaggan, on Islay, on horseback. Her father had been at her side as always, on his black warhorse, Minuit.

'*Se tenir droit, maintenant*,' he said. Sit up straight, now. '*Garder tes talons vers le bas.*' Keep your heels down.

She had been close to dozing in the saddle, her eyes drooping with the fatigue of a seemingly endless journey, but at the sound of her father's voice she had taken a deep breath and made her best effort to come back to the world and pay attention to his instructions. It was cold (why was it always so cold here?), and while it was not raining, the air around her was sodden so that her clothes and hair were damp.

In spite of all the uncounted miles, the discomforts and the homesickness, she had made no protest at any of it – but her father had felt her disquiet just the same. She asked no questions, but still he offered answers.

'It matters that you come here,' he said. 'You matter much more than I do.'

His voice was as soft as the mist.

She looked at him and smiled. She loved him

and she trusted him. He knew it, and the thought of it, the feel of it, was like a bruise upon his heart.

'I do not think there is anyone else like you in the whole world,' he said.

'I do not think there is anyone in the world like you,' she replied, quick as a flash, her eyes loaded with all the seriousness of her words.

He swallowed hard. It was easier when he could treat her like a child – when he was giving her instructions and chiding her for any lapse in posture or behaviour.

'These people are dear to me,' he said. 'They will love you as they have loved me, and that will make all the difference, I promise.'

White mist clung like smoke to the heather and gorse either side of the trackway, and when she looked ahead at the buildings of Finlaggan, the walls and thatched roofs were cloaked in more of the same. It created an air of melancholy that she felt seeping through her damp clothes and into her flesh and bones.

'*Et mettre un sourire sur ta visage,*' he added. And put a smile on your face.

The journey had taken weeks of travel, over land and sea. Home seemed hopelessly far away, and the sensation of longing in her chest – for her mother, her brothers and sister, for familiar sights and smells and tastes – felt somewhere between pain and hunger. In any event she had known there was something she wanted, needed; that she could not have it then and would not be having it again any time soon.

A group of around a dozen men and women had emerged together from an arched gateway in one wall of the largest building up ahead, and walked purposefully towards them. They had been expected in that place – that much she had known.

'Jacques!' shouted a tall, heavyset man at the head of the welcoming party. Having recognised her father, he had broken into a trot. She had wondered once more at the garb of the men living in that part of the world. Tall or short, fat or thin, each lived wrapped one way or another in something like a long woollen blanket that covered them from neck to knee. Folded and pleated, it was draped over one shoulder and belted or tied at the waist. When the weather turned for the worse, as it so often did, some of the folds could be employed as a hood. Those that could afford it wore a loose-fitting shirt beneath the plaid, and every one of them, rich or poor, was armed with sword and knife. It was a place and a people that seemed permanently ready for a fight.

'Douglas!' said her father, as the other man arrived alongside them. He had reached out with a great bear's paw of a hand that entirely enveloped that of her father.

'It's a pleasure to see you here at last,' said the big Scotsman, his arm pumping so hard she feared physical damage might be the result. If he had not been smiling – her father too – then the growling sound of the words exchanged by the pair would have convinced her they were arguing.

'And to be here, I can assure you, Douglas,' said her father.

She gazed at him in amazement, still not used to hearing the new language that came so easily from him. From the moment of their arrival in

Scotland days before, he had conversed with the inhabitants without hesitation and she had looked on with breathless awe, as though seeing him anew. She had wondered then how much else she had still to learn about her own father.

He had jumped down from his horse and embraced the big man, who was the taller of the two by a head. There was much arm slapping, and then each had held the other by the shoulders and leaned back to take a proper look at the familiar face before him.

The one called Douglas had turned then and looked her in the eye.

'She's bonny, Jacques,' he said, smiling. 'A credit to you.'

'She has the look of her mother, right enough,' her father had said, gazing at her with an expression she did not recognise. It had been as though he was seeing her for the first time, and she had felt herself blush at the intensity of the men's attention.

'Is he here?' asked Jacques.

'Not yet,' said Douglas. 'But don't worry, he will come – and soon.'

'The poor soul is exhausted!'

It had been the voice of one of the women in the party. She was thin as a greyhound, with slender arms and legs. Her long black hair was braided and reached halfway down her back. Her face was pretty enough, and smiling, and as she came forward, she held out her arms.

'Jeanne?'

She had clearly wanted to help her down from her horse. Her father had nodded his approval.

'*C'est bien, Jeanne,*' he had said. It's all right.

She stood up in her stirrups and swung one leg over, ready to jump to the ground. As she dropped downwards, she felt the woman's hands on her waist and was grateful for the reassuring touch. When she landed, her legs seemed as weak as unravelling threads, and for a moment she thought she would crumple on to the damp ground. Thin as she was, the woman was stronger than she looked and caught her under the arms to help steady her while she gathered what remained of her strength.

The woman had spoken to her then, and while she had not understood the words, the notes of concern and sympathy were unmistakable. The woman had shot the two men a reproachful look, her dark eyebrows raised and arched so that her forehead creased.

'We must take better care of this one,' she said. 'It's no use wearing her out before she starts.'

She felt a weight upon her shoulders then and thought that she might sink into the soft earth beneath her feet. Her father said she had been chosen to lead the way to freedom, and to God. She would make a king and take him with her, he said. Just the thought of it all, the incomprehensible enormity of it, made her want to lie down and sleep for a year.

The words being spoken around her were mostly foreign to her, and she had watched open-mouthed as both men looked suddenly abashed, brought to heel.

The party had divided in two then, the men remaining with the horses while the women gathered her into their midst and ushered her towards the archway from which the group had emerged minutes before.

She had smelled the dampness of the women's woollen dresses and cloaks, an aroma she would ever afterwards associate with sanctuary. There had been hands on her shoulders and soft words of comfort that washed over her as she stumbled along at the centre of the scrum...

She was brought back to the present, to her captivity, by another question from the nameless, persistent leader. There may have been more from him, while her mind had wandered into her past, but one query penetrated the shawl of memory she had drawn around herself.

By the time he had finished asking it a second time, she was Lēna once more.

'Would you tell me what the angels looked like?' he asked.

19

Lēna concentrated on the popping sound she could feel, rather than hear, coming from her right shoulder. It was not yet painful, but that time would come. One of the younger men, the one called Jamie, had been muttering to their leader about her bindings. Even more than the rest of them apparently, he had been awed by the way she had dispatched his comrades three nights before, and he had several times made plain he felt there was inadequate security in having her bound only at the wrists, hands behind her back.

His suggestions might have fallen on deaf ears but for her sudden return to silence. She had, after all, allowed her inquisitor to feel he had finally penetrated her defences, that her life story was his for the hearing. Her sullen retreat behind her stone wall seemed even to have hurt his feelings.

So it was, she believed now, that he had consented to see her being more securely tied. They had stopped for a while and a new rope had been added – this one around her arms, so that her elbows were pulled towards each other in the centre of her back, in a position that resembled that of a pullet trussed for the cooking spit. As well as limiting her movements even further – making escape that much harder to contemplate – it also felt like a spiteful punishment for her refusal to talk.

The others had seemed abashed by her discomfort. Even Jamie was strangely cowed. Instead of their easy chatter, now there was nothing to listen to but the clinking of the horses' bridles and the popping from her shoulder.

She let her mind wander all the way back to the moment long ago when the damage had been done. She listened again to the clamour of battle all around, the press of horses as her brave Scottish escort had sought to keep her from harm...

The year was 1429, and she was the maiden the French soothsayers had foreseen. The English were unbroken in their resolve. Their king, Henry, was resolute in his claim upon the throne and the land of France. But now the maiden from Domrémy was among them, at the head of an army and a cause made pure by her presence.

Her own mount had been a white charger so broad across the back it strained her thigh muscles just to stay astride him. Arrows from English longbows fell like black rain, and only the shields held around and above her by the brave men of her Garde Ecossaise had kept her undamaged. She was at the centre of a tight protective knot, and beyond it, and all around, men and animals fell dying.

'Keep together!' It was the voice of Hugh Moray, her aide-de-camp, a blond-bearded bull of a man. 'Stay close!'

She wore borrowed armour but was otherwise unarmed, save for her nerve. Instead of a sword she held aloft a great unfurled banner. It was to her and to her alone that the forces would rally in time of uncertainty or need, and she glanced at the reach of it, trailing behind her for the length of two men. It was brilliant white, sown with golden lilies. Near the staff she held gripped in her gauntleted hand was an image of Jesus Christ in majesty, robed in blue and holding the world in his lap, angels by his sides.

They were riding fast, almost at the gallop, and the banner snapped and cracked. For all the death and danger thick in the air, the shouts and cries of men, her heart felt high in her chest – almost in her throat – beating like the wings of a captured bird. Victory was at hand. Despite the sacrifice of her men – indeed because of it – the English were breaking before them, and she felt bathed in the warmth of God's pleasure.

So when the arrow, loosed from somewhere behind her, found its way past the upraised shields and all the way to a gap between the top of her breastplate and her helmet, she thought at first it was a bolt of lightning from above, divine high spirits gone astray. It burned like fire and there was a shout from one of the accompanying horsemen.

'She's hit,' he cried. 'The lady is hit.'

She held the banner tight as ever in her left hand, but her right, the hand controlling her horse's reins, felt suddenly weak as the paw of a newborn kitten. She let go of the leather and felt herself slipping sideways into the gap between her own mount and that of the man who had seen her injury.

'No!' he shouted, and the tight knot began to lose form as men sought desperately to grab her, or her horse's reins, or both. Gravity made the final decision, and despite the efforts of her escort to keep her in place and driving forward to safety, she slumped into the gap and down towards a forest of thundering legs and hooves. The last thing she heard before darkness swept in around her was the sickening crunch of her shoulder, already pierced through by the arrow, popping from its joint...

Lẽna marvelled at the way the memory was vivid while the pain was utterly lost to her. She could effortlessly recall the sights, sounds – even the smells of the battle – but not a trace of the burning agony remained. What she felt now, trussed like a chicken, was no more than indignity coupled with the discomfort of middle age. Although she would

185

have given her eye teeth to massage the spot with one free hand, it mattered little. It was the shattering clap of thunder directly overhead that fully attracted her attention – and that of her captors. The air seemed to fizz and an acrid taste filled her mouth.

'Storm coming,' said Jamie, his ears still ringing from the discharge.

'Do you think so?' said another of the young men, who so far as she could tell answered to the name of Shug.

The others laughed, their leader included. It was as though the thunder had lightened the mood as well as clearing the air, and the return of sarcasm was welcomed by all. A second clap had them all duck down involuntarily, and everyone looked around, wide-eyed with wonder at the ferocity of the sound.

The light of day had gone from the sky. They had ridden through the dusk and now it was all but dark. The prospect of carrying on into a night riven by a rainstorm was an unappealing one, but Lẽna was careful not to allow her body language to suggest as much. Any visible sign of discomfort might persuade their leader to prolong their misery, in the name of putting more of their journey behind them.

She allowed herself a sigh of relief when she heard his voice.

'Look for shelter up ahead,' he said. 'Quickly now.'

20

Crista Fuentes could not sleep. She had said her prayers as usual before climbing into bed alongside her younger sister. Normally she slept curled around little Ana, her nose buried in the five-year-old's dark curls. But this night, sleep was beyond her and she lay on her back instead, listening to her sister's rhythmic breathing that was almost snoring but not quite.

Their parents were asleep nearby as well, on a four-poster bed draped around with white linen. The room, the sole bedroom in their farmhouse, was small, and only the curtain afforded any kind of privacy. Crista had grown used to the soft moans that sometimes rose from beyond it, accompanied by creaking as the bed frame rocked and her father's breathing came in gasps.

Tonight her parents were at peace, however, and Crista concentrated instead on the cause of her own wakefulness. The pain in her middle had been building all day. It had started out as no more than the warning of a need to visit the long-drop privy, but by early afternoon, still with many chores to complete, it had turned into a cramp that felt like a fist clenched deep inside her body.

Another wave of pain broke over her and she screwed up her eyes and pulled her knees towards her chest, breathing out slowly as she did so. She was ten years old – soon to turn eleven –

and a good girl. Unlike so many of the children living on the farms around her, she had never known a day's illness. Her robust good health, while others succumbed to this malady or that, was commented upon by one and all, and so the deepening discomfort in her tummy was as unfamiliar as it was unpleasant. She had meant to say something to Mama about it before now, but the right moment had not presented itself.

She fingered the little silver crucifix on a thin leather thong around her throat, and wondered if Our Lady was upset with her and sending down a punishment from on high. After a few moments she dismissed the thought, shaking her head as she did so but keeping her knees drawn up almost to her chin.

Deciding again that she had to visit the privy, she rolled painfully on to her side, then put her feet down on to the floor and its covering of rush matting. Only able to half straighten her body, she shuffled to the door, holding her tummy with one hand and stretching the other out in front of her for fear of knocking something over in the dark.

Once outside, in the vegetable garden to the rear of the farmhouse, she felt the cramp begin to pass again and she straightened, smoothing the creases and folds out of her nightdress as she did so and taking a breath of air. Despite the lateness of the hour, it was still warm – too warm. The air was as deathly still as it had been in the bedroom – in fact it was hard to believe she was outside and not inside – and she recognised the conditions Papa always said were the forewarnings of a thunderstorm.

There was a half-moon in the sky, but when she looked around from it she saw that its light illuminated the most enormous storm cloud she had ever seen – a giant, flat-topped anvil of a thing that seemed to block out half the sky.

Her hand went involuntarily to her crucifix once more.

'Our Father, who art in heaven,' she mumbled. 'Hallowed be thy name; Thy kingdom come, thy will be done.'

The cramping returned, worse than before, and she fell to her knees, clutching her middle with both arms.

'Thy will be done, on earth as it is in heaven.'

Just when she thought she must surely cry out with the misery of it all, the wave receded from her again, leaving her gasping. She stood, on wobbly legs, and began walking forward. Unsure and unsteady at first, and with no thought as to where she was going, she speeded up, out of the garden and on to the track beyond their fence. Downhill led into the village, but uphill promised high ground and perhaps a breath of cool wind.

'Give us this day our daily bread, and forgive us our trespasses, as we forgive those who trespass against us,' she said, her fist clenching around the cross until she felt the metal digging into her flesh. 'And lead us not into temptation, but deliver us from evil. Amen.'

Briefly enjoying freedom from the pain, but fearful of its return, she pressed on up the steep flank of the hill. She reached the summit, winded, and bent to catch her breath. When she straightened, still panting, she saw the stark outline of the tor, like a pile of rough slabs piled clumsily high by an ancient giant. Sensing a breeze, she pressed on, convinced she would feel better the higher she climbed. She felt a few drops of blessed rain on the backs of her arms and was just raising her face into the sky when a thunderclap burst overhead.

Standing in wonder at the ferocity of the sound rolling and heaving in the air above her head, she held out her arms in a posture like a priest leading his congregation in prayer. A second clap, louder than the first, and closer, ripped the night asunder.

21

Islay, Western Isles of Scotland, 1424

Among other things, before other things, they had come to see the Dewar. Lẽna's father said it was a word that meant *wanderer*, or perhaps *pilgrim*.

Out of what had been a meaningless babble just weeks before, she now distilled words and complete phrases. She was quick – her father always said so – and the tongue of these Scots, which had so eluded her at first and which was called Gaelic, was starting to make some sense at last.

She had known she was to practise the fighting arts – at which, despite her youth and sex, she already excelled – among a people much given to war. In due course it was intended that she be more than any foot soldier, but there were months and years between then and now. Before any of that, she was to be tested in other ways. If she were found wanting, then her time on the island would likely be short.

This Finlaggan, on the island of Islay off the west coast of Scotland, was home to a family and a man called MacDonald. She had asked her father if he was a king.

'Of a sort,' he had said. 'Some of his people call him *Righ Innse Gall* – King of the Isles. Others – MacDonald himself, I think – prefer *Dominus Insularum* – which means *Lord* of the Isles in the language of the Romans.'

Softly he began to sing a sweet dirge of a song:

Do Mhac Domnhaill na ndearc mall
Mo an tiodhlagudh na dtugam,
An corn gemadh aisgidh oir,
A n-aisgthir orm 'n-a onoir.

Ce a-ta I n-aisgidh mar budh eadh
Agam o onchoin Gaoidheal,
Ni liom do-chuaidh an cornsa:
Fuair da choinn mo chumonnsa.

To MacDonald of the stately eyes
Is the gift of what I am giving,
Greater than the cup – though a gift of gold–
In honour of what to me is given.

Though I got this cup free, as it were,
From the wolf of the Gaels,
It does not seem that way to me:
He received my love as payment.

191

He smiled at her, reached out and patted her knee with his rough hand.

'My love,' he said.

They were seated together, father and daughter, in a finely appointed room in a grey stone tower house three storeys tall. One wall was dominated by a great smoke-blackened fireplace in which a veritable forest of pine logs lay blazing and crackling. On the other three were large tapestries depicting scenes of hunting – men on horseback flanked by lean and shaggy long-legged dogs that looked to her like wolves. The window seat they sat upon was plump with horsehair, upholstered with soft fabrics that were blue like a summer sky and golden like the sun. For all the intensity of the flames, the room felt cold to her, and she shuddered.

'If this lord is so important, why are there no battlements – no walls or stockades to protect him?' she asked.

It was true what she said. There were several fine buildings at Finlaggan, the work of skilled craftsmen, but none seemed constructed with defence in mind.

'Alexander MacDonald has no need of such,' said her father. 'None threatens him here. He has more than one hundred warships at his command, and ten thousand fighting men. I'd say he might indeed call himself a king, if he so wished.'

She nodded at the numbers, impressed. There was the sound of someone heavy-footed approaching along the hallway outside, and into the open doorway stepped Douglas, wrapped as always in a great bundle of woollen plaid belted at the waist. Though she had not said so, not even to her father, she thought he looked like an upended unmade bed.

'It is time,' he said. 'The Dewar.'

They stood and walked smartly out of the room, without another word spoken, behind the bulky figure of her father's friend. The pair had fought side by side, this much she knew.

They descended a tight corkscrew of triangular stone steps that made her dizzy, and emerged from a narrow doorway in the semi-circular outer wall of a tower into a courtyard of grey flag-stones. Smoke from many fires hung in the damp air. A few dogs, of the same sort she had seen pictured on the wall hangings, loped around the perimeter in search of scents and scraps. When one passed close enough to touch, she noticed it smelt damp and smoky too, like everything else. A gaggle of people, men and women, were milling about, or talking quietly in huddles, but as she stood breathing the cold air and waiting for the world to stop spinning, she felt all eyes turn towards her and silence fell.

The man who came towards them then wore the plaid as well, but with more panache than big Douglas. His long hair had been black once but was now mostly silver-grey and worn loose to his shoulders. He was bearded and handsome, and not for the first time it occurred to her that he had the look of one of the wolfish hunting dogs that patrolled the place.

He was Alexander MacDonald, Alexander of Islay, Lord of the Isles. She had seen her father talking to him more than once in the days that had passed since their arrival, judged that there was some history between them too, of the sort that was written in battle.

'Let us see then what the Dewar makes of you,' said MacDonald.

He stopped a few paces in front of her and held out his arm. She reached for him uncertainly, as though to take his hand, but she had misunderstood his actions and he merely gestured towards the open door of a small building, a chapel on the far side of the courtyard. She looked at her father and he smiled and nodded, so that she felt it was safe to proceed.

The interior of the little stone building was dark, lit only by two lamps upon a stone altar. The orange lights offered mere smudges of illumination, and she waited in the doorway while her eyes adjusted to the gloom. Kneeling before the altar, at prayer, was a stooped figure in a dark woollen robe. At the sound of her arrival, the figure stood, with some difficulty, and turned to face her.

It was an elderly man, his long face thin and deeply creased, his blue eyes watery like melting ice and his arms and legs seeming no thicker than the rope tied around his waist. In his right hand he held a staff taller than himself and with a curved headpiece, like that of a shepherd but delicately gilded and decorated and gleaming darkly under the influence of the lamplight. His face was kindly, and as he stepped towards her he spoke to her in her own language.

'Come,' he said. 'Sit with me and let me look at you.'

They crossed together to a wooden bench against one wall of the chapel, the only other furniture. She stood and waited for him to sit, before joining him, at what she considered a respectful distance. He looked at her for what seemed ages but his unblinking gaze did not make her uncomfortable.

'They tell me you have spoken of angels,' he said.

She turned away from him, blushing.

'That is no small thing,' he said. 'Is it true?'

It broke her heart to think about what she had seen in her father's garden back home, and her throat burned and tears formed at the corners of her eyes and began rolling down her cheeks. The emotion surprised her, embarrassed her, and she said nothing to the Dewar but only nodded, her hands neatly folded in her lap as her mother had taught her.

'Why do you cry, then?' he asked.

'Because ... I...' Her voice cracked and broke, and she stopped.

'Go on, child,' he said.

'I ... do not think I will ever see them again,' she said. 'And I miss them.'

She was suddenly afraid that he would ask her what everyone else had asked – what they looked like. She feared the question because in truth she had no recall of their appearance whatsoever. All she remembered, apart from their words, was light, and the smell of them, like clean air after a lightning storm. She raised her hands to her face as though she might find there a trace of the scent. Instead she smelled only woodsmoke and cold, and she rubbed her tears and her nose, which had started to run. She wished with all her heart that she had remembered to carry a handkerchief.

She waited for more questions, the inevitable interrogation. The single most extraordinary event of her life and yet recalling the detail was like trying to remember the shape of light, or describing how it felt to be loved. He asked nothing more, however, just sat beside her looking at her profile as a salty tear ran down her nose to the tip, before dripping on to the back of her hand.

'The Angel Michael told me I would fight for a prince and see him made king,' she said.

The thought had come unbidden to her lips and surprised her as much as it did the Dewar. She looked up into his face and he smiled, his head cocked to one side so that for a moment he reminded her of a curious old hound dog.

He was the Dewar of the Coigreach – the keeper of the staff of St Fillan, who had come from Ireland seven centuries before and who had cured the sick. When a wolf killed the ox that was helping him build his church, Fillan had spoken to the beast and taught it the error of its ways, and had had it labour beside him as his beast of burden instead.

The Dewar looked at the girl and wondered what she would say if she could read his thoughts at that moment. His faith was the elder faith, the first, older by lifetimes than that of the Romans and their Pope. He bore an ancient burden, and after many long years spent wandering among his flock he had learned many things. Now they brought this child before him and asked that he judge her. He and he alone would know if she was touched by grace or by madness.

But he did not know and could not know. He prayed every day of his life to hear the word of God and never yet had. Not once. He had known hunger, cold and loneliness, and watched the road stretch ahead of him without end. He had sought blessings for newborns and heaven for the dead. He looked at the girl and saw only the tear-stained face of a child, and knew that he was tired and that he wanted to set aside his burden and sit by a fire. But he also felt the holy air above him and around him, filling the chapel and pressing down upon his head and shoulders, heavy with years.

'How is it that you know how to fight?' he asked. 'Just a girl.'

His question surprised her and she thought for a moment, sensing a trap. She found none, but remained cautious just the same.

'My father leads the militia in our village,' she said, shrugging her shoulders. 'I have always been around men practising their drills, wielding swords.'

The Dewar looked at her anew, noticed that her shoulders were broad for a girl and that she carried herself well, inhabiting her space with confidence and without a hint of shyness.

'They say you are ... especially skilful,' he said.

She shrugged again and was briefly aware that her actions might seem rehearsed.

'It comes easily to me,' she said. 'Tools do the work for you, if you let them, my father says.'

She closed her eyes and thought about that day in the garden when she had been pulling weeds from among the tomato plants. She had smelled that sweet, clean smell and breathed deep and looked around and there they were – Michael, Margaret and Catherine. They were lovely, she remembered that much, and when she had raised her arm in a greeting, the air between her and them had shimmered, or rather it had rippled as though the space had been made of water and she had disturbed its surface. She tried to remember the sounds of their voices but they were gone from her entirely.

'All the way back to God,' she said.

She had not meant to give voice to the thought and she blushed and clapped her hands over her mouth.

'There is no shame in it, child,' said the Dewar, and he reached for her and lightly touched her arm.

'Sit here with me a while,' he said. 'Just you and me – before I give you back to them.'

When at last they stood and walked towards the damp, unwelcoming light of the world outside the chapel, he sent her ahead of him and walked reverently behind. When she emerged alone, there was a brief silence and then cheering.

22

The ground rose sharply and they had to dig their heels into their horses' flanks to keep them moving forward. The air around and above them was thick and heavy, like blame, and Lẽna felt that even time was slowing, turning to treacle. Jamie, Shug and the other of the younger men – the silent one whose name she had still not deciphered – were quicker off the mark and put some distance between the other two in their bid to reach the high ground. Some hundreds of yards ahead, silhouetted by moonlight against a monstrous storm cloud, Lẽna made out the shape of a rocky outcrop. For an instant she mistook it for a ruined building, before realising it was a natural formation.

A few spots of rain were falling now, plump outriders of a downpour to come, and the rocks on the hill's summit offered the only obvious prospect of shelter. The leader cracked the long leads down on to her horse's back from behind her, and the animal whinnied in protest and bolted forward.

Lẽna was rocked backwards in her saddle but gripped tight with her knees and used her stomach muscles to pull herself upright. In his eagerness to reach the rocks before the storm proper, the leader beat his mount's sides until it was first alongside Lẽna's and then slightly ahead. He was still holding the reins and still nominally in control, but no longer watching her as closely as before.

Lẽna had thought of little but her old war wound for the past two hours. The arrowhead had pierced her shoulder front and back, the shaft passing beneath her right collarbone. The surgeon had afterwards found it straightforward enough to snip through the wood of the shaft with a great pair of shears, before pulling it out of the wound. There had been bleeding and pain but nothing compared to the exquisite agony of having her dislocated shoulder reset. They had given her a leather strap to bite on, and when the bonesetter jerked her arm and popped the ball joint back into its socket, with a crack like a slammed drawer, she nipped the thing cleanly in two with her teeth.

Her French countrymen called her the hero of Orleans ever after, and a portent of final victory over the invader.

Fired by the sight of the banner borne by the maiden, they had pressed the English all the harder, until the squatters fled from their trenches and redoubts and the siege was lifted. She had been something clean – something honest. Into a war of sullied men and tainted politics she had arrived from nowhere like a blade freshly forged and mill-sharpened. That she knew the ways of the warrior had been beyond question. They had all of them, at one time or another, seen her stand and fight, cleaving the shield walls and harvesting her foes like wheat. But she came with more – with the strength of angels in her limbs and the very word of God upon her tongue.

Hugh Moray had taken her on to his horse and galloped through the city gates. Within the walls of the relieved city her wounds had been dressed, the arm and shoulder strapped, and then time had done almost all else that was required. The joint, however, had been altered for ever, and while the muscles, tendons and ligaments had adjusted to their new positions, there was always a little … slack.

The years spent working in the forest with axe and hammer had given her new strength, but still there was play around the joint. She found, by accident the first time, while trying to reposition a wagonload of logs, that what had been dislocated once was a little more inclined to dislocate again. Having learned the action required to free ball from socket – and the opposite move to put them back together – she had found it equally painful every time thereafter. But pain could be borne, while other indignities and sufferings could not.

Jamie had applied the second binding himself, but while he had been careful to pull it tight, knot-tying was evidently a skill he lacked. As she rose and fell in the saddle, so her arms had applied rhythmic pressure to the ropes and to the knots holding them. She had been oblivious at first, her mind on Patrick Grant and Robert Jardine and the objectives of the nameless leader of their little company. But then an unmistakable sensation had captured her attention: the tightness around her arms and shoulders had lessened. It was not as though her bindings had come anything like loose enough that she might shake her arms free, but they had loosened nonetheless. It was beholden upon her now to take advantage of the situation.

As her horse pressed on up the rise, she twisted her right shoulder, with all of her might, against the tension of the rope holding her arms in place across her back, and felt the always sickening pop of dislocation. As her arm flopped downwards, so too did the loops around her elbows. While the horses continued uphill, and the leader kept his attention on the way ahead, she shrugged the slackened bindings down her forearms and over her wrists and hands. Knowing only too well what had to happen next, she raised her left foot out of the stirrup and flung her leg over her horse's back. With her right foot freed as well, she dropped to the ground. Landing on her feet, she allowed the momentum to throw her forward. She took the impact on her dislocated shoulder and grunted as the joint was forced back into place.

Sensing chaotic movement behind him and then hearing the sound of a fall, Angus Armstrong looked back and saw the woman sprawled on the hillside. Her horse had continued to trot on without her and he pulled on its reins and those of his own to bring both to a halt. He dismounted and ran back, momentarily disregarding any risk of approaching her unarmed, trussed as she was and now face down in the grass.

He reached her and rolled her on to her back. Her eyes were open, but although she looked stunned, she seemed otherwise uninjured. He helped her rise to her knees, her arms still behind her back.

They were both on their knees and facing the tor when a burst of sheet lightning turned the sky bright as day. On a ledge of granite high above them stood a fragile figure clad in a dazzling white shift. Her face was upturned to the heavens, her arms raised in an attitude of prayer.

23

Another cramp gripped Crista's body, but not as strongly as before.

As it eased, the fist in her gut unclenching, she felt a flow of warmth between her legs. The darkness that had enveloped her, shrouded her, was torn aside by a burst of blinding white light. It flickered and pulsed, its intensity rising and falling, so that it seemed to shimmer, as a third peal of thunder, the loudest yet, rolled over the world like the wrath of an angry God. She blinked, dazzled and momentarily blinded, and then, feeling a second rush of wetness, looked down to see that the front of her nightdress was dark with blood. It was pooling around her feet, and she craned her neck to check the backs of her thighs and saw more there.

From her position on the slope below, Lẽna stared at the vision that seemed to glow as though lit from within. All in an instant she felt her heart flood with a love she thought had left her long ago, and for ever.

The rain fell and her heart beat fast, and as she stared at the vision ... the vision met her gaze. Filled with sudden ecstasy, she felt she was a girl once more, the girl she had been, the girl who had led an army to victory and who had stood with the dauphin, her hand in his, in the moments before he stepped forward and dropped to his knees and the crown was placed upon his head.

As quickly as it had come, the lightning blinked out. Blind in the sudden darkness but filled with a rush of energy and power, she leapt to her feet.

Back in the darkness, Crista ran her hands down the front of her nightdress and felt the thick wetness of her own blood. It was her first bleed, but she was none the wiser – she thought she must be dying. In horror and fear, she dropped to her knees, and pitched face forward on to the shelf of rock.

When the lightning came a second time, just moments later, the ledge was empty – the apparition vanished.

'You wanted to see an angel,' said Lẽna, turning to her captor. 'Well now you have.'

She glimpsed the look of wonder on his face as she brought her forehead crashing down on to the bridge of his nose. Quick as a striking snake, she drew her head back and butted him again, with even greater force.

'But she came for *me*,' she said.

He toppled sideways, semi-conscious, and hit the ground hard. A sheet of rain, so dense it might have been a waterfall, sluiced across the hillside, drenching everything in an instant. The leader moaned, and there came the shouts of the younger men. Another flash of lightning turned night to day, and for the moment that it lasted she saw the three of them, dismounted at the base of the tor and holding their horses by their reins, looking around in near panic.

When the darkness returned, Lẽna sat down heavily. The pain from her shoulder was considerable, but she closed her mind to it as she worked her hands, still tied at the wrists, under her booted feet. She heard movement from the downed man and reached for him where he lay. He tensed at her touch and cried out.

'Jamie!' he bellowed, trying to rise. 'Here to me, now! She's loose!'

He had made it on to his knees and she swung both hands, knitted together at the knuckles, with all the strength she had earned in the woods. She thought of him as the stubborn trunk of a tree as the work-hardened heels of her hands met his jaw and she heard a crunch as some or other bone in his face was parted from its mooring. He dropped to the ground. She felt for his belt and located his knife. Drawing it swiftly, she sat and gripped the handle between her heels, then slid the ropes holding her wrists down the length of the upthrust blade. Her hands parted easily and she was free to turn her attention to the other men, now running towards her out of the dark.

She thought about killing him where he lay – opening the vein in his neck with his own knife and letting him bleed out – but the memory of the vision stayed her hand. She could similarly have dispatched the trio searching for her on the storm-lashed hillside, and her muscles fairly thrummed with the knowledge and skill required by the task. But instead she let them be, and for the same reason.

She had seen the claret red upon the angel's white garb and had understood the message in a heartbeat. There was blood to be spilled on the path back to her God, but not his and not theirs.

The necessary sacrifice was hers and hers alone. She knew it now as she had known it long ago – as she had always known it.

Thunder cracked and lightning flashed around her as she followed the contour of the hill. Her most urgent need was to be out of sight of any pursuers, and she leaned to her left, trailing one hand against the sodden grass of the slope rising steeply beside her. She heard a distant shout and guessed that one of them had found their leader. There were more calls as they sought and found one another in the dark, but she could tell she was putting distance and the curve of the hill between her and them. The torrent washed over her in sheets, like all the tears she had kept unshed down through the years. She realised she was crying too, and wiped the back of her hand uselessly across her eyes and nose.

With sudden anger and disgust she realised she was crying, at least in part, for herself. She wept too for her bold protector Hugh Moray, murdered in his bed long ago, his throat slit from ear to ear on the orders of Robert Jardine. No one had foreseen his treachery, not even she who heard the word of God. Jardine it was who had ordered more deaths besides, seeing to it that a score of his fellow Scotsmen of the Garde Ecossaise were slaughtered in one night, so that he might steal her away and sell her to her enemies for the promise of coins and lands.

When they came for her at Compiègne, they wore the colours of the Burgundians, allies of the English. In truth, though, they were traitor Scots, border Reivers from Hawkshaw with Jardine's

Judas coins in their purses. They had turned their coats and betrayed their French masters. She was the maiden they had been hired to protect, a prize of inestimable value. Now her life and death would be the making of their ambitious Scots master...

The rain stopped – or rather, she was suddenly beyond its reach. Behind her, above her, a near-vertical wall of black, darker than the sky around it, rose towards infinity. Within the mass of cloud, jagged thorns of lightning flashed like signs of life and further crescendos of thunder still rolled in all directions.

The storm cloud was moving away from her, though, and she had run out from under its baleful canopy. She was headed downhill into cooler air, her way ahead illuminated by moonlight. At the base of the slope she looked up at the stars, re-assured herself that she was still heading east-wards, and pressed on. Her clothing was soaked through, and despite her exertions she was begin-ning to feel cold. The hairs on her arms rose up, pulling goose bumps of skin with them, and she shuddered. Her shoulder ached and she wondered if she had relocated it properly.

She was on a clear path, well trodden by people and animals, and she hoped she was back on the same trail her captors had been leading her along. Surely it would pass through or close to some vestige of civilisation?

She almost collided with the horses before she saw them. They were standing in the middle of the track, head to tail for comfort, their bulk neatly blocking her way. As she approached, the closest of them began to shy away. It was the horse she had been riding, a grey mare, as well as the one belonging to the leader, a black gelding with four white socks. A wave of pleasure and relief enveloped her. She looked heavenwards and mouthed a thank-you to providence.

She made a soft shushing noise as she advanced more slowly, before gently reaching out and clasping the tangle of reins that hung low beneath the mare's nose. Next she reached for the other horse, and when she had them properly positioned, she tied the gelding's reins to the long leads that had enabled the leader to control her horse on the trail. She gently stroked her mare's neck, shushing all the while, before hopping one foot into the stirrup and heaving herself into the saddle. Her shoulder complained bitterly at the effort, but she settled back gratefully and turned her mount towards the east once more.

On horseback she had the speed and the freedom she required. If Sir Robert Jardine was somewhere ahead, waiting by the pilgrims' trail – perhaps with Patrick Grant as his prisoner – then she desired to find him first, and in circumstances that were hers to control. She used her heels to coax the mare into a trot, keen to put many miles between herself and her former captors.

She had done enough damage to the leader, she was sure, to make it unlikely that he would be in any condition to follow her that night, and by morning she would be well on her way. For all her elation at the events of the past hour, fatigue hung around her shoulders like a damp shawl. The adrenalin that had coursed through her body had ebbed away and her senses were dulled. She would need to rest, and soon.

It was therefore understandable that she failed to notice the presence, in the deeper dark, of a third horse and the rider upon it.

While he watched her, he thought of Badr Khassan buried in a shallow grave in a cave far to the east, and wondered how many loved ones he would leave in the dark before the end.

It had taken an age to excavate a grave large enough to take the big man's body, and when at last he had manoeuvred him into position, he realised he had not the heart to cover him with rocks and dusty soil. Remembering how they had left Jessie Grant, in the tomb under a nameless cairn on a hillside within a few miles' ride of his childhood home, he had searched outside the cave until he found a stand of long-stemmed white flowers growing by the side of the stream that flowed reluctantly from the cave mouth. He thought they might be lilies, and he gathered armfuls and bore them back to the graveside. When he had enough, he placed them over Badr's body, starting at his feet and leaving his face clear for as long as possible.

Finally he laid more flowers, just the drooping heads and petals, over the Moor's face until he was completely covered and the cave was filled with their heavy scent. He looked down at his clothes and saw they were streaked with sticky golden pollen, like spiders' webs.

'I will hope to meet you on the road,' he said, and turned and walked towards the light beyond the cave.

He had journeyed for many weeks since then and always into the west, before alighting on the pilgrims' path leading from southern France to Galicia and on towards the shrine of St James.

Badr's words in the cave had been his constant companions, holding his hand upon the road.

The Bear had a daughter! She might be his own age by now, or near enough. The very thought of it almost made him laugh, or perhaps cry. And then too there was the big man's lost love, Isabella. What of her?

In spite of those twin fascinations, however, and the lure of Constantinople in the east, it was towards the west and Patrick Grant's great love that he had been irresistibly drawn. Jessie Grant it was who had raised him and cared for him – had died for the love of him – and yet out here in the west was his true source, his wellspring.

In ways that none but he could understand – none save any other gifted with awareness of the spinning of the world, and the journey into the empty dark, and the push of all the souls within his own orbit – he knew with unshakeable faith that he would find her path and cross it.

His own mount was all but worn out by hard travelling and he had been on the point of approaching the mare and the gelding himself, and taking them for his own use, when the push had warned him of another's approach. At first glance the trousers, the heavy boots and short hair of the bedraggled figure that emerged from the darkness of the trail made him assume he was dealing with a man. Only when he had had time to study the body language, particularly the posture adopted in the saddle, did he realise it was a woman who was helping herself to the unexpected bounty.

From the darkness beside the trail he had watched her fix the tack to her own liking, setting the black gelding so that he would have to trot along at her rear. She was well used to horses, that much was obvious, but it was her whole demeanour that had him sit up and pay attention.

She was on the run – and from challenging circumstances by the look of things. From her wrists there hung short lengths of rope, evidence of recent imprisonment, and the droop of her right shoulder suggested a wound or injury of some kind. There was fresh blood on her forehead. All the while she prepared the horses, she kept an eye back down the trail in the direction from which she had come. Despite the signs of trouble, however, and of the possibility of pursuit, she exuded no hint of anxiety, far less of fear. If she had recently been tested, it appeared she had passed and come out on top – and was single-mindedly capitalising on the advantage gained.

By the time she had mounted the grey mare and set out towards the east, John Grant's interest was more than piqued. The push that had preceded this individual had told him someone was coming, as usual. But now, as she and the horses melted into the dark, an entirely new sensation bade him follow. It felt as though some sort of cord was pulling him into her wake. He smiled at the unexpectedness of it, and his inability to resist. He felt as tethered and bound as the black gelding, and he realised, with a not unpleasant shiver, that all the hairs on his neck were standing on end.

'I hear you, old Bear,' he whispered.

John Grant followed at a distance, so far to the rear that his quarry was always out of sight in the darkness ahead. From time to time he heard the clatter of hooves, or the sound of the horses snorting or tossing their heads so that their bridles rattled. At all times, too, there was the detectable presence of the woman herself. He felt like a dog fox following its prey into the night.

He glimpsed movement on the trail ahead and realised it was the rump of the grey mare, her languid, rolling gait faintly illuminated by the half-moon. He had a split second to notice that the horse was riderless before a dark shape flew out of the darkness to his left. Landing lightly on his own horse's back, the figure lunged at him with powerful arms, striking him squarely on the chest so that he toppled, arse over tit, out of the saddle. He landed flat on his back on the soft earth of the trail. Whoever had knocked him from his horse now leapt from the beast's back and landed astride him, one foot either side of his head, before dropping to place one knee across his throat.

He looked up into the face of his attacker and found it was that of the woman. Her left hand was drawn back behind her head, heel foremost and ready to strike down towards his face, and reflexively he raised an arm, palm extended and fingers splayed, to deflect the imminent blow.

His assailant had been all silent, fluid movement, smooth as water over stones. Now she was frozen in place, gazing fixedly at his upraised hand. She leapt to her feet and took two swift paces backwards, out of his range. Her focus shifted from his hand to his face, and he felt her gaze like physical contact, as though she was feeling the contours of his cheekbones and jaw with her fingertips.

'*Ou avez-vous trouvé ça?*' she said, thrown, in her confusion, all the way back to the language of her childhood. How did you come by that?

John Grant had stood by Badr's side in enough battles in France to understand the language, if not the question. His immediate problem was the lack of air in his lungs, and a consequent inability to make any sounds in reply. He had been winded completely by his unhorsing and a silence hung between them until at last he managed to suck down a great draught of air. It seemed to hit the bottom of his lungs and bounce all the way back out again, so that he sat up coughing and choking, shining threads of drool running from his gaping maw. Still fearing a continuation of her attack upon him, he kept his hand towards her, fingers spread in the universal gesture of submission while he fought to gather his senses. He focused on the back of his own hand and saw the ring – the same that had come attached to a scarf wrapped around a scallop shell.

Both shell and scarf he had left with Badr Khassan, tucked inside his cloak and now accompanying him in his grave. The ring he had kept and found that it fitted – albeit tightly – on to the little finger of his left hand.

He moved his focus from the ring to the woman's face – and found she was staring at the little gold band as well.

'Ou avez-vous trouvé ça?' she asked again.

A chilled charge of excitement ran over his skin, so that he shivered. Understanding flooded through him. She meant the ring! She was transfixed by the thing – her eyes focused sharp upon it like a kite's upon a mouse. She had had him utterly at her mercy – had bested him like no one before – and yet here she stood, paralysed by the sight of a little band of gold.

'C'était un cadeau de mon père,' he said. It was a gift from my father.

In all the years he had spent with the Moor, he had never thought of Badr Khassan as his father, far less called him it. The appellation had come unbidden to his lips, and he felt a wave of sadness rising within him.

She backed further away until she began to disappear into the darkness by the side of the trail.

The thought of his father made him think next of his mother. Jessie Grant lay dead in a tomb of stone, uncounted miles and half a lifetime away. A second charge rippled back and forth across his skin, raising hairs and causing him to close his eyes and exhale in a halting staccato of gasps. The ring was one of a kind – Badr had said so. The sight of it would matter only to one other, the one for whom it had been made.

Badr had sent him on his way with his last breaths. Ambushed by death, he had struggled against the mercy of the opium, grappled for any trailing strands of clarity, and revealed to him the existence of two hidden lives. The first had been that of Badr's daughter, surrendered long ago and now passed like a beating heart into John

214

Grant's care; the second had been that of his own mother, the woman who had borne him.

'What's your name?' asked John Grant in his native Scots tongue.

The woman stopped abruptly, so that she occupied a place between light and darkness – a ghost in the space between the living and the dead. She offered no answer but her pause, and something in the way she turned her head, told him she had understood his question well enough.

'Your name,' he tried again.

His voice had regained its power, its certainty.

'Tell me your name.'

Instead of speaking, she began slowly to circle him, anticlockwise, like a would-be predator gauging the threat, if any, posed by the quarry at hand.

'I know you understand me,' he said.

'Your face...' she said.

'My mother used to say I had my father's face,' he said. He stayed on the ground, felt the cold damp soaking his bottom and the backs of his legs. The air between them seemed to crackle, and he feared that if he moved too much he might break the spell and she would disappear entirely into the dark.

'Used to say?' she asked.

'My mother is dead,' he said. 'Or so I thought.'

She kept moving, kept circling, her eyes never leaving his.

'And your eyes...'

He risked a smile.

'My father's too, I believe.'

'You are a Scotsman,' she said.

'Aye,' he said. 'That I am. I get that from–'

'From your father,' she cut him off. 'A Scotsman,' she said again.

'So you've met others like myself?' he said.

He caught an edge of profile and glimpsed there an expression he could not read but that had, within its complex mix, a hint of sadness. Something about her manner made him blush, as though he were the butt of a joke he did not understand.

'We see them all on the pilgrims' trail,' she said. 'Franks, English, Africans ... even Scotsmen. All sorts make their way to the Great Shrine.'

He found that he was captivated by her – by the sight and sound of her. As he stared, he tried to assess her age but found he could not. Her clothes and boots were overtly masculine, as were some of her movements. When she stood still she seemed rooted in the ground, confident and unassailable. There was much besides that was of the feminine as well. Her cheekbones were high and sharp, suggestive of a bird of prey, and she had the countenance to match, but her black hair, flecked here and there with silver, was cut short like a boy's. Her neck, long and slim, showed flexing tendons and muscle, but it was the neck of a woman right enough.

More than anything, it was her gaze that perplexed him and seemed to reach inside him. Her eyes were the palest blue, like the sky nearest the noonday sun, and it almost hurt to look at them. There were fine lines on the skin over her temples and these were thickly marked with the grime of the road. She did not blink, just looked at him

216

evenly. No girl, no woman had ever looked at him that way. He realised he was being sized up in the way his opponents sometimes did. There was no hint of deference whatsoever, no suggestion of feminine wiles. He was being looked at by his equal, maybe his superior.

He was a soldier, a fighting man, and his reflexes were all engaged. The notion, the very idea, that this woman could best him was ridiculous, and he tried to dismiss it.

'What is your name?' he asked again.

She smiled. 'Your fellow Scots had a name for me once,' she said.

He looked her in the eyes.

'They called me Jeannie Dark,' she said.

He had come in search of the woman his father had loved best, the woman who had given him life, if nothing else. He had travelled long and hard in hopes of locating her before the men that were enemies to them both. He had trusted his instincts – known that if she lived still, he would find her.

What he had not expected, however, was that she would come to him on the road.

'No one ever told me your name,' he said. 'But I knew I would recognise my own mother when I met her.'

24

Whoever she was and whoever she had been, Lẽna found herself broken and unbroken, unmade and made anew by his words – like a blade reforged.

My own mother, he had said.

The words hung in front of her eyes, clouded her thoughts and filled her nose and mouth.

Mother.

He had been silent since, content to leave her winded and reeling as though from a punch to the solar plexus.

Before he had said those words, she had seen the little gold ring upon his finger. She had seen it and known it – known it for what it was. But it was the declaration of the fact that had all but knocked the wind from her lungs.

The ring was Patrick Grant's, and here now was his son. Here was *her* son.

She felt disconnected from reality – disconnected from time. The presence of the ring reminded her of when she was young; the presence of the boy reminded her she was growing old.

'Who's hunting you then, Jeannie Dark?' he asked now as they rode. He felt sure he knew the answer, but some private part of him wanted to hear her say it.

They were travelling quietly through the night, two riders and three horses. At first there had been silence between them, a distance made of disbelief and a thousand questions left unasked.

After hours in which the pressure of the silence had steadily built inside John Grant's head, and against his ears, until he felt he was in deep water, he spoke – and too loudly so that she flinched in her saddle as though he had slapped her.

'I would prefer it if you would call me Lẽna,' she said, but she did not even begin to answer the question. Her words, her voice seemed to echo inside his head so that he felt the touch of it like the fluttering of a bird's wings against a window pane.

'You arrived at these horses like a traveller in the desert who had stumbled upon an oasis,' he said. 'You had only recently freed your hands from their bonds and you were plainly on the run. From whom?'

She dropped her chin to her chest while she considered what, if anything, she might tell him. Her thoughts, the explanation of it all, added up to a mountain of sand she had to shift, each word worth no more than a single grain.

'Another of your countrymen,' she said. 'In fact a neighbour of your mother and father.'

The mention of his parents gave him further pause. The thought of them as a man and a woman living together under the same roof, with others like them nearby, busy with lives, filled him with unexpected sadness.

He found it difficult anyway – impossible – to recall his life in Scotland, his life before the coming of Badr Khassan and the start of the chase that seemed sometimes to have lasted a lifetime. Worst of all, he felt the reality of Jeannie Dark rising like

219

a ghost. Rather than face it, face her and accept her for who and what she was, he ploughed ahead with his questions.

'A neighbour?' he asked. 'What do you mean? Who?'

ẽẽna sighed heavily. She had not even begun the tale and yet already she was weary of it.

'What happened to you ... what happened to me ... what happened to your mother and father and to many more besides...'

She stopped, checking the way ahead into her account of it all like a pilgrim surveying a path back over terrain half remembered. John Grant left her words, the unfinished sentence, hanging limply in the air.

'All that has happened – to all of us – is the work, the fault of a man called Robert Jardine,' she said. She was ahead of him on the road and for the first time she looked back at him over her shoulder. 'Do you know that name?'

He smiled at her, though she could not think why.

'Aye,' he said. 'I remember the name right enough. Sir Robert was our laird – owner of the home I had with my mother, our land too. Our master, you would say.'

'Master,' she said. 'He was that all right.'

'What do you mean?' he asked.

'I mean that for him, people – people like your mother and father ... people like me – were property.'

'What does Sir Robert Jardine have to do with you – with here and now?'

'How do you make your living?' she asked.

The question was a non sequitur and took him by surprise. For a moment he felt he did not actually know the answer.

'We are paid to fight,' he said. He still tended to forget that his time as partner to Badr Khassan was now past, and for the thousandth time the realisation of it stabbed at his heart.

'I am a soldier,' he said. 'If you can afford my fee – then I will fight for you.'

Lêna smiled. 'I am not hiring just now,' she said.

John Grant blushed. 'I did not mean... I was not offering my services. I was speaking hypothetically.'

'*Hypothetically*,' she said, drawing the word out like a blade.

He sensed a note of mockery and felt himself bridling. Determined not to rise, he sought to get the conversation back on to something like its original path.

'Why do you ask me about my livelihood?' he asked.

For an endless minute she offered no reply, and he listened to the rhythm of the horses' hooves.

'I am finding it hard to believe that you exist,' she said at last. 'I am trying to make you real to me.'

John Grant felt the blood rise into his cheeks once more. He had been addressing the back of her head for the most part, but her face appeared to him then, in his imagination, and hovered before his eyes against the darkness ... the memory of her looking not at his hand but at the ring upon his finger. He thought of her pale blue eyes and blinked to keep them at bay.

'Sir Robert Jardine is here,' he said.

The effect was so instantaneous it seemed to him her reaction began before the words were fully out of his mouth. Her horse wheeled around so quickly under her it might have been an extension of her own body, taking instruction directly from her thoughts. She was alongside him before he had a chance even to blink, and leaning out of her saddle so that her face almost brushed against his own.

'Are you playing with me?' she said.

Her words were no more than a whisper, but he felt an emotion that was utterly strange to him, and it was fear. He was all at once a boy, and the woman's fierce intent enveloped him entirely. He caught the hot scent of her, like spice.

'No,' he said. 'I am not playing. I swear it. Sir Robert Jardine is here on the road.'

'Where?' she asked again. Her eyes blazed, the pupils fully dilated.

'Half a day's ride from here, and beside this trail,' he said. Her eyes bore into his, weighing the likely truth of his words.

He thought about the day just past and how, as he had journeyed along the road towards Santiago di Compostela, the push had warned him of the presence of men on the road ahead. Armstrong had been hunting him for years. Nowadays John Grant knew to expect his appearance – always, it seemed, at the most inconvenient moments. Since Badr had told him that the archer, together with his master, had history with this woman too, he had been even more wary than usual.

'I left the trail and sought the high ground

above it,' he said. 'In time I spotted them – or their horses at least, tethered by a tithe barn set back off the trail and screened from it by a stand of pine trees. My curiosity was aroused and I dismounted and snuck down the slope to the rear of the building.

'Through an open window I counted a dozen men gathered about an open fire. Some of them had evidently found time to go hunting, and the carcass of a hind was roasting over the embers on a makeshift spit. A store of firewood was stacked against one wall, and here and there on the floor were blankets and other belongings. They had the look of a party that had been waiting in place for days, if not longer.

'They did not, however, have the look of pilgrims. All travellers must carry weapons for self-defence, but the way those characters bore their swords suggested a company more used to fighting together than praying.'

'And Jardine?' asked Lẽna.

'I had seen enough,' he said. 'I certainly had no wish to draw their attention and was about to withdraw when one of them spoke. He was a Scot.'

'Sir Robert?' asked Lẽna again.

'No – but whoever he was, he spoke his lordship's name. He said, "How much longer can we wait for them, Sir Robert? Are we not vulnerable here?"'

Lẽna was bolt upright in her saddle.

'And he replied?' she asked.

'It wasn't what he said; rather it was the way he said it that stuck with me,' said John Grant. 'The arrogance of it.'

'What did he say?' asked Lēna.

'He said, "I do not feel vulnerable – and I have no time for those that do. Wherever I am, wherever I stand and for as long as I stand upon it, then it is Jardine land."'

Lēna was motionless. Even her horse sensed the gravity of the situation and seemed carved from marble.

'I remembered his voice,' said John Grant. 'It's been years, but ... but anyway, I knew him for who he was.'

She stayed silent.

'And yet you were running towards him when we ... when we met,' he said.

He felt his fear dissipate, his familiar sense of control returning.

'So who is behind us on the trail, Lēna? Who bound your hands? Who is hunting you?'

She was silent for a few moments and John Grant almost persuaded himself he could feel the intensity of her thoughts. The air of concentration seemed to radiate from her in waves.

'I do not know the name of the man who held me,' she said. 'But he fights with the longbow.'

John Grant sighed. 'A Scot?' He had no need to ask but felt compelled to draw the moment out.

Lēna nodded. 'All Scots,' she said. 'It would appear your countrymen are everywhere. I am beginning to think there has been an invasion.'

The joke sounded hollow even to her.

'The bowman's name is Angus Armstrong,' said John Grant.

'You know him?' she asked.

'For years and years I have known him,' he said. 'He kills the people I love.'

Lẽna was not hurt by the words. How could she be, after all? But the boy's talk of love and her sense of her own exclusion from it rattled some part deep inside of her – some piece of her she had forgotten. She reproached herself at once, burned by the sensation and the notion – and at such a time.

'I would very much like to see Angus Armstrong again,' said John Grant.

Lẽna looked at him, and he felt her gaze reach deep inside him, as though her fingertips were brushing lightly against his innards. He all but flinched.

'And I would very much like to renew my acquaintance with Sir Robert Jardine,' she said. 'Just for old times' sake.'

His lairdship was dreaming he was walking down whitewashed corridors in a large house, indeed a mansion or a palace. Each side of every wide corridor was lined with doors and he opened them one after another and looked into the rooms beyond. Every one was furnished differently – some modest and some luxurious. He was searching for something, that much he knew, but for the life of him he could not remember what. He was certain, however, that he would know the prize when he saw it, and he scanned every interior with great concentration. The dream seemed to have been going on for ever, and he felt a steadily increasing sense of frustration. He was fairly trotting down the corridors, rounding corners and grabbing for each door handle in turn. These were becoming more awkward too – each harder to turn than the last – and he could feel fatigue, almost cramp, building in his wrists and arms. As his frustration grew and the ache in his muscles increased, so the knowledge of what he sought slipped further and further away, as though descending into deep water.

It had been a good enough day – one of many that had passed since the arrival at Hawkshaw of the message sent by Angus Armstrong. By now, the letter made clear, he would have the woman. She had been concealed all this time by nuns – nuns! – in a convent close by the Great Shrine of St James.

The final obstacle had been distance – separating hunter from prey – but Armstrong was an experienced traveller and had pinpointed both the time and the place for a rendezvous. His arrival, with the woman in tow, would be around the middle of September, he had said. It was many weeks since Sir Robert and his men, hand-picked for the job, had set out from his Scottish estate. For ten days now they had been in place by the pilgrims' trail on the border between France and Spain.

He was impatient now, but in all the years, Armstrong had never once disappointed. The man's determination to finish any task assigned to him was a wonder to behold. Soon enough he would have her. She had been of value then and she was precious beyond price now. The anticipation of all she could mean for him, still do for him, made him dizzy.

All at once, and without warning, Sir Robert was gripped by fear, and he sucked in a great breath and opened his eyes wide. He was awake – indeed, his return to the conscious world was so immediate and complete he felt as though he had never been asleep in his life. He was lying on his back on blankets arranged upon a bed of dried bracken that one of his men had collected and prepared for his comfort earlier in the day. As was his due, on account of his status, he was closest to the fire in the centre of the barn. The rest of them had laid out their bedrolls around the walls of the barn and some distance away from him. So far as was possible in a wide-open space within four walls, he was alone.

He noticed none of that, however – neither the warmth still radiating from the cooking fire, nor the softness of the makeshift bedding. Instead his attention was fixed entirely upon the woman's face six inches above his own, and upon the point of the knife that she had pressed between his lips and which was now drawing blood from the roof of his mouth.

He did not move – indeed, he dared not move for fear that any such action on his part might result in the rest of the blade being thrust through his soft palate and into his brain. She was squatting over him, one foot either side of his chest pinning his arms to the earthen floor. He heard deep breathing and some snoring, all evidence that the rest of the company were sleeping peacefully in the shadows.

Outside the barn, the man who had been on sentry duty was unconscious, courtesy of a blow to the back of the head from a sword butt. He was bound now and gagged, and tied to the trunk of one of the pine trees that shielded the barn from the pilgrims' trail. Just for the fun of it, John Grant had turned the unconscious man towards the tree, resting his slack face against the rough bark of the trunk and wrapping his arms and legs around it, in the manner of a bear hug, before tying him securely. He would have liked to witness his comrades' distress or amusement at finding him there, but by then he and Lẽna would be far away, of course.

Back in the barn, by the soft and flickering light of the dying fire, Sir Robert Jardine recognised the woman straddling him. While the heavy, iron taste of his own blood filled his mouth, he realised he was looking into the face of Joan of Arc.

She had been his prisoner once long ago. She was to have been exchanged for wealth and lands beyond even his imaginings (and his imagination was fertile indeed). Instead she had been stolen from him, spirited away by one of his own, leaving him humiliated, ruined and disgraced. And now here she was, twenty-two years later, sitting on his chest. He prayed with all his heart for the sound of a string being pulled tight on a longbow, but if this woman was on the loose then perhaps the archer had breathed his last.

'Sorry to wake you, Bobby,' she whispered. 'But since you've come all this way, it would be rude of me not to say hello.'

She smiled a dark smile that came from long ago and far away. Sir Robert remained silent, as she intended, his eyes blinking hard with amazement. She slid the knife from side to side slightly, enjoying the sound of razor sharpness upon tooth enamel. His breath was bad, sour, but she could bear it for as long as the encounter had to last.

'You do deserve to die right now, Bobby,' she said. 'We each of us owe a death, of course. But by my estimate, yours is long overdue.'

He squirmed beneath her, as though the spoken threat forced him to react, however pointlessly, however hopelessly. He made a small noise, somewhere towards the back of his throat.

'Hush now,' she said, pushing the point of the blade upwards, minutely, so as to underline her sincerity. He closed his eyes against the pain, felt more blood flow and began to fear he might gag.

'You stole my life,' she said. 'You were supposed to protect me – you were paid to protect me. And yet you betrayed me.'

She stared down at him, noting how the intervening years had taken most of his hair and creased his skin. His teeth, those that remained, were ground down and yellow. But for all that time had had him pay towards his final debt, his eyes were as bright and clear as she remembered. A predator's eyes, shaped for assessing the value and the weakness of prey.

'I should take yours now,' she said. 'Most of me wants to kill you, and it would be so easy for us both. Another inch or two would do it.'

He squirmed again and his eyes opened wider than ever.

'But I have learned something recently. I have been shown something and ... and I think I have been promised something.'

Her face was beautiful to him, and in spite of himself, in spite of the pain and the threat, he felt the leaden weight of his balls and his stiffening prick. She smiled then, almost as if she sensed his arousal – or perhaps she was just baring her teeth.

'I have taken the lives of many men,' she said. 'Thanks to you I have the blood of one woman on my hands as well. I am covered in blood, Bobby – some little of it innocent, and most nothing of the kind – and I stink of it.'

She paused and licked her lips.

'I have had ... a vision.'

She did not look at him while she said this, fixing her gaze instead on the glow of the fire.

'I have been reminded of the blood of the maiden, fresh as new life,' she said. 'I have seen that there is blood that flows, blood that is not mine to take. I have been promised the death that is owed to me. That is the death I care about now – not yours.'

He felt her shift position, rocking forward slightly, and she seemed to be reaching back behind her with her right hand.

I will not kill you tonight, Bobby,' she said. 'But I have something to give you – something I very much want you to have and the last thing of mine that you shall ever receive.'

And with that she swiftly withdrew the knife, brought her right hand forward and smeared a handful of her own firm, warm shit across his mouth and nose. An instant later she used the heel of her left hand to shut his mouth and send him back to sleep.

25

'You should have killed him,' said John Grant.

They had ridden hard for more than an hour, and their mounts' flanks and mouths were flecked with white. It had taken them all of the previous day to reach the barn and they had had to wait long into the night that followed before making their moves upon the men within and without. They had then taken advantage of the cool of the remainder of the night to put distance between themselves and Jardine and his men. Dawn was breaking over a low range of hills ahead of them. Beyond the hills, barely discernible from the sky, was the sea.

'His time will come,' she said.

'I dare say it will,' he said. 'But I would rather it came before mine. You tell me he is the architect of all our ills, all our sadnesses,' he continued. 'You say we and others like us have had our lives altered, and for the worse, by the greed and vengefulness of Robert Jardine. And yet when the moment came and you had *his* life in your hands, you let him slip through your fingers.'

He reined in his horse and she missed the cue. Having overshot him, she had to wheel around before coming alongside. As yet they had no sense of one another and were awkward as strangers forced to dance together. He was scanning the horizon, taking bearings on landmarks and seemingly checking his course.

'Robert Jardine will be judged,' she said. 'Not by me and not by you. He was not ours to judge in that place and at that time. I know now what I must do, and taking the lives of those who have wronged me has no part in it.'

He was shaking his head. She understood his inability to comprehend, but felt forbidden to tell him why. It had been a long time since she had expected others to understand the will of angels. She needed to change the course of their conversation.

'Now will you tell me where it is that you are going?' she asked.

He noticed she had not said 'we', and wondered if she counted herself in or out of what he had planned. Perhaps her interest so far was just curiosity, a diversion while she formulated her own designs. Among a welter of emotions and ideas, he knew at least that he wanted time with her.

'Did my father ever mention the names of men he rode with?' he asked.

He kicked his horse forward once more and she did likewise. If he and she struggled to find each other's rhythm, the animals did not, and he was grateful for their easy mutual understanding as they fell into their stride.

'I think he preferred to leave that part of his life elsewhere when he was with me, which wasn't often,' she said. 'The only name he ever let me hear was Khassan. I know that they were friends, although Patrick did not ever say as much.'

He reeled each time she said the name. That Patrick Grant had known this woman, and she him; that they had made him together, and then parted, seemed impossible. For all that some of him, most of him, accepted the truth of it, some other portion clung to the mother he had known. Dead and buried as Jessie was, and long, hard years ago now, his feelings for the mother he had loved were real as ever. This new knowledge, of this other woman and all that she must now mean, sat in his gut like undigested food.

They rode on in silence for a while, their horses' heads nodding together companionably – the easy instinct of herd animals – while the third was tethered to a lead rein fixed to the rear of John Grant's saddle. Lẽna felt rootless but not quite lost. The tide of recent events had taken her far enough from her home – at least the only home she had known for more than twenty years – so that any pull from it was too weak to affect her path now. The flow of the present might make an eddy that would turn her around and spin her back towards the convent and the shrine – or some other languid sweep might move her further away. She did not know and could not tell. The pull she felt most strongly, however, was towards the boy.

'My father saved Badr Khassan's life,' he said. 'And Badr saved mine in return, and more than once.'

She glanced at him out of the corner of her eye and saw him smile as he said the name.

'Do you ride now to meet with him?' she asked.

'Badr is dead,' he said. 'Angus Armstrong killed him.'

She thought about her erstwhile captor, remembered how she had first beheld him behind the steel head of an arrow pointed at her face and wondered for the first time how much damage he had done.

'How did you find me?' she asked.

He looked her up and down and she felt, for a moment, as though he might be deciding whether or not she had been worth the effort.

'Badr told me where to look,' he said. 'While he lay dying, skewered by one of Armstrong's arrows, he told me about ... about you.'

'How long have you been travelling?'

He made a sound that was somewhere between a laugh and a sigh.

'For a while,' he said. He shrugged his shoulders. 'But it is time that I have, and people I lack.'

She felt as though some small animal was scuttling around inside her stomach. She had turned her back on a life. It seemed to her now that all her efforts at forgetting had merely seen her take the long way round, all the way back to the place from which she had started out long ago. She had turned her back on a child, a baby, and yet the years had carried her far enough to meet him coming the other way.

'How did he know about me?' she asked.

John Grant shrugged. 'Well, let us imagine maybe my father told Badr Khassan that you were my mother,' he said. 'And Badr managed to remember that.'

She snapped her head around to look at him, but he was staring straight ahead, towards the hills and the sun.

There was no emotion in his voice when he continued.

'Badr told me Patrick loved you – that you were the woman he would have ... preferred.'

She looked away from him, down towards her hands resting on the pommel of her horse's saddle.

'I did not ask him and he did not tell me, but I have presumed you did not want to spend your life with him,' he said. 'Or with me.'

She was watching him and saw a glint of sunlight reflected from the thin band of gold he wore on the little finger of his left hand. She had already observed that he led with his left, and for some reason that she barely noticed, far less understood, it pleased her to see the keepsake there on his good hand...

'You want none of it, do you?' Patrick had asked her at the end. 'You do not want me and you do not want our son.'

She had looked into his face and had seen his tears, but when she had reached out instinctively to wipe them away, he had flinched and recoiled from her touch.

The words – any words that might have helped – were lost to her then, and she found nothing worth saying. She felt only hollow inside, like a dead tree still standing in spite of the emptiness within.

He had stood in the doorway of her cottage, an outbuilding of the convent. He seemed uncertain whether to stay or leave. He held their baby in his arms, swaddled in white cotton and pale blue silk, and sleeping. He looked down at the peaceful face, and despite the grief, he pouted at the perfection he found there. By the time he looked up, she had slipped the ring from her finger. It had been his first and only gift to her, and she had wondered at the meaning of the inscription: *No tengo mas que darte*. I have nothing more to give thee.

Even as she had read it that first time, it struck her as a portent of unhappiness, filling her with foreboding. Perhaps he had always known, in spite of all his hopes to the contrary, that their time together could not last.

She tried to press it into his free hand, but he clenched it into a fist, a final act of defiance.

'Please take it,' she said. 'I cannot wear it, I cannot ... bear it.'

The hurt on his face was awful to her, and she cursed herself, wondering why God had seen fit to take away her heart along with everything else.

He looked instead at their sleeping son, and she unfolded one end of the pale blue swaddling, in fact a scarf that had been a gift long ago from her own mother, and slipped a corner of it through the ring. Swiftly she tied a knot to hold it in place. She looked up at him and saw that he had been watching.

'You really do want none of it,' he said, and walked away without once looking back...

It was the soft voice of John Grant that summoned her from her place of memory. It felt for all the world as though he had been reading her mind.

'Will you tell me about my father?' he asked, and his voice sounded, in his own head at least, like a child's.

'And if I do, then will you tell me where it is

that we are going?'

'Yes,' he said. 'Then I will tell you.'

And so she began her tale of Patrick Grant, or as much of it as she knew. To tell it, she had to begin with some of her own story, and that, anyway, was what he truly wanted to hear, and somehow she knew that as well. A story told by one of them was easier for both than the back-and-forth of conversation, and so as their horses trotted, and they rose and fell in their saddles, it was the rhythm of the tale that soothed their hearts.

'I was a soldier too,' she began. 'I am sure that surprises you – the thought of a girl on the battlefield – but it was my ... my calling, I suppose you might say.

'For as long as I can remember, I knew how to fight. I had three older brothers and fighting was their play, of course. I joined in their games, and though younger and smaller than them I soon found ways to defeat them, and easily. It was amusing for them at first – to find their little sister a handful and to have to pay full attention to her as she advanced upon them with wooden swords and spears and laid them low. But the novelty wore off quicker than the bruises and in time they chose simply to exclude me. When I complained to our mother, they told her it was because they feared I would surely get hurt. But my father had watched, and had seen, and he knew the truth of it. There was no anger in the fight for me, no need of the violence – which they did not understand but that he did. It was just ... something I could do, and better than them or anyone else. That is what so displeased them, I

237

think – that I didn't have to try and I didn't have to think.'

'Was he a soldier – your father, I mean?' asked John Grant. She was jolted by the interruption and he regretted it at once.

'My father was Jacques d'Arc,' she said, recovering her place. 'I was young when we left our home and it is the truth when I tell you that I never did learn as much about him as I would have liked. I remember men in the village addressing him as "Sergeant" – and that part of his duty was to prepare them for the defence of our homes in times of need. It is all so long ago for me and I spent many years trying not to remember, but to forget.

'I learned later that my father had indeed been a soldier, and a fine one – brave and loyal. Before I fought the English, my father did too – and alongside more of your Scots. It seems my family has been fated to stand shoulder to shoulder with your countrymen. I know that he was part of the defence of Melun, a walled town on an island in the River Seine. There was a French garrison there, of course, but also many Scots, fighting in defiance not just of Henry, the English king, but also of their own so-called king, James of the Stewarts. Your James was no more than a puppet of Henry then – obedient as a dog. The Scots soldiers were under another's command, a Scots aristocrat called Albany, and they were honouring ties that have bound your folk to my own for longer than the life of any *soi-disant* king.

'But like the rest of his kind, English Henry thought France belonged to him and had crossed the Channel with his hordes to try and prove it. Twenty thousand English besieged Melun. The French and Scots soldiers inside numbered fewer than one thousand, but for half a year they held on, fighting from the walls and also in the tunnels the English miners burrowed beneath.

'When it was over – when the defenders could fight no more and the townspeople were reduced to eating the rats that feasted by then upon their dead ... when it was over, Henry ordered that the garrison commander would spend the rest of his life in an iron cage. And as for your countrymen ... well, most of them were taken and hanged from the city walls as a warning to all. Only a handful survived and escaped back home.

'My father never forgot them – called them friends ever after – and when he decided that my ... my talents should be tested and perfected, it was to his comrades in your homeland that he took me. What I became ... what I have become ... is the work not of French martial arts, but those of your Scots.

'I was trained by the same Scotsmen who fought alongside my father. And when I returned home to carry on the fight against the English invaders, more of their kind came with me as my bodyguard. It mattered a great deal to my father – when I went before our prince to swear that I would see him on his throne – that I was accompanied and supported by men such as those.'

'But why lay so much on the shoulders of a girl?' asked John Grant. 'Even if you could fight – and I can hardly doubt it – what difference were you supposed to make, no matter how skilled?'

She held his gaze, looked deep into his hazel eyes flecked with gold. She felt suddenly foolish, as she always did when she tried to make sense and words out of something she could not readily explain even to herself.

'My father took me to the land of the Scots to practise my ... my art,' she said. 'That much is certainly true.'

'But?' he asked. 'I know you need to tell me something more.'

'But he also sought ... or rather *needed* the reassurance of those he had learned to trust more than other men.'

'Reassurance about what?'

Out of nowhere John Grant suddenly felt the push – not from any unseen stranger, but from Lẽna. He recoiled, and her eyes opened wide as she saw him reel as if he were under attack from an invisible foe. She reached out a hand but he batted her concern away.

'It is nothing,' he said. 'I think perhaps we should look for some food soon. I need to rest and refresh myself, is all.'

He settled himself, breathed deep and collected his thoughts.

'Reassurance about what?' he asked again. 'What else did your father need to know?'

'That I was not mad,' she said.

He said nothing; just raised his eyebrows.

She sighed, resigned, hoping she might breathe out the resolve to withhold her truth from him, regardless of the consequences.

'I fight as I do ... win as I do ... because I fight with the will of God.'

She looked at him and found that his gaze was directed not at her but off towards the horizon and the hills.

John Grant was replaying her words in his head. While he did so, he turned his attention to the rumble of the world spinning on its axis like a giant top. He opened his consciousness to the flight of the planet into the blue and the dark void beyond. The push was still there too – the push from this woman who had given birth to him and sent him away.

She could not know – and he was not about to tell her yet, if ever – about his life at the mercy of the push. She could not know it, but nonetheless she had told her truth to someone who understood what it was like to know what no one else knew; someone who understood how it felt to hear what no one else heard.

He looked round at her and nodded.

She had no idea what the nod meant, but before she had time to puzzle over it, he asked another question.

'If you have the will of God, what did you ever need from my father?' he asked.

She felt the years moving and shuffling before her eyes, backwards and forwards, like the pages of a book left outdoors and riffled by the wind.

She opened her mouth to speak, but before she had time to form any words, the black gelding, tied by a rein to the saddle of John Grant's horse, gave a terrible whinny of pain as it rose up on its hind legs before toppling on to its side.

Panicked by the sound and by the commotion, John Grant's horse reared up too, and he had only a split second to react and to stand in his stirrups as he battled to avoid being thrown backwards. He brought the beast under control and wheeled around. The downed gelding was struggling to rise again, but failing. The cause was suddenly apparent to John Grant as he spotted a foot of arrow shaft sticking out of the animal's right rear leg.

For all that he was fast, the woman was faster. Taking Angus Armstrong's knife from her belt, the same she had used to secure the silent compliance of Sir Robert Jardine, she urged her horse across to the head of the felled gelding and sliced through the leather rein holding it to John Grant's saddle.

'Ride!' she shouted, and brought a hand down sharply on his horse's rump. As they both spurred their animals into a gallop, John Grant looked behind them, seeking desperately for the location of their attacker. He knew without thinking that it was Armstrong, and furious anger rose in his chest.

'I can't see him,' he shouted.

'Just ride,' she said.

He felt an impact in his right foot and looked down to see a second arrow sticking from the heel of his boot. The head was embedded, harmlessly, in the wood of the heel.

'His aim is off today,' he shouted at Lẽna. 'I've never known that bastard miss his target even once, let alone twice.'

'Keep riding,' she said. 'I suspect my parting gifts may be affecting his abilities.'

'I wish you'd finished the job,' he said, leaning forward and keeping his head low. With his right hand he reached down and snapped off the arrow, leaving just the head behind. 'Your mercy towards our foes will be our undoing.'

She said nothing but grimaced instead, aware that he might be speaking the truth. She cursed her decision to leave her captor alive, and then remembered her angel on her shelf of rock and, just as quickly, reproached herself for doubting.

Looking behind them, John Grant finally located the position of their pursuers. There were four of them, clustered by a huge granite boulder in the lee of a hill he and Lẽna had trotted past just minutes before. Three were on horseback. One was dismounted beside them but preparing to climb back on to his horse. They were at the limit of the bow's range, but the dreaded weapon was clearly visible, slung across its owner's back as he climbed into his saddle.

John Grant and Lẽna galloped hard for a short distance over level ground before their path took them steeply uphill. He feared they might soon be within the archer's range once more, and he urged his horse onwards, all the while calling out to Lẽna to drive her own mount as fiercely as possible. She needed no urging from him or from anyone else.

The slope levelled again, on to a terrace of flat ground, and they were able to gain speed. The steep gradient rising ahead of them would be too much for the horses, however, and they swung around to their right, following the level contour into a narrow cleft between two hills.

Briefly relieved to be out of Armstrong's direct line of sight, they galloped hard, desperately trying to put some distance between themselves and their pursuers while also seeking some means of escape, or even just concealment. They followed the narrow valley as it twisted and turned until suddenly, in front of them, a near-vertical wall of rock blocked their path.

'No!' shouted John Grant, wheeling his horse around and looking in every direction for a path worth taking. The valley sides were much too steep, and behind them the path would lead only back towards Armstrong and his companions.

'It's a dead end,' said Lẽna.

Without replying, John Grant leapt from his horse and ran forward to the rock wall. Hunkering down he saw, with a mixture of hope and horror, that there was an opening at ground level not much wider than his own shoulders. At first sight it looked more like an animal burrow than any space fit for a human being, but he lay down and peered into the darkness, the total darkness beyond.

'What are you doing?' she shouted. 'We don't have time for this.'

He ignored her and leaned into the space. Forcing all thoughts of their predicament from his mind, he breathed in deeply, scenting the air. He felt the cool touch of a soft wind brushing against his face. The movement was almost imperceptible but he felt it just the same. Somewhere beyond the darkness, fresh air was finding a way towards him. If air could pass through, then so might they.

In her frustration, Lẽna jumped from her saddle and crouched behind him. She looked beyond him, seeing the cramped opening in the rock for the first time.

'You are not serious,' she said, realisation sweeping over her so that she felt sick with dread.

'Trust me,' he said, reaching out to her and placing a hand on her shoulder. 'You have to trust me. We have no time. None.'

'But why would you even consider crawling into that ... that hole?' she shouted. 'Look at it – there's barely room for a dog!'

'Because they will not follow us,' he said. 'They wouldn't have the nerve.'

She took a deep breath and let it out in one long, whistling gasp. 'But you have no idea where it goes,' she said. 'It may go nowhere at all.'

He shook his head.

'I can feel fresh air,' he said. 'It is not a hole – it's a tunnel, a passage of some sort. I am sure of it. There is a wind blowing through it from ... from somewhere – blowing through from the other side.'

'I would rather fight them,' she said. She knelt down and looked into the opening. Only darkness greeted her.

'We cannot fight him like this – not here,' he said. 'We cannot protect each other. Armstrong will shoot me down and take *you* back – back to Jardine.'

She dropped her chin to her chest for a moment and then looked him in the eye. She knew he was right.

'So be it,' she said.

He nodded once and turned from her, squeezing his body into the opening. She watched the effort it took just to get inside the space and felt her stomach clench.

As soon as he had wriggled in up to his waist,

he was enveloped by the seeming madness of what he was proposing for them both, and he felt his fear taking hold yet again. Some other part of him said it was too late for panic – that there was no *room* for panic. Their options had shut down to this narrow fissure, made by water long ago or created in an instant by some ancient movement of the earth itself.

But there was something else as well, some certainty from deep within him that insisted the way ahead was clear, even if their passage through it might be hellish. He touched the rock wall and felt the distant, grinding vibration of the spinning of the world. The darkness would hide them, and take care of them. Armstrong and his men would not dare to follow. The hunter was driven only by the thrill of the chase, while they sought freedom and life itself. Armstrong had options and time, while they suddenly had neither.

By committing themselves to the unthinkable, they would confound their enemies. To all intents and purposes they would have disappeared into another world.

Breathing shallow, so as to keep his own size to a minimum, he kicked forward into the dark with his knees and feet, concentrating with all his power on the flow of air coming towards him, reassuring him, so that he clung to it like a rope. He let the soft wind take shape and colour in his imagination, saw it flowing towards them and over them, bringing with it the promise of an end to their struggle, of a reward for their daring...

Only when he had disappeared entirely, swallowed up by the earth and the darkness, did Lẽna turn one last time to look at their horses. The animals were unperturbed and grazing peacefully on a patch of coarse grass, oblivious to the predicament of their erstwhile masters. She patted her own mount, the grey mare, relishing the warm, familiar smell of her, and then knelt down at the opening. She had to lie flat and pull herself forward on her stomach. She could hear him in the darkness, scrabbling and cursing, and with her heart in her mouth she began the dreadful business of shimmying forward into the nightmarish space.

In pauses between his own movements he heard her behind him, gasping and fighting for purchase. It occurred to him that if terror held at bay had a sound, then it was the desperate scraping of hands and feet, invisible in the dark.

The tension of the situation kept threatening to engulf him – the looming prospect of suddenly feeling rock in front of his face as well as above and around him. There was every chance that the airflow, the only promise of salvation, came from a space too small to crawl through. Maybe they would be caught like rats in a trap. Perhaps they were crawling into their own graves. Panic threatened to rise within him again, making an enemy of his own body until he felt he was swelling, filling the space and plugging it like a cork. He felt his chest expanding with the need to draw in a deeper breath, but managed to regain control. He focused on the airflow once more, told himself it was growing stronger.

He forced himself to trust his instincts and to concentrate only on his own movements. The fissure twisted and corkscrewed, sometimes rising up and sometimes dropping downwards. Desperate to maintain a handhold on his own sanity, he tried to visualise the shape of the tunnel, even prayed for it to open into some dimly lit cavern where they might look around – look at each other, and remind themselves they still existed in the world. But none came. From time to time he was forced to roll on to his side, almost on to his back, in order to keep making headway.

Facing upwards, his nose occasionally brushing the roof, was worst of all. The sensation of the world pushing down upon him all but convinced him of their doom, and he kicked harder still with his heels until he reached a wider section and was able to turn on to his stomach once more.

Mercifully there were larger pockets of space from time to time – room in which to change position and stretch – but always the fissure narrowed again, bringing the terror of contact with the bedrock all around. The mass above seemed almost to be moving, pressing down like the sole of a giant's boot come to crush them. The near impossibility of their situation kept threatening to smother him, and he felt his mouth dry, his tongue swelling. He heard her make a sound behind him, like a sob, and he stopped and called her name, suddenly grateful for the distraction.

'Just keep moving,' she said. The sound of her words was muffled and seemed to come from somewhere far off, until he felt her head bump against the soles of his boots and she gasped. Her closeness to him in the space made matters worse, and a fresh image flashed into his mind of them reaching a dead end and kicking and struggling against one another as they used up the last of the breathable air and...

'Just keep moving,' she said again. Her voice sounded more urgent than before, and he edged forward to give her more room. And then it happened. He kicked, and instead of moving forward, he felt his shoulders pinned on both sides. The fissure had narrowed even further and he was trapped. He pushed with his hands, trying to move backwards, but he was fixed in place. He moaned and struggled, disbelieving – felt the world collapsing until all that existed was this tiny space, these terrible endless moments. He cried out, a wordless sound, and froze.

'John,' she said.

It was the first time she had used his name, but the sound came from somewhere unreachable.

'John,' she said again. 'Speak to me.'

He was battling for control, the remainder of his sanity flickering and guttering like a candle flame dying in the night.

'Say my name,' she said.

Her words reached him as though through water.

'Lẽna,' he said.

'No, John Grant – say my real name, my given name.'

His face was pressed against the rock of the tunnel's floor. He felt like he was drowning.

'Jeanne,' he said, and felt a flame flicker and glow, as though touched by fresh air.

'I trust you, John,' she said. 'I trust you to get us through.'

He listened to her words and to the sound of his own breathing. He felt her hands on his ankles and flinched, but she held on. Suddenly, with a power he did not expect, she pulled him backwards. It was no more than an inch, but it was all the distance that mattered, all that was needed. His shoulders were freed and he could flex his arms, reaching for a new position.

'Just keep moving, John,' she said.

He took a breath, reaching for control with the tips of his fingers. He found purchase with his hands and kicked gently and nudged forward a fraction. He took another breath, and kicked again, and again. With unbounded relief he realised that his shoulders were beyond the constriction, into a wider section of the passage. Flooded with gratitude, he kicked and pulled and drew his legs forward until his waist, then his knees and then his feet were wholly clear of whatever had held him.

He was drenched with sweat. He felt the salt stinging his eyes but he kept moving, determined never to stop again. It was hot, too. Despite the flow of the cooler air, he felt swallowed within the body of a living thing, eaten alive. To keep his panic at bay, to keep the scream buried, he began counting his own movements, measuring his progress. He had reached one hundred when gradually he became aware of more space around him. Where before the walls and roof of the tunnel had brushed his sides and back as well as pushing up from below in a sickening embrace, suddenly he realised he had room to reach out on either side. He felt a laugh bubbling inside him as he relished the freedom.

What had been a narrow tunnel became a wide, flat cavity, and when he reached left and right with his arms he made no contact with the rock. The roof still pressed down, but there was space either side, and hope and relief began to rise in him. Cautious of the new emotions, fearful that they might yet be their undoing, he battled for calm and careful thought. The movement of air against him was stronger again too, and he reminded himself to breathe, relishing the cool of it, the promise of it.

The seeming proof that he had been right – that his instincts might yet save them – filled him like a blessing and he allowed himself to smile. He heard Lẽna behind him, heard her panting in the new-found space.

'Stay with me,' he said. 'Stay close.'

She made no reply, but he listened as her breathing softened.

The floor sloped upwards and he crawled forward, reaching ahead for purchase and digging in harder than ever with the toes of his boots. It was only when it levelled out that he realised his eyes were squeezed shut.

When he opened them, he beheld something wondrous: the backs of his own hands. Faint though it was, like the first hint of gloom before the dawn, the trace of light filled him with joy, and he redoubled his efforts. The floor dropped steeply away from him again and suddenly, some little way ahead, he saw a triangle of golden daylight. Crawling towards it with renewed energy, he called out to Lẽna.

'Do you see?' he said. 'There's light ahead!'

'Just keep moving,' she replied. He realised that her words had been a chant upon which she had focused her own efforts, perhaps even her sanity.

The walls narrowed either side once more, but there was space above and he found he could rise to his knees. The triangle of light became an opening ahead, filled with the blue of the sky, and he scrabbled his way towards it, panting with blessed relief.

He emerged on his knees, like a penitent, into the light and found himself above a sheer drop into a wide ravine with a broad brown river flowing far below. He was perched upon a cliff like a flightless chick in a nest. He breathed long and deep, revelling in the sunlight and the suddenly limitless open space. Looking upwards behind him, he saw a precipitous face too smooth and steep for climbing. The ledge on to which he had crawled was no wider than he was tall. He heard Lẽna emerging and turned to slow her down.

'Have a care,' he said.

She joined him in the opening and did as he had done moments before – looking first upwards at the giddying height above and then down towards the river. She slumped backwards, leaning against the cliff face beside the mouth of the fissure. He stayed on his knees, wordless, a roaring sound in his head like rushing water. He closed his eyes and breathed, offering thanks to the sky above and the abyss below.

The moments passed and finally he felt able to open his eyes. He settled back on his heels and gazed at the far wall of the canyon.

'Why are you doing this?' she asked. 'Why did you come in search of me?'

He continued to gaze at the canyon wall – at the foliage, even small trees, clinging to the sides and making lives from next to nothing.

'I have lost too many people,' he said.

'We almost lost two more in there,' she said.

He laughed, but it was a bitter sound.

'I knew there was a way through,' he said at last. 'And I was right, wasn't I?'

'You were brave even to try,' she said. 'I would never have done that on my own.'

'Nor I, as it turned out,' he said.

She watched as he played with the ring on his finger, slowly turning it round and around.

'But if you hadn't come looking for me, you would never have found yourself in such a place,' she said.

He nodded.

'I need something new to remember,' he said. 'The people, the things I have known, and that I remember – they were not mine.'

'They loved you,' she said. 'They gave their lives for you.'

'Their lives were taken from them – that's different.'

'Why did you come looking for me?' she asked again.

'How could I not?'

She blushed and raised a hand to the hot skin of her face.

'We are strangers,' she said.

'One way or another I have spent my life with strangers,' he said. 'I loved Jessie Grant. I loved

253

Badr Khassan. But they were not my own.'

'That is ungracious,' she said. 'They were not obliged to love you. They chose to, which is a greater gift.'

He looked hard into her face then, and when she returned his gaze she glimpsed a question flickering there.

'You still haven't told me about my father,' he said. 'About Patrick Grant.'

'You say he saved the life of Badr Khassan.'

He nodded.

'Well he saved mine first.'

'Tell me,' he said.

'First tell me where you are going,' she replied.

He dropped his shoulders in frustration.

'I have my own debts to pay,' he said. 'In the city of Constantinople ... there is a girl.'

'Do you love her?' she asked. She felt the question curl and uncurl inside her like a serpent's tail while she asked it.

'Love her? I do not even know her.'

'Then who is she?'

'She is his daughter,' he said. 'Badr Khassan's. Her mother's name was Isabella. He asked me to find her – to take care of her.'

'Constantinople is half a world away from here,' she said. 'How do you propose to get there? You do not even have a horse now.'

'I travel light. I just have to follow this river to the sea, and then find a port, and a ship heading east, and a captain who needs another crewman.'

He looked at her face but found he could not read the meaning of the expression he found there.

'I have told you my destination,' he said. 'Now you must tell me about my ... my father.'

Without another word, Lẽna stood, strode forward and leapt out into the void. John Grant gasped and reached for her. He almost toppled into space and gasped again as he regained his balance and then sat down heavily. By the time he had done so he heard the splash and leaned out again in time to see her head break the surface of the water. She turned and looked up at him on his perch, and raised both arms out of the water in a questioning, beckoning gesture.

'I followed *you*,' she shouted, and the sound of her voice echoed around the canyon.

He rose to his feet and looked down at the surging waters.

'Follow *me* and I will tell you what you want to know!' By then the river had carried her further away from him and her words were all but lost beneath the roar of the water. But he had heard enough.

He took three steps back, until he felt the rock wall behind him, and then sprinted forward and out into the nothingness.

Lẽna glanced upwards in time to see him leap, and for an instant, before the fall began, he seemed, to her at least, fixed there like a bug in amber. It was an image she would carry for the rest of her days, as he seemed to float, perfect and beyond the reach of either earth or sky.

More than anything else she would recall how completely he gave himself to the moment. His head was thrown back and he looked not down towards the murky depths but up and out and

255

into infinity. His arms were extended behind his back, so that he had the look of a crucified Christ, lost in an ecstasy of agony. And then the moment passed and the fall began.

PART THREE

Siege

26

Constantinople, 1453

'Tell me about the fat Turk, and how he drowned that poor baby.'

'He wasn't a baby. He was two years old – a little black-haired boy. Walking and talking.'

'*Nearly* two years old, you always say. That's still a baby to me.'

He felt her settle down beside him, like a child.

And he began ... the way he always began:

'While some of this must be true, and some of it might not be, it is all I know...'

His fingers fluttered in the dark and a black shape moved against a blue sky painted on the ceiling above their heads. Grotesquely fat, its pumpkin head topped with an outsize turban, the shadow might have been comical.

She hissed at the sight of the villain while she moved closer on the bed where they lay.

Armed only with paper cut-outs, his own clever hands, slivers of metal and glass mirrors, he had become a talented illusionist. His shadow characters loomed and diminished, danced and fought, flew and ran. In the darkness of his room his broken body was no hindrance to his art, and all the while his figures moved and lived at his command, he was like a little god – master of his creations. The room was a world of their own,

259

one split into light and dark, real forms and shadows.

'A man in his middle years, Ali Bey was a leader among his own people. In his homeland he would have been the one giving orders, dispatching others to exercise his will. He seldom felt any sense of superiority nowadays, however. Just as the hairs were slipping from his scalp in alarming numbers, so his self-esteem was sloughing off him like dead skin.'

Ali Bey was all at once replaced in the tableau by the shadow of a snake – one shedding its skin so as to become a bigger, fatter version of itself.

She snuggled deeper into the bedclothes, lulled by the familiar words and all but hypnotised by the interplay of his voice and the light and dark. The sounds of the city all around them seemed far away, inconsequential to the precious moments here in the jasmine-scented gloom of his bedchamber.

'Now more than halfway through his allotted span, he felt thwarted. A son of chieftains, Ali Bey had been convinced he was destined for glory.'

Ali Bey's fat shadow floated on high, suddenly ghoulish above the heads of a crowd of tiny figures.

'In a favourite dream he floated above his fellows, so that they had to crane their necks to gaze upon him.'

She cupped her hands around her mouth and booed.

'Here among the splendours of the palace of Edirne, padding quickly past elegant courtyards and quadrangles, he was just another servant of the sultan.'

Suddenly Ali Bey's silhouette was that of a young man, lithe and strong, while the shadows of lesser men fell at his feet.

'In his youth he had won fame as a wrestler, and his strength and speed had not quite left him. Even now, fat as a pig, he moved with feminine grace. But while once his body had been widest at the shoulders, now the circumference of his waist was the larger measurement.'

She dutifully catcalled as the youthful wrestler departed the scene and a bloated mockery of his former self was left behind, watching the other go.

'Finally he arrived at the double doors of the harem.'

A pair of shadow doors parted and a figure stalked through them, dripping pompous self-regard.

'All at once the fat man was confronted by the eunuch, Quadir.

'"What is your business here, Ali Bey?"'

The voice he used for the eunuch was high, almost shrill. Its shadow was as large as Ali Bey's, but muscular and with a bare, shaven head as smooth as an egg. The figure grew larger for a moment, imposing, while Ali Bey's drifted out of focus.

'Ali Bey wasn't even through the door and already the eunuch's tone was irksome. What would the atmosphere be like, here in the women's quarters, when he had finished what he had come to do?

'Quadir, whose duty it was to oversee all the business of the seraglio, had uttered Ali Bey's name like an insult. The eunuch was a towering figure, half a head taller than Ali Bey, and slowly he folded his arms across his chest.'

A tap, tap, tapping, made by a fingernail upon part of the bed frame, was the sound of Quadir's agitated foot upon a tiled floor.

The shadows came together as one, almost comically, and then parted, with Ali Bey's in control and striding ahead.

'Rather than reply, Ali Bey used the fading skills of the wrestler he had once been to unbalance his challenger and push him aside. Eunuch or not, Quadir had commanded respect for half a lifetime, and here in his own domain such effrontery was shocking. The fat man was past him, however, and looking around at doorways and corridors leading in all directions. He turned to face the eunuch once more.

'"Little Ahmet," he spat, his voice wheezing and thick with the effort of the confrontation. "Where is Little Ahmet?"

'"You have no business here, Ali Bey," the eunuch said, his anger coiled, ready to strike. "Must I summon the guards and have you rolled out of here on your fat belly?"

'"I am here on the sultan's business," said Ali Bey. "The boy's mother is in the throne room, at his majesty's pleasure, and he has sent me to collect the child. Where is Little Ahmet?" he asked for the last time.

'Quadir smiled. The suggestion that Mehmet would have sent this man – any man – to collect a child from the harem was ridiculous. Something in Ali Bey's sweaty manner, however, gave the eunuch pause.'

The shadows came together a second time, and a flash of light, created by a flick of the illusionist's wrist, suggested a glimpse of steel.

'While he stood in what he hoped appeared like calm contemplation, Ali Bey stepped lightly forward and struck Quadir just beneath his breastbone. Knocked backwards by the blow, the eunuch stumbled. He raised a hand to massage the sore place and found dampness there. Looking down, he was surprised, and only surprised, to find his hand covered in blood. He snapped his head up to look at Ali Bey. Only then did he glimpse the blade disappearing, like a darting fish, back into the folds of the other man's sweat-damp robes.

'There were many things Quadir wanted to say to Ali Bey then. But his mouth only opened and closed, twice in quick succession. Like a fish, he thought.'

Now the eunuch's shadow stood alone against the painted sky, while suns, moons and stars passed over his head.

'All at once, and for the first time in many a long year, he remembered standing buried up to his chin under a boiling hot sun after the priests had held him down and cut away the puny seahorse of his penis, the shrivelled seeds of his testicles. The searing agony when the bamboo stalk was inserted into the wound was long gone, unrecoverable, but the heat of his burial, neck deep in the scorching sand, washed over him like a blast from the baker's oven.

'Quadir, chief eunuch and confidante of wives

and sultans, back in the mind of his eight-year-old self, was dead before his face hit the floor.'

The shadow eunuch's fall was as graceful as it was tragic. His audience, his audience of one, buried her face in her hands as she always did at this moment in the telling.

There were no shadow puppets for the murder of the baby boy, only soft words and a sky flecked with clouds and birds and with a fiery sun at its centre. The muffled hubbub from beyond the windows – the cries of traders in the market, iron-shod hooves on cobbled lanes, the chatter of passers-by – might have been the grief and ululations of mourners.

'There were moments at the end, a handful at least, when peace and quiet replaced the frenzy of the struggle. All sensations were set aside and Little Ahmet was suspended in the silence, hovering there. The fat man was gone and there were no hands upon him any more, forcing him under. He floated on the surface, legs splayed and arms outstretched. He was face down, his hair arrayed like the fronds of some aquatic plant. While he had thrashed and fought, his eyes had been squeezed tight shut, another way of resisting. But the pain and fear were gone now. His lungs had filled with water but there was no more choking. That time had passed.

'Not so very long ago he had been a creature of water and the womb, and in the little life that remained, he remembered. His dying eyes opened into a shimmering light, and as he gazed into its warmth he heard her voice, clear as notes from a bell. He could not see her face – only dappled light

264

– but her voice was all around him. As soon as he heard her call his name he began to fall deeper, slowly descending through still, warm water towards the source of the light and the sound. He was not afraid.'

They lay quietly together for a while, letting the words settle around them like birds.

'And Ali Bey?' she asked, finally.

'The sultan executed him, had him hanged, as you well know.'

'Even though it was he – Mehmet – who had ordered his baby half-brother's murder,' she said.

'Even though – yes,' he said, indulging her need for repetition. 'That's what makes Ali Bey's dream so satisfying, don't you think – when he looks down upon his fellow chieftains. It came true when their upturned faces were the last thing he saw, with the noose around his neck

'And they really called the baby *Little* Ahmet?' she asked. 'It just makes it all the sadder.'

'He was his father's last son, sired when the old man was nearer death than life. And he was, as well, a silent, listless scrap of a thing at birth, and premature. No one expected him to live beyond his first breaths.'

'His mother's love, though,' she said, wistfully.

'Whatever it was, he thrived, apparently. They loved him.'

'So that is our foe,' she said. 'A man who would kill his own half-brother, a baby, to secure his throne.'

They were silent for a little while, and then he said:

'They all do that. It's what makes them men.'

265

'You're wrong,' she whispered. 'It's what makes them sultans ... and emperors.'

They lay in the dark, a boy and a girl in a darkened bedchamber. Above them, the ceiling of the room was all aglow so that there seemed to be two worlds – one made of day and the other of night; or two times, the past and the present.

We draw back from them now, out and away from them, and their room is revealed as part of a palace built of white stone. It is hard to tell if it is the stone itself that is white or if the brightness of the structure is due only to the heartless light of a wintry sun. Higher still and their city, once the greatest city, is revealed as a web of streets, lanes and alleyways, with lives and buildings great and small trapped within.

As we rise higher, in an ever-widening gyre, the city's place in the landscape is made clear. It sits at the end of a triangular peninsula of land shaped like the snout and horn of a rhinoceros. The squat stump of the horn thrusts up and out into the sea, so that there is water on two sides. The neck of the peninsula, the throat of the beast, is cut across by a great white wall like a collar or a livid scar, and flowing towards it like an unstoppable wave is a horde of people and animals – the massed forces of Sultan Mehmet II.

It is April, but spring has been slow in coming and the misery of winter is all around, so that a million sets of hooves and marching feet have made a mire that stretches in every direction. Their progress is slow, painful and accompanied by the shouts and groans of men and the complaints of beasts of burden.

266

However long it takes, whatever effort is required, their advance upon the wall and the city will not stop.

27

From high above it looks like an anthill, clinging to a precipitous slope. A white structure, rising into the sky and surrounded by tiny creatures, thousands upon thousands of them, moving in ordered lines or gathered in clumps. Hither and thither the lines weave and criss-cross, filled with purpose and intent. Not a moment is wasted as they work tirelessly in concert, inspired it seems by a common goal.

Closer to the ground now, hurtling down towards the mass of it, and we see the creation for what it is – a castle of pale stone surrounded by massive walls. The creatures moving busily in all directions around it are not ants but men. This is Rumelihisari, a great fortress of the Turkmen that erupted almost overnight, like a puffball in a field. Since the work began a little over four months ago, the hubbub of frenzied activity has never stopped. By day the men toil beneath the unforgiving sun. Stonemasons and the lime burners tasked with making their mortar; carpenters and joiners, and the smiths to make and sharpen their tools; hod-carriers and labourers and practitioners of another score of trades besides.

Such is the Ottomans' desire to raise this

clenched fist into the sky, so as to cast God's shadow over what remains of the Byzantine Empire, even the sultan's nobles toil ceaselessly alongside their underlings. From behind the walls of Constantinople itself – only six miles downstream from this latest audacity of their Muslim foes – the Christians can only watch and pray.

In their eyes it is a monstrosity. Its growth is frighteningly fast, like that of a cancer, and there is a rumour that even Mehmet is to be seen there, stripped to the waist and heaving stones into place with his bare hands. By night, their efforts are illuminated by a thousand fires and a hundred thousand lamps.

Like all of his ancestors, this latest sultan has spent a lifetime dreaming of Constantinople. The Prophet promised the city to his followers long ago, and it has been part of Islam's destiny ever since, an article of faith. They must place their hands around the Christian neck and throttle the life out of it...

From the windows of Prince Constantine's apartments in the Blachernae Palace in Constantinople, the tops of three lead-roofed towers – the threatening pinnacles of the new Turkish fortress – could easily be glimpsed. Its walls reached from the very waves breaking upon the shore of the Bosphorus to the summit of a ridge more than sixty yards above the water.

The prince lay in his bed, propped up on many pillows, but his teacher Doukas stood at one of the tall windows, the only one not shuttered against the sunlight. Constantine had already complained about the light, and Doukas was careful to allow only a sliver of bronze to intrude. In fact he was standing upon the window seat, the better to survey the distant scene.

'How far, would you say?' asked Constantine.

Doukas turned from the window and was silent for a moment while he allowed his eyes to adjust to the gloom of the interior.

'No more than six miles, Costa,' he said, turning back and continuing his observations on tiptoe. 'I have thought about this and I believe the infidels must have chosen to squat upon the ruins of our Church of St Michael.'

'Nice spot,' said Constantine. 'Lovely views.'

'Just so,' said Doukas. He was as plump as a pot-bellied pig and Constantine smiled at the sight of him, his rotund silhouette like a child's spinning top.

'This sultan of the Ottomans fears nothing and no one,' said Doukas. 'He does as he pleases while your father, the emperor...' His voice trailed away.

'Does nothing, Doukas?' asked Constantine. 'Is that what you were about to say?'

The teacher pretended he had not heard the question.

'Do not forget that Constantinople has shrugged aside the shadow of the Muslim scimitar for century after century,' said Constantine. 'Why should my father doubt the strength of the city's defences now, after all this time?'

Doukas did not answer and instead began listing the statistics of the new fortress.

'Walls as wide across their tops as three men laid head to toe,' he said. 'And as tall as eight men standing on each other's shoulders. The towers are greater still. Truly it is a marvel.'

'I hear talk of magic in the mix as well,' said Constantine. Doukas turned to look at him, saw that the prince's eyes were wide, his teeth glinting.

'I wonder about you sometimes,' said the teacher, resuming his survey and squinting into the sunlight. 'Where you find pleasure.'

Constantine warmed to his theme. 'They say the mortar was mixed with ram's blood, for strength and good fortune.'

'There's hardly anything magical in that,' said Doukas. 'Heathen superstition – no more and no less. Damn them all.'

'What about the layout of those walls you're so impressed by, then?' asked Constantine. 'I have heard their lines trace the shape of two names intertwined – the sultan's and the Prophet he serves...'

'For one who spends so much time in a darkened room, you don't miss out on idle gossip,' said Doukas.

'God forbid my father's subjects should keep me in ignorance,' said Constantine.

Doukas clambered down from his perch at the window and crossed to the bed.

'Never mind the prattle of hoi polloi,' he said, taking a seat by the prince. 'The facts are more sinister than any fancy. Sultan Mehmet has built his own castle within sight of our walls – and no more than six miles from the Golden Horn. He even calls his abomination *Rumelihisari* – the fortress on the land of the Romans!

'No captain dares pass the Ottoman fort without first allowing his ship to be boarded, the cargo checked and taxed.

'The walls are festooned with guns – big enough, they say, to hurl stones from one side of the channel to the other. No ship is safe.'

Now that his eyes had properly adjusted to the near darkness, Doukas noticed that the prince was considering a sheet of parchment pinned to a board. On the parchment was a sketch plan of the new fortress and the territory around it.

'You have to admire the gall of the man,' said Constantine, tapping his finger on the outline of Rumelihisari. 'Right where the channel is narrowest – at the Sacred Mouth.'

'Have you heard what the people have taken to calling the thing?' asked Doukas.

Constantine looked up from the plan and shook his head.

'*Bogaz Kesen*,' said his teacher. 'The throat-cutter.'

'Oh, I like that,' said Constantine. 'Has a ring to it.'

Doukas shook his head, exasperated.

'I call it a tumour,' he said. 'A tumour in the Sacred Mouth.'

28

Within the view framed by Constantine's windows, but much too small to be noticed from six miles away, a figure mounted on a fine white mare surveyed the latest symbol of his intent.

271

He was Mehmet, hero of the world, son of Murat, Sultan, son of the Sultan of the Gazis, frontier lord of the horizons. His age was twenty-one years and he had been sultan for nine of them. His mare, Hayed (which meant *movement*), was on heat and would not settle beneath him. She turned this way and that, even rearing on to her hind legs.

'Calm yourself now, Hayed,' he said firmly. He was strong, and a masterful horseman, and the challenge to his authority only made him smile as he used his knees and heels to enforce his commands. She came to a standstill and he stroked her neck, feeling the long, coarse hairs of her mane between his fingers, smelling her sweat.

Suddenly an explosion tore apart the peace of the morning and Hayed reared up once more, so that Mehmet had to rise in the stirrups and lean forward over her neck to retain his balance. When she settled back down on to all four hooves, he turned his head in the direction of the sound. It was the report from one of his heavy guns newly installed along the seaward-facing walls of the fort. A thin veil of dark smoke rose into the sky, betraying its source.

Glancing upstream to his left, he saw why his gunners had sprung into action. A galley, small and slight as a water beetle when viewed from so high above the strait, was travelling downstream from the Black Sea as fast as its oars would propel it. Mehmet counted three sails on the craft as well, all filled with a wind that favoured its line of flight down the channel and on towards the Great City.

Still the little ship came on, and now there were shouted threats as Mehmet's soldiers warned the crew of the consequences of attempting to evade inspection and the payment of tolls. A second shot rang out, and clearly the time for warnings had passed. A stone cannonball weighing almost half a ton missed the galley's bow by no more than the length of a man.

Moments later, a second ball, as big as the first and moving slowly enough that its passage just above the white tops of the waves could easily be tracked by Mehmet's sharp eyes, blasted into the galley. The hull cracked like an eggshell and seawater gushed into the void.

The sultan watched impassively as the shattered vessel began to turn turtle. The tiny figures of men scrambled over the sides and into the water – striking out desperately for the shore or clinging to floating wreckage. Less than a minute later, the galley was gone and only a clutter of men and flotsam remained to show it had ever existed.

Hayed seemed strangely mollified by the display, as though she had watched it as well and found that the outcome suited her mood, and Mehmet had to dig his booted heels into her flanks to get her moving – down the slope and towards an entrance to the fortress.

Armed guards at their posts lowered their heads as he passed, careful to avoid his eyes, but Mehmet kept riding hard, through an elegantly arched gateway in the shadow of the north-western tower, and on down a cobbled thoroughfare. Rumeli-hisari had been built with all possible speed, but his masons had been under orders to create

273

something beautiful, worthy of God.

He glanced beyond the battlements and glimpsed, shining in the sun on the far side of the strait, Anadoluhisari, the fortress put in place by his great-grandfather, the Sultan Bayezit, half a century before. Now his own work completed the set, a pair of stone hands poised to wring the infidel's neck.

He spared a thought for Bayezit, whose own siege of the Great City had failed, along with so much else in the end. He thought of him brought to battle by the Mongol Timur the Lame and defeated and kept for the rest of his days in a cage pulled behind the victor's dogs. Mehmet spat the memory of the khan from his mouth and spurred Hayed all the harder.

By the time he had reached the sea wall, craft crewed by his own men were already fishing bedraggled survivors from the water. Scores of soldiers and robed officials looked on from the battlements, clapping and jeering, and it was some moments before anyone noticed the sultan's arrival. At once there was a clamour as men ran forward from all directions to help him dismount.

Mehmet shook his head at their approach and Hayed, still skittish and ill-tempered, shied backwards, away from the press.

'Leave me be,' he said, jumping easily down and straightening his clothing. 'Let us see who has been first to challenge our authority.'

He received the prisoners in the guardroom on the ground floor of the massive twelve-sided tower that loomed over the waterfront above the middle portion of the sea wall. He was seated on a tall wooden stool, the hem of his sky-blue robe skimming the flagstone floor beneath his feet, so that he had the look of a bird on a perch, with folded wings. His face was long and thin, the profile aquiline. The avian appearance was intensified by a nose hooked like a beak.

Those closest to him might fear him, but they found much to admire as well. For all that he was headstrong and impulsive, he was clever too, and learned. A keen student from childhood onwards, he was a master of languages, a poet and a great reader of books. The exploits of Alexander the Great he had learned by heart, and he knew history and geography, science and engineering.

He was accompanied by a dozen armed guards but his confident air suggested he felt no need of their protection. All was silent, and then the sound of iron shackles dragging on stone announced the arrival of the prisoners. Mehmet was distracted, gazing at the light from a window high in one wall, but turned his hazel eyes to the door as they entered, preceded by two heavily muscled guards armed with scimitars unsheathed.

'How many are they?' he asked, as the line of bedraggled figures trooped slowly into the room.

They were chained at wrists and ankles and still soaking wet. One looked to be a boy of perhaps ten or twelve years. While they lined up in front of the sultan, water ran from their clothes, darkening the guardroom floor. The flagstones were red and the spreading dampness had the look of freshly spilled wine, or blood.

Mehmet considered the faces before him. All were dark, save the boy, who was fair, and he detected family resemblances among the group – as though brothers had found places aboard for brothers, fathers for sons.

'A crew of twenty-five, your majesty,' said a clerk who had brought up the rear of the line and now stood as close to the sultan as he dared. 'Plus their captain.'

At the mention of the rank, a prisoner in the centre of the line raised his bearded chin. Mehmet noticed the movement and addressed the man himself.

'Your name?' he said.

The bearded man looked the sultan in the eye before responding.

'I am Captain Antonio Rizzo, your majesty,' he said. 'Our home port is Venice and we pass this way many times each year.'

The man looked to be around thirty years old. His dark hair was curly, unruly and just beginning to show grey by the ears. The face was not handsome, but open and pleasant. He had a bangle of silver metal on one wrist. Around his neck he wore a silver locket and on his left hand a silver ring. Taken together, Mehmet thought, the assemblage suggested a loved one, if not a wife.

'Kneel down,' said the sultan.

Rizzo looked left and right at his men, and they at him. Mehmet saw trust in the looks they gave him, even affection. They certainly intended to take their cue from him.

'KNEEL!' bellowed one of the guards, and all of them dropped, the captain included, as though poleaxed.

There was silence then, broken only by the

sound of water dripping from clothes and the ends of noses and unwashed hair.

'You know it is against our wishes for any ship to pass through these waters without payment of a toll,' said the sultan. There was no note of a question and he delivered the information as a simple fact.

'Yes, your majesty,' said Rizzo.

'So you knowingly and openly defy us?'

'We were a week overdue, your majesty,' said the captain. 'With a cargo of beef that had already begun to spoil. It was my intention to settle our debt on the return leg of our journey.'

'Indeed, said the sultan. 'Well the meat is well salted now.'

He turned his attention to the clerk.

'We have no time for debts,' he said. 'They will settle their account immediately. Keep the boy.'

The clerk took a thin wooden board from under his arm and made a swift note on a sheet of parchment fastened to it. Mehmet wondered what it said, but not enough to ask.

'And put the good captain where everyone may see him,' he said. He stood up from his stool and walked out of the door, followed by his guards.

Within the hour, all of the Venetians were dead – all save the boy, whose youth and appearance had pleased the sultan. He was Rizzo's son, and the fair hair was the gift of his mother. He was placed within the harem. Each of the other crewmen was swiftly dispatched with the sword. Rizzo was impaled, however. Before any of the beheadings were carried out, and while all looked on, two strong men held the captain face down on the courtyard in front of the tower, his arms manacled behind his back and his legs spread wide by a length of wood tethered between his ankles. A third man, less heavily built than the other two but with specific skills, then thrust the sharpened end of a long wooden pole as thick as his arm into Rizzo's anus. He used a heavy mallet next, to drive the point onwards, like a tent peg, into the abdomen. Rizzo was still alive, and bleating like an abandoned calf, when the pole was raised vertically and the tail end slotted into a waiting socket between two flagstones by the battlements. From a distance it might have looked like a toy for a child – one of those on which the arms and legs of a jointed figure jerk up and down when a string is pulled.

29

The sultan did not stay to witness the executions. Instead he departed for his capital at Edirne, three days' ride to the west of Constantinople. As he turned his back on the Throat Cutter, and while his retinue fussed around him on the road, he smiled as he remembered the flight of the colossal stone ball that had doomed the Venetians and their ship. He had seen the store of ammunition at first hand, like gaming pieces for a giant, and for all that each missile was as fat and big around as the greatest wild boar, the bombard had tossed it across the strait like a pebble. His hand clenched involuntarily into a fist as he considered the power. Just as the hulls of ships would splinter in the face of such weapons, so too would the ancient walls of the city that had defied his forebears, his own father, Murad, Bayezit, and all the rest.

It was late afternoon on the third day of the journey when they reached Edirne, and with the sun hanging low in the sky like a copper coin, he saw the earthbound infernos of Orban's furnaces. Without a thought of going first to the palace, he hastened towards the crowd of men labouring ceaselessly to add to his steadily growing collection of city-takers.

One of the foremen caught sight of Mehmet's approach, accompanied by his attendants, and shouted out to the assembled founders, masters and labourers. All turned towards the sultan and as one they stopped what they were doing and dropped to their knees, heads bowed. Nearby were two long, low couches on which the sultan's most trusted advisers had been seated to observe the massive labours. They too had risen at word of Mehmet's approach but he waved everyone away – insistent that his arrival should do nothing to interfere with the job at hand.

'Continue! Continue!' he shouted, as he reached the casting pit in a specially prepared site outside the city walls and jumped down from Hayed's back. All leapt to their feet once more and he strode excitedly to towards the commanding figure of Orban, the master founder. Fully a head taller than the sultan, though not as powerfully built, he took care to stoop uncomfortably low.

Mehmet was hungrier for a progress report

than any show of deference.

'Well?' he asked, eyes wide.

'You have timed your arrival perfectly, majesty,' said Orban, straightening and leading the sultan on a quick walk around the perimeter of the pit.

It was itself a colossal creation, as deep as five tall men, and the width of four. Rising from the centre, to ground level, was the rounded top of a huge cylinder of clay that had been mixed with grass and shredded linen to form a robust mould. In fact the mould was in two parts – one inside the other like a sword inside a sheath.

What was visible to Mehmet was the outer shell of clay that had been painstakingly shaped and then lowered into position over the slightly smaller inner mould, leaving a void all around – like the air gap around a finger in a loose-fitting glove. Into this space, several inches wide, would be poured the torrent of molten copper and tin that would form the bombard itself. Packed tightly around the mould was a framework of huge logs and iron rods, which had in turn been surrounded with a fill of earth and stones so that the weight of the bronze might be supported while it cooled in its cavity.

'We are about to pour a slurry of wet sand down and around the outside of the mould,' said Orban. 'It will absorb some of the metal's heat and prevent the mould from cracking.'

Mehmet nodded. His was no casual interest. Rather he had immersed himself in the lore of metal casting – indeed ever since Orban had offered his services. The founder had told him he had learned his art in Hungary, the land of his

280

birth. He had impressed the sultan with his frankness then, admitting that he had tried first to ply his trade in the Great City. The emperor had been keen enough but lacked the funds to suitably reward his endeavours – and so he had sought out the sultan of the Ottomans instead.

Mehmet had spotted Orban's value at once and had thrown down a challenge:

'These weapons you say you can make – will they bring down the walls of the Christians' city?' he asked.

Orban had nodded.

'I am certain of it, sire,' he said.

Since then the Hungarian had made the guns mounted on the walls of the Throat Cutter – one of which had utterly destroyed the ship of the Venetians. Now he was poised to create his masterwork, the greatest bombard the world had yet seen.

While Mehmet and Orban watched, the labourers piled yet more earth and sand over the top of the pit until only a small hole remained leading into the cavity inside the mould itself.

Content that all was as it should be, Orban had the men turn their attentions then to two huge furnaces built of clay bricks. They had been alight for days, fed continuously with charcoal so that each interior blazed like the sun and roared like the mouth of hell. Orban bade the sultan keep back, but Mehmet needed no instructions to stay many yards from the scorching heat.

His viziers were still on their feet awaiting his pleasure, and he gestured at them to take their seats. He joined them, on a throne raised on a dais set between their couches, and while sweat coursed from every pore on their bodies they watched as the founders and stokers approached the furnaces.

Clad in thick robes, mask-like head-coverings that concealed all but their eyes, heavy leather gauntlets and slippers, the men tended huge crucibles, one within each furnace. With wooden poles as long as the masts of galleys they stirred the molten metal. The hellish soup of copper and tin – spiked now and then with coins of gold and silver for good luck – swelled and bubbled. Noxious fumes rose from the mixture and the observers strained even to keep their eyes open as they gazed upon the spectacle.

All the while the sultan had hastened back from the Rumelihisari, Orban had overseen the preparation of the metal. It had been three days now – the fires fed by air pumped continuously into the flames by sets of bellows worked ceaselessly by rotating teams of workers. Having cast a practised eye over the brew one more time – and contented himself that the soup glowed with precisely the right shade of cherry red – Orban ordered the commencement of the pouring.

Now was the most dangerous and telling moment of the whole exercise, and Mehmet hunched forward on his throne, shielding as much of his face as possible with gloved hands as he struggled to watch. His eyes felt dry as paper, and stung in protest.

The founders started up a rhythmic chant, calling out to God as they used long poles with metal hooks on the ends to reach into each furnace and tip the crucibles forward until their liquid contents poured into carefully positioned gutters of fired clay leading to the hole in the top of the mould.

While the red rivers flowed, the workers ran up and down alongside the channels using yet more long poles to prod and cajole the liquid, easing out air bubbles that might enter the mould and leave a weakness in the casing of the finished bombard. All was measured, deadly serious activity until the mould was completely filled and the overspill flowed across the earth, hissing and throwing up clouds of smoke and steam.

Orban called a halt and almost at once the plug that had formed on the top of the mould began to change colour, fading in brightness until what had seemed like a flow of dragon's blood turned dark and strangely lifeless.

Unable to contain himself, Mehmet leapt from his seat and rushed towards the master founder. Sensing and seeing the sultan's approach, Orban turned from the mould and hurried over – anxious that his master should not come too near to the heat. Mehmet said nothing, but his expression carried the question he dared not ask.

'I am pleased,' said Orban, nodding. 'All is well.'

In the thrill of the moment, Mehmet quite forgot himself and slapped his founder on the shoulder with boyish excitement. He shook his head in honest wonder at all he had just witnessed.

'God is with us,' he said. 'He sees to it that I shall have what I need to complete this task.'

Orban bowed his head. Experience had given him the strength to withstand the heat of the furnace, but the intensity of the sultan's gaze was altogether too much for him to bear.

If the creature's conception had been a wonder, a breathtaking union of elements, then its birth out of the earth that had cradled it was a clumsy affair of stumbling men and bellowing beasts of burden. By morning, Orban had judged the metal would have cooled enough to permit the excavation of the mould. Hours of heavy labour followed, as the sun rose ever higher in the sky, until the great seed had been wholly unearthed. Ropes and tethers were fixed around its massive bulk and teams of horses were used to haul it up and out of its pit until it lay on its side on the sand.

The sultan had retired to his palace and his bedchamber soon after the completion of the pouring. Orban sent word to invite him to gaze upon the product of a week's endeavour only once the clay of the mould had been cracked away and knocked clear of the interior. By the time Mehmet arrived with his retinue, the bronze had been buffed to a golden sheen. Supported upon massively stout wooden trestles, it gleamed with a terrifying lustre. It had the scale and appearance of something made not by men but by the almighty.

Mehmet reached out a hand towards the glow of its surface, but such was the reverence he felt, he stopped short of touching it. He walked the length of the cylinder and found it took him a dozen exaggerated paces to travel from its rounded base to its gaping maw. While he rightly decided it was beneath his dignity to do so, he saw there was room enough inside the barrel for a man of his size to crawl comfortably inside and turn around.

He turned to face the master founder and saw

that his face was bathed in golden light reflected from the bronze.

'A blast from this trumpet would have toppled the walls of Jericho,' he said.

30

With the memory of the bombard gleaming before his eyes, Mehmet returned to the palace and made for his private quarters. His favourite room had windows on three sides and all were open to allow soft breezes to freshen the air.

He crossed to an eastward-facing window and looked down into the courtyard. There, on a tall pole at the centre, ruffled by a breeze, was an elaborate banner with a braided horsetail as its centrepiece. He remembered when, weeks before, he had ordered it set in place. At the sight of the thing, a great cheer had gone up from those passing nearby, and the sound had spread, carried on a sudden wind and infecting all who heard it, until it echoed from one side of the city to the other.

Mehmet turned his back on the courtyard, walked to the centre of the room and cast himself down gratefully upon the cushions and pillows heaped there. Another breeze, and as welcome, came this time from the westward-facing windows and caressed his skin. He imagined his commands carried upon it like the scent of blood, into the most distant reaches of his realm.

Within minutes of the raising of the banner,

messengers and heralds had been dispatched far and wide, taking with them the news that their sultan had finally set his eyes upon the greatest prize of all – the Great City.

They would be close to him now. From Edirne he would lead them – professional soldiers and impassioned volunteers alike – to Constantinople.

Soon now, within the hour, he would set himself to the task once more and not rest this time until it was done. The great bombard and city-taker was ready, the final piece in the complex puzzle he had been assembling for many weeks. When he rose again and rejoined his throng, he would be at the centre of a whirlwind of his own creation – shaping and directing it, feeding it like a living thing and coaxing more power from it. There would be no end to his efforts until either the goal was reached or life itself was taken from him. For now, for a few final moments, he was alone with his thoughts. Muhammad himself had foretold that the city raised by Constantine would, in the end, become home to the people of the Faith. He trembled, and wondered whether it was the chill of the breeze that stirred him, or the will and pleasure of God.

There would have been no need of force, he knew, to bring the masses to him from every corner of Anatolia – to have them form his armies and fight for him. Rather they would come like guests to a wedding. The only injustice would be that felt by those left behind, those deemed too crippled, too old or too young. Even they would make the march to the mustering points – as many boys as could shake off the grasping hands of their mothers, as many old men as could drive their old bones over the intervening miles, as many of the halt and the lame as could drag themselves across the unforgiving earth.

They would be lured not only by his command but also by the prospect of glory. For the city of Constantinople – just three days' ride to the east of his palace at Edirne – dangled in the faces of the faithful like the reddest apple, the sweetest fruit of all. Those blessed with the chance to reach out for it would either taste its flesh or, harvested themselves by the cruel blades of the infidel, rise to the paradise promised only to martyrs.

Mehmet's breathing had grown shallow and fast with the thrill of it all.

'They shall be as numerous as the stars,' he murmured. 'My armies will flow towards the walls of Constantinople like a river of steel.'

He lay back upon the pillows, luxuriating in the softness and the cool. Once he embarked upon the campaign, comforts would be few and far between. He would spend the necessary weeks and months – however long it took – at the centre of his forces. Young as he was, he had passed enough time among besieging armies to know they made for foul and pestilent company. They would stew in their own juices, basted by misery and hardship, until the Wall of Theodosius itself was finally brought low. Only then, when his river of steel had burst its banks and flowed into the streets of the Great City, would he savour any freshness.

Slowly he became aware of a new sound, building like a thought. He ignored it at first, dismissing it as nothing more than the hubbub of the palace and of the city beyond. But the noise grew steadily in volume and intensity so that it elbowed its way to the forefront of his consciousness. It had something of the ebb and flow of waves upon a shore, a great booming, rhythmical roar that rose and fell with a life of its own. He sat up slowly, realisation dawning. Suddenly flooded with understanding, he leapt to his feet and crossed to the open windows once more. Looking out, beyond the palace walls, he saw men – hundreds, thousands of men, and countless animals besides. His army, his people, had arrived at his city walls at last. In ordered ranks they advanced upon Edirne, banners flying and horns blaring.

'It is begun,' he said, and he brought his hands together beneath his bearded chin and raised his eyes to heaven.

31

Constantinople, April 1453

Prince Constantine flew high above the city, beyond its walls and out over the sparkling waters of the Sea of Marmara. A chill breeze swept over him, through him, ruffling his clothes and hair and filling his lungs. He was free, and filled with the joy of it and the endless possibilities. Far beneath him, formations of oared galleys practised their moves upon the blue. Lithe and fast as sea serpents, they cut with predatory purpose between the portly merchant ships plying back and forth, every which way – sharks among dugongs.

The waters around Constantinople were always busy, yet another means of approach to the centre of the world. The pull of the Great City attracted a ceaseless flow: pilgrims and merchants; makers of war and preachers of peace; madmen and malcontents; paupers and princes, and all else in between. They came on foot, on horses and on wagons and carts; on the broad shoulders of elephants and upon the cross-draped backs of donkeys; in boats and ships of every size and shape and in every condition imaginable. The prince's city was irresistible and he marvelled anew at the colour of it all, and the energy.

He was dreaming, of course. The flying dream was his favourite – lived to the full for as long as it lasted and bitterly mourned when it ended. Sometimes he drifted gently back to consciousness, landing among his bedclothes as lightly as a leaf parted from a tree on a windless day; often the return to the waking world was presaged by a sudden, sickening fall, a headlong, flailing dive towards rooftops, desert sands or cresting waves. Soft landing or hard – each return to earth near broke his heart.

At other times he dreamed he was weightless in water, sweeping across an undersea world in the manner of a dolphin, or a seal – or better than either, able to breathe there, to suck down lungful after lungful of energy-giving oxygen without the need to return to the shackles wrought by gravity for the world above. But just as with the dream of flight, the thrill of the deep never lasted – or not long enough.

Always there was the sudden loss of ability followed by a terrifying plummet. In the dream of the sea it was a plunge, stone-like, into deeper water. Blue turned black and then his crushed lungs would blaze in his chest until he awoke gasping into the captivity of reality, weighed down by the anvils of his crippled legs.

This time he experienced the least familiar option, and the one he found most troubling of all. Having spent many happy minutes soaring and swinging in the sunlight, he became aware of heaviness in his legs. Instead of trailing straight out behind him, they began to pull earthwards of their own accord, as though his feet were suddenly encased in lead. His forward motion faltered and then failed completely. He was falling now, feet first towards the water, faster and faster, looking now not at the waves but into the empty vastness of the clear blue sky above. After too many desperate moments, tensed for impact but with no way of knowing when it would arrive, he awoke instead, with a jolt, sweating and panting among a chaos of sheets.

While he waited for his breathing to return to normal, he focused on the circular ceiling of his room. At his own request it had been painted like the sky – azure blue and flecked with white clouds. There were birds here and there, doves, starlings and sparrows and a single white gyrfalcon. Most of it, though, was empty blue and at the centre of it all the noonday sun, golden and with wisps and tendrils of fire coiling away from the rim. It was the sky he loved and flight he longed for – the chance to shake off the bonds of earth and rise up, weightless and untrammelled.

'Costa?'

He heard her soft voice as though from far away. After a few moments, it came again. 'Costa? It's me, are you awake?'

It was Yaminah. Even now she sought his permission before coming into his room.

'Yes ... yes – come in, come in,' he said, his gaze still fixed upon the ceiling.

She opened the door no more than a few inches and slipped inside. The heavy fabric of her dress made a shushing sound as she turned to close the door before stepping quickly over to his bedside. An observer might have thought her an intruder, someone who did not belong, and yet Yaminah had lived in the palace of Prince Constantine's parents for six years. It was the only home she had and she was made welcome, but still she moved through its rooms and corridors as though in mortal fear of discovery by the guards.

She knelt down and took his right hand in both of her own. She stroked the slim, elegant fingers as she talked.

'They're here,' she said.

'I know,' said Constantine softly. He looked down at the top of her head, bowed as if in prayer. She remained focused upon his hand rather than his face. 'They certainly like their drums.'

'And their horns,' she added, and sniffed drily. 'I suppose it's safe to assume they would have us be in no doubt about their presence. Or their intentions.'

'I expect you're right,' he said, and he smiled. The vulnerability of the pale skin of her scalp, revealed by the neat parting of her long brown hair, made him think of the child she had been when he first saw her, perched like a bird of paradise on a balustrade inside the Church of St Sophia all those years before. All those years before his old life had ended and a new one began. He reached for her face with his free hand, caressed her cheek as softly as a wish. He felt her expression change beneath his fingers as she too began to smile.

His touch, the reassurance of it, seemed finally to give her the peace of mind she needed, even if it would not last. She looked up into his face for the first time since she had entered. There was always shyness in her manner towards him, though she knew it pleased him every time she walked into a room. She had made his world smaller than before but she filled the space entirely.

Even from where she knelt on the tiled floor by his bed she could see that his legs were awkwardly arranged – out of line with his top half – and that he was, as always, unaware of it. He looked broken, a sapling toppled by a storm. He *was* broken, and she wished with all her heart that she might fix him – or at least straighten him, as she would have smoothed the sheets upon which he lay. But even to attempt to do so would wound what remained of his male pride, she knew, and she let him be.

He lay there like her own private Christ: come to save her and her alone, and paying an awful price for his good deed.

'Do you still want to go through with it?' he asked. 'Now that all these uninvited guests have shown up? I mean, heaven alone knows what we're going to feed them.'

Despite the seeming lightness of his question, the hearing of it made Yaminah's smile vanish like day turned to night.

'How dare you ask me that?' she said, two hot tears pricking in her eyes. He might as well have struck her. Her gaze was fierce, an outright challenge, her chin raised towards his face. 'And why say it like that – I'm not about to *go through* with anything. I want it even more now.' Her voice sounded brittle. 'Don't you? *Don't you?*'

The speed of Yaminah's emotions – their arrivals and departures – was a fascination to the young prince and sometimes made him want to laugh out loud, but this time her sudden momentary seriousness, and the accompanying hurt, banished his own smile as well.

'Me too,' he said, nodding, and he cupped her heart-shaped face with both his hands. With his thumbs he caught her tears, then lightly traced the lines of her cheekbones, as though opening a book to a favourite page. 'Me too.'

When he had asked her to marry him, weeks before, he had known she would say yes. In truth he had felt he owed her, although sometimes in his heart he wondered if the gift he had to give was a blessing or a curse. She loved him – he knew that – but was it fair to bind her to him for a lifetime?

His father's hearty approval of the betrothal had surprised him most of all. Since his accident, the prince had remained out of sight of most. His absence from court life had seemed to meet with the emperor's approval, and so when Constantine had broken the news of his plans to marry Yaminah, he had expected a sharp intake of breath at the very least.

A wedding would place the prince centre stage after all – bringing him back to the forefront of everyone's attention. He had thought therefore that there might be a note of caution from his majesty, if not outright disapproval – and yet the emperor had sounded only surprised at first, and then sincerely enthusiastic about the whole idea.

Yaminah's smile returned, replacing her frown like sunshine after rain, but the clouds remained, threatening. She snuck up on to the bed then, suddenly feeling tired, and curled beside him like a cat. She placed her head on his lap and tapped his thigh, just above his knee, three times with one thin finger.

'Tell me stories,' she said. 'To make up for your stupid question.'

Constantine had watched her finger jab at his withered flesh, stretched thin over bone, but had not felt it, and when she settled her hand upon his leg he detected only a vague suggestion of its warmth. He could, however, just about register the weight of her head in his lap, and he closed his eyes as his heart beat faster. There was a sudden hint of heaviness, and of need, between his legs, and he might have groaned, but did not.

After a moment or two he opened his eyes and reached behind his head. With his left hand he felt for a set of dangling cords, each attached to some or other part of a network of little pulleys and weights above the bed. He made a few brief tugs and adjustments until heavy curtains and slatted blinds moved into their desired positions over tall windows, the room made all but dark. A single shaft of sunlight remained, lancing down on to the top of a wooden cabinet by the bed. Upon the cabinet stood a dish of highly polished bronze, four inches across and fixed to a stand by small brass screws. A turn here and a twist there made the gleaming dish swivel and turn like a roving eye.

With a practised hand Constantine manoeuvred the gadget until the beam, thinner than Yaminah's wrist, was caught and reflected back up on to the ceiling. All at once the painted sky was lit up, bright as noon. It was an effect Yaminah never tired of, lying in the gloom beneath the apex of an upturned cone of light through which dust drifted like stars in heaven.

From a drawer in the cabinet Constantine produced a handful of black-painted rods, each of them topped with a different, exquisitely crafted, two-dimensional blackened figure or shape. There were crowned emperors and empresses; kings and queens; princes and princesses; mounted warriors; foot soldiers – singly and in ranks; crescent moons and stars, towers and battlements, lightning bolts and storm clouds – the props for any story the prince might weave.

Yaminah let out a contented sigh that was almost a purr, and her saviour prince began his tale as he always did:

'While some of this must be true, and some of it might not be, it is all I know...'

And into the beam of light he brought the first of the figures and shapes so that their shadows were cast large against the blue, or passed across the face of the painted sun with its tendrils of flame. Armies advanced and clashed, fought and fell, triumphed or retreated; horses cantered and galloped; emperors made their empresses by marriage as required, and consorted with their mistresses as they wanted, while those empresses sought their own lovers; fortresses were raised and flattened, suns set, moons rose, stars roamed free and tears were shed for all of it.

'..."Let him who loves me follow me,"' roared Mehmet, sultan and lord of all,' said Constantine, while Yaminah yelped, her face in her hands.

'Out of his bedchamber he charged, shrugging off his robe of sky-blue silk, trimmed with the white fur of the Arctic fox, while courtiers rushed in all directions like startled birds.'

Shadows danced against a painted sky, and a prince and princess, a broken boy and the girl whose fate it had been to break him, lay together in a circular bedroom in a palace in a great city. He sent his stories up into the sky to fly alongside his dreams, and she, like an angel, could fly there too for as long as each tale lasted.

Sometimes the cast of characters remained only shadows; at other times, when the warmth of his body and the softness of his voice conspired to lure her into the space between waking and sleep, they seemed to come fully alive. Then their shapes would fill with colour and be transformed into flesh and blood, so that it was as real men and women that they played their parts.

'"Let him who loves me follow me!" said Constantine again, more of a bellow this time as his shadow sultan strode forth, while grim-faced men rallied to his call, issuing from every doorway of his palace and flocking to his side.

'A letter was clutched in Mehmet's right hand – indeed he gripped it so tightly that his knuckles shone white like bone. The poor soul who had brought the missive remained on his knees in the bedchamber, his forehead pressed tightly against cool floor tiles, eyes closed.

'Like everyone else he had no idea what news he had carried, and his lips moved silently as he prayed that its contents would not cost him his life. Only when the shouts and clattering footsteps faded from his hearing did he risk a sideways glance, first left and then right.'

Constantine flicked the messenger's shadow from side to side, an elegantly exaggerated move that always made Yaminah giggle.

'Content that he was alone, he risked a hitching, tearful breath.' Constantine mimicked the panicky sob, making Yaminah giggle even louder. 'Before rolling on to his side, still curled into a ball.'

Constantine turned the little figure then, made only of stiffened paper, until the man's shape was reduced to nothing more than a black line beside a four-poster bed upon an otherwise empty sky.

Yaminah clutched his hand. For all that it was a tale she knew well – how Sultan Mehmet II had learned of the death of his father and had set out in all possible haste to seize the throne – it was Constantine who made it real for her, made it all true, and she held him tight.

'Whatever storm the messenger had unleashed had passed him by,' said Constantine, whispering now, 'leaving him unharmed.'

It was in this way, lying in the warm, perfumed darkness of her prince's bedchamber, that Yaminah had learned the history of her city, of the empire of Byzantium and of those, like Mehmet's Seljuk Turks, who would harm it.

'Out in the corridors it became apparent to one and all that Mehmet was making for the stables, and men began shouting ahead, issuing orders for the grooms to ready the horses,' said Constantine, his voice high, in harmony with the thrill and foreboding of it all.

'Mehmet's gaze was fixed straight ahead, as though focused on a point far in the distance that only he could see.'

Constantine played a tiny mirror, cupped in his free hand, to make a momentary blinding flash.

'None dared speak to him for fear of rebuke or reprisal. Instead they stole glances at his face in search of understanding.'

'What age was he?' asked Yaminah, momentarily breaking the spell of his storytelling. 'When he learned his father was dead?'

'No more than seventeen,' Constantine replied, still playing with the mirror and moving the thin shaft of light around the walls.

'So young,' she said. 'And why such urgency? The throne was his.'

He laughed. 'The throne might go to whoever had the will and the strength to seize it,' he said. 'It is the way of the Ottomans. Where there are many sons – and that is what their harems and seraglios are for – each may claim the throne on the death of the father.'

'So they murder babies too – just to be sure,'

she said.

'Little Ahmet,' he said. 'I sometimes wish I had spared you that tale.'

'It is no tale,' she said. 'In what sort of world is a tiny child a threat to a sultan?'

'The Turks are hardly alone in that cruelty,' said Constantine. 'Do not forget my own family. Plenty of my ancestors have done away with kin. One of them blinded his own son and also his three-year-old grandson, just to keep them from his throne.'

Yaminah closed her eyes and turned away from him.

To distract her, Constantine returned to his shadow play. All at once, two parties of horsemen approached one another, stopping while they were still separated by a respectful distance.

'A great horde – common people as well as grand men – rode out from the royal capital to greet him as he approached. When they saw Mehmet and his party on the horizon, they dismounted. Leading their horses by the reins, they progressed in silence while the new sultan came on – and then he too climbed down from his horse and his followers did likewise.'

Constantine brought the shadow parties together so that they appeared as one thronging mass.

'As they came upon one another, a great call went up – a wailing cry of mourning for the dead sultan, and the ululations rolled across the wide plain. As abruptly as it had begun, the wailing ended, and then every man and woman knelt down before the new sultan and offered him praise.'

32

Rome, eighteen years before

It was still half dark, but the sunrise was close.
Isabella's right shoulder was exposed to the air.
Keeping her breathing shallow and with movements slow, she reached for it with her left hand.
Her skin was cold, like that of a corpse. It was
just as well. She could not risk falling back to
sleep, and the chill made her more determined to
rise and be away.

Shrugging aside the covers, she swung her legs
off the bed until she could sit upright. Only then,
with her back turned, could she allow herself to
look down at him over one shoulder. Given the
gloom, she sensed rather than saw that Badr was
lying on his front. His face was turned away from
her, which was a relief. Somewhere outside and
far away, a bird began to sing, heralding the rising
of the sun. The fragile notes broke her lover's spell
and she closed her eyes, promising herself she
would not look at him again.

She heard him groan, mutter some words she
did not catch. He was feverish still, radiating the
kind of heat that came only from illness. Soon he
would be awake. She hated to take her leave of
him while he was unwell, but part of her knew it
was the perfect time to make her getaway.

She slipped out of the bedroom then, without a

backward glance, and stole along the narrow hallway. There was a dim glow from tall windows high up on the walls, and when she stopped to dress by the main door, she could see well enough. There was a mirror on the wall beside her and she paused in front of it for a few moments, long enough to check that she looked respectable, nothing more. Her long fair hair was loose and reached more than halfway down her back. There was no time to fix it now, and pausing only to throw a wrap around her shoulders, she opened the door of the town house and stepped out into the dawn. Black-headed seabirds squabbled on the rooftops above, their keening cries full of hunger and sadness.

As she made her way along a narrow pavement touched by the sun's first rays, she remembered some of Ama's words. An old lady now, blind and frail, Ama had been Isabella's nurse from the moment she drew her first breath. As full of stories as with love, it was Ama, more than Isabella's mother or anyone else, who had cradled her and loved her. Needed her. As the gulls' pleading, lonely cries sounded high above and out of sight, Isabella was reminded of Ama's talk of souls and their twins.

Such a notion was tantamount to heresy, of course, or heathen nonsense at best. The thought had been entrusted to Isabella among many other confidences shared by the pair. Ama had loved her stories, kept them close around her in place of any family of her own, and Isabella couldn't hear enough of them.

Now old age had taken Ama's stories along with

so much else. The woman who framed Isabella's childhood, who featured in every other memory, had been robbed of her own power of recall. She embodied Isabella's past but had access to none of her own. Her stories too had departed one by one, like guests leaving a party in the wee small hours; time to go. She existed now in a warm haze of confusion. Still in Isabella's family home, though mostly unaware and untroubled by the blur of it all, Ama haunted the tumbledown remains of her own life.

When Isabella had asked where the idea of twin souls came from, Ama said it was a story that came out of the East – from India maybe. Whatever its origins, it had pleased Isabella as a little girl just as it pleased her now. Maybe she wasn't alone – or at least, not for ever.

Ama said that for the most part each twin followed a separate path, without encountering its other half. But from time to time in an infinite universe they must come together, by accident or design, and the result then was greater than the sum of two parts.

It was only the souls that were identical, of course, said Ama, not the people who embodied them, so the individuals concerned need not look alike. Geography and distance created by the accident of birth played their parts, often keeping twins apart. Gender had its role as well. One soul might be incarnated in a male body, while its twin was female. Sometimes the souls got out of step with one another so that one was newborn when the other was old – and all points in between.

'They may meet as parent and child, as lovers,

as enemies, as strangers from opposite ends of the earth,' Ama said, brushing Isabella's dark blonde tresses until they shone. 'Every once in a while, though, their time coincides, and for as long as they are together there must be consequences.'

'Will my soul have a twin?' Isabella had asked at once, gazing into Ama's face reflected in the mirror. Ama bit her lip, wondering if it had been a mistake to dangle such a hope in front of a heart as needy as little Isabella's. It was too late. The bait had been swallowed, and the hook was fast.

'No one knows that about themselves, sweetheart,' she said, smiling. Ama was as warm and soft as new-baked bread, and Isabella pushed back against her nurse's tummy as though it was a cushion. Ama stopped her brushing then and rested both hands on the girl's shoulders. She adopted a serious expression, as of the schoolroom, so that Isabella might pay attention and remember.

'But here is the most important part ... you must never, ever go looking.' She was improvising, making up rules that did not exist. 'Never imagine you have a twin. Better think of it as a story to make you smile. But if you did have a twin soul and...' she was drifting helplessly back into her story, 'you were to meet, then so be it. You cannot make it happen, though ... must not try.

'And anyway,' she said, bending down to plant a soft kiss on Isabella's cheek, 'what need have you or I of twins, when we have each other?'

She winked at their reflection and Isabella gasped, her heart filled to the brim with the possibility.

'Maybe we are twins!' she said. 'You and I!'

Ama smiled. 'Maybe my darling,' she said. 'Maybe.'

Back in the present, back in the early morning of the Eternal City, Isabella felt the memory of the moment like a lump in her chest. An old memory, but one with such power – a light unfocused by great distance but burning bright.

But for all she had enjoyed the possibility that she herself might be blessed thus – gifted a partner for eternity, one she might encounter in this life or in some other yet to be – the thought made her sad today as well.

She felt she might have loved the man she was leaving behind, but he was not her soul's twin; of that she was certain. He had caught her eye the first moment they met, but truly they were different people (she had learned that much, at least) and therefore – she was quite sure – theirs were unconnected souls. She realised she was nodding to herself as she reviewed the situation.

It was, however, no fancy thought of souls, entwined or otherwise, that had persuaded her to cut him away and for ever. She might have kept him, twin or not. It wasn't the infinite possibilities suggested by the world invisible that had persuaded her to turn her back on him. Instead it was the straightforward understanding that if she did not give him up – and if their liaison were discovered – her father would have his life snuffed out like a candle's flame. She would put away her own sorrow for now, ready to be unpacked later when the job was done.

'Enough of all this,' she said out loud.

She was shaking her head, suddenly filled with

self-reproach.

Again and again her father had told her she was trouble, and that she had to be watched, and he was right! Stolen moments with one lover might be dismissed as an indiscretion; even predictable in the case of a girl kept always on so short a leash. But with two?

She raised her hand to her mouth to stifle ... what? A laugh? A groan? She was not sure herself, and she quickened her pace to distract herself from her line of thought.

Now there was another soul to be considered, of course – the baby growing inside her. A new life. She allowed herself to imagine that her unborn child might have a twin somewhere, a fellow traveller already out in the world and unaware. She was scared by her new-found circumstances – terrified – but the wonder of it all transcended every other consideration.

Her father would be appalled, furious – that much was certain. When he found out, he would roar at her, and shout obscenities. He might call her a whore and say she had disgraced him, brought their family name into disrepute. He would want to hit her – just as he sometimes hit her mother. But she was certain that in spite of the temptation, and the undoubted provocation, he would not raise his hand against her.

Philip Kritovoulos was a violent man, but never to her. She was his most precious possession (possession was quite the right word), and he would not allow her to be damaged, even if her recent actions and their consequences would see his reputation dragged through the mire.

Next, she thought about her lover, lying on his sickbed. Badr Khassan was a good man and would make a good father one day. But their situation was hopeless. If he were to stand by her side now, it would bring down his death sentence, nothing more.

She thought about Badr's friend, Patrick Grant, and what he had said when she had confided in him, told him about the baby, and that she was leaving...

'Badr loves you – you should tell him,' he had said. 'He will be a good father for the baby, a good husband for you.'

'I know he loves me – that is precisely why he must not know. I have to leave him behind. It is the only way. And since I have to leave him, since we must part, there is no good in telling him. There will be pain enough to bear – I would spare him the worst.'

'This cannot be right,' he said. 'There must be something more that I can do.'

She had smiled at him and raised a hand to his face.

'Apart from anything else, more than anything else, you are his best friend,' she said. 'He will need you now.'

He had turned from her then so that he was beyond her reach, and began walking away with his chin down on his chest like a chastened child. She left her hand extended towards him, but he did not turn back, and some small part of her was glad.

He was right, in any case. Badr would be a good father for her baby, and a good husband. But not here, and not now.

Two men concealed in the shadows of a dark alleyway waited until Isabella was long out of sight before stepping into the dawn light and crossing the street...

It was Patrick who came for him in the burning bedroom half an hour later – Patrick who found that the flames had already taken hold beyond any hope of extinguishing them. Crawling on his hands and knees beneath the worst of it, he had found his friend by touch rather than by sight. The big man was unconscious, half in and half out of the bed, some of his clothing already on fire.

'Wake up!' Patrick bellowed, as he hauled and pulled at the dead weight. 'Come on, Badr! Wake up!'

33

Yaminah opened her eyes. The room was quiet now, the storytelling over. Much to Constantine's annoyance, it often happened like this. He would be in full flow, almost lost in the tale, when he would become aware of the change in her breathing. No matter how many times she told him it was a compliment – that he made her feel so safe and relaxed here on his bed with him that a peaceful snooze was all but inevitable – still he preferred to take offence.

'Some teacher I am,' he would say, when the

time came to wake her. 'Even the attention of a classroom of one is too much for me to hold.'

'You're not my teacher. I have plenty of those. But sleeping with you – falling asleep with you – is my favourite thing,' she would reply, sitting up and brushing the creases from her clothes, fixing her hair and checking the corners of her mouth for trails of drool. 'Lying here, with you. Your voice is like soft music to me ... it leaves me powerless.' She would pretend to swoon, falling backwards on to his bed.

He would snort and busy himself putting away the props, opening the curtains and blinds once more so that the daylight might banish the intimacy, like a traitor.

What he overlooked, and what she was careful never to remind him of, was how she pleased him in sleep just as she did when she was awake. Her calm invariably pulled him down like quicksand, so that he almost always followed her into unconsciousness. He was happiest beside her, in this realm or any other.

This time, however, it was different. She awoke with her head in his lap, as always, but now there was a hardness there, unmistakable against her cheek. Gently she raised her head to see if he was awake, but unlike any time before, she had been first to resurface. His eyes were closed, his breathing slow and deep. Gently, so gently, she reached out a hand and touched the solid ridge beneath the sheet. It felt hot, and emboldened by the strangeness of the situation, she stroked it lightly. It twitched against her hand. She almost laughed out loud, but sensed a seriousness and a certainty at the same time and bit into her lip instead. Here was a bubble not to be lightly burst.

Constantine was wont to say that he was half dead already, dead from the waist down. Here, however, hard and heavy as a length of lead pipe, lying tensed and ramrod straight against the lower part of his stomach, was the surest sign of life.

Yaminah, still a virgin at eighteen, had dabbled with boys and they with her – kisses and caresses and wandering hands. She lacked her mother's height, but the curves that had arrived with her adulthood, coupled with quick wits and a mercurial, spirited manner, meant she had attracted male attention from early on. She was a bolt of energy, enlivening any room she walked into, and boys and men reached for her like a will-o'-the-wisp in hopes of luck and a better life.

Her heart was Constantine's – always had been – but given the circumstances, there had been dalliances along the way. She had been held tightly enough by one admirer or another to know when a man wanted her. Here now, long after she had accepted things as they were, was proof of Constantine's desire – like a longed-for guest at a party and certainly better late than never. This might change everything – and if perfection was out of the question, here at least was the hope of a few steps in the right direction.

On an impulse she bowed her head and placed her lips upon the outline of its tip, the gentlest of welcoming kisses. The hardness twitched again, pushed against her mouth of its own free will, and to her surprise she pushed back, softening and opening her lips to feel the whole of it. She felt a wetness, in her mouth and between her own legs.

Constantine groaned, a heavy, gravelly sound deep in his throat, and she stopped at once, suddenly mortified. She sat up, blushing crimson, set both feet back upon the floor and glanced at him over one shoulder. His eyes were open but he took a moment even to notice she was still there. Quickly he bundled his sheets across his middle and ran a hand through his thick black hair. She knew at once that it was not the first time – that he had felt this way before today. She felt a fluttering in her chest and looked away.

'Some teacher I am,' he said, as usual.

Yaminah laughed, too loudly. Constantine looked at her with an expression close to pity.

'I have somewhere to be,' she said, standing quickly and making for the door.

34

He lay in a tangle of sheets. The paradox of the disarray did not escape him – quite a confusion for a man who moved so little in bed. Rather than his own limited movements, it was Yaminah who was the messy sleeper. Always when they slept together he awoke to the chaos left behind by her dreaming.

There was a tangled knot inside his head as well. After six years tethered to his own lifeless legs, hope of anything more was a dangerous thing, a threat to the world he had built out of light and dark, and shadow shapes, and then accepted as his all. He had Yaminah too, a brightly coloured bird with whom to share his cage. Her devotion had clipped her wings, clipped them as surely as his own – and hope ... well, hope might change everything.

Here was an interloper, a newly arrived ... possibility ... a wandering salesman offering goods of uncertain provenance and unproven value. There was no denying the change to his status quo. For weeks there had been, from time to time, moments of feeling between his legs. The sensation was there now, while he stared at the bump of it, beneath a rumple of bedclothes. It amazed him he had even recognised the feeling for what it was after all this time, faint but unmistakable.

He dismissed the notion like a sometime friend who might yet make him look a fool. He turned his face towards the windows instead and reached back behind his head for the ropes to open the blinds and shutters. Winter sunlight poured through them, and he squinted and then closed his eyes against the glare, hoping it might have burned away his fantasies of a different life, perhaps a better life; his old life.

In the midst of his tortured thinking he noticed that the sounds from beyond the window glass were louder than usual, almost a cacophony. Threaded through the normal symphony – the hustle and bustle of the city dwellers, the shouts and cries of the traders in the markets, the hubbub of conversations conducted in a score of different languages – was an unfamiliar, discordant note. Anxious voices rose and fell with questions, accu-

311

sations and prayers. From some of the womenfolk came the ululations for a death in the family.

The Turks were at the walls once more right enough, and their arrival was like a terrier's appearance by a nest of ducklings. If there had been anywhere for the locals to go, they would be gone. Trapped as so many of them were, between their walls and the sea, they could only quack and clamour, panic and pray.

His city, he knew, was well accustomed to the arrival of would-be conquerors. While he ignored his toes – and everything else below his waist – he lost himself in the paintings and maps around his bedroom walls. The story of Constantinople, from inception until now, was laid out in sequence before him like the moments of a life that might flash before the eyes of a dying man.

Though no one's intention – neither the artists who made them nor the teachers who hung them there for his pleasure – together they revealed a sad decline. The product of work spread across a millennium, they showed what had once been, as well as what Constantinople had become. He closed the shutters once more, plunging the room into near darkness, and used the reflected light from the polished bronze dish – the same that illuminated his shadow plays – to pick out each work in turn.

Obvious in the oldest was the ordered tartan of streets laid out by Constantine the Great. Order and control on the eastern frontier; Western civilisation self-consciously realised in the East. Rome had felt, to the new emperor and his generals, too far from the empire's frontiers, and so they had

312

built *Nova Roma,* New Rome, to take her place.

Prince Constantine gazed in admiration, undiminished by years of scrutiny, at the result of six years of labour completed more than a thousand years before. Conceived and realised as heaven on earth, New Rome grew to beguile and captivate all who saw it, a lustrous white jewel set between the twin sapphires of the Golden Horn and the Sea of Marmara. They were Romans in a new Rome, but soon the inhabitants took to calling the place Constantinople in honour of their benefactor.

In more recent centuries, in artworks by locals and visitors, the diamond's flaws lay unintentionally revealed: a once lovely woman, ripe fruit of many mothers and fathers, now trading on memories and hiding from her own reflection.

As the later maps and paintings had it, Constantine's Constantinople was made mostly of empty spaces, a gap-toothed grimace in an ageing maw. A dream made real, it had been a place fit for Roman emperors. Colonnaded streets, their towering pillars taller and wider than trees; elegant squares filled with sculpted gods and emperors; grand buildings styled to humble passers-by; trophies looted and pilfered from old Rome and from every town and city in between; marvels from elsewhere grafted on to the body of the newborn wonder of an ancient world.

Admirers had been drawn from the beginning. But what once had seemed unattainable and out of reach fell prey in time to grabbing hands. Constantine played the dish's light from one work to another, exposing the fall from grace.

Six years, much of the time spent in this same

313

room, had made the young prince unusually sensitive to the approach of others. Yaminah, wary as a fawn, sometimes arrived at his door without his knowing. Mostly though he felt he was becoming some sort of spider, his chamber the heart of an invisible web that twanged and jangled with the vibrations of intruders. So it was now, and he turned the dish to fix the beam on his closed door. He heard shuffling feet, and before their owner could speak he called:

'Come in, whoever you are – I can hear you breathing.'

The handle turned and the door was pushed inwards. Into the beam of light stepped the plump figure of Doukas, one of his father's closest confidantes and chief historian of the empire.

'Sorry if I'm disturbing you, my young prince,' he said in a voice as warm and rich as melting butter. 'But I feel the need of conversation, yours most of all.'

Doukas was holding one hand up to his face to avert the glare of the beam, but he was un-mistakable even before he spoke.

Realising it was friend and not foe, Constantine swung the dish away so as to let his teacher's eyes adjust to the near darkness. He returned the beam of light to a painting depicting his city's darkest hour – a devastation meted out not by heathen Turkmen but by Christian soldiers bearing the sign of the cross.

During the past eleven hundred and more years, he knew, the place had been besieged over and over again. The great defensive wall – two in fact, one behind the other and fronted by a deep, brick-lined moat they called the *fosse* – stretched from the waters of the Golden Horn in the north to the Sea of Marmara in the south. They had stood for a thousand years at least, a wonder of his own and any age, and never breached.

Constantine kept his light fixed upon the huge painting, one that had outlived its artist's name. In harrowing detail it portrayed the coming of Christian crusaders two centuries and more before his birth, and the havoc they had unleashed in their bitterness and envy. Denied all other hope of spoils, they had ripped their way through every street and avenue, every lane and alleyway, every home from the lowest to the highest. Men and women and children were raped, and most of them finished with the sword or other cruelty; their corpses were set alight as kindling to feed flames that left less than half the city standing. Ruined and defiled and never fully to recover, Constantinople lost her beauty for ever, to puckered scars and crooked bones.

'You're a gloomy lad, Costa,' said Doukas, crossing to the prince's bed and sitting heavily beside him, so that Constantine fairly bounced upon his mattress. While he looked at the highlighted painting of Greek maidens cowering in the shadow of a porticoed church frontage and being put to the sword by wild-eyed crusaders, their hands red and dripping, he reached out and patted the boy's thigh.

'And do you remember the words of our fellow historian on the subject of the razing of our city by those we ought to have been able to count as our brothers in Christ?' he asked.

315

Constantine smiled and leaned his head back against his mounded pillows. His eyes were open but he let the world split apart – like a pomegranate and as full of crimson moments – so that he was freed from his broken frame and walking instead along the paved surface of the Mese, the middle way that was the backbone of the old Roman city.

'Ah, now,' he said. 'Let me think. You mean, of course, our friend Akominatos ... Nicetas Akominatos.'

'Good. Now go on,' said Doukas, lacing his chubby fingers together on his luxuriously upholstered lap.

He had schooled his pupil in the Socratic tradition, insisting that all meaningful knowledge be committed to memory. On their first morning together as teacher and pupil, when the prince was just eight years old, Doukas had begun by telling him that memory and only memory was the path to wisdom. According to Socrates, said Doukas, writing was a distraction from the path of truth.

He began to quote from the master.

'This discovery of yours will create forgetfulness in the learners' souls, because they will not use their memories,' he had told the boy, revelling in the notion. 'They will trust to the external written characters and not remember of themselves. The specific you have discovered is an aid not to memory but to reminiscence, and you give your disciples not truth, but only the semblance of truth.'

Constantine began to recite what he had learned by heart and by rote.

'How shall I begin to tell of the deeds wrought

316

by these nefarious men!' he said, summoning the account laid down by Akominatos more than two centuries before, when memories of the deeds were warm like torn flesh.

'Alas, the images, which ought to have been adored, were trodden underfoot!' he continued easily, strolling in his mind through a version of the city he had conjured from maps and other images but never known, never seen.

He had nonetheless learned to use this creation of his mind's eye for the safe stowage of his learning. The street he walked was filled with people, and with incident, but silent. For Constantine it was as though his head had been plunged into deep water.

There was action all around: people gesticulated wildly at one another and their mouths moved in impassioned speech, men and women fought and died, children cried or ran. But there was no sound for the prince beyond a dull roaring in his ears. He turned into a well-remembered side street to his left and watched, unsurprised, as a broken and bloodied saint, clad in filthy robes and holding a battered gilded cup, emerged from a doorway and stumbled and fell beside an open sewer. An armoured man ran to his side, as though to help him, and instead used the toe of one foot to roll the prostrate figure into the foulness. His plight triggered his recitation of the next section of the historian's account.

'Alas, the relics of the holy martyrs were thrown into unclean places! Then was seen what one shudders to hear, namely, the divine body and blood of Christ was spilled upon the ground or

317

thrown about. They snatched the precious reliquaries, thrust into their bosoms the ornaments which these contained, and used the broken remnants for pans and drinking cups...'

Doukas watched enthralled, and not for the first time, as his student spoke from a far-off place. For Constantine it was a walk through familiar places. The anonymous passers-by were dimly lit, or in faded hues, so that the principal figures upon which he relied – vivid and bright, commanding his attention – had centre stage at all times.

He turned right and followed a street parallel to the Mese. Fine buildings lined the way, columns and pillars, statuary and towering doorways of ancient timber. Off to his right he glimpsed one curving end of the hippodrome, built for Constantine the Great and topped with four bronze horses, miraculous and enormous, the work of the genius Lysippos. Ahead of him, beyond the end of the street, stood the unmistakable edifice of the Church of Divine Wisdom, the Church of St Sophia. The pale blue dome of its roof, a bulging eye, stared unblinking into heaven above, wilfully blind as always to the suffering of her faithful.

'Nor can the violation of the Great Church be listened to with equanimity. For the sacred altar, formed of all kinds of precious materials and admired by the whole world, was broken into bits and distributed among the soldiers, as was all the other sacred wealth of so great and infinite splendour.'

From the main doorway of the church poured a river of unspeakable horror, human and animal excrement bearing whole and partial corpses of men and women, as well as of beasts. The surging river of filth broke around the base of a great stone column a hundred feet high. Atop it stood a colossal sculpture of Justinian, the last great Roman, seated upon a mighty horse. He was styled after Achilles, with gleaming breastplate and helmet topped with a cock's comb. In his left hand he held a globe that declared that the shadow of his grasp stretched across the whole world.

Constantine strolled towards the torrent unsurprised and unafraid. Among the waste and the bodies of the dead were holy relics – reliquaries and ossuaries, vessels of gold studded with precious stones, all of it borne upon a tide of still-warm piss and shit.

'When the sacred vases and utensils of unsurpassable art and grace and rare material, and the fine silver, wrought with gold, were to be borne away as booty, mules and saddled horses were led to the very sanctuary of the temple. Some of these, which were unable to keep their footing on the splendid and slippery pavement, were stabbed when they fell, so that the sacred pavement was polluted with blood and filth.'

He was inside the church now, watching soldiers fight among themselves, rolling in all manner of foulness as they wrestled one another for this or that scrap of gold or silver. From the wellspring of the torrent of filth arose an unmistakable figure – Mary, mother of God, clad in soiled and soaking robes that clung to her body and revealed every curve and fold. While she had the look and shape of the Virgin, she was pure no longer. Her pale blue raiment was torn so that her breasts were exposed. Her legs too were clearly to be seen, and, most alarming of all, a wanton smile played upon her too-red lips.

The imagery was vivid and uncompromising, as Constantine had learned it had to be if memory was properly to be stimulated, goaded into recall.

'Nay more, a certain harlot, a sharer in their guilt, a minister of the furies, a servant of the demons, a worker of incantations and poisonings, insulting Christ, sat in the patriarch's seat, singing an obscene song and dancing frequently...'

Outside once more, the defiled church behind him, he made his way back home, taking this turn and that at random, sure that he would encounter all he needed to summon the rest of the words of the long-dead scribe.

In a doorway a couple struggled. A man, clad in mail, had the near-naked woman by the throat. His free hand held a cruel blade, the point drawing blood from a spot beneath her ribcage. Her skirts were forced up around her waist and he had forced himself between her legs. His hips were grinding against her and into her and his gaping mouth was at her neck while her tears fell. Elsewhere, wailing fathers were dragged from their wives and children and carried off, or cut down before them. Children begged and wept and howled, and mothers tore at their clothes and hair and fell upon the ground.

'No one was without a share in the grief. In the alleys, in the streets, in the temples, complaints, weeping, lamentations, grief, the groaning of men, the shrieks of women, wounds, rape, captivity, the separation of those most closely united.'

His recitation at an end, he felt the city of his imagination disappear behind him. Ahead of him was his bedroom, always his bedroom. He saw himself upon the bed, his teacher beside him. He closed his eyes.

'Excellent, my dear Costa,' said Doukas, turning from the painting and looking into his student's eyes. 'Most excellent.'

After a minute or so, the prince opened his eyes and fixed them squarely upon those of his friend.

'The Turks encamped before the wall – how many?' he asked.

Doukas looked down at his lap for a moment, and then back into Constantine's face.

'The word from our lookouts is that they number perhaps five thousand,' he said.

Constantine smiled as he considered the frown lines etched deep into his teacher's brow.

'But...?' he said, raising his chin to emphasise the question.

'But there are many more on their way. Of that there is no doubt.'

Constantine said nothing, just kept his eyes on Doukas's plump face.

'Many, many more,' said the scholar. 'Mehmet advances from his capital at Edirne with every man available to him. Those of our people who have already faced them say the assembled host is ... uncountable.'

Constantine nodded. 'I am sure that is how it appears,' he said. 'I must admit that part of me would relish seeing such a gathering at first hand.'

'I have no such ambition,' said Doukas. 'Unfortunately we will both have the opportunity to gaze upon them in their glory before the week is out.'

'What keeps them?' asked Constantine. 'I'm sure they're more than keen to get on with it. What do the heathens call our wall ... the bone in Allah's throat?'

'Indeed, my prince – the bone in Allah's throat,' said Doukas. 'Sad to say, he hasn't actually choked on it yet.'

'Now, now, Doukas,' said Constantine, raising an eyebrow. 'Are we not all people of the Book? Muslims, Christians, Jews – same father, different name.'

'Different people,' said Doukas sadly. 'I doubt if Allah means us any harm. But Mehmet and his hunting dogs?' He left the thought floating in the air between them, like a bad smell.

'Dogs? Dogs? Come, come, Doukas – first you wish harm on our Father in heaven, and now you call his children names.'

'All his children,' said Doukas. 'And therein lies the disgrace of it. There may be as many Christians as heathens marching towards us, under the sultan's banners. Perhaps it is the end of days, right enough.'

'Faith, my friend,' chided Constantine, placing a hand gently on one of Doukas's chubby thighs. 'Now is the time for faith. How many sieges has our city faced in a thousand years?'

'More than a score,' replied Doukas, without looking up.

'Twenty-two,' said Constantine. 'Allah has been trying to cough up the Wall of Theodosius for a thousand years. I fail to see why you should imagine the twenty-third will end any differently from the others.'

Doukas looked calmly into his student's face.

'I look at the sea and I watch the waves,' he said. 'I watch the waves and how they never stop moving. I look at our sea walls and see how they are locked in place. These Ottoman Turks are the sons and daughters of a restless people. They do not love cities as we do – rather they despise them, I think. Just as the sea rolls endlessly, without a moment's rest, so these Turks remain always on the move. Their hearts are happiest not in palaces or on city streets, but on the journey. We are only in their way. Our walls are an offence to everything they believe, everything they are. The waves must roll and walls must fall.'

'So why do they tarry on the journey to Constantinople?' asked the prince. 'If our presence here is so abhorrent, why don't they come at a gallop?'

Doukas stood from the bed and walked over to the windows. He looked out for a few moments, his attention caught by a long line of hand-wringing citizens walking in procession, heads down and mumbling, behind a party of priests carrying a life-size statue of the Virgin.

'They are burdened with great … machines,' he said, still watching the desperation of the faithful as they begged ceaselessly, day and night, for divine intervention.

'Machines?' said Constantine. 'Of what sort? Catapults, battering rams? All have been arrayed against the wall and always they have failed. The bone in Allah's throat can neither be coughed up

323

nor swallowed down.'

'I lack the words to describe these latest creations,' said Doukas. 'Our people in the villages beyond the walls – those who have already been defiled by the passing of the Turks – send word of great bombards.'

'Bombards?' asked Constantine, frowning. 'But we have those.'

'Not so, Costa,' said Doukas. 'Those who have seen them and lived to tell the tale describe machines longer than a house is tall, big enough for a man to stand inside.'

Constantine waited for his teacher to continue.

'The largest of them launches a stone as big as a hay wagon for a distance of a mile and more,' he said. 'I have heard them called "city-takers" and so cumbersome are they it takes a hundred men and as many beasts to haul the things a mile or two a day.'

'City-takers,' said Constantine. His tone was all at once dark, like clouds gathered for a sudden storm. 'Perhaps Allah's fingers are finally long enough to reach down and pluck the bone out once and for all.'

35

All the while Mehmet and his force are advancing upon the city, a lammergeier soars high above.

Reflected upon the sheen of his golden eyes, the Great City beneath appears a tattered patchwork.

The encircling walls still seem immutable as a mountain range, yet even these have been ground down by years, like an old lady's teeth. Built more than a thousand years before, they defy every attacker that seeks to challenge them. Behind the walls, hunkered in their shadows or exposed to the light of day, the citizens live their lives amid a web of streets and alleyways and ancient buildings. Some structures are grand enough, the churches and shrines especially, but the city now is made as much of empty spaces as anything upstanding. Constantinople is in the process of forgetting herself.

She has never truly recovered, after all, from violation at the hands of Christian men, soldiers of the cross who came by sea in 1204. That rape, and by her own brothers, was more than she could bear, and the hurt inflicted then has never healed. Now, too, the dementia of ages is at work, like a rising tide of darkness and absence.

Where once there were homes and businesses, streets and lanes crowded with workshops and market stalls, places of industry and endeavour, now there are swathes of scrubby heath – grasses, bushes and even trees reclaiming and smothering the work of men. Saddest of all is the mighty hippodrome – once the home of charioteers and baying crowds. What was then a wonder is now in precarious decline. Empty plinths lament the absence of the great bronze horses sculpted for Alexander the Great, trophies of a distant war but looted two and a half centuries before.

Mehmet and his Turkmen might covet the place like no other, but the once perfect picture is growing smudged and indistinct, blind spots fogging and blurring the image, piece by piece. The Great City is like a book left open in the rain, and now half the words are washed away. Some of the loss is the product of neglect, but much is just the merciless erosion of old age, the inevitable failing of one who has lived long enough, or too long.

A city is a dream shared by its inhabitants, and now the blissful sleep of Byzantium is past and cruel awakening morning approaches. In sleep she dreams she is young and lovely, as she was and thought she always would be. But when she looks at herself in the mirror, in the first light of day, she will see that time has caught her.

Where once the dream made perfect sense, now many scenes seem meaningless and vague, doomed to the oblivion of forgetfulness. All around the place are statues and memorials whose very names the people have forgotten. Above their sorry heads, on walls and sculpted porticos held aloft by fluted columns, are fine inscriptions, but the origins and meanings of those thoughts and words are mostly lost as well.

The dream, the original, essential truth that bound it all together, as mortar binds bricks, is turning to powder and blowing away on the wind. Since the inhabitants no longer remember, or even care, what stories once explained their city, those have been replaced by superstitions and rumours and by folk myths and tales to frighten children.

This siege by the Ottoman Turks is in many ways the lesser of two evils, for Constantinople is already busy dying from the inside out.

Just visible on the outer edge of the bird's vision

are the incoming tides of two Ottoman armies. It was no accident that set Mehmet out from Edirne on a Friday. Rather, he chose the holiest day of the Muslim week so his soldiers might not fail to grasp the sacred nature of their quest. He rode out from his capital accompanied by his holy men, his sheiks and his viziers, on the crest of a wave of soldiers and animals that seemed, to all who witnessed its passing, to reach from horizon to horizon. Horns blared and men howled and cheered as they poured away from their city and out across the landscape.

Impressive though it is, driving before it a flotsam of terrifying rumour that is itself enough to engulf and sweep away all save those who follow the Prophet, still it is only half the sultan's army. For every soldier or cavalryman that departed Edirne in the west, the same again flocked to a second mustering station, at Bursa in Anatolia, and those too are on their way to the Great City, from the east. Constantinople is a solitary white rock in the path of an encircling torrent surging towards it from all sides.

Ready for them – as ready as he can be at least – is the Christian emperor Constantine. He is more than twice the age of Mehmet. He has had his chancellor's office seek out every man within the walls who is fit to fight, and now the task is complete and there are fewer than eight thousand names on the list.

The emperor is a stag at bay, horns lowered towards the snapping jaws of many foes. But he has fought before, and often, and must put his faith in the wall, and in God.

To add to the citizens' woes, there are Christians by the thousand among the advancing force. At the core of the army are the sultan's janissaries – professional soldiers, cavalrymen and gunners. Born under the cross, they were captured as boys and turned to Islam under the shadow of the scimitar. There are Christian mercenaries too, soldiers of fortune ready to side with the Muslims or anyone else in return for gold and silver.

Like the emperor, his subjects also put their faith in the wall, and in God. Constantinople is a city built as a heaven on earth, with the emperor as God's anointed and appointed champion. Prayer and ritual are everywhere. Bells ring and wooden gongs boom and the holiest of holy icons are ceaselessly on the move through the streets, giving hope to the faithful. Here is a stone from Christ's tomb, his crown of thorns, the nails from his cross. Here too the bones of his apostles and the head of John the Baptist.

While the market squares and taverns of other cities might ring to different talk, in Constantinople every man speaks of religion. Every man knows God's will better than his neighbour. They bicker among themselves and dismiss as heretic and apostate any whose opinion differs from their own by word or deed. In this way they make enemies of all – especially their fellow Christians in the West. Even as they damn their neighbours, so they are damned themselves.

They look up to heaven, but only the birds look back.

Close to the city, almost in the shadow of the wall now (having departed weeks before the guns), are the crews tasked with transporting Orban's bombards. The Great Gun alone requires a team of hundreds of men and scores of draught animals. It takes up the length of three wagons, chained together to support the barrel, its early lustre dulled now to a malevolent glimmer. Oxen moan and haul and their handlers struggle beside them, yard by yard.

Yet more teams of men – labourers, carpenters and craftsmen of every sort – busy themselves further ahead again, levelling a path and building bridges to ease the passage of the Great Gun and the rest of the artillery train.

Also on the move, almost insignificant but important nonetheless, are other figures, with other plans. Chief among these, moving like water beetles upon the surface of the Sea of Marmara, is a flotilla of three ships. As they alter course to make for the entrance to the Golden Horn and the imperial harbour within, the lammergeier's attention is briefly fixed upon them.

Just within reach of his sight, like dots before his wondrous eyes, are the figures moving upon the deck of the foremost vessel.

36

Prince Constantine was hardly alone in mourning all that had been lost to the Crusaders in 1204. The Byzantine heart had broken then, and while it kept on beating, its ancient rhythm was lost for all time.

Aboard the ship leading the little flotilla towards the royal harbour of Constantinople, Lẽna's mind too was filled with the city's plight. As a student of war she had been taught the sad tale by her father, so that she knew it by rote; as a willing soldier of Christ, she felt the pain of the city's wounding like a knife in her own gut.

She breathed deeply, relishing the clean, fresh taste of the salt air and letting it cleanse her thoughts of all the horror that had unfolded in the city in the name of Christ.

She felt as though life itself was re-entering her body with each new breath. It was the first day since their sea voyage had begun weeks before that she had felt anything like well. For almost all of that time she had been beyond miserable, racked by a seasickness that swelled to fill every corner of her being. For more than two weeks, the fat-bellied carrack had wallowed and rolled in the ceaseless swell. Truth be told, her incapacity had served its purpose by keeping her below deck and out of sight. Despite her pleasure and relief in the open air, she took care to keep a scarf loosely draped around the lower half of her face.

She gazed towards a thin white line etched across the landscape in the distance – part, she assumed, of Constantinople's sea wall. The feature was barely visible through mist and haze, and all the while she peered ahead, she massaged the aching and tender muscles of her stomach.

When John Grant had first informed her that he had secured passage for them both, all the way to the city, her delight had matched his own. The

330

bloodstained angel on the tor had reminded her who she was, after all. While the lightning flashed and the thunder roared, she had seen the path she must follow. Her death postponed – a martyr's death – had been a near-unbearable burden. She had escaped the flames but had allowed herself to be carried into hell just the same. Her guilt had lain upon her life with all the crushing weight of a gravestone, until everything good had been squeezed out of her like juice from an apple, leaving only a husk.

But the angel had come back for her, had revealed herself and given her the strength and the reason to remember who she was and what she was for. She had been given back her child, the son upon whom she had turned her back, and now she would follow him to the end. He was bound for Constantinople in hope of saving a girl. Lẽna would go there too, and the soul she might save was her own.

The price John Grant had paid for their transport was the promise of their service in the war to come. Their ship would be one of three commissioned to carry a force of armed men to Constantinople, and the addition of two more professional soldiers was apparently welcome. Lẽna had passed for a man before and would do so again provided no one paid too close attention.

John Grant would do the talking and she would provide silent, brooding backup. Given the anonymity afforded by the always grim and dehumanising conditions aboard a troop ship, it would only be a matter of keeping her face obscured, and shunning contact with the ship's company. As it had turned out, her sickness put her below with all those dozens similarly afflicted. For the duration she had been just another heaving mess curled in a corner and best avoided.

The commander of the operation was a Genoan noble, and the money for the whole enterprise – the private army of eight hundred men, their arms and the vessels to carry them – was coming out of his own purse. All of it was in answer to the latest desperate cry for help from the emperor himself.

It seemed their own need to reach Constantinople was in tune with a greater calling that was penetrating the distant reaches of the world like ripples from a stone tossed into a pond.

'Badr was right,' John Grant had said on his return from the harbour and his successful negotiations.

'About what?' she had asked.

'About the Ottomans. Badr said years ago they were on the rise – and we fought for them together more than once. But I wonder if even he would have predicted how high they might reach.'

Lẽna had nodded, her eyes raised so that she looked beyond him.

'Their desire for Constantinople is as old as their heathen faith,' she had said. 'Their Prophet foretold the fall of the city into their hands. They have believed it ever since.'

'Well it seems a reckoning is at hand,' he had replied. 'If the winds of the same storm might drive me where I wish to go, then that is well and good.'

She had shrugged and set herself to gathering up her few possessions. His casual dismissal of the threat posed to a Christian city by a Muslim horde had caused her pain, but she held her tongue.

Their journey so far, from the claustrophobic confines of the tunnel to the sour-smelling belly of the carrack, had taken most of a year, certainly more months than she had bothered to count, and they carried only what they needed to survive. The miles that remained, separating them from their goal, mattered little. The force that drew her towards Constantinople now was greater even than that driving John Grant, though she would not have revealed as much to him.

She had spent almost the entire voyage in a miasma of nausea, either heaving the emptiness of her insides into a wooden bucket or sipping brackish water that did little more than keep her alive. From within the depths of her suffering she had recalled the long-ago journey with her father to the western isles of Scotland and the home of MacDonald of Islay. She had been just a girl then, and while the necessary sea crossings had made her queasy, out of sorts for their duration, there had been nothing to compare with the misery of this first sea voyage made in adulthood. She would have prayed to God for death except that even in extremis she had been wary of making demands upon the almighty when so much else was at stake.

More than that, seasickness aside, she was somehow at peace.

'I did not know a person could turn such a colour,' John Grant had said on one of his regular visits to her side. Despite her suffering, his attentiveness pleased her for reasons she preferred not to dwell upon. That said, if anything could make her feel worse than she already did, it was the presence of someone, anyone, who was so visibly well.

'Leave me be,' she had said. She wanted not to talk, but to listen, and the making of words had burned her raw throat so that she felt she was swallowing hot sand.

'The good news is that the captain says we'll be in the Sea of Marmara by this time tomorrow,' he had said.

'And the bad news?' she asked.

'No bad news,' he said. 'Giustiniani says the weather is changing for the better at last. The wind is behind us ... or athwart, or ... on the side of us ... or ... or anyway it's precisely where he – that is we, and especially you – would want it to be.'

'Quite the navigator, you are,' she said.

'Indeed I am,' he said. 'And I can also tell you that we will be in the city in no more than a day or two.'

Those conversations – only hours before – seemed to her like distant memories already. Whatever storm clouds were building above the Christian empire of Byzantium had apparently stirred the sea for a thousand miles around – but their weather had changed as predicted and she had awoken from her latest fitful sleep to find a sea smooth as oil and the ship steady upon it.

The near-instantaneous transformation of her condition had seemed almost magical to her and she had offered up a silent prayer of thanks. All at once she had felt able to rise – and better yet to climb out of the fetid confines of the cramped and stinking quarters below decks.

John Grant had seen her emerge through the hatchway and had joined her at once. There was still a distance between them – some wariness each retained regarding the other's intentions – but she detected something in his manner that seemed almost like hunger for her presence.

'How's your new friend?' she asked.

She was referring, he knew, to the man whose personality permeated every inch of the ship – and of the others in the flotilla.

Standing close to Giovanni Giustiniani Longo felt like proximity to a flame; in his presence there was the prospect of both warmth and danger. A head shorter than John Grant, he was as muscled as a cat. He was clean-shaven and his features were fine, with full, almost girlish lips and dark, blue-black hair. It was his eyes, however, that captured and held attention. Large, dark and deep-set beneath heavy brows, they shone with an inner light, suggestive of sharp intelligence but also of sadness, or regret. His clothes, though obviously expensive and well made, were dishevelled and worn. He seemed never to be at rest – always moving among the men, asking questions, checking gear or holding court.

As Lẽna spoke, they both watched their new-found leader busying himself with a mariner's astrolabe.

'He is in fine form,' said John Grant. 'If we must go to war, then it is good to go with one such as he.'

She said nothing in reply and he turned to look at her, troubled by her silence.

'Are you sorry you came?' he asked.

She shook her head. She had already told him she had business of her own in Constantinople.

When she had first said it, as they sat drying themselves by a hastily built fire on the riverbank after their flight through the hellish confines of the cave, he had doubted her.

He had long known that the Great City was in peril – that the Turkmen were pressing the last redoubt of Christendom in the East. Every soldier had known it for years – and some'd been drawn to the place already in hopes of rich rewards.

Both sides were paying for the services of fighting men after all – Christian and Muslim – and the swords of mercenaries would go to the highest bidder. He'd fought for both empires in his time, alongside Badr Khassan, and would have cared little for the outcome. His only motivation now was his promise – the safety of the girl. If that put him on the side of the Christians, then so be it.

But it seemed word of the city's plight had reached even Lẽna's hiding place in the convent at the Great Shrine. She knew too – and it seemed she cared, though why or how much he could not tell.

The city walls were growing clearer, rising out of the sea like a cresting wave. Their ship rode up on the back of an unexpected swell and dropped into the trough beyond. Lẽna felt her stomach turn over, and she reached above her head to grab hold of a rope and steady herself.

'What is your business here – really?' he asked. 'Why have you come?'

The nausea peaked and passed, leaving her breathless. She swallowed thickly before answering.

'I am afraid I have your Angus Armstrong to

thank for setting me on the path,' she said. 'If he had not taken me, I would not have ... I would not have got the message. That is why I spared his life.'

'Message?' he had asked.

'I had been hiding too long, is all,' she said. She ran a hand through her hair, smoothing it into shape. 'By taking me he ... he brought me back into the world.'

He knew she was leaving something out of her testimony, perhaps a great deal.

'Why there of all places?' he asked. 'Why the shrine of St James?'

'Patrick Grant's idea,' she said. 'Just somewhere far away.'

'From what?'

'From Sir Robert Jardine,' she said.

'Tell me,' he said.

She felt her skin prickle with discomfort. It was all so long ago, and breathing upon the embers of her memories filled her with heat that made her blush. She pulled the scarf up to the bridge of her nose. For all that the story pained her, the need to tell him about herself was stronger still.

'Years ago – many years ago, when I was young – I went to war.' He raised his eyebrows.

'I was a better soldier than any of them,' she said. 'I had trained as long, or longer. I was born to it, born *for* it. I do not know why – it is only the truth. My father saw to my training, as I have told you, and when we returned from Scotland I was taken before the dauphin, the man who would be king.'

He watched her scarf move as she spoke, found it easier than looking into her eyes.

'They walked me into a room full of people. I

337

should have recognised no one – I was just a peasant girl and those were great men of the realm. But as soon as I saw him, I knew he was the heir.'

'How did you know?' he asked.

'I have told you,' she said. 'God talks to me through his angels, and I listen.'

'God pointed out the prince?'

She looked at him pityingly, and he regretted his teasing tone.

'I let go of my father's hand and crossed the room towards him, and when he turned around I knelt before him.'

'And what happened?'

'What happened? People gasped is what happened,' she said. 'People gasped and then clapped and the dauphin took my hand and helped me stand.'

'And what did he make of you – just a peasant girl?'

She smiled at him indulgently.

'He made me commander of his armies,' she said. 'I was God's instrument, he said, and only I could rid his kingdom of the English.'

'And my father?'

'I was accompanied at all times by bodyguards – Scotsmen. Sir Robert Jardine was among them. Serving him – and serving me, as it turned out – was Patrick Grant.'

'Serving you?'

'Once we had our victory – when the English were on the run – Jardine saw the bigger prize. He betrayed me – betrayed all of us. He had his men murder the rest of my protectors and took me prisoner – bore me away to my enemies.

'Because I said I heard the word of God, the English called me a heretic and a witch. They held a trial for me and found me guilty and condemned me to burn in their fire.

'On the night before the dawn of my execution, Patrick Grant came for me – freed me from my prison and carried me away.'

'You talk as though the memory of it makes you sad,' said John Grant. 'My father spared you a dreadful death.'

'I do not deny that,' she said.

'So what is wrong?' he asked.

'What is wrong is that another died in my place,' she said. It seemed she could not bring herself to look at him as she said the words, and she gazed out to sea instead.

'The English commander could not bear the loss of face,' she continued. 'Rather than admit to my escape, he had his men seize another girl – a peasant girl like me, but one who had done them no harm. It was she who suffered my fate instead. They cut her hair like me and dressed her like me – told the waiting crowd she was me. She had done no harm – to them or to anyone else – and yet they tied her to a stake and had the flames consume her.'

John Grant was quiet, considering her words.

'The death of that other girl should not be your burden,' he said at last. 'You were not there. You could not have known.'

'I let him take me,' she said.

'What do you mean?'

'I was afraid,' she said. 'I was afraid to burn in their fire.'

'Blame my father, then,' he said. 'He was the one who carried you away.'

'I could have stopped him,' she said.

'Who?'

'I could have stopped your father, accepted my fate.'

She looked him squarely in the eye.

'I can stop anyone,' she said. There was no note of idle boasting in her voice, only a statement of fact.

'Well what have we here?'

The question came from a man standing behind them. Like the rest of the mercenaries aboard, he spoke in the Tuscan dialect, and both Lẽna and John Grant understood him at once. So engrossed had they been in their own conversation, they had not noticed he was close enough to overhear.

They turned sharply to face him. Out of the corner of his eye John Grant saw that Giustiniani had heard the question too – or more likely its angry tone. While the three of them stood eyeing one another, more and more men on deck became aware of a sudden change of mood in the air and stopped what they were doing, the better to watch.

'What have we here?' the man asked again. He was in his middle years, lean and muscled – the product of hard work and harder fighting. Realising he had gained an audience, and relishing it, he raised his voice for all to hear.

'This one has a lady friend,' he said, gesturing at John Grant. He made a grab for the scarf that partially concealed Lẽna's face, but she stepped smoothly out of his reach. There was a laugh, and some catcalls as the watchers warmed to the moment. It had been a long and uncomfortable voyage, and here, suddenly, was a wholly unexpected and welcome distraction.

John Grant shot a glance at Giustiniani. The commander had set down the astrolabe and was watching the scene with an expression that was somewhere between surprise and dismay. For all that he seemed interested, his stance suggested he was inclined to let natural justice run its course.

'Well let's have a look at you, then,' said the soldier, and this time he stepped forward as though to grab Lẽna by the shoulders. Despite the enervating toll exacted by the seasickness upon her muscles and her senses, the lunge might as well have been made in slow motion. As her assailant began to close the distance between them, she stepped not away from him but towards, turning her right shoulder as she did so and dropping into a half-crouch. His momentum, coupled with the rolling movement of the ship, was suddenly to her advantage rather than his. Her right hand grabbed the man's crotch, her left snapped shut on his throat, and in one graceful, effortless movement she propelled him into a forward somersault over her knee.

He landed flat on his back on the deck with a solid sound that made the onlookers grimace and raise their shoulders in sympathy. When she knelt down on him, her knee on his neck, the point of Angus Armstrong's knife was hovering just above his right eye.

'Hold there!'

It was the voice of Giustiniani, and he was striding towards them. By the time he reached

341

them, Lẽna had straightened and stood up. She spun the knife in the air so that she could catch the tip and offer him the handle. He stopped and stared at the weapon. Like everyone else, he had missed the moment when she had made it appear. He held his hands up and shook his head.

'No, no,' he said. 'That clearly belongs to you – but I would rather you put it away.'

She slipped the weapon blade-first under the cuff of her right sleeve, until it was out of sight once more.

Giustiniani looked at her questioningly, and in reply she raised a hand and pulled away her scarf. She looked him in the eye without blinking, and he returned her gaze evenly.

'What business have you here, madam?' he asked.

John Grant opened his mouth to speak, but the commander held up a hand to silence him.

'I have deceived you,' she said. 'But if it is war you are bringing to the Turk, then I too have skills that are of use.'

Giustiniani looked down at his winded and bested soldier, who had just begun to move – rolling on to his stomach and rising to his knees, his eyes wide and staring. He was a veteran of many battles. The commander had seen him stand and fight and hold his own when others might have fled. Yet this woman had tossed him aside like an empty coat.

'My battles are not fought by women,' he said.

'More fool you,' she said. 'And so what would you have me do? We travel together, this lad and I, and we fight together.' She glanced at John

Grant and he nodded.

'I have no time for this,' said Giustiniani. 'We make port in a few hours and my fight is there, not here on this ship.'

He pointed at John Grant and addressed him directly.

'*You* are in my service,' he said. 'What arrangements you seek to make for your ... your travelling companion are your own affair.'

He turned away, waving at them with one large hand. In his mind's eye he watched once more as his soldier turned a somersault in the air before flopping on to the deck like a landed fish.

Without turning back he said:

'I would ask only that you do no more harm to any of the men.'

There was laughter at this, as one by one the onlookers began talking among themselves, marvelling at what had just happened.

The soldier Lẽna had overpowered was on his feet, brushing down his clothes and wiping his face with his hands.

'Who are you?' he asked.

'I am Joan of Arc,' she said.

37

Yaminah could feel the blood pulsing hot in her face as she hurried from Prince Constantine's bedchamber. The heels of her shoes clip-clipped on the stone floor of the corridor, and she raised one hand to her cheek to conceal the signs of her embarrassment. It was a needless gesture. The palace was all but empty. So close to the walls, and to the sight, sound and smell of the Turkish army, any and all that could had departed for less unseemly circumstances.

Even the air inside the palace reeked of the cloying damp of a winter without end, mixed with dread of whatever was to come. The cold, humiliating stench hung like a shroud, ready to enfold the dead. Yaminah made her way through halls and courtyards that smelled of the death of the world.

Constantinople was old, older than memory. The city had been pawed by more enemies than anyone had counted, and gnawed at from within by greed and neglect. Now it was the Ottoman Turks come to bait the tethered bear, and their hunger seemed insatiable. Bite by slavering bite, plain by plain, hill by hill and city by city they had consumed the empire until all that remained was the Great City itself.

Yaminah knew her focus should be on the present need of Constantinople. But she was a teenage girl, and youth and hope bubbled within her, alongside fear and dread. Her mind was therefore filled with thoughts of what the prince's recovery – even his partial recovery – might mean; all that might change between them. For six years she had known him only as he had been from the moment of their catastrophic meeting in the Church of St Sophia – first the boy and then the man, but always without feeling or movement in his legs.

Mostly bedridden, he was a soul set apart from

other people, from other men.

She had never once heard him complain, and his stoicism made his predicament harder to watch. Broken as he was, he carried an awful weight – the reality of his existence – and did so lightly. He was first to poke fun at himself, always quick to relieve the tension that might arise out of the thoughtless remarks of others.

From time to time she glimpsed an unfocused look in his eyes, as though he had allowed himself to drift in dreams towards a place where his legs obeyed his will, but she never asked him to share those thoughts, or to confess any sadness, and he never had.

She could not bear the word *cripple* and was quick to admonish any who used it about him in her hearing, but it lurked in the shadows just the same. Always she had liked him, and soon she loved him, but his handicap was between them every minute of the day. It was his dark half, never mentioned.

She had done this to him – or at best they had achieved the result together. She had not asked anyone to save her when she fell, but she was grateful nonetheless. He, and no one else, had had the nerve to step beneath her with arms outstretched, in defiance of gravity. He had broken her fall and she had broken his back – it was as simple as that. Then, in the aftermath, when her own fate had been uncertain (orphan that she was), it had been Constantine who had surprised everyone by insisting that *he* would take care of *her*. From his bed, while physicians shook their heads and his parents grieved for a son transformed – or an empire burdened with a crippled heir – he had summoned her.

Before all of them he had declared that she had been sent to him by Our Lady, and that having caught her it was his duty to keep hold of her ever after. His father the emperor, moved by his son's words, had consented to his wishes.

In fact it had been the emperor's companion and consort, Helena, who spoke first. Crossing to his bed, she had looked down at him, wordlessly, for what seemed an age. She was tall, so that in his dreamlike state it seemed her face floated high above him, and her dark beauty reminded him of the sharply delicate features of a hungry cat.

He lay confined and fixed upon a wooden frame that had been assembled on the orders of Leonid, most senior of the physicians – indeed a man so old his actual age was beyond the reach and knowing of everyone else at court. Leonid had declared that the prince's best hope of recovery lay in being held immobile, belted and braced within a rigid structure that might give his body the chance to mend itself.

At last Helena had reached out to Constantine, seemingly meaning to take and hold his hand in her own while she spoke. But a sharp sound, somewhere between a hiss and a tut, stayed her hand. She snapped her head around in search of its source, and her dark eyes met those of Leonid, standing by the door of the bedchamber with three grim-faced colleagues. The sound had been involuntary, escaping his lips only when he sensed she might raise the injured prince's arm, move him in any way, and the expression on his face showed he was already rebuking himself. Helena's gaze softened and she smiled at the old man until he allowed himself an apologetic grimace in return.

'Prince Constantine's words reveal to one and all the kind of boy he is ... the kind of man he will be,' she had said, pausing to look at each of the assembled, anxious faces in turn. Her own face, illuminated by sunlight through the high windows, shone with righteousness so that it was hard to look at her.

A murmur of approval had passed around the room then, like a breeze bringing relief to a room filled with stale air.

Constantine lay motionless, his eyes clouded with pain. He had been dosed with opiates but his senses remained within his control. He looked up at his father's lover, keen to hear what else she might say.

'The orphan Yaminah's veins course with imperial blood from her mother, our sister so recently laid to rest, indeed from the line of Komnenos – the same who harried the Turkmen all the way back to their homeland two and a half centuries ago,' she continued.

She paused again, and this time the low rumble of assent from her audience in the bedchamber made it clear she understood the will of the room.

'Prince Constantine has accepted the child as a gift – and who are we to gainsay him after he risked and nearly lost his life in his determination to keep her from harm? And so in his wisdom he has made us her family now. In truth, she has always been one of us.'

Having said her piece, Helena had walked purposefully back across the room until she was beside the emperor once more. Constantine Palaiologos had reached for her hand and grasped it firmly. For a moment he had seemed smaller than the woman by his side, the lesser – but who knew whether it was his own sadness or her bravura in the face of grief that had made the difference?

'So be it,' he had said, his voice fragile with the emotion of the time and the moment. 'So be it.' Without another word and with his pale eyes shining, he had led Helena from his son's bedchamber, followed by all but the physicians, who had gathered once more about the boy's bed, eddying aimlessly there like the waters of a stream about a stubborn rock.

Since that hour and day, Yaminah had been a princess of the Byzantine Empire in all but name, raised alongside Constantine, his companion and his comfort all the while. Helena had been as good as her word, and Emperor Constantine along with her. Yaminah had grown to young womanhood with their every blessing. But like a flower grown in the shade, she had struggled for want of light. She lapped up warmth like a house cat laps milk, and found most of what she needed at her prince's side.

She loved Constantine with a sharpness that sometimes made it hard for her to take a deep breath, but as the years passed and her girlish needs began to give way to those of a woman, the certainty that they could never be with one another as man and wife was a shadow on her heart, a draught of cold air that chilled her.

But now this! It was as though the golden,

warming light of the sun itself had made its presence felt, unheralded and unexpected, through a break in the clouds. She had felt the hardness of him, the heat of him. Might there be new life after years of winter? Would the warmth newly returned venture further south? And would this late spring see him walk again as well?

It was all too much to hope for and she knew it. She closed her eyes and shook her head to banish the dreams. But for all her efforts to force herself back into the world of before, back into reality, a half-smile remained immovable upon her blushing face.

Gradually, Yaminah became aware of where she was. She had taken her leave of the prince in such a state of discombobulation she had climbed stairs at random and rounded corners into a less familiar part of the sprawling palace complex. Lost in her private thoughts, she had wandered far from her own territory, indeed right into the part of the palace reserved for the emperor's consort.

She was thrust fully back into the here and now by the sound of two voices – one a man's and the other that of Helena herself. The conversation, a heated one, drifted into the corridor through a half-open door a dozen paces ahead of her on her left. It was the mention of her wedding that stopped her.

She stepped to the wall and pressed herself against the cool stone, one hand up at her mouth as though to stifle the sound of her breathing while she listened.

'It is more important now than ever,' said Helena. 'It is about the appearance of legitimacy

... of the rightful order of things ... of confidence!'

Yaminah could not identify the man's voice, but whoever he was, he sounded fearful – submissive to his mistress.

'Of course, of course,' he said. 'I understand, of course – and you are right, my lady. I meant only to enquire whether you still felt this was the best use of your time. There are so many demands on your attention now.'

'Do not patronise me,' said Helena, her voice quiet and controlled so that the threat loomed all the larger in the softness of her tone.

'The people watch our every move now,' she said. 'These are the blackest clouds ever to hang over the city. If we are seen to falter ... if any action or statement reveals a lack of resolve ... well, think about the consequences. These are the most superstitious citizens on God's earth. We must treat them like the children they are. Give them a party and they'll smile and forget, for a little while, what waits beyond the walls.'

'Of course,' said the man once more. 'All is well.'

'All must *seem* well,' said Helena, her voice rising in pitch. 'All must seem well, and while they are still celebrating the union of a prince and his bride, we shall take whatever action is required. The empire needs a backbone, and Constantine's is broken. He shall not be their undoing. He shall not be *our* undoing.'

Yaminah pressed even harder against the wall, as though to penetrate the very fabric of the building and disappear. The tiles were cool to the touch but her whole body burned, twisting in the flames of Helena's threat. She felt the colour rise higher in her cheeks. There was a jagged lump in her throat too, like a half-swallowed shard of glass, and for a moment she thought she might cry.

For all that she burned with the blood pulsing through her body, the chill of the palace pressed all around her. She was often cold within its walls, regardless of the season, but now she felt as though she must be glowing, that the light and heat radiating from her body must surely give her away, like a glow-worm in a cave.

What was this? *Why* was this? Helena meant Constantine harm – that much seemed clear. All in an instant, and for the first time, Yaminah saw life in this place for what it was. The palace, the whole city, was constantly awash with rumour and plotting, that much she had always known. Some courtier was on the rise while another was out of favour. This wife was consorting with a lover half her age while that one was drunk on wine by noon every day.

Hour by hour the dramas and intrigues flowed like currents rippling the surface of the Sea of Marmara. Often blood was spilled. Guilty or innocent – who could tell? The key to survival was to turn a blind eye. Yaminah kept track of as much as she could – which was a great deal. Often she had had to clamp a hand across her mouth to stifle a gasp at some or other revelation. But now she felt the tide, a power far greater than her own, pulling at her feet and threatening to sweep her away. She clung to the wall for fear of losing everything.

There was movement in the room beyond. The conversation had drawn to its close and there was the shuffle of footsteps and the rustling of expensive garments. She must not be found here at such a moment. She had no real business near Helena's apartments after all; even without the complication of having been in a position to overhear such words – private, sinister words – she would have struggled to explain her presence there. If Helena were to catch her eavesdropping ... well, the mere possibility replaced her blushes with a prickling chill. The urge to turn and run was all but overwhelming, and it was some other, better part of her that had her stand firmly in place. Any attempted flight over marble flagstones in hard-heeled shoes would have betrayed her utterly; instead she remained still, fixed like a flower pressed between the pages of a book.

Helena, tall and dark, slipped from the room like a resident ghost. For a moment she paused, and Yaminah would have sworn the woman raised her nose a fraction, as though sniffing the air around her. In one hand she held a walking cane, topped with an ivory heart. With the fingers of the other she fondled the contours of the carving, and for a split second Yaminah imagined her raising it above her head and turning to pounce upon her where she stood transfixed.

A single bead of sweat pricked in the small of her back. It trailed, like the tip of a dead finger, down the curve of her lower spine and all the way to her tailbone. She closed her eyes and imagined Constantine, asleep upon his bed and surrounded by cloaked and hooded figures bearing swords in upraised hands. The tension of the stretched and endless moment tugged at her heart and she almost spoke, just to break the spell. When she opened her eyes, Helena was nowhere to be seen.

All at once Yaminah was aware of a roaring, pounding sound inside her head and realised she was holding her breath. Slowly, painfully, she exhaled – taking care to let the trapped air seep soundlessly from between her lips. She realised too, with a shiver, that she had no idea which direction Helena had taken. For a moment she contemplated the possibility that the consort had seen her there, eyes tightly shut and pressed against the wall. Might it have suited Helena to know she had been overheard and yet to leave the eavesdropper dangling like a leaf in autumn? She dismissed the thought as nonsense and shook her head to clear it. Deciding to retrace the aimless steps that had so nearly delivered her into disaster, she turned from the door and walked away as quickly and as quietly as the flagstones allowed.

Any relief at having been overlooked at the scene of her crime was short-lived, however. Yaminah's system had briefly coursed with adrenalin, but those moments of heightened sensation were past now, leaving dismal desolation in their wake. Reality bore down upon her narrow shoulders and she felt her knees might buckle, pitching her helplessly on to the floor.

Almost harder to bear than the new-found knowledge of the threat was having no one alive in the world, save Constantine himself, with whom she could share her burden. She had been taken into the care of his family, and of the wider court. He had spoken up for her from the depths of his own suffering to pledge his determination to care for her. But in spite of his patronage, she was and always would be an orphan. Her mother's absence was a yawning emptiness at her centre, and while Constantine's devotion made a bridge across the void, still she felt hollow.

She had cultivated acquaintances among the girls and young women whose orbits intersected her own, but always she had felt a need to maintain a distance. In part it was out of fidelity to her mother – some belief that her memory would remain untarnished only if no other woman or girl came between them.

But there was also an understanding of the reality of life within the gilded cage of the Blachernae Palace. At best the rarified world she inhabited was a rumour mill in perpetual motion. At worst it was a hive of venomous, hard-shelled creatures searching ceaselessly for the chance to land a mortal wound upon challengers both real and imagined.

Denied the bulwark of family, of elders and siblings bound to her by blood, she had grasped from the outset that her long-term security in the palace depended upon keeping her own counsel as much as possible, ensuring that at least a portion of her thoughts remained private. But above all, she knew she depended on Constantine. He was hers and she was his. All this time she had assumed others valued him as she did. The realisation that some of those closest to him might wish him ill struck her with the force of a thunderclap.

She scolded herself, furious at her own lack of awareness and maturity. Constantine was all she had. It was therefore her responsibility to spot danger at a distance, and yet she had allowed her own feelings to blind her to the intentions of others. Now a potentially lethal threat was close by, and only by chance had she learned the truth, like a splash of iced water to the face.

Childish ... childish! she scolded herself.

She made her way back through the corridors like a convict approaching the place of execution.

'Yaminah?'

She was almost back on familiar territory, where she belonged, and within a minute's walk of the sanctuary of her own quarters, when Helena's voice reached out from behind her like an unseen hand. For the second time in the space of as many minutes she felt the rush of hot blood in her cheeks. How long had Helena been behind her? Had she followed her?

'I am perfectly well, madam,' she heard herself say.

If it was physically possible, her face felt even hotter than before. The non sequitur burned on her lips. She was so overheated she felt she might catch fire, and she was painfully aware of dampness on her brow and on her top lip. She ached to wipe away the beads of perspiration with the sleeve of her dress but resisted the temptation. Part of her wanted to run. An adult she might be, but the child within was alive and well. More than anything, she wished for darkness – cool, cosseting darkness in which to be unseen and unobserved.

Surely Helena must smell the sweat of her anxiety? She had read that animals could detect fear by scent, or some other sense, and she was not even sure she couldn't smell it on herself now.

'I am pleased to hear it, daughter,' said Helena. The expression on her face made clear Yaminah's comment had arrived uninvited.

Helena was in the habit, when it suited her, of adopting what Yaminah regarded as an overly affectionate tone. There was no familial or legal relationship between the two women, no tie of blood or of marriage, and sometimes Yaminah felt the emperor's consort used the word 'daughter' not as a term of endearment but rather as some kind of put-down. If nothing else, it underlined the pecking order, as if there was any need to do so.

Unable to stop the flow, seemingly determined to answer questions before they were asked, Yaminah heard herself ploughing ahead into an increasingly difficult furrow.

'It is time for Prince Constantine's therapy,' she announced, too formally, the words falling over each other in their eagerness to be out. She blinked hard and imagined them scurrying around Helena's well-turned ankles like needy lap dogs. 'He will be expecting me.'

Helena's demeanour softened nonetheless. Here was a subject of conversation that might serve as common ground, certain to deflect any aggression. Yaminah's devotion to the prince was an accepted fact of life at court, and no one had ever questioned any tenderness she extended towards the young man who had so famously sacrificed his well-being and put her life before his own.

Whatever Helena's intentions might be, she was commanded by custom and practice to respond favourably to such attention to duty – even, it seemed, when there were no witnesses. It was a gesture and a set of consequences that fitted easily into the thinking of a society desperate to demonstrate and to witness the fruits of Christian charity. With the enemy at the gate, just beyond the walls, all those who were trapped within felt the need to live up to the ideal, however inconvenient it might be. Here was self-sacrifice – indeed self-sacrifice that had inspired more of the same. Prince Constantine had saved Yaminah's life, and she, without ever having been asked, had offered him her own in return.

'Do you really love him?' asked Helena.

38

It was Leonid, senior physician at court, who had advised that since the prince was incapable of moving his own legs, then efforts must be made by others to move them for him. Leonid himself had devised and prescribed the treatment, a routine he called 'the therapy'.

Constantine had remained in his frame of wood and metal, immobile as a statue, for many days. That, said the old doctor, would allow any and all natural healing of wounds to take place. Leonid's training in anatomy had allowed him to perceive that the prince's attempt to catch his falling angel had tested his own young frame beyond its limits. Beyond black and purple bruises, he bore no visible outward signs of damage. But the shattering impact had somehow severed the connection between the upper and lower halves of his body. Control of the legs had been put beyond the reach of the lad's own will.

After weeks and then months of waiting for spontaneous repair, Leonid had begun to observe the wasting of the boy's limbs. Inactivity, he deduced, was causing the muscles to dissolve, the tendons to shorten.

Should the day come when the power of movement returned to the royal legs, it was Leonid's avowed intention they would be fit for the fray. And so it was that the clever, cantankerous physician had set about devising a programme of exercises to counter the deterioration and stop the rot. If the prince could not move his own legs, then they would be moved on his behalf by others more able.

At first it had been Leonid's fellow doctors who had undertaken the time-consuming and laborious business of flexing and straightening the prince's lifeless limbs. The air of Constantine's bedchamber was thick with incense, and while the medical men worked, a group of young priests standing beneath the shuttered windows of the room kept up a low, steady chanting – all of it designed to soothe the prince and keep him in a state of restful calm.

Yaminah, however, had found reasons and excuses to witness the therapy from the outset, and since everyone had to agree that her presence soothed Constantine – gave him peace and, more importantly, the patience to put up with the indignity of it all – no one was allowed to chase her away.

'I don't know about you, Yaminah,' the prince would say, 'but I'm exhausted just watching myself. I must have not walked for miles!'

Constantine's seemingly bottomless reserves of good humour only made his predicament harder to witness. She would remember to smile at his stoicism, his endlessly inventive self-deprecation, but in truth it added to her own pain and feelings of guilt.

Soon enough she began even to inveigle herself into the application of the therapy itself. Having begun by watching from the point in the room furthest from the bed, skulking there like a dog with a heavy conscience, slowly she had edged inwards on an ever-decreasing circle, seeking forgiveness.

The doctors had tsked and tutted and generally fretted at the presence of a girl in such intimate circumstances, but she was impervious to their discomfort. Only the suffering of her prince mattered to Yaminah, and she blithely ignored their attempts to discourage her as she drifted ever closer.

Then came the day when she asked Constantine if she might help. His brow and face had been beaded with sweat, for the manipulation of his feet and legs – and indeed the rest of his slender frame, since Leonid prescribed exercises for his hands, arms and shoulders as well – took its toll. As always, though, when she spoke to him, his discomfort was apparently eased.

His doctors protested as though with one voice. Surely such an indignity ought not to be visited upon a royal personage? But Constantine's own voice cut cleanly through the clutter of protest.

359

'I should be delighted,' he said, so that she blushed. 'If there must be hands upon me, then better that they be cool and soft like I imagine yours to be.'

Yaminah had been barely thirteen years old at the time, and the flirtatious words from one who was already becoming a man sounded nothing less than scandalous even to her. There had been gasps and palpable shock from the assembled doctors, but Constantine pressed ahead boldly, gaining strength it seemed, and resolve, from the wave of indignation buffeting his bed.

'Please show young Yaminah here how best to encourage some sap back into these broken sticks of mine,' he said, his eyes on hers. And then addressing his doctors directly he added: 'In any event, I am sure the time and undoubted experience of such learned men as yourselves would be better spent elsewhere. Train this girl as your replacement and perhaps she may yet relieve you all of a duty that must be onerous at best, if not completely pointless. If this dead horse must be flogged, then let it be done by younger hands.'

At this last apparent acceptance of defeat, a shadow somewhere between self-rebuke and regret flitted across the prince's face. He batted it away, as unwelcome and troublesome as a fat bluebottle, and regained his good humour.

'Gentlemen,' he said, his gaze fixed not on any of them but on Yaminah once more, 'what can it hurt?'

39

Yaminah pulled the darkness around herself like a blanket, letting it smother her, and conceal her from the world above. She held, cradled at her breast like a newborn, a handful of finger bones.

'Tell me what to do, Ama,' she said.

From beyond the darkness, beyond the walls that contained it, came the sound of horns wildly blowing, and the cheering and jeering of many men. Even here, deep below the palace, where the foundations met the bedrock of the world, the first of the besieging Turkmen could be heard dimly, and Yaminah clasped her hands more tightly around the slender bones.

'Is Mum with you today, Ama?' she asked, and while there came no answer, there was at least comfort in the sound of the words ... *Ama ... Mum* ... soft and warm and smooth, and more pleasing than any others she knew.

She had already told them everything Helena had said. She always told them everything. For want of a family, for want of the warm flesh and blood of loved ones, Yaminah had her box of bones. There were, anyway, those parts of every person's life that were best kept secret, and perhaps especially from family. No matter the love between any two people, there were always thoughts and glimpses of self-knowledge that would not endear the one to the other – and so they were placed in a concealed room made only of imagination and memory; a room in the mind, the very existence of which – let alone its contents – was neither confessed to nor discussed with another living soul. What Yaminah might not have told her mother's nurse in life, she could at least tell to her relics.

Once, long ago, almost lost in the palace gardens, she had chanced upon an elderly beekeeper tending his hives. She had been afraid at first, trembling at the sight of the insects, hundreds of them, as they drew their unerring straight lines towards or away from their little homes. The hum of them was soothing, though, like the sound of a crowd far away, and soon she relaxed and let the beekeeper, tall and stooped with the weight of years, tell her some of what he knew.

First and foremost, he had said, it was vital to tell the bees everything. A bee landed on the end of his hooked nose but he seemed entirely unconcerned. His eyes crossed, momentarily, as he noted the presence of the visitor, then focused once more on the girl.

Staring at the insect as it crawled up his nose and on to his forehead, she had enquired exactly what he meant by everything.

'Just that, little mistress,' he had said. 'Everything that happens – to me and to each member of my family – everything. They are especially concerned with births, marriages and deaths, but I do my best to keep them fully up to date with even trivial details.'

'And what happens if you don't?' she had asked. 'Tell them everything, I mean?'

'Now that would be a dreadful mistake on my part,' he had replied, shaking his head. 'The bees would know I had left something out.'

'And then what?' she had asked.

Before he answered, he raised his right hand from where it had been dangling by his side. There was a bee on the web of skin between his thumb and forefinger and he reached towards Yaminah until his hand, and the insect, was right under her nose. She looked closely and saw that the bee's stinger was buried in the old man's flesh. She gasped, and reached out to swat the thing.

Smoothly, calmly, he withdrew his hand. With the other he began gently, oh so gently, to nudge the bee – tapping its side. Under his patient direction, the little creature began to move, slowly describing an anticlockwise circle. It was almost comical, its tiny legs sidestepping like a high-stepping pony. After a couple of complete rotations, its stinger came free of the keeper's skin, and for an instant Yaminah saw that the little thorn was twisted like a pig's tail. The old man's coaxing had enabled the bee quite harmlessly to unscrew its weapon.

'Do you see?' he said, looking down into her face. 'If you or I had knocked him from my hand, his stinger would have been torn from his body. He would have been terribly wounded and certainly would have died. By helping him free himself, I let him live to fly on – and to make me more honey, of course.'

Yaminah nodded, mouth open, her subconscious noting the value of avoiding instantaneous reactions fuelled by hurt. Then she remembered her question from before and asked it a second time.

'What would happen if you left something out, if you did not tell them everything?'

'Ah, yes,' he said. 'Why then they would leave me, of course.' His old face was a picture of sorrow at the thought. If the bee's sting had caused him any discomfort, he gave no sign. It was only the notion of losing his bees that caused him pain.

'The whole lot of them would up and leave me, never to return. They would make a new home somewhere else, start over with someone more attentive and forthcoming, and I would never see them again.'

With all that in mind, Yaminah had taken care to treat her bones the way the old man treated his bees. For fear that the memory of her loved ones might leave her for want of attention, she kept the bones in their wooden box; she visited them as often as she could; and she told them everything. She had already lost too much, she reasoned; she certainly could not afford to lose any more.

She sighed, rolling the bones between her fingers before raising them to her face. She closed her eyes, and then opened them. It made no difference, for here the darkness was total, her sense of vision made wholly redundant, so that her other senses had to close ranks and fill the gap.

She inhaled deeply, but there was no odour of decay from the relics. Ama had been gone a long time, after all. She had died on the same day Yaminah was born, in fact. *(The Lord giveth and the Lord taketh away.)* Yaminah's mother Isabella had liked to say that it made her happy to know that her two favourite people had existed together for a little while, overlapped for a moment in eternity.

After many years, much handling and careful storage, the bones were clean and dry. Exposed to daylight they would have shown, in places, a pleasing patina.

'Mother of God and Virgin, rejoice, Mary full of grace, the Lord is with thee,' Yaminah whispered softly, fondling the bones like worry beads. 'Blessed art thou amongst women, and blessed is the fruit of thy womb, for thou hast given birth to the Saviour of our souls.'

She was seated on a flagstone floor, her back against a wall and her legs stretched straight out in front of her. With the finger bones still in her left hand, she reached with her right into the wooden chest by her side. By touch alone she identified Ama's skull. As was her habit, she placed the palm of her hand over the empty eye sockets, her index finger over the triangular cavity once occupied by a nose.

'I miss you ladies,' she said. 'I promise I will take you with me if I can.'

She stroked the smooth, cold bone of Ama's forehead.

'I shall carry you, Ama,' she said, and smiled. 'And you shall carry Mum, just as you used to long ago.'

Minutes passed; perhaps an hour. There in the dark with the memory of her mother, and her mother's ancient nurse, Yaminah breathed low and slow.

More than any other physical feature, she remembered her mother's long dark-blonde hair. When Yaminah was very little, her mother would stoop over her, bending low until a heavy curtain of fair tresses enveloped her completely. There were soft kisses to be had in the impromptu privacy, the rubbing of noses. Yaminah leaned her head back against the wall and felt once more the tickle of that warm mane upon her face, pursed her lips in expectation of a kiss.

She slept. In dreams she replayed the conversation with Helena, remembered the itchy prickle of sweat in her armpits and the dryness in her mouth.

'Do you really love him?' Helena had asked.

While she had spoken, she had reached out towards Yaminah with her cane and used the tip of it to free long strands of chestnut hair from the girl's sweat-damp neck. There was something close to intimacy in the touch, the nearness, and Yaminah had thought for a moment that she detected the woman's own scent, mingling lasciviously with her own.

The question had taken her by surprise. The moment, the context, was entirely wrong and Helena was too close.

'Of course I do,' she said. 'Of course I love him. We are to be married!' This last was delivered too loudly, the truth of it undermined somehow by the shrillness of her tone.

Helena smiled. 'Marriage is hardly proof of love,' she said.

Yaminah had offered no denial of the obvious, and concentrated only on holding Helena's gaze.

It was as uncomfortable as standing too close to a fire.

'Why do you love him?' asked the consort, tilting her head towards one shoulder as though the answer truly mattered. 'He cannot protect you. He cannot even make love to you.'

'He is stronger than me,' said Yaminah. 'He is stronger than you.'

She bit down hard on her own impertinence before continuing. 'He has already borne a heavier burden than any of us has ever carried, or ever shall, God willing.'

'Is that love?' asked Helena.

Yaminah did not know and did not answer and so the consort pressed on. 'So you admire him – we all do. Perhaps you pity him as well?'

Yaminah felt bitter anger rise in her chest, bubbling into her throat. Carefully she took three deep breaths, using them to smooth down her temper like she might have used her hands to smooth creases from her clothes.

'He has made me a better person,' she said quietly, firmly. 'I love him for that. I am the person I am because of Constantine – in every way – and I would not change it.'

She felt Helena's gaze like a physical intrusion, reaching inside her head. There it was again, another pulse of Helena's intoxicating, heady scent.

'And he *can* protect me,' she said. 'He always has.'

Suddenly the older woman closed her eyes, lifting her chin as she did so and seeming to let the moment pass.

'I can protect him too,' said Yaminah. 'I always will.'

Helena opened her eyes and seemed, for a moment at least, unsure of where she was. Yaminah met her gaze squarely, and while she expected to find malice there, ill will, she glimpsed only another question. But this one was left unasked. Without another word, Helena turned and continued on her way, passing her cane from hand to hand as she did so.

Yaminah awoke in the darkness with a jolt. How much time had elapsed she did not know, and the complete absence of light made it impossible to judge. She was not afraid. Here she was never afraid. The bones of Ama's fingers were in her lap, cradled in the folds of her skirts, and she returned them to their chest, all save one.

Finding the lid by feel, she replaced it and stood to place the casket inside a small stone sarcophagus beside the place where she had sat. Content that all was as it should be, she turned and took three confident, practised steps that brought her toes up against the first of a flight of twelve stone steps. Before she reached the top of them she felt the hair on the crown of her head brush against the underside of a wooden trapdoor. It was heavy but opened easily, thanks to the design of the hinges, into a basement beneath the apartment she and her mother had once shared.

The basement was dark, but light fell here and there through gaps between the pine floorboards that formed its roof. She walked quickly across to a flight of wooden stairs and climbed them. At the top was a landing and a heavy oak door. Taking a long-shafted key from a pocket of her skirts, she unlocked the door and opened it, gingerly.

There was silence beyond and she pulled it wide enough to allow her to look out into the corridor beyond. There was no one around – there never was – and she stepped out, taking care to lock the door behind her as quickly as possible.

Viewed from this side, the door was nondescript, without adornment, and therefore apt to be overlooked by passers-by. Pocketing the key once more, the key to the kingdom of her memories, Yaminah crept silently along the corridor, opened a larger and altogether more impressive set of double doors, and began making her way back towards her quarters. In one hand she held the small, smooth bone. She did not look at it, merely grasped it tightly in one hand before slipping it into her pocket alongside the key.

It was indeed time for the prince's therapy and she needed the chariot. Since Constantine flatly refused to have it anywhere in his line of sight when it was not in use, it stayed always in Yaminah's rooms.

For her own amusement, and partly due to her fondness for the dark, she closed her eyes. She focused on the sound of the hems of her skirts brushing lightly on the flags of the corridor and made her way by memory alone, taking turns left and right. Rounding the final corner, she counted fifteen steps before reaching out with her right hand and finding, with faultless judgement, her own door handle. Only when she was inside, with the door closed behind her, did she allow herself to open her eyes.

Her suite of rooms was flooded with dazzling wintry sunlight and she blinked hard. While her eyes adjusted to the brightness, she crossed the room to one of the tall windows and, by touch as much as anything else, located the chariot. She placed her hands on the handles, turned it smoothly towards the door and set off towards the prince's quarters.

After years of what felt like hiding in the palace, of behaving like an interloper or an intruder, she felt infused suddenly with a sense of ... right. As she made her way towards the man she had just sworn to protect, she realised for the first time since her mother's death that she had an important role to play and a duty to perform. This time it was Constantine who stood on the edge of the abyss. This time it was her turn to catch *him*.

The chariot, so-called, was a wheelchair of sorts. Leonid's masterstroke had been to conceive and then design a contraption that would perform, simultaneously, the two functions he felt were key to Constantine's well-being. While he had denied himself the luxury of saying so, it had troubled the old man that his patient was confined to his bedroom, trapped like a moth in a jar. The interior of one room, well-appointed though it might be, lacked the stimulation necessary for the maintenance of a healthy mind, he thought.

That he was unable to repair the prince's body drove Leonid almost to distraction. But he was equally determined to care for the boy's mind. That much, he felt, was not necessarily beyond him.

In the end it had been Yaminah's devotion that

had provided his inspiration. As one of her early sessions of exercise and manipulation of the prince's muscles and joints had drawn to its close, Constantine had glanced away from his young carer's attentions and so caught sight of his physician standing silently in the doorway. Quite how long Leonid had been observing them, the prince could not guess, but he identified concern in the old man's eyes.

'You have to agree she's a dedicated student,' said Constantine, trying to lighten the mood and brush away, as always, any sign of pity.

Yaminah had been completely absorbed by her task, vigorously massaging the calf muscle of the prince's right leg. She had her back to the doorway and so had been entirely unaware that they were being watched.

While she and Constantine were alone, physical intimacy between them seemed natural and unaffected. Young as she was, she had never once felt awkward in his presence. It was as though any barriers between them had been obliterated in that moment when their lives collided, deep in the cavernous heart of the Church of St Sophia.

And yet for all that, the sudden presence of another, an observer, made her instantly self-conscious, and the sound of Constantine's voice addressing his physician made her stop what she was doing and stand to attention like a little soldier.

After a moment or two, she allowed herself to glance over her shoulder at whoever had joined them. When she saw it was Leonid, a man whose age and authority made her more nervous almost than any other, she stepped away from the bedside and turned to face where he stood in the doorway.

Leonid said nothing at first, but approached the pair quietly, his eyes on Yaminah.

'Hmm,' he murmured, a rumbling low in his throat. To Yaminah's ears there was agitation in the sound, like a fly trapped against a window pane.

'I have long since lost count of the miles this girl has walked on my behalf, and with my legs,' said Constantine. He was reaching for levity, hoping to coax something light-hearted from a man for whom humour was an always unsettling companion.

Yaminah realised she was wiping her hands, slick with scented oil, on the fabric of her dress. She wanted desperately to assess the damage done, the inevitable staining, but forced herself to remain as motionless as possible.

Leonid was notoriously taciturn, and when he finally spoke, both Yaminah and Constantine were faintly startled.

'It is not enough,' he said.

'Yaminah tends to me every day,' said Constantine, almost crossly. 'Or at least every day that I let her.'

The old man waved one hand, impatient at the misunderstanding.

'No, no,' he said, doing his best as far as he was able to lighten his own tone. 'I am not talking about the frequency of the treatments.'

Yaminah inadvertently made eye contact with him as he said this.

'Nor their thoroughness,' he added, apparently

for her benefit. She lowered her eyes, but she was pleased by the old man's seeming praise for her efforts.

'What then?' asked Constantine. 'She could not give any more of herself to the task – nor I, for that matter.'

Leonid shook his head slowly as he came closer to the bed.

'No ... it is not enough that you remain here in this bed, in this room, day after day and week after week,' he said. 'Your legs are not the only part that wastes away for want of stimulation.'

Without another word Leonid had turned and left them, his tattered black robes flapping behind him like the untended wings of an ailing crow.

Yaminah sighed with relief and returned thankfully to the application of the therapy – switching her attention to Constantine's left leg. As she did so, she looked him in the eyes, questioningly. The prince said nothing; just shrugged his shoulders.

A month later, the physician returned, preceded by an assistant pushing an outlandishly complicated-looking chair on wheels. All the while it advanced, it made a clicking sound like an incessantly dripping tap. The contraption was reminiscent of a little cart that might be pulled by a pair of miniature horses, with a shaft that protruded from beneath the seat and extended for a distance of a yard or so. A pair of pedals, or stirrups, was mounted either side of the shaft, and these revolved all the while the assistant pushed the chair forward. When he stopped, in the centre of the prince's room, so too did the stirrups.

Constantine was in his bed, propped up on

pillows and cushions and reading a book. Yaminah was perched upon a window seat, enjoying the warmth of sunlight on her back and shoulders. Having been briefly transfixed by the arrival of Leonid and his assistant, and most of all by the wheeled contraption, she looked at the prince. His expression was one she had not seen before – some way between amusement and suspicion – and she waited to hear what he would say.

He let out a long, whistling breath and allowed his book to fall forward into his lap.

'I am impressed, Professor,' he said. 'Now tell me what it is.'

Leonid clapped his hands once, and the assistant, understanding the instruction, turned from the chair and quickly exited the room.

'This is the next stage of your treatment, your highness.' Leonid's eyes were not on the prince but on his invention.

'Treatment,' murmured Constantine softly. 'It is without end.'

'It will end when you can walk again,' said the physician sharply.

His choice of words was bold, as was his tone. Despite his age and experience – and therefore the status that came with them – he was nonetheless addressing his superior. The suggestion that he, and not the prince, might determine the duration of the treatment was clearly open to challenge, if not a downright rebuke.

But something else in Leonid's tone, a note of implicit and deeply held commitment to Constantine's well-being, was unmistakable and also touching. The old man usually exuded only crustiness and lack of sentiment, and this confession of determination to make good caused the breath to catch in Yaminah's throat. She looked again at Constantine and was relieved to find there only affection for the good doctor.

'And this will help me how?' asked the prince, gesturing towards the chair with one hand.

'This will help,' said Leonid, suddenly more animated than either Yaminah or Constantine had ever seen him, 'by performing two tasks simultaneously.'

'How so?' asked the prince, warming to Leonid's enthusiasm.

The physician walked to his contraption and grasped a pair of handles mounted on either side of the chair's backrest. He turned it until the seat faced the prince and pushed it towards the bed, and Constantine watched once more as the stirrups turned in sympathy with the forward motion.

For the first time he noticed an intricate mechanism mounted beneath the seat, a set of interconnecting wheels of different sizes. Around the rims of two of the wheels – a large one beneath the seat and a small one between the pair of stirrups – were protruding teeth. Captured in the teeth were the links of a chain that looped around both wheels, each link taken in turn by one of the teeth and passed forward to the next. Two more chains connected other smaller wheels beneath the seat to those mounted on each of the four wheels on the chair's legs. Constantine noted with fascination that some cunning interaction between the mechanism of wheels and chains, and the forward motion achieved simply by pushing the thing, caused the stirrups to rotate.

'It is not enough that you spend all of your time in this room,' said Leonid. Again he was looking not at Constantine, but at his invention. The prince saw a rare expression of fondness on the old man's face as he regarded the chair, of a sort he had never seen directed at any human being of the physician's acquaintance.

'From a healthy mind comes a healthy body,' said Leonid. 'And your mind is being denied nourishment by remaining within these few walls. You must sally forth once more. A change of scenery will be to your brain as good food is to your blood and bones.'

'And so you would have me mount this wooden steed of yours?'

'An excellent choice of words,' said Leonid, either missing or overlooking a note of scepticism in Constantine's voice. 'Yes – a wooden horse that will carry you out of this room and back into the wider world.'

The physician clapped his hands once more, and this time two large men entered the room.

'With your permission, we will place you into the chair and you will see at once the benefits to be had from so doing.' The old man raised his eyebrows questioningly, seeking royal approval.

Constantine glanced at Yaminah, who had remained motionless and silent throughout. She nodded her head vigorously. The prospect of seeing the prince leave the confines of his room was nothing less than thrilling.

Constantine dropped his shoulders in submission and sighed. There was something about the idea of being pushed around the palace, helpless in a wheeled chair, that struck him as demeaning. Mingled with his uncertainty and hesitation, however, was an undeniable desire for a change of scenery.

'All right then,' he said. 'Back in the saddle it is.'

Yaminah leapt to her feet in excitement as Leonid and his two heavily muscled assistants crossed to the bed. She joined them there and, without even bothering to ask permission, quickly pulled back the sheets covering Constantine's legs. He was clad only in a white cotton nightdress, and the sudden sight of his frailty, of the almost transparent skin on his lower legs – and in the face of such large and able men – stabbed briefly at her heart. Dismissing the pain, she stepped back to let them get to him. For big men they were surprisingly gentle in their handling of him as they raised him from the mattress and transferred him easily into the chair.

Still conscious of his inadequate attire, Yaminah grabbed an embroidered blanket from the end of the bed and wrapped it around Constantine's shoulders, covering his torso and also providing a layer of softness between the wood and his bony back.

Leonid himself set about gently raising the prince's legs and flexing them into position so that his feet fitted into the stirrups. Content that all was as it should be, he turned suddenly to Yaminah. It was the first time he had acknowledged her presence since he had entered the room, and she was instantly flustered by his attention. Unperturbed, he cocked his head to one side and flashed her a smile. She had never before seen such an expression on his face and she stepped backwards in surprise.

'Well?' he asked. 'Will you show us how it works?'

Tentatively she stepped behind the chair and grasped the handles. She pushed it forward, slowly at first; then, realising that it would be easier if she applied more force, she speeded up. She raised her head and saw with amazement that Constantine's legs were moving, his knees rising and falling in a smooth and rhythmical motion. It looked for all the world as if he were powering the chair forward with his own efforts.

'Do you see?' asked Leonid, excitement and satisfaction obvious upon his face and in his voice as he watched. 'Do you see?'

Almost every day since then, Yaminah had taken Constantine for what they came to call their excursions. Sometimes he was keen, and other times less so. It seemed to her that he was always torn between a desire to be out of his room and on the move, and an ever-present sense of humiliation at being dependent on the physical abilities of others.

In any event, he would allow Yaminah and no one else to push the chair – or the chariot, as she called it. Sensitive to his feelings, she scheduled their excursions either just after dawn or late in the evening. In this way she sought to ensure there were fewer people around to see him. Beneficial though the exercise was, she understood Constantine's discomfort.

He had been especially hesitant at first, insisting

on being taken only to the great throne room of the palace. Having first ordered the place cleared of all occupants, he could relax while Yaminah pushed him around and around the empty perimeter. With no one to see him, his legs cycling endlessly and his knees rising and falling helplessly, he could forget the absurdity of it all and lose himself in conversation with her.

Perhaps it was because so many of their first conversations were conducted in this way, without eye contact, that they grew so comfortable with one another, and so quickly. They had been all but strangers when they met, after all. Until then, each had been to the other nothing more than a vaguely familiar face. The force of their coming together had somehow and instantly broken all the boundaries that normally separated people. Having collided – been joined in an instant into a bundle of legs and arms and crumpled clothes that had to be untangled by witnesses to the fall – it seemed they had never quite been separated again, or at least not entirely. Some unbreakable bond, an invisible glue, remained between them ever after. Countless conversations only reinforced the strength of it, burnished its gloss.

There was a gap of six years between them. When he caught her in his arms she was twelve years old and he was nearly nineteen. It had felt like a wide gulf at first, but gradually it mattered less and less. He began by treating her as the child she was, and she saw him only as an adult. But as days turned into weeks, weeks into months and months into years, so the distance contracted until in time she came to see that she was more than his companion. They were travelling together into the darkness of the unknown, and he needed her. She needed him too and could not escape him, not that she wanted to. She was the moon to his earth. Her face was always turned towards him and together they spun through the void, as dependent on one another as they were oblivious to all the rest.

When it finally came, the sound of his voice was a surprise. He hardly ever used her name when they were together, and it surprised her. Normally nowadays their excursions took them through the lamp-lit corridors of the palace, passing closed doors and the private lives lived behind them.

Often they would invent intrigues involving the occupants, some of the hundreds of people who formed the royal court, thrilling each other with fantastical rumours and scandals. Now of course the apartments were mostly abandoned, their occupants having sought sanctuary elsewhere.

On this day, however, Yaminah had been distracted from the moment of her arrival in his rooms, and without thinking she had brought him to the throne room, the venue for those first, self-conscious excursions long ago. He had noted her silence, but let her be. Companionable silence was no less enjoyable, provided it was hers.

They'd made two slow orbits of the huge room and were embarking on a third before he spoke.

'What's wrong, Yaminah?' he asked softly.

She had been immersed, as though in deep water, in her own concerns. Even the throne room, at once so familiar, seemed to harbour in-visible dangers.

What secrets lurked in the shadows high above them? The figures on the tapestries draped around the walls, depicting scenes from the lives of the emperors – what were they whispering about? What did they know that she did not? She felt the towering space above her, felt it bearing down on her head and shoulders. She might as well have been at the bottom of one of the great cisterns that kept the city's inhabitants supplied with water.

So his question, when it reached her, was like a hand thrust down into the depths to save a drowning soul, and she reached for it gladly. Worse than knowing was Constantine not knowing, and while it might break her heart to tell him what she now knew, if she kept it secret she felt it would choke her to death as surely as a swallowed peach pit.

She took a deep breath, like the first breath of a head suddenly above water after much too long submerged.

'I heard something today, Costa,' she said...

We begin to rise above them, the girl and the broken boy, and towards the shadows of the ceiling.

'While some of this must be true, and some of it might not be,' she says, 'it is all I know...'

Higher still and we can no longer hear her words. They are both small now, and getting smaller. The height and the distance make them seem like children, fragile without the protection of adults. While she talks, the girl keeps pushing the contraption of wheels and chains and the broken boy's legs keep rising and falling, so that he looks like part of a toy.

40

As Giustiniani's ships drew closer to the city, they were spotted first by the members of a welcoming party. Men and women dressed in expensive gowns and robes lined the water's edge. At the centre of the gathering was a tall and elegant figure, more simply dressed than the rest – in the manner of a soldier of Byzantium, in fact – but noticeable as a result. His hair was light brown and hung to his shoulders in long, loose curls that might have seemed feminine. He was handsome, however, with a broad chin and wide cheekbones. His mouth was wide, the lips thin but well shaped, his eyes a blue so dark they were almost purple. Suddenly catching sight of the flotilla's commander aboard the foremost of the vessels, he raised one arm in greeting.

'Giustiniani!' he shouted. 'Not a moment too soon! The sight of you pleases me more than could any other!'

The Genoan leapt up on to the gunwale of the ship, grabbed hold of one rung of a rope ladder leading to the rigging as he did so, and leaned as far out over the water as he could without tipping into the drink.

'Where else would I be at such a time, your majesty?' he replied. 'I have brought every man I could. I only wish they were ten times as many.'

'Or a hundred times, old friend,' replied Emperor Constantine. 'Or a thousand.'

When Giustiniani's vessel finally came alongside the wall, men aboard and on land sprang into action – tossing and securing ropes, positioning gangplanks. The desire to get off the always rolling deck and on to firm ground, after so long at sea, was overpowering for most, and individual commanders had to bellow orders as they strove to maintain control and ensure the disembarkation was carried out as smoothly as possible.

John Grant and Lẽna hung back from the press of those men most eager to leave the ship, hoping their own sudden and unwanted notoriety might be lost in the excitement of arrival. He was grateful for the moment of quiet for another reason too. Having learned long ago to keep his own counsel, he revealed nothing of what he felt. In truth, he was close to breathless with anticipation and his heart was beating so hard in his chest he feared it might be heard by anyone standing close.

He had approached the strife of war many times and Badr had prepared him well. He knew to expect and to accept a rush of excitement. He knew also that such a feeling was not to be trusted – that it could be his undoing. He had seen enough of killing and dying on the battlefield to know what happened to those who gave in to the thrill and let it carry them away, heedless of danger.

What he experienced now, however, as the city of white and gold loomed larger by the moment, was altogether different. All his life he had been aware of the movement of the world he stood upon. He sensed both its rotation and its forward flight. But a lifetime of awareness of it had given him the balance to cope, as well as the strength to accept it. Truth be told, he simply ignored the sensations for the most part, and gave in to them only when he had time to revel in the pleasure they brought.

Up till now he might as well have been standing on a log tossed by a river's rapids – but his body made unconscious adjustments born of instinct and experience that countered the momentum so that he felt only smooth and level flight.

What was happening now, however, had never happened before. Here beneath the sea walls of the Great City he could have sworn he felt the world slowing down. In the moments that remained to him, he gave himself over to the fall … and found it all but gone. It was as though the white water of a lifetime was behind him, and what lay ahead was glassy calm.

He was almost giddy, felt the need to make his ears pop, but those feelings were overpowered by another – that he was finally, after so many years, approaching the hub of the wheel.

'Come on.'

It was Lẽna, and she was pulling him by one arm, making for the gangplank. He shook his head to clear it and followed her.

Giustiniani had been first to go ashore, and John Grant watched as he strode forward into the waiting arms of the emperor. Some gasped at the intimacy, the apparent breach of etiquette, but the two men paid no heed.

It was then that he noticed the girl standing by the emperor's side and also watching the embrace. All other thoughts, all the overwhelming emotions of before, were brushed aside. He felt raw, like something newborn, and his skin tingled as though his nerve endings were exposed to the elements for the first time. His knees weakened and he breathed deeply of the cool air, clinging to it as though it was a rope.

Just the sight of her had filled him, all in an instant, with sadness. Her face was a perfect heart, her lips darkly red, eyes as black as a bird's. While he stared, she opened her mouth slightly, as though to speak, but said nothing. More than anything, he wanted to hear her voice – to know what she was thinking right there and in that moment. A wind was blowing onshore and the fabric of her dress was held tight against every curve, but it was no base desire that he felt. In place of the familiar need and want, he experienced for the first time something akin to panic ... as though time might be running out.

His mind filled with things to tell her, and only her – thoughts she alone inspired so that they appeared spontaneously, fully formed. Now that he had seen her, it mattered a great deal to him, more than anything in fact, that no more moments should pass before he made her understand the importance and the urgency of it all.

Lẽna had felt the intensity of his attention, his distraction, and following his line of sight, she spotted the girl as well.

'What is wrong with you?' she asked.

Even though he had been caught out, his mouth open like a freshly caught fish lying stunned on a riverbank, for a few moments more he kept his eyes fixed on the vision. Then he turned to Lẽna.

'Hmm?' he said.

'See something you like?' she asked. 'The little lovely standing in the emperor's shadow, though clearly not eclipsed by him?'

John Grant said nothing, just turned to seek her out again.

To his dismay, she had moved further back into the crowd of onlookers and all but out of his sight. He glimpsed only the top of her head, the long chestnut-brown hair in a centre parting.

Pulling himself together, he tried to pay attention to whatever Giustiniani might be saying.

'Interesting times,' said the Genoan, leaning back from the embrace with the emperor so that he might gauge his friend's expression.

'Indeed,' said the emperor, and John Grant saw him smile a hard smile.

'I expected a hotter welcome from your Turkmen,' said Giustiniani. 'Where is the fleet you warned me about?'

Emperor Constantine placed an arm around the other's shoulders and began guiding him away from the ship and towards a gateway leading into the city.

'They have vessels by the score,' he said. 'But they are galleys – powered by oars and low in the water. For all that they have the numbers and the speed, they would not dare confront high-sided ships like yours in open battle.'

'So they do not yet hold all the advantages,' said Giustiniani.

'Not quite,' said the emperor. 'Or at least, not yet.'

'Have you sealed the city?' asked the Genoan.

'Even as we speak,' said the emperor. 'We are an island now.'

He picked up the pace and gestured towards the land walls.

'We have horses nearby,' he said. 'Quickly now – their first attack may come at any moment.'

Most of the men aboard the first ship had followed their commander ashore, and now the other carracks slid in behind. John Grant stepped on to the harbour wall, followed by Lẽna, and they began following the rest of the party into the city. He looked ahead, straining for a glimpse of the girl – and spotted her by the emperor's side.

'My, my,' said Lẽna. 'Quite the first impression.'

High above, impassive and imperious, a lammergeier flew, riding columns of warm air and surveying the movements of the tiny figures trapped upon the world below. Above and beyond the prattle of shouted greetings and commands, he listened instead to the collisions of the currents of air that kept him aloft and aloof, while he scanned the landscape for whatever he might want.

He had watched the ships, like insects scuttling on the surface of a pond. They were still now, he noticed, and lines of men poured away from them burdened with loads that bent their backs and slowed their progress. Longer and longer grew the procession, passing in single file through gaps in high white walls and winding along cobbled paths that led upwards, away from the water and towards a wide square of gleaming white flagstones. It might as well have been the progress of ants, or termites.

All at once the bird's senses were assailed by something new.

An array of dots was fixed always in his view – the product of proteins in his eyes conspiring with the light of day to set free clouds of electrons that helplessly aligned themselves upon earth's own magnetic field. Like twinned souls travelling together for eternity, each one of the pair sensed the rightness of its other; unbreakable bonds keeping them connected, regardless of distance between them. The infinitesimal crumbs were entangled, united by an invisible stickiness that came from the heart of the universe itself, and for the bird the consequence of that union was an unfailing sense of direction. For all the apparent magic, he experienced only the unmoving pattern, permanently in his vision and always showing him the way north.

But it was away from north that he turned now, and towards the east, where his peerless vision had detected food. Downwards he spiralled, closing on his target – the body of a man. It was that of Rizzo, the luckless Venetian ship's captain, still mounted upon a tall pole above the battlements of Rumelihisari, a warning to all. The elegant processes of decomposition were well under way, but still his body was whole. His arms and legs moved gently in the breeze, an obscene mimicry of life.

Down flew the lammergeier until it could alight on the battlements below the corpse. The bird was a large and baleful presence and his sudden arrival scattered the crows and other, smaller winged scavengers that had been busying themselves upon what little remained of the exposed flesh of the captain's head, hands and feet, so that for a few moments he had the feast to himself.

Having looked left and right, and contented himself that there were no people or other dangers close at hand, he hopped forward on to the corpse, burying his talons in one bloated thigh. With his powerful beak he tore at the flesh and connective tissue there, flapping his great wings to add purchase and force to his efforts. With a wet, tearing sound, the leg detached itself from the whole and fell heavily to the ground. The lammergeier followed the limb and continued the work of tearing away at the mess of it. Unlike most scavenging birds, he had no interest in the flesh, and deliberately eschewed the darkening, putrid meat. He was only satisfied when his efforts had freed one of Rizzo's femurs, a long thigh bone. He rose into the sky once more, bearing the livid, glistening trophy grasped tight in his talons.

Triumphantly he flew, up and up into the burning blue of the sky. It was only by chance that his flight took him back towards the west, over the city that had preoccupied him minutes before.

It was calculated intent, however, that had a second of his kind spy him and his prize and set itself the task of stealing it. The first bird had sought only to place himself high above a hard surface of the sort that would shatter a fallen bone and expose the marrow within – the favoured foodstuff of all his kind. In his stomach was an acid so strong it would dissolve even the bone itself.

His casual flight put him above the same square of white flagstones he had observed minutes before. The line of men was filing across it now, carrying weapons and other possessions in readiness for a fight. Satisfied with his position, he released his prize and, moments later, set himself in a spiralling descent behind it.

It was then that the second bird – a female of the species and slightly larger – made her move. She had waited, tens of yards above, until the other lammergeier let go of the bone. Sensing her moment, she adopted a yet steeper dive and plunged downwards in a tight, corkscrewing flight while the prize tumbled end over end.

Far below them, John Grant (blessed or cursed with the power to detect the approach of foes unseen) sensed movement in the air above his head and, without any conscious thought, reached up and out with his good left hand and caught the falling thigh bone even before he saw it.

There was a gasp from somewhere in the line – followed by cries of fear and surprise. The noise rippled through the men, and all turned to investigate the cause. Emperor Constantine, along with every last one of them, was looking in the right direction in time to see the birds. So too was the girl.

While John Grant held the stinking bone up high, both lammergeiers, talons extended, alighted upon it. For a moment, as each struggled to win the prize from the other, they seemed fused as one. The emperor stood tall, frozen in the moment. By his side, Giustiniani cried out at the sight and dropped to one knee.

Men turned from John Grant, and from the huge birds mantling upon the bone he held above his head. Those soldiers saw their commander kneeling, with his face upraised to the spectacle, and beside him, the Emperor of Byzantium. As though for the first time, they paid heed to the imperial emblem on his chest – the double-headed eagle of the house of Palaiologos.

Turning back to John Grant, they watched in silence as he let go of the thigh bone, slippery with gore, and the birds, still grasping it between them, still fighting for supremacy, rose together into the sky. One had its head turned to the east, the other to the west.

There was a heavy moment of quiet then, interrupted only by the beating of wings, and then a great roar of approval. John Grant, with Lēna by his side, turned from the sight of the birds rising higher and further away, to find a thousand men cheering, their faces shining.

He looked from one to another and then found, by chance, the face of the emperor. He saw too the image of the two-headed bird on the tabard, and the hairs on his arms and neck rose in excitement. The emperor held out one hand, beckoning him. John Grant turned his attention instead to the girl by Constantine's side, and their eyes met for just an instant before a thunderous explosion of noise seemed to split the world in two.

All flinched and dropped and turned instinctively in the direction of the source of the din, and as they did so, a whole section of the city wall – an edifice that had been in place for longer than memory – collapsed in a heap, a gigantic plume of mortar dust rising from it like the ghost of a lost loved one.

This could not be, and men cried out at the wrongness of it. Not since an earthquake a thousand years before had any harm come to the Wall of Theodosius. The quake then had utterly levelled the wall and the whole population had rallied, working tirelessly and unstintingly to rebuild it. Since then, it had defied everyone and everything. It was a fixed point in an uncertain universe. And now part of it was gone, punched through as though by the wrath of God.

Moments later a second blast, that near deafened all that heard it and dropped every man to his knees in fear and disbelief, rolled across the world. This time a tower that had kept watch over the landward approach to the city for century after century fell crashing to the ground as though crushed from above by an invisible fist.

While men knelt and cried, a third blast rang out, and this time a ball the size of a bull soared over the top of the wall and crashed into the bell tower of a church on one side of the square. For a few moments, a perfectly round hole gaped high in one wall, before the entire structure crumpled earthwards and another ghostly cloud of dust and dirt rose against the sky.

'To me!' shouted Emperor Constantine. 'To me!'

He turned then, away from John Grant and the miracle of the birds, and began running towards the ruptures in the city's defences, and all ran with him, baying for the blood of the infidel.

41

A mile from the emperor (and from John Grant and the lammergeiers) and a few hundred yards beyond the wall, Mehmet stood open-mouthed and awestruck alongside his chief smith. A wreath of smoke coiled around them like a serpent.

The preparations for this first firing of his guns had taken weeks. The teams tasked with their transport had advanced across the landscape between Edirne and Constantinople at a speed of no more than a mile or two each day – slow as lava from an erupting volcano, but as unstoppable. Mehmet had ridden alongside them at times, cajoling and cursing by turns. Men and beasts had groaned and strained with the effort of hauling the huge cylinders of bronze and brass, and the sultan's calls had mixed into the din, or even rose above it, as he urged them forward with threats and promises.

The first of his fighting men had reached the city days ahead of the artillery train, and the sight of them would have been enough, Mehmet knew, to fill the citizens there with dread. He had put out his call to arms and a force numbering in the hundreds of thousands had rallied to him from all across his empire.

Most of the seasoned warriors had been provided by Mehmet's sipahis – noblemen raised and trained in the saddle and able to fight with the bow or the lance. They were his shock troops, spiritual descendants of the mounted hordes that had ridden out of the desert long ago, whose horsemanship and skill with weapons was the stuff of legend. While foot soldiers advanced into battle from the centre, cavalrymen formed the curving, encircling wings of the attacking line – riding out to goad and to punish, tormenting the static foe and moving around him like a swarm of bees.

A sipahi occupied a position in Ottoman society that would have been recognisable to any Christian crusader knight, and he fought for honour first and last. Each held land from the sultan and the size of his holding dictated the number of warriors he was obliged to equip and to train at his own expense. These armed and armoured retainers were usually related to him and so they fought out of loyalty to their own blood as well as obligation to the sultan.

Closest of all to Mehmet, though, were his janissaries – several thousand elite infantry soldiers entrusted with his life and with the lives of those dearest to him. Christian-born, they had been captured and enslaved in boyhood and raised as Muslims. Janissaries lived lives made separate and almost holy by their own strangeness. They fought and died as a class apart.

But it was perhaps the seemingly uncountable mass of impassioned amateurs that had flocked to the side of the professional soldiers that inspired real terror in the hearts of any who encountered them. Who after all would stand against such a reckless wave of men and boys armed with little more than the tools of their working lives and driven only by passion and by faith? Certainly not the inhabitants of those few Christian settlements still in existence outwith the walls of the city itself. All but a few of those souls, in towns and villages strung along the coastlines of the Black Sea or the Sea of Marmara, or in the hinterland before the walls, had been harvested unto God by the vanguard of the Turkish force. The only ones left alive were those whose own town walls had proved strong enough to withstand the horde. If they had held out stubbornly enough, the attackers' interest waned and they moved on to torment more submissive prey.

Mehmet had timed his force's advance to ensure that the crest of the wave broke and lapped against the Wall of Theodosius on the dawn of Easter Sunday. Mehmet knew that the Christians cowering in their churches and shrines would have felt especially protected by the advent of their holiest week. Whatever else might befall them in the days ahead, surely almighty God and the mother of his son would spare them for their prayers and devotions at that special time? Yet despite all the howled appeals to their most sacred icons and to God above, the ringing of hundreds of bells and the wafting of veritable storms of incense, the Turks had arrived on the doorstep on the very anniversary of their Christ's resurrection. Instead of salvation, it had been a tented city of wrathful enemies that came in response to their prayers – sprouting out of the soil overnight like a crop of poisonous mushrooms.

The sultan's sappers had set to work at once, clearing the ground before the wall of every movable obstruction. Buildings and boundaries, trees and scrub – whole orchards and woodlands, in fact – had fallen to their hammers and axes so that the guns, when they arrived, might have a clear field of fire. An eighth of a mile in front of the wall, and parallel to it, they had dug out a great ditch that stretched from the Golden Horn to the Sea of Marmara. The earth and stones from their excavations they had heaped in front, as protection for Mehmet's precious bombards. A screen of wicker fencing was then strung along the top, so that the activities of the gunners (precious too, but less so than the guns) might be obscured from the defenders' view.

For a millennium the wall had stretched for four miles across the neck of the peninsula of land that had the city at its apex – and for more than seven hundred of those years one Muslim foe after another had jealously studied its construction. Mehmet and his sappers knew its dimensions and complexities by heart.

Any and all who had business in Constantinople, and who made their way towards it across the plains of Thrace, eventually came face to face with not just one wall, but two – running parallel to one another and trapping between them a lethal killing field. An enemy force that might breach the first would surely be cut down by defenders safe behind the battlements atop the second, armed with crossbows and bombards, spears and boulders, boiling oil and Greek fire.

Even before tackling the outermost wall, attackers had first to find a way across the fosse – the deep moat lined with bricks – a veritable mass grave prepared for the corpses of any men fool enough to confront it; so that taken together, the city's landward defences amounted to a barrier sixty yards wide and thirty yards high. Both walls were interspersed along their lengths by nearly two hundred towers, giving yet more advantage to armed men keeping watch over the terrain beyond.

All along the length of the walls were the gates – some great and some small. Each had at least one name and some had seen so much of the life of the city that they had earned many. In any event, sultan and citizen alike knew of the Gate of Charisius, which was also the Cemetery Gate; the Reds' Gate that was also the Third Military Gate; the Gate of Rhegion; the Gate of St Romanus; and the Golden Gate, through which emperors had processed in better times with their trophies of conquest. There was the Gate of the Silver Lake; the Gate of the Spring, the Gate of the Wooden Circus and the Gate of the Boot Makers, and many more besides. All were barred now to Mehmet and his kind, and some or all would have to be breached before he could fulfil his destiny.

When news of the arrival of the sultan's outriders had reached the city, Emperor Constantine had immediately given the orders to have it sealed tight. All the bridges across the fosse were withdrawn or otherwise destroyed; all gates through the walls were closed, locked and barred.

All of this Mehmet had considered – in dreams as well as in the waking world. He had known too where best to look in search of the realisation of those dreams. The terrain the walls stretched across was not flat, and its undulations meant that some stretches of the defences dropped into low ground and shallow valleys before rising again. On the ridges above such depressions an attacker might find positions that actually looked down on to the top of the wall – even into the interior beyond – so that impregnable though it had always been, still the Wall of Theodosius offered maddening glimpses of hope for anyone seeking to penetrate it, especially someone armed with the sort of weapons Mehmet now possessed.

It was in a lofty position in front of the Gate of St Romanus – one of those entrances made weak by high ground overlooking it – that Mehmet had positioned not only his own tents and those of his bodyguard, but also the greatest of Orban's bombards, chief of all the city-takers. Either side of it were more guns, made small only by the sheer size of the giant. In time they would come to know the grouping as the bear and her cubs, and the family's claws were cruel. It was in the hulking shadow of the mother bear that Mehmet was to be found standing when the artillery bombardment began.

The massive barrel had been set in position in the trench dug in front of the wall, on a wooden platform that could be raised and lowered – and thus its angle of attack adjusted – by the judicious use of chocks and wedges. The gunners had poured their black powder into the gaping maw of the thing, followed by a circular wooden block as big around as a tabletop and cut and shaped to fit the barrel precisely. This they had hammered home with iron rods before manhandling the ball itself, a carefully crafted sphere of stone that two large men would have struggled to link arms around. Once the projectile had rolled down into the darkness, into position against the block, the barrel had been braced all around with great timbers buried deep into the earth to help absorb the force of the coming explosion.

All had then retired to a safe distance – all save the man tasked with applying a smouldering taper to the touch hole bored close to the behemoth's base.

A mile away, in the centre of a square of shining flagstones, John Grant's lammergeiers had risen into the sky, grasping their trophy between them. That same instant, back at the gun, a tongue of flame had darted into the darkness and ignited the pounds of powder packed inside the barrel. The sound that followed was that of the birth of a new age, and Mehmet, son of Murad, was its father.

A column of flame burst from the end of the gun, followed by a huge and billowing cloud of dark smoke. Out of the midst of that miasma shot the ball itself, and Mehmet watched mesmerised as it drew its monstrous arc across the sky and crashed like the fist of God into part of the wall beside the Gate of St Romanus.

The effect was as of an earthquake, and the ball shattered into a thousand jagged fragments that rained down on to the landscape or splashed into the waters of the Lycus river, which flowed beneath the wall and into the city, the only welcome guest.

But it had been neither a solitary detonation, nor a single flight. All along the line, every single one

399

of the guns had been fired in concert with their giant overlord, and it was this combination of forces that caused the very earth herself to shake and buck until it seemed the entire wall must fall as one under the onslaught. As it was, whole sections of ancient masonry shivered and collapsed. Towers too toppled over like felled trees or dropped into their own foundations like hanged men.

'*Alhamdulillah*,' Mehmet mouthed silently, his breath all but stolen by the force he had just unleashed upon his enemies and the world. All praise and thanks to God.

If Mehmet had lost his voice, then the majority of his followers had not, and while he wondered at the sight of masonry falling and clouds of dust rising, his prayer of thanks was somehow taken up by the host, rising and falling among them like a murmuration of starlings taking to the air.

'Do you see, majesty?' shouted Orban, jumping up and down with joy at the destruction wrought by his creations. 'Do you see that I am as good as my word?'

Mehmet stepped forward and, casting aside all thoughts of propriety, threw his arms around his smith's neck and kissed him on both sides of his bearded face.

It was Orban's turn then to be stunned, and he gazed into the young sultan's face, his own eyes shining with the reflected glow of his master's pleasure.

'It is the will of God!' said Mehmet, finding his breath and his voice at last. '*His* will!'

And back behind the wall, beneath the Blachernae Palace too, the earth shook, and one world was understood to have ended while another had begun. A broken boy, who had seen neither the two-headed bird nor the stabbing tongues of flame from a hundred city-takers, sensed a change in the order of things nonetheless.

The sultan's guns had sent a wave before them that shocked every heart for a dozen miles around. Underneath the trembling, in spite of it, Prince Constantine felt something else – a different vibration entirely, and older, that troubled him more deeply and preoccupied him much longer than any work of men.

42

John Grant had grown tired of being the centre of attention.

Since his moment in the square, he had felt eyes upon him at all times. For a day or so the novelty had appealed, and he had walked tall, aware of every movement he made and every expression on his face.

It was Lẽna who was first to say he would live to regret having made himself such a spectacle (though privately she had been as moved by the scene as any other who witnessed it), and she was right.

There had been little time for celebrity in the first moments after the birds rose up and away from the soldiers, still vying with one another for ownership of the trophy.

Once the giant stone missiles began raining down, the emperor had called for horses and departed for the palace and the wall, accompanied by Giustiniani and his closest aides. The rest of the newly arrived force had struggled across the city any way they could. Wagons and carts had been gathered from all around – gratefully accepted from those who offered or taken forcibly from those less willing. The weapons and the rest of the equipment they had brought with them were ferried to where they were needed, at the land walls, with all possible haste.

Once begun, the bombardment continued relentlessly, like a man-made volcanic eruption. The ground shook, a foul reek of burned gun-powder filled the air and hot rocks fell from the sky like judgement.

Underneath it all was another sound – that of hundreds, thousands of voices crying out together in fear and sadness.

There had been portents of disaster after all. The days and weeks ahead of the Turks' arrival had been laden with evil signs. Before the guns began their hellish shuddering chorus, the earth herself had flexed her aching back and sent tremors that rippled beneath the city, toppling statues, breaking windows and sending cracks and fissures through walls.

Even spring had found reasons to disappoint the citizens of Constantinople; while they might have expected clear skies and warmer air by now, banks of fog draped themselves thickly across the Bosphorus, and snow had fallen.

For all that John Grant had been filled with a new and unfamiliar clarity – a powerful sense of having arrived in the right place, and at precisely the right time – he was aware too of an all-pervading feeling of dread wrapped around the city. A population in need of a clear view of heaven had felt a shadow fall instead. Desperate for a breath of clean, fresh air, they were trapped inside a cooking pot, and now the lid was being lowered upon it. He stole glances at Lẽna, and her expression, as she took in their surroundings, told him she laboured under the sensation too.

More than anything else, he was troubled by the guns. He had in fact been in the presence of such contraptions more than once, and found little to fear. With Badr at his side he had heard and felt the blast of them right enough, and witnessed at first hand the erratic impact of cannonballs. The Moor had hardly rated the technology, and dismissed those guns he had seen as little more than noise-makers.

'They are more trouble than they are worth,' he had said. 'So heavy they can scarcely be moved … so clumsy they cannot be aimed in any meaningful way. If you ask me, they pose more of a danger to those poor souls tasked with serving them than they do to any enemy.'

John Grant had agreed, and harboured infinitely more respect for bowmen like Angus Armstrong, or any warrior skilled with sword and knife. But these new bombards of Mehmet and his Ottomans were altogether different. Never before had he even heard talk of anything like the weapons now trained upon Constantinople. He had been taught that castles and cities surrounded by stone were impervious to assault, and knew as well as any soldier that a few good men shielded by high stone walls had little to fear from hundreds, even thousands of enemies thrown against such defences.

But now he knew different. Now he had seen stone balls pass through buildings like darts through paper. Worse, he had with his own eyes witnessed the fall of whole sections of the city's legendary wall.

He had thought he would have time in this place. He had travelled knowingly into the heart of a war, but had been confident he had little to fear. He trusted his skills and his senses. He had Badr's daughter to find and had believed the sanctuary of the Great City would protect her well enough, at least until he could track her down and make himself known to her. Now he realised with a jolt that time might be of the essence.

It was not the push that told him so – rather it was his own two eyes.

Many of the Genoan men-at-arms had spent time in the city before, and they set the pace towards the walls, sometimes marching and sometimes jogging along a route that kept the safe anchorage of the Golden Horn always to their east and on their right-hand side.

The sound of tolling bells, from church buildings all across the city, was constant, and John Grant wondered why a population pressed by a besieging army was more inclined to pray than to rise up in arms.

'Less time on their knees and more on their

hind legs with swords in their hands,' he said to Lẽna. 'Badr said that God loved a fighter – and I believe him.'

All around was evidence of sad decline. For all that John Grant had been told about this place, what struck him most forcibly was a sense of despair. There were great buildings here and there, evidence of past glory, but even those had the cast of age and neglect upon them. Wide-open spaces were as common as anything built, and from among the vegetation sprouted ruins, stubborn shards of what had once been.

The Genoan commanders said Giustiniani would meet them again at the Blachernae Palace, home of the emperor and the headquarters of the defensive efforts. By the time they arrived in its shadow, Constantinople was plainly a city at war. Time would tell when and if the citizens would choose to attend to the present need and take action, or remain absorbed in their appeals to the almighty.

The palace had already suffered the attentions of the guns, but the sight of the building, freshly wounded or not, was enough to stun John Grant into silence. Never before, in all his travels, had he felt so dwarfed and humbled by the works of men as he did now. The stonework of Blachernae was so finely wrought it looked more like something grown out of the earth itself than fashioned by mortals.

He was pulled back from his wondering by the sound of a man's voice.

'You there – have you come to fight or to sight-see?'

He turned to see a man of advanced years, yet heavily armoured and with an unsheathed sword in his hand. He was backed by half a dozen more soldiers, similarly attired.

'To fight,' said John Grant.

'The woman,' said the soldier, gesturing towards Lẽna with the point of his sword. 'For the love of God – what is she doing here?'

Lẽna stepped forward and spoke quietly and on her own behalf. Her voice caught and held the attention of her inquisitor.

'It is the love of God that brought me here,' she said. 'And I fight better than any man – better than you, I say.'

Her audacity might have earned her a beating, but no one in his company seemed minded to attempt the job.

'We are few enough,' said the commander. 'I will accept the help of any willing and able to do their duty. Just keep out of my view and out of my way.'

With that he turned away and strode towards a set of stone steps leading up towards the battlements on the inner wall, looming high alongside the masonry of the palace.

'Minotto,' said a voice from among a gaggle of the Genoans, standing closer than she might have liked. Since the incident in the square, she and John Grant had drawn followers like honey attracted wasps.

The foremost of them, a soldier in his middle years and clad in chain mail of a quality that declared he was a man of substance, was evidently the speaker.

'Girolamo Minotto,' he said again. 'Venetian

diplomat, but a warrior by inclination. I believe he has taken up residence in the palace.'

Lẽna shrugged and turned to make for the steps Minotto had climbed. John Grant followed along with the rest of their group. It was like being attended by courtiers.

The view from the battlements drove every private thought from the mind of every soul that gazed upon it then. Spread out across the rolling landscape beyond the walls was an entire city – but one in which the buildings were made of canvas and silk rather than timber or stone. From the Sea of Marmara to the glistening waters of the Golden Horn, there was barely a patch of ground left unoccupied by the sultan's force. For all that it was a temporary creation, it had all the order of a settlement that had been in place for months. The conical tents of each fighting unit were neatly grouped around that of the officer in command. Corps by corps they had formed themselves, square after square, column after column. A chaotic rabble might have been easier to look upon. Instead, the sense of order and control, of relentless purpose, added an air of quiet menace.

In a broad strip of cleared ground – between the tented city and Constantinople's outer wall – John Grant saw the livid scar of the hurriedly excavated trench that was home to the sultan's bombards.

It was while he struggled to take in the scale of the army ranged against the city, like flood water rising behind a levee, that the emperor spotted him. He had been talking urgently to Minotto, hearing the Venetian's assessment of the damage, when Giustiniani, standing by his side, noticed the new arrivals on the battlements and tapped the emperor's arm.

'The man who summons eagles out of the sky,' said the emperor, his voice loud enough that all of them heard his words.

John Grant dropped his head resignedly. He had not meant to make himself a focus, but there it was.

Emperor Constantine, accompanied by Giustiniani and Minotto, walked slowly towards him, his arms stretched out in a welcoming gesture. He placed his hands on John Grant's shoulders, and then turned to address his audience.

'Long before the shadow of Islam fell across the land of Persia, the people there had their own name for eagles such as those commanded by our friend.'

He gripped John Grant's shoulder firmly, like a brother, or a son.

'They called them *huma,* and said that the very sight of them brought joy, and the promise of good fortune. Any man who brings such messengers among us is welcome here.

'You shall be our talisman! And I say to all of you – any who fights by this man's side shall likely share in that good fortune.'

The emperor reached out a hand to summon Giustiniani, and took him by the shoulder as well.

'To you, old friend – a thousand thank-yous, for bringing this one among us.

'Now tell us – what is your name?'

Those watching seemed to take in a collective breath, as though expecting to be reminded of something they already knew.

'I am John Grant,' he said. 'I have come to fight for you and yours.'

'And so you shall, John Grant,' said the emperor. 'Giustiniani – I urge you to make good use of this one.'

As quickly as it had begun, the performance was over. The emperor turned and strode off along the battlements, followed by Minotto and a handful of his lieutenants.

Giustiniani did not move. Instead he looked into the eyes of each man, as though weighing his soul. Last of all he looked at Lӫna, and found he was not surprised to see her there. She returned his gaze without any outward show of emotion. From behind them came the sound of many footsteps, the clatter and clank of armoured men. John Grant turned to see that the rest of the Genoans – all forty score of them – had reached the rendezvous and were now looking expectantly at their commander.

Giustiniani seemed charged by their arrival, fuel to his flame. He looked away from them for a few moments, out at the Turkish encampment, and slowly passed his right hand across the whole expanse of it. There was a roar from close by and another cannonball found its mark, pounding into a section of wall beside the nearby Gate of the Wooden Circus, close by the palace. This time, the missile shattered harmlessly and the masonry held firm.

'We are here of our own free will,' bellowed Giustiniani. 'We come as free men, beholden to none. A few short days ago we were safe in our homes, and now here we stand, in harm's way. This is where I prefer to be, and I hope and pray that none of you would say different.

'I have not come to fight for an empire. I have not come to fight for my God. I have come here to slaughter the Turk because he is the enemy of my blood. I will not turn away from him, or from those who side with him, while there is breath in my body.

'I make one promise to you, and one promise only: if this grand adventure shall be the death of me, then when you gather up my remains and wrap me in my shroud, you will find no wounds upon my back.'

None spoke. No one moved. Every man kept his own counsel.

Elsewhere on the battlements, Minotto was keeping pace with Emperor Constantine.

'I know the legend of the *huma*, majesty,' he said. 'I noticed you stopped your account before the part that says that whomsoever falls under his shadow is a king-to-be, a sovereign in waiting.' He raised his eyebrows questioningly.

'Only sovereigns make sovereigns,' said Constantine. His expression was hard, his eyes cold. 'Hear me when I say it.'

43

'Tell me again about the birdman,' said Prince Constantine.

Set against the relentless percussion of shattering impacts upon the wails, the level tone of his voice seemed faintly surreal. Unperturbed by the intrusion, the assault upon his whole world, he focused his attention upon his hands, deft and swift.

'I just wish you might have seen it for yourself,' she said. Her own voice sounded brittle inside her head, along with the rest of her, as though a fine web of cracks was spreading from within. She felt she might soon shatter into a thousand tiny pieces.

Despite the constant danger posed by the Turkish bombardment, which had continued day and night, he refused to abandon his quarters in the palace. They would concentrate their fire on the walls, he said, and he had been proved right.

While the occasional missile was sent hurtling into the city, to strike at random buildings or sweep away luckless citizens like dust from a board, the gunners' focus had been and remained the ancient defences. The Blachernae Palace had been damaged too – particularly on the first day, as the gunners found their range and aim – but Constantine's apartment was located on the side of the building facing into the city and with its back to the onslaught. Many hundreds of yards of rooms, corridors and courtyards, all of it comprising massive masonry, stood between his rooms and the facade of the building most exposed to the Ottoman artillery.

He had said anyway that he was not worth worrying about – a useless cripple unable to mount a horse and sally forth, or to wield a sword upon the battlements. His words grieved Yaminah, but to her dismay it seemed that no one but her – not even the emperor himself – was minded to dispute his stance.

She sensed that his father's acceptance of his decision to stay in harm's way burned the prince somewhere deep down inside himself, but he would never have admitted it – and certainly not to her. Emperor Constantine had merely nodded when told of his son's determination to stay put. For Yaminah, the growing realisation that the man she loved was being casually left adrift in stormy waters was one that ran around inside her head like a cockroach.

From the moment they had come angrily to life, the guns had been driven ceaselessly by their masters, like tortured beasts fit only for screaming and roaring in hot agony. Their howls provided a constant punctuation to the day, and the intermittent blasts, followed by the sound and sensation of the impact of the projectiles, became part of the fabric of life, like the onset of chronic pain. Even now Yaminah struggled to recall the days before it began, before her life was one lived inside a constant round of destruction, and beneath a darkening pall of fear and dread.

Sometimes the firing stopped, but only to allow

waves of attackers to swarm across the open ground towards fresh breaches in the walls. So far the fosse had defied these suicidal attempts, but the howl of the men as they came on was as hateful to her as the hammering of the guns. Costa said they were the most desperate of the sultan's volunteers – peasants and the like who had thrown down their tools and answered the call to arms in hopes of riches or, more likely, a martyr's death.

Constantine seemed strangely immune to it all, his own domain a glass bubble left inviolate at the heart of a storm. Beyond his rooms, beyond the palace, men and women ran, fetched and carried, while children cried out. Orders and commands echoed around the palace in a near chaos and yet on the edge of it all, overlooked and all but forgotten, he passed his days as he had done for the past six years and more. His isolation – and the absentee court's indifference to it – left Yaminah sick to her stomach.

He had spent the morning shaping new characters for his shadow plays, and as he asked his question about the birdman, he brought his latest creation to life. His commitment to something so fragile in the midst of pounding stone and shrieking metal made her want to kiss him or strike him, she was unsure which.

There upon his ceiling, silhouetted by the slim finger of sunlight reflected from his polished bronze mirror, was a warrior borne aloft by a pair of eagles. Prince Constantine manipulated thin rods to create the illusion of beating wings.

'They did not carry him away,' she said. 'As I have told you several times already, *he* held *them* in place. It was … magnificent.' She sighed, and he did not miss her show of emotion.

No matter how many times she recalled the moment, and the vision, always she felt her heartbeat increase its pace. The heat that the thought of him left inside her made her blush and she was thankful for the dark. She was anxious to change the subject.

'The emperor is keener than ever that our wedding should go ahead as planned,' she said. 'He even said as much to me in front of the Genoan, Giustiniani.'

'I know,' he said. 'Even Doukas is full of talk about the grandeur of all that is planned.'

'And so he should be,' she said. 'It is in times like this, in the heart of darkness, that light is needed most. Our wedding is no longer just about us, if it ever was. Our coming together at this moment, of all moments, will be a hopeful sign for all – a show of belief in happiness to come.'

'I admire your optimism, I really do,' he said.

She scowled at him, unsure of his sincerity.

'No, really,' he said, raising his hands in a placatory gesture. 'I admire you and … and I love you.'

She was taken aback, and only stared at him. For all that she understood how much she meant to him, he seldom expressed it in words. To hear him say out loud that he loved her made unfamiliar feelings of guilt uncoil in her tummy.

'I love you too,' she said. And she meant it.

She meant it, but she was troubled too, and by her own words. She thought again, for the hundredth time, about the one her prince called the birdman. She was furious with herself, and confused. Here she was, days from marrying a man she had loved since ... since she was no more than a child. Here she was on the point of joining for a lifetime with a man who had all but given his life for her, and yet her thoughts returned moment by moment to this *birdman,* and to that look he had had on his face when their eyes met, and for just a second.

She looked at her prince and told herself to believe that all was well – that all was as it had always been. It was better, in fact. She thought about the moment just days before when she had awoken with her head in his lap to find they might yet be lovers and parents after all. She had loved Costa when he was, as he insisted on saying, dead from the waist down. If that dead half came back to life, then anything was possible – indeed a whole life together as man and wife.

With all of that, why then, she asked herself desperately, did her thoughts keep returning to a glimpse of a stranger? She had met his eyes for only an instant, and yet in that glance she had seen another world. All in a moment she had understood that he might take her to that world, and far away. Why now, when so much might be possible, was she waking in the night from dreams of that face – that face shadowed by the beating of wings as it came ever closer to her own? Then just at the moment of coming together, eyes to eyes and lips to lips and ready to be ... consumed, she would awaken breathless and sweating, alone in the dark.

Loneliness took her by surprise then and pooled around her like cold, dark water that sapped the warmth from her bones, and she looked at the floor.

'I miss my mum,' she said, able at least to give voice to some of her thoughts. 'I miss her every day, but I miss her now more than ever.'

She wanted Costa to reach out for her, maybe take her hand and hold it, but he remained still on the bed, looking at her with an open expression on his thin face.

'I wish you could have known your father,' he said.

She gasped. While she was aware that he knew about her parentage, the truth of it was always left alone between them.

She was silent, and to fill the gap he pressed on.

'I think ... in fact I know that what I really mean to say is ... *I* would like to have known him.'

'Why?' Her voice was fragile, like a child's.

'Because I love you.'

There it was again – his second declaration of love in less than a minute!

'And *because* I love you, I feel the need to know the people who ... who made you. I knew Isabella a little – enough at least to see how she fits into the person that is you. But I would like to have ... I don't know – heard your father's voice, maybe got a sense of the sort of things that made him laugh, or angry...'

His voice tailed away as though he was embarrassed by what he was saying.

Out of nowhere, unbidden and unwanted, she was aware of the memory of the man who had been her mother's husband. The man she had been told to accept as her father but who had been no such thing – neither husband nor father.

'I am glad they had one more time together – if only for such a little while,' she said. She realised her words were an extension only of her own thoughts and that she would have to say more if he was to understand.

'If only you had had the chance to ... even to look at each other, see each other's faces,' he said.

She thought about the birdman's face and looked down at her hands, folded neatly in her lap as always.

Her mother had confessed the same sadness, and many times.

After many years of wanting to, and trying to, Isabella had got a message to Yaminah's real father. They had a daughter, she wrote. She was more sorry than she could say that she had kept the truth from him, but she needed him to know. And he had come, even though she had begged him not to. He must put aside any such thought, she had written. It was much too dangerous.

Isabella's father, Philip Kritovoulos, another prince of the realm and mentor and friend to the emperor, still nursed a furious anger. And if he was not enough of a reason to stay away, then her husband, Martin Notaras – who had done them all such a favour by marrying her and giving his name to the child – was every bit as vengeful. Even though there had been no connection be-tween Notaras and Isabella (he had been drafted into the role of husband, and father to Yaminah, only after the fact and as a favour to the family), his venomous nature had allowed him to back-date his hatred.

That her real father had wanted to come – in spite of the danger and in spite of her mother urging him to stay away, for all their sakes – mattered more to Yaminah than she could say.

'Tell me how they met,' said Constantine, snapping her back into the present.

She took a moment to collect her thoughts. She had never told the story to anyone before, and it mattered to her to find the right words.

'My grandfather had travelled to Rome,' she began. 'He was sent on the emperor's behalf – the leader of a delegation. My mother told me that the rest of them were churchmen and that they sought an audience with the Holy Father so that they might secure promises of help and support in the face of the Turkmen's relentless advances into our territory.

'My mother went with him. She said it was because he was so possessive of her that he feared the consequences of leaving her behind.'

'What consequences?' asked Constantine.

'My mother loved my grandmother, and was loved in return,' she said. 'My father did not understand, had no time for ... for love. She loved her nurse, Ama, perhaps even more. All that my grandfather saw was people wanting my mother to be happy. She said that as far as he was concerned, her happiness mattered not at all. To him she was a bargaining piece, to be played at just the right moment in the long game of life at court. Rather than see her value squandered – on love or any other foolishness – he took her everywhere.'

'For all the good it did him,' said Constantine. 'I mean ... by the sounds of it.'

She smiled at him, enjoying the fact that he evidently understood the irony of her grandfather's actions.

'My father was among the bodyguards – soldiers sent along to keep the delegates from harm. My mother told me he was the single most beautiful man she had ever laid eyes on.' Yaminah relished the thought and rocked back in her seat and closed her eyes.

'Would I be right in supposing he laid more than his eyes on your mother?' asked Constantine. She opened her eyes wide and stared at him, mock horror on her face.

'How *dare* you?' she said, but she smiled again. It felt like they were taking sides – she and Costa conspiring against the memory of her grandfather – and she was surprised by the pleasure of it. The thrill came from a secret sealed away long ago, but it tasted sweet just the same.

'She said she noticed him as soon as she stepped aboard the ship,' she said. 'He told her later that he had spotted her waiting by her father's side on the dock – that it had pleased him to know the first sight was his alone.'

'What did he look like?' asked Constantine.

She glanced down at her hands once more.

'I only wish I knew,' she said.

'I know that. Of course I know that,' he said. 'But how did your mother describe him?'

'He was dark,' said Yaminah. 'Darker than her, anyway. She said the tone of my skin was from him, and my hair too, I suppose.'

'What else?'

'Well, he was quite the grand physical specimen, apparently,' she said. She blushed at the thought of her father the giant, and while she had no such memory, she allowed herself to picture him picking her mother up off the ground and spinning her around like a toy.

'And you such a little thing,' said Constantine.

She scowled at him again.

'That is all the picture I have of him,' she said. 'My mother spent more time telling me how gentle he was, and kind … how he would look into her eyes and tell her he could hardly believe she was real.'

'And so they became lovers,' he said.

'And so they became lovers. My grandfather and the rest of the delegates were kept busier than any of them had imagined, I think. They were in Rome for weeks and my grandfather had no option but to leave my mother to her own devices. He attended meeting after meeting after meeting. My mother and father stole some time alone together and … and I was the result.'

She held her hands out to her sides, palms upwards, as though inviting him to consider her existence for the first time.

'I am delighted to hear it,' he said. 'And she kept you a secret?'

'From him, at least. She said as soon as she realised she was going to have me, it was like awakening from a dream. She knew at once what it all must mean, the consequences…'

'And so what happened?'

'She left him,' she said. 'Left my father. The delegates were due to depart for home – and since the bodyguards were not regarded as necessary for the return, they had been paid off. She waited until the last possible moment and then left him behind.'

'And that was the last she saw of him?'

'Until five years later, yes – when she gave in to the need to tell him about me,' she said. 'She got a message to him somehow ... somewhere. And he came to her.'

Constantine began moving his hands once more, and when Yaminah looked up at the ceiling, she saw the figure of a man transported across the sky by giant birds. She caught his meaning and smiled in the dark.

'He found his way to her somehow,' she repeated, still watching the show. 'She was married by then, of course, long married. My grandfather had seen to that, and Notaras had been happy to oblige. My mother was ... she was lovely.

'She was alone, except for her servants. I think my father must have kept watch until he was sure it was safe. My mother said I was out with my nurse and that my father seized the moment and ... and he came to her.

'She said she found scars upon his back and on his legs, and when she asked about them, he told her men had come on the day she left him. They had barred his door and set the house on fire. He only escaped because his friend rescued him.'

'A friend indeed,' said the prince.

'His best,' said Yaminah. 'Anyway, they talked and talked and ... and they were together when my ... when her husband returned.'

'So what happened?'

'There was a fight. My mother did not tell me

exactly what happened. There was a fight and my father killed Martin Notaras. My mother said my father begged her to leave with him – to find me and for us both to leave with him.'

'And why not?' asked Constantine.

Yaminah shrugged, hopelessly.

'Where could they ... we ... have gone?' she asked, not expecting an answer. 'She made him leave us behind. And he ... and so he did.'

They sat quietly for a few moments. Finally Constantine reached out for her and held her hand, as she had wanted him to all along.

'My mother said his last words to her were some kind of an apology.'

Constantine kept silent, just stroked the back of her hand with his thumb.

'He told her he was all the trouble in the world,' she said.

'Do you know his name?' he asked.

'Of course I do,' she said, looking up at his face. 'My father was Badr Khassan.'

PART FOUR

Wedding

44

The days of siege passed in the Great City like a malady endured. Through it all – every moment, it seemed – the emperor was with his soldiers on the battlements or among his frightened and fearful people. Where they prayed, he prayed – in the Church of St Sophia and in a score of other holy places besides. When they processed through the streets carrying their most revered and trusted icon – the Hodegetria depicting the Virgin and her child – he was always to the fore, head bowed like the rest beneath the weight they shouldered.

To Giustiniani he had entrusted the care and defence of the walls, and this had been among his best decisions, for the Genoan brought not only a lifetime of experience of warfare, but also instinctive tactical genius. As soon as he was able, he set about the work of assessing the walls – all twelve miles of them. Battered and bruised they most assuredly were, but still strong, still good.

'But they are failing,' Minotto had informed him, as soon as the Genoan had arrived at the palace. 'These torments of the heathen are too strong. We are lost before we have even begun to fight!'

Giustiniani said nothing, but shook his head. He had looked around him then and from among his men selected a twenty-strong party to ride out with him and survey the worst of the damage.

Almost as an afterthought, it had seemed, he pointed at John Grant.

'At such a time, we need all the luck we can get,' he said. He had smiled, and John Grant found himself smiling back. Feeling an inexplicable need, and surrendering to it, he looked for Lẽna. Their eyes met for a moment and she nodded, as though her approval was required, as though it mattered to him.

'Let us see if your eagles come along,' said the Genoan.

Embarrassed, John Grant looked again for Lẽna, but she was gone. He looked around the battlements and down towards the interior; there was no trace of his mother.

The little group crossed to the outer wall, where great holes had already been punched, ragged and raw. Only the fosse – simplest of the defences, yet priceless now – stood wholly intact in the attackers' way. Giustiniani was the most agitated John Grant had yet seen him, first riding back and forth behind the tumble of rubble lying heaped in the gap, and then dismounting and climbing upon the blocks until he could look out over the fosse and into the no-man's-land beyond.

'They have made this a war of stone upon stone,' he said. 'And have found the results to their liking.'

'What can we do?' asked Minotto. His words were measured and delivered quietly, but John Grant sensed the tension beneath.

Giustiniani squatted to the ground and picked up a fragment of masonry the size of a man's fist. The damp spring had kept the ground soft, puddled in places with thick mud and ooze. He straightened and tossed the stone, and all of them watched as it landed in a patch of mire with a wet plop.

'See there?' he said. 'See how the softness catches and holds the stone?'

John Grant understood at once, but held his tongue, unwilling to place himself in the spotlight again.

'It is all we have time for anyway,' said the Genoan.

'And so?' asked Minotto.

'And so we will plug these gaps with soil, and anything else that comes readily to hand. It is muck we have and time that we lack. We cannot be about rebuilding these walls with blocks and mortar while the Turks are firing upon us. But we can surely heap soil and sand and anything else that can be piled in barrows and pushed into cavities like this one.'

'That we can,' Minotto had said.

He had been slower than John Grant to understand the beautiful simplicity of the proposed stopgap, but once he grasped it, he clung to it. 'And it requires no skill – no masons or other craftsmen. The good folk of Constantinople – women and children too – can bend their backs to this and be a part of the fight.'

Orders were issued and quickly circulated. Within hours, the citizens had begun pouring from the city. First in their hundreds and then in their thousands – just as their ancestors had done a thousand years before, when the earthquake levelled the walls. This time it was a different threat, but the response had been the same. Like white blood cells rushing to the site of a wound, the people rushed to minister to their own hurt.

Under Giustiniani's directions, his soldiers erected a rough frame of wooden stakes, planting the ends of the shafts within the topmost level of the rubble. Into and on to this scaffold teams of workers piled earth, sand and stones. Vegetation was harvested too, and brush, bushes, branches and even domestic rubbish added to the mix. Since men would have to stand and fight there, barrels were filled with yet more sand and soil and these were placed in ranks, three and four deep, along the levelled top of the spoil to create crenellations behind which soldiers might stand to, or simply take cover.

From dusk of the first day the citizens had worked, on through the night that followed, until by the dawn their efforts were nearing completion. Blinded by darkness though they had been, still the Turkish gunners kept up their fire through that night, and for those labouring among the rubble there were hellish seconds to be endured until the sounds of impact elsewhere told them they had been spared.

When the light of day allowed the Turks to survey the walls, they found to their dismay that all the inroads made by their blessed guns had been swallowed up, so that it appeared they had never been. Now some of the teeth in the grimace they beheld were black, or brown, but they were teeth just the same.

In furious anger the gunners turned their fire upon the ad hoc repairs, but when their missiles found their marks, the result was like a conjuror's trick. Where before there had been great explosions and thrilling sounds of destruction, now there was silence. The stones, even the greatest of them, simply vanished into the softly heaped soil and became, as they did so, further reinforcements to the structure.

John Grant had laboured among the rest, never shirking a moment of the toil. He had watched women and children sweat beside him and had seen the grief upon their faces and felt their fear – and so understood as never before that he had done right by coming here. Around and above him it had seemed a darkness thicker than the night was forming. At times he had reeled upon the roiling sea of sensations, and he had struggled to reach through the fog of it in search of understanding.

It was as the dawn came on that he finally succeeded in seeing through the welter of chaff to the grain he had known was there within. With the task of plugging the gaps all but completed, the workers began to slow their efforts and to lean upon picks and shovels. There were a few moments for quiet conversation, the swapping of stories of the night's adventures and misadventures, and as the sun rose milky behind a thin blanket of cloud, John Grant reached all the way down and felt the push.

He had suspected it was there, swamped and all but overwhelmed by the clutter of anxiety around him. In the respite and calm he had had the time to listen and to feel and he had known, all in an instant, why it had been so hard to pinpoint. While he had stood in the cool of early morning, his skin damp and cold with the residue of the night's efforts, he had felt a pressure rising through his body from his boots. The soles of his feet, soaked by the dew, were tingling. In fact, when he moved, it was almost as though he was walking upon the rounded ends of broom handles.

It was the push, all right – and it was coming from under the ground. The realisation had washed through him like warm relief, like the sensation of finally summoning a lost name from within the muddled depths of memory. At first he had hardly known what to do with the knowledge. He had understood at once that it mattered and that he could not and would not keep it to himself. But how best to ensure it was turned to the advantage of all?

He had heard Giustiniani's voice then, and turned to watch him moving between groups of weary soldiers and civilians. The certainty that this man would at least listen appeared in his heart unbidden, and he had immediately run to the commander's side.

Sensing his approach, the Genoan had turned to face him, hands on hips.

'The birdman,' he said. 'And all in a flap.'

John Grant blushed, and slowed his approach.

'What is it?' asked Giustiniani.

Aware as always that the push gave notice, but only so much, he had resolved to express his instincts in as straightforward a way as possible.

'I believe the enemy is digging beneath the walls,' he said.

45

Fog like wet linen hung loosely draped about the night. The light of the moon did its best, struggled to penetrate the murk but seemed content in the end only to cast a dark, grey gloom that felt like forgetting. Lẽna had been drawn by it, into it. There was something dreamlike about her progress towards the Ottoman lines, she thought, coupled with the faintest sense of watching herself from afar. The more she thought about it and allowed the sensations to wash over her, the more she realised the city itself had seemed like the setting for a dream.

More than that and besides that was the unmistakable notion that every moment she had experienced since their arrival in the harbour had happened before. She had no words to describe the feeling, but the longer it lasted the more she felt a tingle of excitement that was almost indecent; sacred and profane. If she had a destiny then it was close enough here, it seemed, beyond the city walls, that she might reach out into the gloom ahead and touch the hem of its garment as it led the way.

Constantinople was a city besieged, huddled in the shadow of war and worse, and yet its citizens had about them the air of a people enchanted or otherwise befuddled. She had known it was a city of superstition and rumour, its folk given to trusting portents and signs more than the action of their own hearts and hands. The people here had long since learned to accept fate and to see everything as the will of God. But their plaintive beseechings for help from elsewhere fairly set her teeth on edge.

Lẽna loved her God, even if he must be silent, but always before she had been, and even now she was, imbued with the certainty that some part of her fate was her own responsibility. While she sought to find and follow her own path wherever it might lead, those citizens of the Great City had the look and feel of the herd. They were scared, that much was obvious and understandable. They feared their God was disappointed – or worse, that he was angry with them and vengeful as a result.

But for all that they might cast their gaze to the sky and to heaven in search of more signs, more portents, there was something in their dull and impotent acceptance that struck Lẽna as ... *bovine*. Their necks were stretched ready for the butcher's blade, their eyes wide and imploring and their mouths agape. She had come to help them – more specifically to give all of herself in service of the greater need – but found to her dismay she almost hated them as well.

The city had defied a score of sieges after all. The sights and sounds of an enemy baying for their blood were nothing new. Perhaps the experience of being besieged, of being put upon by one lustful foe after another, was the destiny of Constantinople.

Only by an act of collective will could they deny

the unworthy claimants to their place on earth. Was she judging them too harshly? She shook her head as she advanced into the swirling djinns of fog. Let them be, she thought. Let them face what they must, and how they must. Tired of deep thoughts, she turned her attention to the job at hand. She had come to pay what she owed.

She had found it easy to leave the city, to pass beyond the walls and into the no-man's-land that separated the foes one from another. Men paid most attention to other men in times of war, and while the great gates were heavily barred against the threat of soldiers and men-at-arms, the lesser posterns were more porous to those who seemed to pose no threat. It was via one of those that she had left the city behind, beyond the palace and at a point where there was no fosse to negotiate. If any guard had noticed her passing, she had evidently mattered not at all.

Warrior though she was, she had given little thought to any plan. It had seemed enough merely to put herself in danger. She was close to God there – closest of all – and in the valley of the shadow she feared no evil.

She thought about the girl who had burned at the stake in her place, and about all the years she had gained while the innocent's blackened bones had turned to dust. From that day to this, all the intervening heartbeats and breaths had amassed somewhere as a terrible debt, and she was ready to settle her account.

She thought too about Jacques d'Arc – wondered, not for the first time, if he was alive or dead. After Orleans, the whole family had been raised by the king to nobility, but while her mother Isabelle had enjoyed their improved circumstances, her father had cared little for the grandeur. He had known his daughter for what she was and had only bent his will to seeing her fulfil her potential. He had listened while she described the visions and the voices, and had believed her with all of his heart. He had understood she was born and made to fight for the glory of the crown, and God – and he had done all in his power to make it come to pass – but more than anything else he had loved her like a father should. It had broken his heart when she went off to war, and she had scarcely dared allow herself to wonder what awful harm had been done him by news of her tortured death.

'Forgive me, Father,' she said.

The sense of having been this way before was like a warm wind from a far-off place that seemed briefly to caress her face before parting and passing either side. Figures from her past were there too, woven through the fog like wraiths. She thought of her mother and feared her grief. She thought of her brothers, Jean, Pierre and Jacquemin, and wondered if they too had survived the fighting, if they lived still, perhaps with families of their own. She thought of her sister Catherine, dead in childbirth long ago. She thought of Patrick Grant.

Had there been any there to witness her advance towards the Turks, it would have seemed to them like the progress of a penitent bound for a place of pilgrimage. She would have appeared distracted, preoccupied with her own thoughts while the ropes and tendrils of fog coiled around her like living things, or their spirits.

It was as the first of the Turkish pickets saw her and lunged towards her out of the gloom that she heard her father's voice.

'To MacDonald of the stately eyes is the gift of what I am giving,' he said. 'Greater than the cup – though a gift of gold – in honour of what to me is given.'

She had already raised her sword, sweeping it upwards from within the folds of her cloak to parry her enemy's clumsy blow, when she glimpsed Jacques by her side. He was unarmed, but clad in his soldier's garb as of old. She disarmed the hapless sentry – spun him past her and knocked him unconscious with a blow from the pommel of her sword, and watched him sprawl heavily on to the soft ground – then turned to look properly upon her father's face.

He was beautiful. He was clean and bright-eyed and younger than she ever remembered seeing him in life, and she knew at once that he had come to her from among the peaceful dead.

'Forgive me, Father,' she said again, tears in her eyes and a tremble in her voice as she turned from him to deal with a second attacker.

The expression on the Turk's face was one of plain astonishment; instead of crying out at the sight of her, and thereby summoning more of his kind to his aid, he came at her in silence, dumbstruck in fact, but with curved sword raised.

For Lẽna the sensations of a dream were all but overwhelming, and it was only the smell of the man's sweat and fear that reminded her he was

435

real, that this was real. She stepped wide of his downward blow and turned and brought the pommel of her sword down for a second time and upon a second head. She had hit him harder than she intended, felt the crack of bone and only hoped he would wake up.

'Though I got this cup free, as it were, from the wolf of the Gaels,' said Jacques d'Arc, 'it does not seem that way to me: he received my love as payment.'

Her father's voice was a wonder to her, even more so than the sight of him. As she watched his form shimmering and shifting within the folds of mist and fog, he mirrored her movements in the combat and smiled approvingly at her as he did so.

For any vouchsafed a vision of the fighting – the dark-haired woman and a succession of attackers – it might have seemed like the steps of a carefully choreographed dance. The fog made of every encounter a self-contained vignette; the sight of each concealed from every other and all of the sounds muffled so that no general alarm was raised, and she moved among them one by one like a nameless fear.

She dispatched a third man and a fourth, and in the moment of calm that followed, her father smiled at her, stepped close and reached out with one rough hand and caressed her face. He leaned forward until his smooth cheek brushed her own.

'My love,' he said, and was gone.

She looked around, her face wet with tears. She had gone alone among them in hope of finding the death she deserved. She had offered herself in combat – been ready to face them en masse and to fall beneath a forest of swords and awaken in the peace of heaven.

But it was not to be. Another angel, her own father, had come to her and to her alone, and she had learned from him, and for the second time, that the good Lord would receive her when he was ready, and not before.

46

Yaminah felt a familiar hard knot of tension in her stomach as she made her way through the corridors leading to the throne room of Blachernae Palace. She was following the lady-in-waiting who had brought the summons, and to steady her nerves she concentrated on the soft sound of the woman's robes sweeping rhythmically across the ancient flagstones. They had not exchanged a word and the woman ahead seemed keen to have her duty over with.

Yaminah had been with her prince, busy with the daily task of massaging scented oil into the wasted muscles of his legs, when her efforts were interrupted by a light knock upon the outer door of Costa's rooms. For all that the rest of the city was now utterly absorbed by the threat looming over them, the girl and her broken boy had wrapped the folds of their private world ever more tightly around them. Their shared rituals mattered more than ever, more than everything.

Yaminah had told him every detail she remembered of her encounter with Helena, and about the overheard conversation that had preceded it. Inwardly he shared her concern about the consort's tone and choice of language, but he consoled himself with the thought that it had been in the context of plans for their wedding. If such a ceremony was still going ahead at such a time, then that was enough to be going on with. They could hardly ask for a greater demonstration of commitment. That Helena had been heard, in a private conversation, bemoaning his disability in a time of war was hardly surprising. He had sought to calm his betrothed and to allay her fears, and he felt he had succeeded, at least in part. Regardless of his outward show, however, he harboured doubts of his own.

The knock at the door came again, louder than before.

'Join us,' Costa had said.

There had been a moment or two of hesitation while whoever it was, beyond the threshold, had assessed the unfamiliar choice of words, and then the door had been pushed open and a young woman Yaminah recognised from the court had entered hesitantly.

'I have a message,' she said. 'My lady wishes to speak with Yaminah, and at once.'

Yaminah had looked up into her prince's face, and then, aware that such a summons could hardly be delayed, far less ignored, she had picked up a cloth and wiped the oil from her hands. She had left him without a word, but with a sense of foreboding.

The emperor had been solicitous of her time of

late, almost disturbingly so. He had demanded her presence at his side for the arrival of the Genoan ships; indeed, he had chosen her over his consort. Yaminah was aware of what men thought and felt when they saw her, and she understood, with some undeniable satisfaction, that he had wanted to be seen in the company of one who would be envied and desired. The emperor might be God's representative on earth, but he was also a man.

The summons had come from Helena, but the venue for the audience – in the palace throne room – made Yaminah certain the consort would not be alone. She expected the emperor to be waiting as well, and in spite of herself, the thought was exciting as well as troubling. A shadow of danger hung over her prince, but it was shapeless.

To learn more, properly to understand the threat, she needed to spend time with those who might threaten him. She pulled herself up straight and arched her back. She slowed her walk too, just a shade, and paid more attention to the movement of her hips.

The lady-in-waiting approached a narrow wooden door that Yaminah recognised as one leading to the rear of the vast room beyond, behind the dais upon which stood the throne itself. She opened it and stepped aside so that Yaminah might proceed alone.

She listened to the echoes of her footsteps rising like a flock of startled birds towards the domed ceiling. There was the throne – an absurd-looking confection, she had always thought. Around the luxuriously upholstered seat and back were four elaborately carved stone pillars. Atop these, and supporting a dome of burnished bronze that both sheltered the seat and underlined the imperial character of whomsoever sat upon it, were four doves carved from white marble. Of all the ostentatious decorations that still adorned the palace – those that had survived the depredations of the crusade two and a half centuries before – the throne had always struck Yaminah as the most preposterous of all.

Today, however, it was empty, and she looked around in search of life. Finding none, she walked beyond the throne and then out from the walls until she was in the centre of the huge room.

It was all too strange. Game-playing was not in Helena's repertoire, and the emperor would hardly set aside his preoccupation with the city's defence to make mischief such as this. She had almost persuaded herself it was some work of the lady-in-waiting when she heard the heavy note of the closing of the door through which she had entered the throne room minutes before.

Startled by the sound, and with its reverberations still rolling around the cavernous space, she turned towards its source.

Standing before the throne, diminished by the scale of the room but unmistakable even at such a distance, resplendent in robes of white and gold and with a gleaming bejewelled coronet resting on his head, was Costa.

47

The cloying stink of blood was heavy on the air. Unusually, Mehmet had overseen the executions himself. The job was done now, though, and he was seated with his back to the carnage, still nursing his wrath.

What was to be done?

Not one of the men standing in front of the sultan would dare to open their mouths before he himself had spoken, and so they waited, avoiding his eyes. How much difference had been made by the events of a single day and a single night.

Just twenty-four hours ago, the atmosphere around Mehmet had been filled with excitement and possibility. After more than a week, the relentless bombardment had taken its toll so that the walls, indeed the entire city, seemed to vibrate, giving off a deep note like that won from a struck bell. The Turkish gunners had mastered their routines to such an extent that they had been able to bring a concentrated fire to bear upon that part of the outer wall directly in front of Mehmet's own tents. He had stood by the largest of the guns, the fattest of Orban's children, as it delivered its deadly cargo.

After the third firing of the day, however, Orban had run forward and chased off the men pouring olive oil on to the barrel, as they had been instructed, to cool it. He had peered closely at the metal, too hot to touch, and brought his hands as close to its steaming surface as he dared. In an agony of anxiety he had rushed to the sultan's side.

'We must let him cool,' he said, speaking about the bombard like a father fearful for the welfare of his favourite son. 'We will concentrate on the others – until tomorrow?' Mindful that he was suddenly giving rather than receiving instructions, he had turned his last words into a question just in time.

Without even looking at his gunsmith, Mehmet had shaken his head.

'The walls of Jericho, you said. You promised me this contrivance of yours would have dropped the walls of Jericho. Then find me a way through the Wall of Theodosius.'

Chastened by the exchange, the Hungarian hastened to his masterpiece and oversaw the loading of another ball, this one of grey stone and as big as a crouching bear. When all was ready, he called to the sultan, begging him at least to retire to a safer distance, but Mehmet stood firm as though he had not heard the warning.

The order to fire was given and a young gunner, stripped to the waist and sweating, placed a long lighted taper against the touch hole. With an ear-splitting roar the barrel bucked and split into a dozen pieces that scythed through the air in every direction. Anyone not felled by chunks of cherry-red metal was knocked to the ground by the ac-companying shock wave. A few seconds of stunned and deafened silence followed, before those still living got to their feet, ears ringing and hearts pounding.

Mehmet was among those able to stand, and men rushed to him from all sides, astonished to find that he was unhurt. Brushing his courtiers aside, he rushed towards the remains of the gun. Every man of the crew – all two dozen souls – had been sliced and blasted into bloody lumps of flesh and hair and ragged clothing. Orban the gunsmith was cloven neatly in two at the waist. Mehmet looked down into the lifeless eyes that stared back at him from a face strangely peaceful and unmarked, and experienced no emotion beyond frustration.

A great shout went up and the sultan turned from the lifeless Orban to investigate the cause of the outburst. All eyes were focused not on the dead gunners and the remains of their erstwhile charge but upon the wall. There beside the Gate of St Romanus – the central point in the ancient land defences – a yawning gap had opened, product of the great gun's dying breath. Already the figures of men and women could be seen rushing towards the rupture, desperate to set about the business of repair.

Swiftly regaining his composure, Mehmet shouted orders to those of his lieutenants who still had eardrums intact. The fire of the three nearest guns was to be brought to bear upon the gap more heavily than before, so as to deter those defenders who were even now beginning to heap soil and other materials upon the piles of rubble. He himself would lead a mass charge to the fosse. Wagons were to be loaded immediately with anything and everything that might be used to infill a section of the huge brick-lined ditch.

Within minutes there was amassed around the young sultan a great horde of his *azaps* – Muslim levies swept into the ranks of his attacking force from every corner of his demesne. The resolve of those game but untrained volunteers was stiffened by the presence of a company of janissaries, and with Mehmet to the fore and to the accompaniment of a great cacophony of horns, pipes, cymbals and drums, the whole mass of them advanced downhill towards the wall. The sun had set, and by the time they reached level ground beside the river, a half-moon was rising above the city.

Mehmet and his professional soldiers were mounted upon warhorses, but they held themselves to a pace that could be matched by the trotting infantrymen. Down the slopes they poured, and when they came within range of the gap, the defenders rained hell upon them from their own guns, and from their crossbows and longbows besides.

The janissaries clustered around their sultan, shields upraised. Understanding all too well the likely consequences of allowing any harm to befall him, they seemed far more concerned for his safety than their own.

The dying of the *azaps*, unmistakable in their bright red caps, was a horror and a wonder to behold. The Christians, realising that the Turkmen were too close for the useful firing of stone balls, loaded the barrels of their own smaller bombards with lead shot and iron nails instead, and blasted the lethal hail into the faces of the foe. In this way, even heavily armoured janissaries were cut down, while the *azaps*, simply clad and protected only by shields (which many had thrown aside anyway in their haste to get in among the Christians), were butchered ten and twenty at a time by every discharge, missiles passing through man after man without losing velocity.

Despite the carnage, still they came on. Reaching the fosse, they heaped all manner of material into the void, even their own tents and many of their dead, until a vile slurry of timber and stone, fabric and flesh began to fill a section of the ditch wide enough and deep enough for men to cross.

The continued fire of the Turkish guns brought down blow after blow upon the walls, and upon defenders and attackers alike. Emperor Constantine had watched the Turks advance from the inner wall and had sent out orders to sound a general alarm. In the city behind him, all the church bells tolled and into the darkening streets poured thousands of terrified citizens, crying and tearing at their clothes and clawing at their faces in their maddened panic.

The Turks crossed the fosse by the score, and, armed with long wooden poles topped with hooks, set about dragging down the barrels of rubble and soil, the better to expose the defenders on top to the violence of the guns and to their own blades and crossbows.

The last of the light bled out of the sky until the only illumination was that of the moon and the lightning flashes from the guns. Sensing victory, the *azaps* surged on to the earthen rampart, each man pushing at the rear of the one in front so that they began to reach the summit in great numbers.

The janissaries, dismounted now and fighting shoulder to shoulder with the rest, pushed hardest of all, and for many dreadful minutes a great press of Christians and Muslims came face to face under the watchful moon.

Mehmet, stalled at the base of the rampart, stood baying at the sight of it, at the moon and at the tumult of the fighting – urging and cursing as men of every creed slashed and gouged at one another in the claustrophobic confines of the fissure. But for all the sultan's earnest vows and dire imprecations, the momentum of his forces began to wane, breaking like a spent wave, until in a sudden flurry of retreat they fell back down and away towards their own lines.

And now it was the early morning of the day that followed the night, and Mehmet sat and brooded. He was in the open space in front of his own conical tent of red and gold, protected from prying eyes by a circular timber palisade that surrounded and formed his private enclosure. The most senior of his attendants, his chief vizier, Halil Pasha, felt the heat more than most. Spring was properly on its way at last, but it was hardly the warmth of the day that made him feel faint. Neither was it hunger, for although a Muslim army on campaign ate but once a day, at sunset, his stomach felt like a mere pebble.

In hopes of lowering the temperature of the sultan's furious disappointment, a company of prisoners had earlier been paraded before him. The luckless party had been taken during the retreat, bundled among the fleeing Turks and carried back to their encampment.

Mehmet had watched impassively as they were tortured and abused with hot knives, and then blinded. They had had little to reveal anyway, and he had lost interest before even half of them had been defiled. Instead he had had each man strung up by his feet from a hastily erected timber frame. One by one they had been sawn in two with long blades, from crotch to shoulder. Mehmet had heard that these Christians valued their heads and so feared the consequences of being separated from them. He had therefore spared them the indignity by leaving their heads upon their shoulders. Now all of them were dead, steam rising lazily from their remains.

'I am saddened,' he said.

No one replied, not even Halil Pasha, who valued his own head as much as did any Christian.

'I have provided the tools required for the task, and yet here I sit outside the walls while the emperor looks down at me from on top of a heap of dirt. Explain to me why this is so.'

Halil Pasha stepped forward, but before he could speak, Mehmet continued.

'I am sad about these infidels,' he said, gesturing behind him with a wave of his hand. 'In spite of all my encouragement – my love – you have fallen short, every one of you. And all you can think to do is bring these men to me – these brave defenders – and have me watch while they are tormented.

'I am saddened,' he said again.

Sensing the building of a wave that might sweep him and the rest away, Halil found his moment to speak.

'There is another possibility,' he said.

Mehmet was quiet for a long minute. Finally he sighed and motioned with his hand in front of his face, as though savouring a scent and wafting it towards his nose. Halil recognised it as a gesture to continue. He was long in the tooth now, having served and outlived Mehmet's own father, and well practised in reading his masters.

'It has always been thought that the Great City, and the walls surrounding it, were built on solid rock,' he said.

Mehmet looked his vizier in the eye for the first time since the audience had begun.

'But among our mercenaries are men who say different.'

'You have my attention,' said Mehmet.

'They are men from the north, from the land of Saxony,' said Halil. 'They are miners of silver, and masters in the art of digging and cutting away mountains. To their tools, it is said, marble is as beeswax and the black mountains of their own land are as piles of dust.'

Mehmet watched his vizier, enjoying the visible tension and the need to please. He knew too that Halil would be happiest watching his sultan swinging from a noose with his feet cut off at the ankles.

'And so what do they say about the rock here?' asked Mehmet.

'That is the point, sire,' said Halil. 'Among them are men who say they have seen terrain like this in their own country – that while there is a hard crust over much of the surface, it can be cut through.'

'And then?' asked Mehmet.

'And then, the Saxons say, it is sand and soil and boulders – that it is a matter only of tunnelling towards and then under the walls.'

'We have mountains of black powder for our guns,' said Mehmet. 'And more on the way. If I cannot knock down the walls, then perhaps I may blow them to the heavens. I had thought mining impossible in this terrain, but if what these Saxons say is true...'

He stood up and walked towards his vizier, who unconsciously took three steps backwards.

'...then perhaps the bone in Allah's throat may yet be loosened.'

48

'Buckets and bowls?' asked Giustiniani. 'So it has come to this?'

The Genoan's tone was gently mocking, but he had acceded to the young Scotsman's request just the same. When John Grant told him that the Turks were tunnelling under the walls – that they might burst from the ground at any moment or under cover of night (like Greek warriors of old, from their giant horse), he was sceptical for only a few moments.

Giustiniani had spent the larger part of his life commanding men in war. Along the way he had learned the value, indeed the necessity, of trust. Among his company were several men he trusted with his own life. He knew too, with an intensity of feeling that was almost painful, that all his soldiers had placed their trust in him. Most of all, however, he trusted his instincts, and since their first encounter aboard the ship, he had had a feeling about John Grant.

He would have struggled to say out loud quite what it was, and did not even fully understand it inside his own head. Some of it came from the manner of the woman who had been by his side. She had had to be twice his age and yet she had followed him into a war, disguising herself as a man in order to do so. He had discerned no hint of romantic attachment between them, and so it had been something else that placed her close to him and kept her there.

And then, he had to admit, there were the eagles. He had watched dumbfounded with the rest as the giant birds had come together upon the legbone the lad had held aloft in one hand. He had gasped at the sight of it – and at the way the birds had seemed for a moment like the incarnation of the double-headed eagle on the crest of the house of Palaiologos – and he had gone down on one knee.

There was something in the boy, he was sure of it – something unknown and unmeasurable. There were always men upon the field of battle to whom others were drawn. Call it luck, call it good judgement, call it magic – there were those soldiers who always saw the surest path and took it, and survived as a result; men who made the right choice in a split second, the choice that saved their lives. And other men noticed – others on the field sensed the one among them who seemed guided, perhaps sheltered by an angel's wings, and he gave them faith and belief. They were drawn to such men and made of them lucky charms.

With his own eyes Giustiniani had watched his soldiers seek out the young Scotsman. Since that moment in the square they had seemed pulled in his direction, drawn to his side. The truth was, Giustiniani felt it too – felt a quality about this young man – and so when John Grant came to him and said he believed tunnels were being dug beneath the walls of Constantinople, he believed him.

For days now, in addition to fending off assaults on the fosse and upon the outer wall, the defenders had had to become preoccupied with bowls and buckets. When Giustiniani had accepted the truth of what John Grant had had to say, he asked next what was to be done about it. And the Scotsman's answer had been to call for hundreds of vessels for holding water.

He had filled one and placed it on the ground at the commander's feet.

'Watch what happens,' he said, walking away from the bowl. 'Keep your eyes on the water.'

When he was a dozen paces from Giustiniani, he turned and stamped his foot. 'Do you see?' he asked.

The Genoan smiled and nodded, watching the telltale ripples on the surface of the water.

Having received the go-ahead for the deployment of his early-warning system, John Grant had had receptacles of every sort distributed at intervals across the space between the outer and the inner walls, placed directly on the ground where the vibrations from any nearby activity would be at their strongest. Women and children were tasked with keeping watch on them; special attention was to be paid to those bowls closest to the walls themselves.

John Grant was on the battlements of the outer wall when it happened. It was a moonless night and he was seated among a company of weary soldiers taking comfort from a fire lit inside an iron brazier. The siege was in its third week, and the defenders, few enough to begin with, were spread thin as gossamer around the city's perimeter. In the end it was their own silence that saved them.

'Listen,' said John Grant. He was warm enough, but the hairs had risen on his arms and he felt a pressure beneath him like the uplift from a soft swell in deep water. His nerves had been jangling for days, assaulted by threats and doubts, but now there was a sound as well.

'Listen,' he said once more, and the men around him sat forward, straining to hear.

After a few moments, the faint but unmistakable ring of a pickaxe striking rock reached out to them from the dark.

'I hear it,' said one of the soldiers.

'Digging!' said another. 'I hear it too.'

'Get word to Giustiniani,' said John Grant, to the first who had successfully picked out the sound. 'And to the emperor. Go!'

The rest of the men grabbed their weapons and bolted down the steps leading to ground level. John Grant was ahead of them and sprinted to the location of the nearest of his bowls. He stood motionless beside it. Nothing. He ran on to the next, a wooden bucket, and gazed at its surface, lit by a flaming torch on the wall above. Pulsing there, with an even rhythm like that of a distant heartbeat, was the proof of all he had said.

It was one thing to read the ripples and know someone was digging somewhere, quite another to pinpoint the location of the tunnel itself. He could already hear the sound of approaching horses. It would be the commander – perhaps the emperor as well – and they would want answers.

In the moments that remained to him, he closed his eyes and reached out towards the push, searching for its centre. The world turned and hurtled into the void on its endless flight, and John Grant, witness to the journey, imagined the force of it scouring away dust and sand to reveal a lost jewel.

'Where is it?' It was the voice of Giustiniani. 'Where are they?'

John Grant heard horses beside him but kept his eyes closed and was motionless while he concentrated.

'Well?'

He moved forward, walking at first and then breaking into a trot as he realised he knew where he was going, and how far. He stopped abruptly and turned to look for Giustiniani – and his eyes met those of the emperor instead, mounted upon a white horse.

'Well?' asked Constantine.

'Here,' said John Grant, and he gestured at the ground between his feet. His voice was calm and filled with certainty. 'We dig here.'

49

Lēna's breathing was shallow and slow as she stood in the shadows of the balcony above the throne room in Blachernae Palace. Unusually adept in combat though she was, fast as a striking snake and as strong, she had also mastered stillness and silence. Just as John Grant had been transfixed by the sight of the girl standing by the emperor's side when they arrived in the royal harbour of Constantinople, so too had the Maid of Orleans. Had she been on her own, she might have missed the face in the crowd of onlookers. What she had noticed instead was her son's concentrated gaze, and when she followed it, and found the girl who had so captivated him, her breath had caught in her throat.

As soon as it had been possible, she had absented herself from the fighting men on the battlements and gone in search of her. The pressure from the siege and the barely contained chaos it had created in the city meant comings and goings to and from the palace precinct were less well controlled than they might otherwise have been. Lēna was, in any case, more than capable of sidestepping a guard or two and finding her way, by stealth and guile, into the vast and sprawling interior of the building itself.

Luck had played its part as well, and it had been as she made a circuit of the cloister surrounding all four sides of an elegant courtyard, with an extravagantly appointed ornamental pond and fountain at its centre, that she had observed the progress of two women. They had been on the far side of the courtyard and moving in the direction opposite to her own.

Her attention had been drawn first by the urgent speed of their walk – not side by side like friends or colleagues, but in single file, the one leading the other. There had been a tension about the pair, and it was as she scrutinised their movements that she realised the rearward of the two, the one following, was the girl from the harbour.

Blessing providence, she had looped quickly around the courtyard so as to follow the pair at an inconspicuous distance. After a few minutes they had arrived at a dark and heavily panelled wooden door. The girl leading the way had opened it on to what appeared to be a huge hall or chamber, and the second girl had entered, without any sign of hesitation, while the other stood by. Lẽna had looked around before deciding to follow the corridor around a corner to the right, and so give the impression she had business of her own to attend to.

She had spotted an open door leading to a flight of stairs. Guessing that it might put her in a position above the interior of the space the girl had entered, she had taken the steps two and three at a time before arriving, as she had hoped, in a vast and darkened gallery lined with wooden pews and designed to give an audience a discreet view of anything happening in the huge hall below.

She had taken a moment or two to admire the

cavernous scale of the place. She had heard the sound of a solitary pair of feet clicking on a stone floor, and while she could not yet see the girl, with her eyes she followed the echo of her footsteps up into a domed ceiling impossibly high above. Had she not been reminding herself to remain silent and undetected, Lẽna might have gasped at the immensity and the grandeur.

It was the booming sound of a door slamming shut – no doubt the door through which the girl had entered, she thought – that pulled her back into the present. Carefully she walked forward, still concealed by shadows, until she could observe the scene below.

The girl, the beautiful girl with the long chestnut hair and a perfect face made to fit neatly into the cupped hands of a lover, was so rooted to the spot in the centre of the chamber that she might have grown out of the floor. For all that she was dwarfed by the immense space, she was nonetheless its focal point, like a diamond in its setting, and Lẽna felt her heart swell and rise in her chest at the sight of her.

'Costa?' the girl had said, and at the sound of it – the sound of certainty and disbelief mixed in equal measures – Lẽna was transported back to the moment when she had known the dauphin, without understanding how or why. The angels had not spoken to her, had not told her which one of the many men she should honour with her attention, and yet she had felt their wisdom wrapping around her like a following wind that moved her in the right direction.

'Costa?' The bittersweet sound of a word from

a heart made naked by hope and doubt rose from the girl's lips and flitted, like a bird, between the curls, curves and twists of stone forming the details of the ceiling high above her.

Reluctantly tearing her eyes from the girl, Lẽna followed the line of her gaze, as if the desperate heat of it had burned a path across the distance separating her from its object. It was a young man, tall and lean. He was robed and garbed as a prince, in shimmering white and gold. Shafts of light from windows high in the walls made him shine so that he was almost too much to look upon. On his head, resting lightly on his temples, was a coronet of gold the colour of rich butter and set with many gems, polished *en cabochon*. Had she not known better, Lẽna might have mistaken him for an angel.

'Hello, Yaminah,' he said.

For the first time, and at the sound of his voice, the girl moved. Rather than towards him, however, she took a step backwards and away. She stopped and craned her head and neck forward as though that couple of extra inches might sharpen the sight of him. Visibly gathering her courage around her like the folds of long skirts, she began walking hesitantly towards him, turning her head slowly from one side to the other as though favouring each of her eyes in turn, the better to examine him. Lẽna could not fail to notice that the girl had stopped saying his name.

The young man did not move; rather he stayed firmly in place with his feet slightly apart and his hands on his hips.

'Stop there, Yaminah.'

At the sound of the new voice, the girl froze.

Lẽna turned her head to locate the speaker. It was a woman, stepping out from the shadows beneath the gallery opposite. She was closer to Lẽna's age than that of the girl or the young man, with long hair as black as night. She was tall and stood straight to maximise every inch of the advantage it gave her. In one hand she carried a black walking stick topped with a white carving. The distance was too great and Lẽna could not see the shape clearly, but while the woman walked she fondled the decoration with the fingers of her right hand.

Lẽna's heart ached for the girl. Although she had stopped when commanded by the woman, she had not for a moment switched her gaze away from the young man's face. Her eyes seemed to plead wordlessly with him, or for him. Her hands were together, the fingers worrying at each other like squabbling siblings. Lẽna looked at him again and found that he was smiling.

All at once the intensity of the moment was ripped asunder by the sound and percussion of a pounding impact nearby. The girl dropped to her knees and put her hands over her ears; the young man briefly crumpled too and turned to look for signs of damage or danger. There were none, and Lẽna had realised faster than they that whatever part of the palace the cannonball had hit, it was somewhere out of sight of the great room within which they were gathered. She saw too that the middle-aged woman had been least affected by the intrusion. She had ducked her head, no more than that, and regained her composure almost at once.

'Makes a handsome bridegroom, does he not?' she asked.

Yaminah collected herself and stood up straight. She turned from the young man (straightening too and brushing at his clothes, as though they mattered most) and looked at Helena. The girl's confusion was palpable, and Lẽna realised that she had been holding her breath as she watched. She let it out, slowly and silently, while the girl spoke. Her gaze flickered between one and the other as she did so, as though not sure to whom her enquiries were best directed.

'How can this be?' she asked.

Almost before the words were fully out of her mouth she began moving forward once more, her pace somewhere between a walk and a run. She was still wringing her hands together and Lẽna was sure she had begun to cry.

'Stop, Yaminah,' the woman said. The girl slowed and hesitated for a heartbeat of time, but her desire to get closer was evidently overwhelming, and despite the woman's repeated commands, she kept closing the distance. The woman was closer to the young man, and simply by walking smartly she was at his side by the time the girl arrived, stopping several paces in front of them.

The similarity to Costa was undeniable. When she had first seen him, from the distance made by the greatness of the throne room, she had believed her prince was standing before her, healed of all the hurt. Surely it was he? He was the same height, of the same slight build.

Never before had she seen him stand, and the

459

sight was utterly disorientating, like viewing a familiar map upside down. Only as she had drawn closer had she noticed that while his face was thin, and beautiful, it was not Costa's.

His smile was good, best of all in fact, so that its similarity to the smile she loved above all others tugged at her heart. As she had come closer, though, she had seen that his eyes too were wrong – the same shape and the same colour but a shade darker so that they lacked the light that gleamed in Costa's gaze and warmed her soul. His voice too, still echoing inside her head if no longer in the ceiling above, was deeper than that of her prince.

This approximation might fool many, perhaps all if they did not examine him too carefully. But from closer than fifty strides it could not, and never would again, fool Yaminah.

'You are not Prince Constantine,' she said. She raised her hands to her face and closed her eyes.

'What trick is this?' she asked, her voice breaking. 'Why?'

Another voice spoke; a man's voice.

'This is the man you shall marry in front of all the thousands of your guests. He shall be your Prince Constantine and you shall be his Princess Yaminah, and the congregation shall cheer, and the miracle of it all shall delight them and give them new strength to endure – and to take up arms and to triumph.'

Yaminah had opened her eyes and was staring through a mist of her own tears into the emperor's handsome face. In her confusion and sadness, all thoughts of etiquette were driven from her mind and she made no sign of deference. Her mouth had dropped open behind her hands but she had no words. It had all taken on the texture of a dream, and somewhere in the background of her consciousness she wondered why the sound of the cannonball's strike had not been enough to awaken her.

'There in the Church of St Sophia, close by the spot where you fell six years ago into your prince's arms, you shall be wed,' he said, raising his arms like the spreading branches of a tree as he warmed to his theme.

'Your fall was such, of course, that the breaking of it broke my only son's back. God and heaven had thrown you together with such force it left him a cripple, unable to take on the duties of a prince, far less a husband.

'But now, in this hour of our greatest need, Our Lady will be seen to have blessed us all. Just as she reached out her hands to spare you, so she will seem to have touched my son and healed him. The people shall see you walk together through the doors of that great Church of the Divine Wisdom, into a future made newly bright by hope, and they shall understand, every last one of them, that if a broken boy can be raised up once more by the love of God, then a shattered city can be made whole again as well, and the infidel Turk shrugged off like sour foam from the surface of the ocean.'

'I won't do it,' said Yaminah.

Her arms were by her sides now and she had thrust out her chin. She thought of her Costa, lying all unknowing in his bed, and felt anger deep in her gut. She thought of all that he had lost – that she had knocked out of him with her clumsy fall.

461

She imagined it was he standing before her now, clad in shining robes and coronet, and her heart fairly burned in the fires of her guilt. For all that he should have been and all that he should have had, she mourned. His had been a kingdom, and now he lay uncomplaining in his silk-lined prison cell and contented himself with shadows and stories while others – those who should love him – made plans to pretend he no longer existed.

'Who is this anyway?' she asked, gesturing with her chin.

At her words, the terse dismissiveness of them, the young man bridled as if he had been slapped.

'I am man enough for you,' he said.

He was about to say more, but she cut him off.

'Prince Constantine is ten of you – ten of any man,' she said. As she spat the last of it, she turned deliberately to the emperor. 'I would live with my prince – and die with him – broken as he is, before I would stoop to accept the hand of any ... any impostor.'

She turned back to the facsimile of her love. 'Who are you?' she asked. 'Who are you that would give up himself, give up his own identity, in hopes of donning the robes of his better?'

He stepped forward and was about to speak when the emperor held up his hand, demanding his silence.

'He is the fruit of a long and careful search,' he said. 'An empire cannot have a cripple for its heir. While you spent your days ministering to the prince's needs – and we thank you for your care – our agents were abroad in the land. Each carried a memory and a likeness of our prince, and

462

sought to find one who resembled him in every way.'

'Well they have failed,' said Yaminah. 'My prince finds better likenesses with his shadows than your lackeys found in all their searches. He fools none but another fool.'

'You are quite wrong, Yaminah,' said Helena, stepping closer and taking the false prince's hand in her own. 'They have done well.'

She leaned back to take a long, appraising look at the young man.

'Among our Varangian Guard they use a word of their own Norse tongue to describe one who is mistaken for another. It is *vardoger*, and means a spirit double – a phantom that goes in place of the real person and convinces all who encounter it.'

'Spare me,' said Yaminah.

She felt alone and desolate among them and therefore free to speak her mind. The need to be with Costa, to hold his hand, look into his eyes and listen to his voice, was overwhelming. She wanted nothing more than to be curled by his side on his bed, in the darkness of his chamber, while he told her again about the world of before.

'I tell you now I will not play your game, far less accept the hand of your ... your phantom.'

'You will do these things, Yaminah,' said Helena.

Yaminah looked away from Helena while she spoke and glanced at the emperor, but his gaze was above her and beyond her. He seemed to be looking through the windows of the throne room as though he had said all he wanted and had moved on to other matters in his head.

'You will marry this man and you will smile as

you do so, and wave to your witnesses as they greet the happy couple,' said Helena. 'You will do all of this or you will never see Prince Constantine again.'

Yaminah stared at her, expressionless but with some soft parts of her insides feeling as though they were being ground under the heel of the emperor's consort.

'As it is, you will not see Costa now until after your wedding, at the earliest,' Helena continued. 'If you do as you have been instructed, then the two of you shall meet and you may be reassured that all is well with him.'

'And then?' asked Yaminah. She felt fingers of panic grasping at her soul. 'After that, what then?'

'After that you will leave the city,' said Helena. 'Together with your new husband you will take ship for Venice, there to establish our imperial court in exile. If needs be – if the city must be lost – the emperor will join you there to make plans for whatever must be done to take the empire back from the Turk.

'At the very least, the citizens shall see that the line of the House of Palaiologos is safe – that there is hope beyond hope, and beyond despair. All of this you will do, or your prince shall perish.'

Yaminah lunged towards Helena, her hands clenched into fists, but the doppelgänger was faster and came between them and caught her by the wrists. Furious, she spat into his face, even if it be the shadow of Costa's face, and rammed her right knee into his groin. He made no sound, merely opened his mouth wide as he fell.

'Take her!'

It was the emperor's voice, and Yaminah looked round in time to see a company of armed guards advancing towards her at a run. A door was open behind them, and before the first of them reached her, she glimpsed an unmistakable figure framed there. He had clearly intended to remain unseen, but for a split second before he ducked out of sight she saw the portly figure of Doukas, teacher and erstwhile friend to Prince Constantine.

50

'Who will tell Mehmet this time, do you think?'

'I would rather dig these tunnels – and hide forever in their darkness – than go before him with news of another failure.'

'How many has it been now?'

'Ten, I think, maybe a dozen. It is not my job to count them, nor is it yours. All we have to do is shovel out the spoil. If I ever leave this damned place, with my skin intact, I will count myself lucky.'

'How can it be that they know – that they always know where we are? How can it be that whatever line the Saxons take with their workings, however deep we burrow with our picks and shovels, they find us?'

'You know as well as I do it is not *they* who find us ... it is *him*. Every time it is the same one who is first to break through the roof above ... the same one who orders our tunnels flooded with the fire that sticks to men's clothes and skin and burns them alive ... the same one who leaps among us with his knives.'

'I saw him slice off a man's face with a shovel – one sharpened so the edge gleamed like silver in the light of the dying flames of the inferno he had unleashed'

'Did you see it yourself, Tekin? Or did you only hear about it from one who did?'

'I saw it, Hebib, with these same eyes that are looking at you now. He leapt among us from above and he brought the shovel up from below so that it found the man's chin first and then sliced onwards and upwards to his forehead. The poor bastard was still alive when he fell, I tell you, his face no more than a side of meat.'

'I did not know you had seen the devil for yourself.'

'Well I have, Hebib. And I hope never to see him again. May Allah see to it that I am always to the rear of the miners from now on – and never again among them while they work.'

'So what does he look like? Is he a giant, like they say? Is he strong like a carthorse? Is he crazy like a cut snake?'

'I am sorry to disappoint you, but he is slight, slender as a reed. I swear I could snap his arms in two if I ever got close enough – may Allah see to it I am never that close.'

'Do his eyes blaze like the fire he rains upon us?'

'It is you that is crazy like a cut snake if you think I have been close enough to see his eyes.'

466

'Have you heard him speak a word of his hatred?'

'Hatred?'

'Well surely he must hate us? I believe he must wish that the whole world had one neck – and that he had his hands around it.'

'He is silent always. I have heard the Saxons say he makes no sound at all when he attacks – that his feet seem hardly to rest upon the earth, so that he floats among them like a ghost. I have heard what they call him, though – the word his men cry when they want him back.'

'And what is his name, Tekin?'

'The miners say it is foreign even to them. But when the heathens need their devil's attention, they shout "Jon-grant".'

'Perhaps this Jon-grant *is* the devil, says I. Trust the infidels to have the devil himself on their side.'

51

'What say you, John Grant?' asked Minotto, the bailey of Venice, standing sword in hand. The armour that had gleamed like a newly minted coin when John Grant had first laid eyes upon it was grimed now and dull, and bearing fresh dents from recent fighting. 'A good night's work?' Minotto bent and slapped him hard on the shoulder. 'A good night's work indeed,' he repeated, before striding off.

John Grant only nodded in reply, and smiled grimly at the Venetian's departing back. He was slumped against the wall of a sentry post beside the Caligaria Gate, a cup of water in his hand. He was filthy, and he tasted only blood and dirt. And he was tired – in fact as exhausted as he had ever been. For ten days they had fought either on the outer wall or beyond it – sallying forth from the postern close by the Caligaria Gate to howl and hack and slash at the *azaps* struggling to fill the fosse, or even to cross it on those occasions when they managed to work through the night, shielded by the dark, and bridge the abyss with debris. Then the janissaries would follow, sometimes on horseback – but always they had been driven back by the slowly dwindling army of defenders. The toll was scarcely bearable and a force spread thin as fat on a poor man's bread could not last much longer.

The emperor and the rest of the great men still promised help from the West – still rallied their wearied comrades with talk of a crusade, white knights with red crosses on their breasts, leaping from ships and riding out to drive off the filthy Turk.

John Grant listened with the rest – even felt his hackles rise at the prospect of relief from out of the setting sun. But it was not crusaders that he saw every day and every night; rather it was Turkish levies, and while he cut down every one he could reach with sword or knife, or with the karambit that appeared in his fist whenever it was needed, still he had learned to admire them for their courage and their obedience.

They were to be pitied, though, he thought, those *azaps*. Brave they surely were, driven by their masters or their faith or by a lethal combination of both. But they were poor souls just the same, perhaps the poorest – straight from the fields where they had gleaned their livings, and thrust face first against the greatest obstacle in the wide world.

When he came close enough to see their faces, John Grant saw their eyes gleaming sometimes with hatred, but most often with hope. When he struck down at them from his warhorse, felt his sword passing through them, or when he took them in his deadly embrace and opened their stomachs and throats, he watched their eyes grow dim and felt only sorrow.

But most exhausting of all was the work in the tunnels. First his mental strength was sapped by the enervating effort of finding them – studying the ripples in the bowls and calling upon his senses to locate the miners themselves. Then it was the physical graft of dropping vertical shafts, two and three at a time through the brick-hard topsoil and into the softer material beneath that could be carved like chalk, in search of their burrowings.

He either patrolled the digging sites, tirelessly and obsessively, to encourage the workers as they bent their backs to the endless labour, or gave in to his frustration and leapt in among them to wield pick or shovel with his own hands.

Tonight's events had been the worst so far. He had been sitting in just this same place, by the gate, but with a bowl of red wine cupped in his two hands. He was watching the tiny crimson bubbles lining the rim, relishing the prickling dryness in his throat in the moments before the first gulp, when the opaque surface had suddenly risen in the slightest of perfect circles. And he had known they were back again, and a sudden tingle in his feet and on the side of his face told him just where they were.

Quickly he had pinpointed the workings, but the tunnel itself had been the deepest yet and he had begun to doubt himself as his men dug further and further downwards without finding any sign. Desperate with the need to reach the foe and drive them off, he had climbed down the wooden ladders – two lengths of them – and thrown his own muscle power behind the effort.

Suddenly the ground beneath their feet had given way unexpectedly and they had plunged – John Grant and four others – into the tunnel. The soil and rubble they brought down with them had extinguished the enemy miners' torches and buried the first of them alive, and it was in a hot, inky blackness that they struggled to right themselves and find their bearings.

The collapse had briefly silenced the foe, but all at once there were cries and angry shouts as they too began to orientate themselves in the blanketing dark. John Grant was quickest as always. He had no memory of going for his weapons, but there in his right hand was his long-bladed knife, in his left the karambit, curved like a little crescent moon.

He was slicked with sweat, beads of it stinging his eyes as he blinked uselessly in the dark. He heard his own men behind him, but they were diggers rather than fighters and he was, anyway, blocking them from the foe. In a heartbeat he reached out and assessed the dimensions of the tunnel, and found to his dismay that there was barely room enough to crouch, far less to stand. He was on his knees and the air was thick with panicked calls and the stink of men's sweat and fear.

On a reflex he thrust forward with his right hand and felt his blade part flesh and strike bone. When his hand, wrapped around the hilt, struck home behind it, he recognised the feel of that place immediately above the topmost curve of a man's hipbone, on the left-hand side. He heard the groan and felt the body fold towards him. A bearded face brushed his own and he slashed upwards with the karambit in his left hand – felt the cutting edge slice across a throat and the flow of hot blood on his fingers.

He was pushing the dying man to the floor when he was struck from behind – by one of his own seeking only to find and perhaps help him but instead causing him problems he did not need.

Another hand came out of the dark in front and above him, fumbling and feeling for him. He felt fingers in his hair, grappling for a hold, and in desperation he rolled over on to his side and lunged upwards with both blades. He felt a knife enter the second man's body, just below the rib-cage, and before it went slack with hurt he twisted and pushed the weight clear until he could gain an upright position once more, still on his knees and with the top of his head brushing the roof of the tunnel.

471

The air was filled then with a sound like thunder, and he was smothered and bent double, his head crushed on to his knees. His ears rang and his mouth was dry and he wanted to cry out, but the weight of the roof collapse had emptied his lungs as completely as a pair of leather bellows. He flexed his arms but they were pinned by his sides. He was immobile, fixed like a fossil in rock, and his lungs burned, screaming for an intake of breath. Before his eyes were bright flashes, whole starbursts, and the noise inside his head was deafening. Just as he felt he was letting go, slipping downwards into his own deeper darkness, he felt hands grasping at his ankles. He had a momentary flashback to the tunnel through the rock, and Lẽna reaching for him, and then he was moving, being dragged backwards. His legs were straightened beneath him, like an opening penknife, but he was helpless still, his mouth and nose filling with dirt as someone pulled him clear of the roof fall. Then he was beyond the collapse, and gasping and choking as someone he could not see rolled him on to his back. He sucked in air – hot and damp, but blessed nonetheless. He swallowed more soil and choked again and rolled up on to one side and coughed and vomited, emptying himself of strings of bitter bile and then sucking down more merciful draughts of air.

'You're all right,' said a voice, familiar but stricken with concern. 'You're fine, you're fine,' the words babbled like a prayer.

He was carried then, arms around his shoulders and under his legs as he was passed, still in a sitting position, to the base of the first ladder.

They would have fixed ropes and hauled him bodily up the shaft to the surface, but he brushed them away and found the rungs for himself and slowly made his way upwards into the night.

He reached the top and was pulled clear of the shaft by many hands. While he gathered himself, shaking and breathing deeply of the cooler night air, more soldiers poured down the ladders. Bronze cylinders filled with the makings of Greek fire were lowered then, their flammable, oily contents pressurised by hand pumps.

Once in place, the deadly mix was pumped out through a short pipe and ignited by a flaming taper fixed on its end. Mixed with the oil was wood resin, sticky as honey, so that the resultant fire that reached far into the tunnel clung to the clothes and skin of the men it found there.

The Turks in the tunnel, the living and the dead, had a few moments of light by which to consider one another's startled faces before the flames engulfed them. As the air below ground was consumed by the white-hot blaze, more was sucked down the shaft and the inferno inhaled deeply of it, and all and everyone was incinerated. The timber props burned too, until they could no longer support the weight pressing down upon them and they crumpled, so that scores of terrified men were either burned or buried alive.

John Grant sat close by the lip of the shaft, watching smoke coiling wraith-like into the sky as his comrades emerged coughing and spluttering, and triumphant. Behind them they dragged a pair of prisoners, Turks who had leapt from among the flames into the waiting arms of their tormentors.

'Let us see what these fine boys may tell us about where the rest of their friends are hiding,' said one.

'Rats travel in swarms, do they not,' said another. 'I'm sure these ones can be persuaded to point out more of the nests.'

John Grant watched as the hapless *azaps* were led away towards a nearby guardroom, and then he leaned back and looked up at the sky. There was no moon, no stars. Instead a blanket of cloud lay over the city so that the place had the feel of a corpse wrapped in its shroud.

Behind him, to the east, a barely perceptible light presaged the dawn. Despite his fatigue, he knew sleep would elude him for now. He put his head down on his knees and gave himself over to the fall.

52

'Did you say why your good lady is neglecting you today?' asked Doukas. Since he had offered to push the wheeled chariot, the question had to be addressed to the back of Prince Constantine's head.

'I am sure she has more and better things to do than push a wheelbarrow around the palace grounds every day,' said Constantine. 'To be honest, I like to think of her going about her business unburdened by the weight of my carcass.'

He delivered the lines in what he hoped was a

breezy tone, but privately he was surprised by Yaminah's absence, and without a word of explanation. She had made no mention of other appointments or commitments and yet now it had been a night and a day since he had last seen her. It was unusual, and in spite of his light-heartedness in front of his old teacher, he felt uneasy.

'Your wedding will be a marvel,' said Doukas.

They were doing laps of a courtyard (the same, as it happened, beside which Lẽna had spotted Yaminah). Constantine would have been happy enough in his rooms, but his friend had all but insisted on wheeling him out into the fresh air.

'It seems senseless, if you ask me,' said Constantine. 'The Turks are even now at work pounding us into submission with their bombards. Yet more of them are burrowing under our walls night and day. And here we are preparing to shepherd thousands of our people into St Sophia's to hear two of their kind – or at least one and a half – joined in marriage. It is madness. One lucky hit on the dome, for God's sake...'

'But you are looking at it from quite the wrong angle, Costa,' said Doukas. 'This is a city and a people that needs proof that life goes on – that our way of life is not easily extinguished. You two will be a light in the darkness.'

'Their enthusiasm would be best spent upon the walls, with swords in their hands,' said the prince. 'I only wish that I might join them there and do something that matters.'

The bombardment rolled around them like a storm. Every few minutes there came the sound of another eruption from one of the guns, followed by an impact somewhere along the four-mile stretch of the land walls. Heavy all around was the smell of burned gunpowder, and hanging over everything was the unmistakable sense of the end of days. And yet in the heart of the Palace of Blachernae, two men took the air – one young and painfully thin and seated in an outlandishly odd wheeled contraption, his legs cycling in front of him in an imitation of life; the other older and portly and gamely pushing as though in need of the exercise.

'Why do you stay here, Costa?' asked Doukas. 'The Turks are so close I would swear I can smell them. They concentrate so much of their fire on the Caligaria Gate, right beside us; the place is little more than a barracks. And yet here you are...'

'It suits me to carry on,' said the prince. 'This is my home. You say our citizens need to see life being lived as before ... well, here I am, doing just that.'

Doukas kept pushing, watching Constantine's whip-thin legs as they rose and fell in turn.

'What are we calling that beast of a thing they have looming above the river?' asked Constantine.

'Ah, you mean the Royal Gun,' said Doukas. His tone switched at once from that of a friend making conversation to a teacher luxuriating in his knowledge. 'I am pleased to report that that horrifying and extraordinary monster is no more; it blew itself apart days ago, along with the swines attending it.'

Warming to the thought of reverses lately experienced by the foe, he continued.

'You say you wish you could be on the walls?' he said. 'I only wish you had been on our sea walls to watch the humiliation of the Ottoman fleet.'

'How so?' asked Constantine.

'It was marvellous, Costa, truly marvellous – the work of God himself, I should say.'

Sensing a story, and happy to be lulled and transported by it, far beyond the walls, Constantine relaxed his neck and shoulders and let his head loll back against the chair, eyes closed.

'It was on the morning of the twentieth day of April that our lookouts spotted four carracks driven hard into the Marmara by a wind from the south,' Doukas began. 'They were Genoese, and dispatched by the Holy Father himself. For all that he may despise our faith, still he grieves the loss of so many children.

'As they came on, they were sighted by the Turkish fleet – waiting and ready in the mouth of the Bosphorus. I leave you to imagine what orders were received from Mehmet when he learned that a flotilla loaded with good Christian men, weapons and supplies was approaching the city, bringing much-needed hope to a fearful and put-upon people.'

'You really must write a book,' said Constantine. 'Your flights of fancy deserve a wider audience, I promise you.'

Doukas cleared his throat, made suddenly self-conscious by the prince's teasing.

'In any event, the Turks set out in their war galleys – scores and scores of them, like swarming ants attacking four grasshoppers. While the

477

carracks sought the safety of the Horn, the oarsmen in their galleys worked harder still to cut them off.

'Our citizens flooded from their homes in search of high ground from which to watch – climbing church towers and any other structure that gave them sight of the Marmara. Your father was among them, garbed as a soldier as always, and cheering with the rest.

'The first fire came from the galleys, and the carracks were raked with stone balls and burning javelins and anything else the Turks could fling against the hulls. The bold Genoese struck back with bolts from their crossbows and stone balls from their own guns. Smoke and fire was everywhere, but still the carracks came on, drawing closer to the Horn and to the sanctuary it promised.

'I swear to you, Costa, it was like watching great bears tormented by snapping dogs–'

'You said ants and grasshoppers before,' interrupted Constantine. 'Now it is bears and dogs. Which is it to be? I need clear images if I am fully to engage with your account.'

'And then,' continued Doukas, pretending the prince had not spoken, 'just when it seemed our ships would clear the pack and make the turn towards a safe harbour, and while our people cheered from the rooftops and from the heights of the hippodrome ... the south wind ceased and the carracks were all at once becalmed.'

'Bears brought to bay,' said the prince. 'Grasshoppers with their ... tiny ankles tied? Do grasshoppers have ankles?'

Doukas ploughed ahead, his own sails still full of wind in spite of the prince.

'Seizing the moment, the Turkish commander ordered his fleet to close with the stranded vessels. First one by one and then in ranks the galleys rammed their bows into the hulls of the carracks, or else let the current bring them alongside.

'The fighting then was hand to hand as the Turks battled and struggled to climb aboard the carracks, while the Genoese sailors and soldiers beat them back with swords and clubs and grappling hooks. Marksmen in the rigging and out on the yardarms picked their targets and skewered the Turks with bolts and with arrows.'

Doukas stopped pushing for a moment and placed both hands upon the prince's shoulders, then he raised his arms above Constantine's face and his chubbly fingers writhed like fronds of weed in a stormy sea as he recalled the scene.

'Costa, it was as though an island of wood and sail had risen up out of the water,' he said. 'All four of the carracks came together and ropes were thrown between them so that they became one – a castle of timber with the poop decks looming like towers in the midst of it all.

'Around them were the Turkish galleys, and the whole mass of it – like dry land, I tell you – swarmed with men hacking and slashing at one another, fighting with fists and feet and teeth.

'All the while the fighting raged, the current of the sea drove the mess of ships closer and closer to shore. I heard later that Mehmet was so incensed, so maddened by what he was seeing and sensing victory must be his, that he jumped on to his horse and rode it into the sea. He then stood up on his saddle, the better to harangue and abuse his captains.'

'Now that I would have liked to see,' said Constantine. 'Tell me now that he so lost his temper, he overbalanced and fell into the sea and was drowned.'

'I promise that what happened next must have pained him more than death itself,' said Doukas.

'Just as it seemed that our men were at their limit – firing the last of their missiles and with their strength failing after hours of brutish struggle – the wind returned and filled their sails once more.

'What had seemed dry land was torn asunder as the carracks separated and then gained momentum and crashed through the surrounding flotsam of the galleys. While Mehmet screamed his fury and threatened his men with messy murder, the Genoese broke clear of the last of their assailants and sailed safely into the haven of the Horn.

'What say you to that, young Costa?' asked Doukas. He had worked up quite a sweat with the telling of his tale, and he wiped at his brow with the sleeve of his robe.

'I say pity the Turkish sailors who lived to feel their sultan's wrath.'

'Quite so,' said Doukas. 'Quite so.'

53

John Grant was blissfully asleep, curled in a ball against one wall of the guardroom, when Lěna found him. She considered his peaceful face for a moment and then knelt by his side and shook him gently by one shoulder, murmuring his name as she did so.

He surfaced like a diver returning from deep water, and while his eyes were still closed he was a little boy once more and it was his mother's voice that he heard. He smiled and opened his eyes and found not Jessie, but Jeanne d'Arc.

'What is it?' he asked.

'Your girl,' said Lěna. 'I have found her for you.'

Still wrapped in the befuddlement of sleep, he sat up, his back against the wall, and rubbed his face with both hands.

'My girl?'

'The girl from the harbour ... standing with the emperor ... the one whose beauty left you looking like a stunned fish?'

She had his full attention now and he sat up straighter.

'What about her?' he asked. 'Why do you wake me to tell me this?'

Lěna paused before continuing, shuffling words in her head.

'You must come with me,' she said. 'She is in danger.'

John Grant would have sworn he felt the push, but it was hopelessly faint and he chose to ignore it.

'Where?' he asked. 'How?'

She straightened then, and he leapt to his feet and followed her silently as she turned and jogged out of the guardroom. His thoughts spun inside his head.

'Where is she?' he asked.

'They have her in a dungeon in one of their prisons,' she said. 'I am taking you there now.'

'She matters to me,' he said. 'I had no idea she mattered to you.'

'She matters,' said Lẽna. She stopped running and he turned to look at her. The madness of what she was about to say was all but overwhelming. Only the certainty that she was right nonetheless gave her the will to go on.

'I think... I am sure she is the girl you came here to save.'

John Grant's mind was flooded with questions and confusion.

'Badr's daughter?' he asked. He shook his head and sighed. 'How could you know that?'

She had begun running again, and he caught up with her before continuing with his questions.

'How could you possibly know?'

'I promise I will tell you,' she said. 'But not here and not now. That is the stuff of a conversation for another time and in another place.'

Their path led through covered cloisters and narrow ways until they arrived in the shadow of a building close by the palace.

'What is this place?' he asked.

'It is the Anemas prison,' she said. 'I doubt we would ever manage to find our way inside in peacetime – and I am certain we would not want to – but now ... well, let's say that for now the guards' energies are required elsewhere. The place is all but abandoned.'

They found a door through the massively built wall of the prison compound, and a guardroom beyond occupied by two slumbering sentries. They were grimed with dirt and looked to John Grant as though they had only recently returned from more arduous duties elsewhere.

The citizens of Constantinople should not, he reasoned, be further imperilled by an unnecessary winnowing of their dwindling crop of defenders, and so their lives were spared. Both were quickly and quietly incapacitated nonetheless – their sleep made deeper by well-placed blows to the neck – and now they lay bound and gagged.

'Sweet dreams, bonny lads,' said John Grant as they passed through the guardroom and on into the darkened building beyond.

'How will we find her?' he asked, as they made their way through the interior and beneath lofty arches that soared overhead. The only light was that provided by tallow lamps in sconces along the walls. Some had failed for want of fuel, and the umber glow provided by the remainder was barely enough to see by.

For all that the place seemed near empty, still there was a detectable scent of human waste and sweat and misery. It hung in the air like a humiliating memory.

'I think the finding of her is down to you,' she said.

Before she had finished speaking, he felt the push for the second time that night. It came from beneath his feet, beyond the flagstones of the floor.

'The dungeons are below ground,' he said. 'We have to find some stairs.'

At the end of the chamber, through a doorway so low they had to stoop to pass beneath its lintel, Lẽna found the topmost stair of a spiral flight of stone steps leading downwards into Stygian gloom. John Grant counted fourteen steps before he reached the floor of the prison's basement level. By the faint light provided by more tallow lamps, he saw heavily bolted doors stretching away from him along both sides of a passageway.

From behind some came low noises, moans as well as words spoken too quietly to be heard. Convinced the place was unguarded, they walked easily through the gloom. At the end of the chamber was a final, larger dungeon. As well as a bolted door there was a barred window that revealed the interior beyond. Sitting on a wooden chair by a large square table, head in hands, was the girl.

Lẽna stepped to the window and grasped two of the bars as she spoke.

'Yaminah,' she said.

John Grant was rooted to the spot.

The girl dropped her hands to the table and turned to face them. She stood, pushing the chair back across the stone floor and so making the loudest sound they had heard since entering the prison.

'How do you know my name?' she asked.

'I was in the throne room when you were presented to your husband-to-be,' said Lẽna. 'I heard them call to you.'

Yaminah's eyes flashed as she considered how much of her predicament was now known to his stranger.

'That actor will never be my husband,' she said. 'I will ... I will not.'

She cast her gaze down to the floor of her cell.

'Do you know where the keys are kept?' asked Lẽna. 'Who locked your door?'

The girl shook her head, confused and uncertain.

'Two men ... guards,' she said. 'Filthy creatures – looked like they had been sleeping in a ditch.'

Understanding at once, John Grant turned and ran back through the chamber. He raced up the stairs two at a time and then retraced his steps to the guardroom.

Inside, one of the men was stirring – groaning as he began to regain consciousness. Without slowing his pace, John Grant ran to him and kicked him in the back of the head, harder than was necessary. Kneeling down, he frisked the man's clothing. He found a pocket knife and a spoon carved from horn, but nothing else. Crawling over to the second guard, he repeated the process, and this time, dangling on the man's belt, he found a bunch of keys, the toothed ends gleaming silver from much use.

54

'I believe I know who you are,' said Lẽna.

'What do you mean?' asked Yaminah.

'What is your mother's name?'

'My mother is dead.'

'I am sorry,' said Lẽna. 'Please forgive me for this. We have little time remaining to us. Please tell me your mother's name.'

Yaminah stared into Lẽna's face. There was no aggression in the look, not even suspicion. All Lẽna read was sadness.

'Izzi ... Isabella,' she said. 'My mother's name was Isabella. Why do you ask me this?'

'I honestly do not know where to begin,' said Lẽna.

She smiled at the girl, smiled at the face that was so familiar. Almost on a whim, she thought of another question.

'Do you speak the language of Galicia?'

Yaminah's face was suddenly a study in surprise and confusion.

'What?'

'*No tengo mas que darte,*' said Lẽna.

'I have nothing more to give thee,' said Yaminah.

'Who taught you those words?' asked Lẽna. Her heart was filled with sadness and there were tears in her eyes.

'My mother,' said Yaminah. None of it made sense to her, but she felt the other's need and her soul reached outwards. 'Those were my mother's words.'

Before they could say any more, there came the sound of another's approach. It was John Grant, and both turned to see if his search had been successful.

He could hardly bring himself to do more than glance at the girl. Instead he moved Lẽna away from the door and began trying one key after another. Finally, and with a gratifying click, the tumblers within the lock were satisfied and the door opened inwards with a sigh.

He looked at Yaminah then, felt his face flush and blessed the gloom for concealing it. He felt the push too, and stronger than before.

'The birdman,' she said.

'Come now,' said Lẽna. She was standing in the doorway holding out one hand. Yaminah crossed to her and took it and followed her into the hallway. She looked around at John Grant for a moment and he followed her, wordlessly.

They climbed the stairs and ran into the gloom of the chamber beyond. It seemed dreamlike to John Grant, and a wave of déjà vu washed over him as he watched the two women running hand in hand in front of him.

They were halfway to the guardroom when Lẽna spotted movement ahead. There were figures moving there – tending to the unconscious men. She halted, and then changed course, pulling Yaminah over towards the left-hand wall. John Grant saw the figures too and cursed himself for ignoring the faint warning he'd felt in the dungeon. In the moments that remained to them, he rushed to Lẽna and the girl, where they stood concealed.

'Take her,' said Lẽna. 'Stay in the shadows and keep moving forward until you are against the wall of the guardroom – close by the door.'

'What about you?' It was Yaminah's voice, and they both turned to look at her, as though they had momentarily forgotten she could speak.

Lẽna smiled an ancient smile and turned to address John Grant.

'Tell her she has no need to worry about me,' she said, and she pushed him in the chest to get him moving.

'I will see you soon,' he said.

On a sudden impulse – before she could react and before he took Yaminah by the hand and led her away – he stepped back towards her and placed the lightest of kisses on his mother's lips.

He and Yaminah had reached the far wall, no further, when the figures burst into the chamber. There were three of them – men, and altogether better dressed than the two lying senseless on the guardroom floor.

He watched Lẽna as they sprinted towards her. She glanced at him and their eyes met, and then she turned and ran for the spiral staircase leading to the dungeons.

'Where best to go?' he asked Yaminah. They were outside the prison, beyond the towering curtain wall. Her hand felt cool as they stood together in the light of a gibbous moon. She seemed almost bashful, momentarily uncertain. He wondered if she was uncertain about her hand in his or about where to go in hope of sanctuary, and hoped it was the latter.

'Come with me,' she said, tugging at him. 'I know.'

To his surprise she led him into the palace, on a complicated route through courtyards and into a maze of corridors. Finally she stopped by an anonymous-looking door. She reached into a pocket in her skirts and produced a key. She held it up in front of John Grant's nose, so close he had to squint to focus on it.

'The key to the kingdom,' she said, and smiled.

She opened the door and led him inside and down a flight of wooden stairs. The basement was dark, but thin shafts of light infiltrated the windowless space via cracks between the floorboards that formed its ceiling.

'What place is this?' he asked.

'We'll be safe here,' she answered. 'My realm.'

'But seriously, where are we?'

'I lived here when I was a child,' she said. 'Not this basement, but the rooms above. It was home to my mother and me.'

'Isabella,' he said. 'Was your mother's name Isabella?'

She looked at him, hard – the sort of look that might leave a bruise.

'Who are you, birdman?' she asked. 'And the woman – who is she? Why did you come looking for me? How do you know my mother's name?'

'I am at a loss,' he said.

John Grant's mind reeled. Could it be? Was Lẽna right? Was this girl really Badr's daughter? Possibilities and impossibilities jostled for position in his thinking.

For all that they were strangers, they were standing close together. He ached to touch her. More than that, he wanted desperately to hold her tightly, to crush her against him until her bones cracked. The longing was so intense he felt he might lose control of it, let go of it and lunge at her, bite her flesh, or do her some other harm with the force of all that he felt, that he was holding back like a wall of water checked by a dam.

'Tell me how you know about my mother,' she said, and the sound of her voice gave him something to hold on to.

'I don't ... that is ... I have never met her,' he said. 'My father ... or, well, rather, the man who took care of me after my mother died ... or I should say the woman I thought was my mother, the one who raised me...'

In spite of the tension, even because of it, Yaminah felt a laugh rising in her chest like an air bubble. She raised a hand to her mouth to stifle it.

'Do you even know who *you* are?' she asked.

He was suddenly crestfallen, embarrassed by his stammering attempt to explain himself. She saw his discomfort and felt an urgent need to reassure him.

'What happened in the square – the day you arrived?' she asked. 'What happened with those eagles?'

Relieved by the change of subject, he brightened, remembering the moment and how it had felt when the birds mantled their wings and he had thought for an instant that they might lift him into the sky.

'It was the bone they wanted,' he said, and

shrugged. 'That foul-smelling bone. I was just the one that caught it.'

'Where did it come from?'

'From the birds, I suppose. One of them must have been flying with it and then dropped it. I caught it and then they both made a grab for it.'

'It was quite the spectacle, all the same,' she said. 'You know the emperor took it as a message from God – a sign that his house will rise again?'

John Grant smiled.

'But what did you think?' he asked.

Then it was Yaminah's turn to blush. She found that rather than watching his eyes while he spoke, it was his mouth she was drawn to. She found it hard anyway to look into those eyes. Even in the half-light of the basement she could tell they were hazel; more than that, they were flecked with gold that caught the light and sparkled like little suns.

Before she had known what colour they were, she had imagined them. She had listened to Constantine's voice and felt them upon her, as though he was watching from a distance. She had held Constantine's hand and wondered what the birdman's would feel like, what scent it would leave on her skin. He was here now and Constantine was not, and she wished she might feel guilty but she didn't.

There in the gloom, where everything was indistinct and not quite certain, she felt freedom. They were strangers after all, and she knew – just knew – that here there was no point in being less than honest. They were strangers and yet somehow not. Before being honest with him, she was honest first with herself, and she had to admit that

491

when their eyes had met across the square, while he held the eagles aloft, there had been nothing like strangeness between them. That was the first time she had laid eyes on him, she was certain of it, and yet ... and yet the feeling that had struck her in that brief moment was recognition.

She felt a powerful urge to kiss him – or otherwise close the remaining distance between them.

'I thought that I would never forget the sight of them, or of you,' she said.

They were standing in the bare room hardly moving, and he wondered how much time had passed since he had pulled the door closed behind them. He felt he had a thousand things to tell her, and only her. He needed her to know how much their being together – here and now – mattered to him, that it was important and that it was everything to him.

'I was sent here, to you, by a man called Badr Khassan,' he said. 'Do you know that name?'

She stared at him, and motes of dust drifted between them like tiny planets adrift in the universe.

'Badr Khassan is my father,' she said.

'He saved my life,' said John Grant. 'Many times over. It was his wish that I should come here to the Great City and seek you out and see to it that you are safe and well.'

'Why is he not here himself?'

'Badr is dead,' said John Grant. The words, the fact of it, shocked him anew, and he thought again about the cave, and the way Badr had said the word *daughter*, and the smell of flowers.

'Isabella is dead too,' said Yaminah. Her sudden sadness then was like dark water too deep to swim in.

She fumbled in her pocket for Ama's finger bone. She found it tucked in a fold and took it into her fist. She felt a lump like broken glass in her throat and she swallowed and closed her eyes against hot tears and felt his lips on hers. He kissed her face then and her eyes, tasting salt, and she gasped and put her arms around his neck as he found her lips once more. His arms were around her and he was pulling her against him, crushing her to his body, and then he broke the kiss and held her tighter still, pressing his face into her hair and kissing her neck. She opened her eyes and looked beyond him, over his shoulder, and saw that a finger-thick beam of light through a knot-hole in a floorboard above was making a shadow of them upon the wall of the basement.

All at once she saw them for what they were, lovers hidden in the dark. She heard Constantine's voice in her head telling a story of a faithless empress, and she remembered the feel of her prince's cool hand in her own – and she knew that she loved him still, as she always had. Then she was pushing John Grant away and stepping backwards, almost falling over in her need to be apart from him.

'What's wrong?' he asked.

'I'm sorry,' she said. 'I want... I think...'

'What is it?' he asked again.

His voice was soft, filled only with concern, and confusion flooded her and she wanted him again and she shook her head to be free of the thought.

'*This* is wrong,' she said. 'This cannot be.'

'I don't understand,' he said.

She paused, breathing heavily and with her heart hammering, like the fists of someone trapped behind a heavy door. Searching for calm and reason, she flung her mind back in time, in hope of hearing her mother's voice.

'When I was little, my mother would tell me about soul twins,' she said.

He breathed out hard through his nose, and shook his head.

'What?'

'She had it from her nurse, who was called Ama,' she said.

She put her hand back in her pocket and felt for the little bone and played it in her fingers so that she could feel its contours.

'Ama told my mother, and my mother told me, that while most people travel alone through eternity, some lucky few have a twin. They don't look alike, but they have a ... a connection, I suppose.

'Sometimes, in some lives, the twins meet. They might be man and wife, parent and child; sometimes one is old and at the end of a life, while the other is newly born and just beginning.'

John Grant looked at her evenly. He had never heard the like, but his need for her made him wait and listen to what she had to say.

'And this means...?' he asked.

Yaminah sighed and looked down at the floor.

'I don't know what any of it means,' she said. 'I just feel – I just know that it's no accident that you are here now, with me in this city.'

John Grant held his hands up, as though surrendering and admitting defeat.

'I do not understand,' he said. He pronounced

each word slowly.

'Nor me,' she said. She looked up again, met his gaze squarely before taking a deep, halting breath and continuing.

'And I am betrothed. I am to be married.'

'Married?' he asked. 'Tell me.'

'Married.' She nodded as she spoke. 'And in three days' time.'

Suddenly desperate for the clear light of the world above, Yaminah half ran towards the wooden stairs. Before she had covered even half the distance, he had caught her by the arm and turned her to face him.

'How can you be getting married in three days?' he asked. 'You were in a prison cell when we found you, locked up like a common criminal – hardly the usual routine for a bride.'

'There is too much to explain,' she said. She was trying to pull free of him, to shake off his hand, but his grip was unexpectedly strong.

'I promised your father I would take care of you,' he said.

She gestured over her shoulder with her thumb, to the spot where they had been standing moments before.

'I suspect that was hardly what he meant by taking care,' she said. 'I would call that helping yourself.'

Her sudden anger surprised her as much as him. He let go of her arm and turned away from her. Instantly contrite, she reached out for him and placed a hand gently on his shoulder. She pulled on it and he turned back to face her once more.

'Listen to me, please. I am as confused as you

are,' she said. 'But it is true that I've thought about you and little else since I saw you in the square.'

His eyes were fixed on hers, and she forced herself to hold his gaze while she continued.

'You remind me of what my mother always said about the moment she first saw my father – Badr Khassan.'

John Grant said nothing, but raised his chin expectantly.

'She said he was the most beautiful man she had ever seen.'

He kept looking at her and she felt the blood rise in her face again.

'You are beautiful, birdman,' she said. 'You may even be the most beautiful – but I have promised myself to another.'

'So where is he?' asked John Grant. 'How is it that you were in that miserable cell if you are to be married? Where is he?'

'I expect he is where he always is,' she said. 'In his bed.'

He looked at her with frank disbelief, pulling his head back in a motion that reminded her, just for a moment, of a tortoise retreating into its shell. She laughed out loud at the madness of it.

'In his bed?' asked John Grant.

'And I think you may be just the man I need to get him up.'

He put his head on one side. One moment a tortoise, the next a puppy dog. Her heart filled with the need to hold him, but she resisted.

'If you will be patient, I will try to explain,' she said.

'I am listening,' said John Grant.

55

John Grant lay on his back in the guardroom by the postern near the Caligaria Gate. It had been hours since he had left Yaminah – at her insistence – and returned to his duties. The story she had had to tell was hard to believe and had it come from another source he might have dismissed it as fantasy. Despite knowing her hardly at all – and although his emotions still reeled from her brief acceptance of his desire, followed by swift rejection – he felt compelled to trust her and to believe her.

But as he lay on his straw-lined pallet, his mind spun like the planet beneath him. For want of distraction from her plight, he stretched his arms out by his sides and placed his hands palms downwards on the earthen floor. He spread his fingers, exhaled softly and surrendered to the flight into the void.

As though he had leapt from the edge of a cliff into space, his stomach seemed to rise inside his body. His head felt light and he thrilled at the speed of it. But while the feeling of the planet's journey had always overwhelmed any other, possessing him completely, tonight the rumble and grind of the earth's revolutions vied for dominance. He felt the thrum of it in his fingertips, stronger than ever before, and then, with a force that had him open his eyes wide and clamp his mouth shut so that his teeth fairly rattled in his skull, he felt a jolt against his back like a kick from a horse.

His ears were left ringing and he lay still and stiff, almost afraid to move. The jolt was followed by more impacts, each less powerful than the one before, until at last they stopped and the only sensation was the familiar, steady vibration, almost like the jangling from muscles tensed by excitement, or by fear.

He raised his head and looked around the room. He would not have been surprised to see the place in disarray – as in the aftermath of an earthquake – but the rest of the room's inhabitants slumbered peacefully. He glanced at the table and saw cups and glasses still in their places, their contents undisturbed. Standing up, he walked to the door, left open for fresh air, and looked outside. A handful of men, soldiers by the look of them, were crossing the yard some hundred yards or so away. They were talking quietly, without any hint of excitement or agitation.

Confused but no less certain that what he had felt was real – that it had happened even if he alone had noticed – he returned to the guardroom and lay down once more, in faint hope of sleep.

Half a world away from John Grant and the Great City, and the girl and the broken boy and the Maid of Orleans, an island in an ocean then unknown to any soldier of Christ had ceased to exist, leaving nothing but a bottomless crater deep beneath the waves.

The greatest explosion in ten thousand years had blasted Kuwae, an island in the Pacific and home to hundreds, into mere fragments that rose into the sky and then lowered upon the wide world like the very shadow of death.

Trees in forests would be strangled, left starving for want of the warmth of the sun; crops in fields would be smothered by dust and debris; tempests and torrents and snowstorms would bury whole cities and blanket the earth, and everywhere and anywhere the hearts of men would be broken in the endless shade.

56

Alone in his bedchamber, Prince Constantine felt sick. He had awoken in the wee small hours before dawn with a feeling close to dizziness or vertigo, the like of which he had not felt since the early aftermath of his broken spine. He could imagine no physical cause that might explain it, and so he decided it was the worry of Yaminah's absence that made his head spin and his stomach churn.

He spent the remaining hours of the night in tortured contemplation, seeking answers and explanations and possible outcomes. Where could she be? And why? Over and over he reviewed what she had told him – about the emperor's consort and all that she had said. There was the wedding to be considered too, of course. For all her passionate insistence, all her tears and heartfelt talk of how much she loved him and wanted to be his wife, had reality set in at long last? Had she properly considered her future – a lifetime devoted, of necessity, to a man unable to stand, to walk, to make love, far less to make with her the children she deserved? Was she absent now, just days from the ceremony, because the very sight and sound of him had become painful and too much to bear?

There were more thoughts in his head as well – born of a steadily growing sense of anticipation. Woven through the leaden feeling of dread caused by the siege, and the anxiety about Yaminah, was something close to excitement. Given the circumstances, it was inexplicable. But there was no denying it. At loose somewhere in his mind, flitting between the conscious and the unconscious, was the notion that events were unfolding as they should ... and that something was about to happen.

It was as he was mulling and musing, his forehead slick with cold sweat and his eyes dry and itching, that he became aware of a sensation he had not known for many years. Once he had noticed it, at first buried among his trials and tribulations, it rose to the surface and declared itself loudly. Its advent overwhelmed all other considerations, and his thoughts turned, all and only, to the feeling.

He remembered how, as a little boy, he would often awake in the morning to find a seemingly dead arm in bed with him – lying cold across his face or across his chest so that it had to be flung aside with the other. He would move, sometimes with much effort on account of the lifeless limb, until the deadness could be dangled out of the bed. Slowly then would come the return of sensation, as warm blood made its way to his fingertips and began the work of resuscitation. Sometimes the return to life was close to agony, or at least a confusing mix of pain and pleasure.

For some little while then he was distracted by an unbidden memory of his mother. She had been gone from him too long for any recollection of her face. Instead he recalled smooth, cool hands and soft words, the floral scent from her hair and skin as she bent over him and kissed him.

No one ever mentioned her now – and not for the longest time. She had been not a wife to his father but a mistress. Her place in the world, he imagined, left formal union out of reach. Only the boy, her boy, had been of value. She had tended him at first, as a nurse perhaps, until such time as he was old enough for his education to begin, and then the currents of court life had taken him away from her, or she from him.

He lay on his back and remembered the sound of her voice. It was she who had heard him cry out about his dead arm the first time it happened – she who had come to him and described it in a way that made sense to him then and stayed with him ever after. She had shushed and stroked him, and held his pudgy arm and told him it was just a dream.

'Your arm has fallen asleep,' she had said. 'Let's wait and see what happens now.'

She had sat with him that time, and many others, and gently massaged the skin and muscles while life returned.

He lay on his back and gave himself over to the

feeling in the lower part of his right leg. Where before and for all the years since he'd caught Yaminah there had been only an absence, now there was a tingling like a thousand needles against the skin. He thought again about his mother's words and reasoned that while a limb was asleep it would have no feeling at all. The tingle and the jabbing of the needles meant quite the opposite, therefore. The sensation came instead from a leg that was awake.

57

Hours had passed since John Grant had felt himself kicked in the back not once but a dozen times, and yet still he felt not quite properly in touch with the world. It was the last hour before dawn. He was due back on duty, patrolling the walls and monitoring the bowls, but he dreaded the prospect of setting his mind to the task.

For one thing, he felt almost numb, and all over. There was a faint hum in his head too, as of the last vibrations from a glass struck with the handle of a spoon. It seemed to him that he was wrapped in an invisible blanket that kept him from properly feeling anything around him. It was a hangover without the pain. He even pinched his nose and tried to make his ears pop, but there was no relief to be had from the distance he perceived between his own self and everything around him.

As distracting, if in a wholly different way, were

his thoughts of the girl, Yaminah. He tried to concentrate – to consider the consequences of neglecting his duties and missing an attack from the Turks – but always her lovely face appeared before his eyes like that of a djinn.

As it turned out, the necessary distraction from his ills arrived with the first light of day. From the outer wall came the sound of men shouting, sounding the alarm. He grabbed his sword and dashed from the guardroom. More men followed, running behind him, leaping up the steps and on to the battlements high above.

For a moment he thought he was confronted by an illusion, some trick of the mind that was yet another symptom of whatever malady had beset him. Then the continued howls of the men – all of them pointing and staring, first into one another's faces in search of explanation, and then back at the cause of their alarm – persuaded him that here was no hallucination.

Just in front of the outer edge of the fosse, and looming over the battlements he stood upon, was a massive square tower. It had evidently been constructed as a huge timber frame, then covered with animal hides and timber cladding. There were arrow slots from top to bottom, through which could be glimpsed the movements of the enemy within. Worst of all was the sight of Turks on the topmost level of the thing, peering from behind timber crenellations and actually looking down, from a superior height, on to the walls and into the city beyond.

'Dear God,' whispered John Grant under his breath.

The next voice he heard was that of Giustiniani. John Grant turned to look at him, finding reassurance in the sight and sound of the man. They had been fighting for weeks, doggedly repulsing every attack, and yet the Genoan seemed as full of energy as he had on the day they had arrived into port. Every time a section of wall was crumpled by the Ottoman guns, Giustiniani was there, rallying the workers, urging them on as they sought to plug the gaps with rubble and soil and their own sweat and tears.

'These Turks have all the cunning of Satan himself,' he shouted.

Now beyond the shock of the first sight of the monstrosity, John Grant began to study it in search of weakness. To his amazement he saw that the tower had a tail – a trench leading all the way from its base to the Turkish lines many hundreds of yards away. Covered with timber and more leathery hides, it provided the foe with the means to supply their construction with men and materials without fear of injury.

While he watched, the tower's central purpose became shockingly apparent. From the base came a steady flow of debris, rubble and sand and much else besides, that was filling the fosse at an alarming rate. If something was not done – and soon – the workers in the tower would have created a bridge wide enough for the advance of an entire army.

'They must have assembled it in the night,' said Giustiniani. Scores of men had gathered to him and were listening intently as he assessed the threat. 'And then hauled it upon wheels across no-man's-land and to the very edge of the ditch.'

Before he could say another word, a series of monstrous blasts rang out in quick succession, followed by harrowing impacts. The Turks were concentrating their fire on the section of the wall close by the Gate of St Romanus. Looking towards the enemy lines, John Grant saw a cluster of gun barrels, evidently the heaviest and longest of those remaining. While he watched, a great cheer went up from the Ottomans, along with a blaring of horns and a pounding of drums and wooden gongs. Another gap, the widest yet, had appeared in the wall beneath a massive cloud of dust. An even greater roar, men's voices raised in expectation of triumph, rose into the air, and moments later a wave of Turks began pouring down the slope towards the breach.

'With me!' shouted Giustiniani. 'Come with me!'

While the wave came on, the defenders – fewer by far in number but as fired with bloodlust – ran for the gate, or mounted horses if they had them and galloped to the site.

John Grant was among the first to arrive at the breach, close by the commander. Together with the emperor, who had taken the Gate of St Romanus for himself, they mounted the rubble and debris and looked out upon an awful sight. The Ottomans had evidently done more than construct their tower overnight. Here too there had been preparations made under cover of darkness, and a wide section of the fosse had been all but filled with yet more debris.

Although the widest of any gap punched

through the wall so far, it was quickly plugged, not with earth and barrels but by defenders. Shoulder to shoulder they stood, grimly ready as the first of the Turks lunged towards them, cruelly curved swords held high above their heads. John Grant glanced at the men nearest him, considered their expressions. There too was Minotto of Venice, his armour crazed with the gashes left by scimitar and axe, and three more Genoese: the Bochiardi brothers, Antonio, Paulo and Troilo, who had come to the city at their own expense, and bearing their own arms.

Next he turned to Giustiniani, to the fore as always and poised on the balls of both feet, ready for the off, and Don Francesco di Toledo, a maverick captain from Castile. For an instant he was filled with pride and thought that he might cry, not out of fear but out of love. If he had to die today then let it be here, he thought, in the company of men made brave by love of their own folk, sure and certain in the knowledge that should all be lost, they would know at the end that they had given every last ounce and breath, their own lifeless shells falling as final obstacles between family and foe.

At the front of the attackers was a man-at-arms, breastplate gleaming and flashes of sunlight dancing along the edges of his blade. Giustiniani met his eyes and leapt forward, but the boulder he landed upon was loose underfoot and he stumbled as the janissary loomed above him, sword poised for the strike. John Grant raised his own sword and lunged towards his commander in hopes of shouldering him out of danger and parrying the blow. Fast as he was, he was beaten to the clash by Paulo Bochiardi, who came in low and fast as a cat, swinging his straight blade like a woodcutter, and severed both of the janissary's legs above the knees.

First blood drawn, the mass of the opposing forces came together in a frenzy of hacking blades and spear thrusts. John Grant lunged and slashed and felt flesh and bone parting and splitting beneath his sword. Out of the corner of one eye he spied a splendidly attired Turkish warrior, six and a half feet tall or more, looming above the rest with the tails of his brightly coloured robe snapping in his wake. Suddenly before him, blocking his way, stood another giant, a citizen defender, and as they began to circle one another, the sight of them gave other men pause. Both sides fell back then, transfixed by the moment of single combat.

Swung with terrible force, the crossed sword of the defender and the crescent of the scimitar of the Turk came together like bolts of lightning fusing in the midst of a storm. Steel squealed and the warriors roared into one another's faces. Blow after blow was swung or parried until the Turk, his robe swirling like smoke, dropped low and aimed for his enemy's knees. Quick as thought the giant defender leapt into the air, pulling both legs up towards his chest so that the scimitar passed harmlessly beneath his feet. Landing clean, and while his attacker was still unbalanced by his miss, the Christian swung his blade high and with a howl of rage brought it scything downwards. The mill-sharpened edge found the space between the Turk's shoulder and neck and the massive force behind it had the sword sweep through his body to his right hip so that he was cloven in two.

John Grant would have cheered, but in an instant, and as the two halves of the dead Turk settled into the dust and dirt, the attackers surged forward as one and felled the Christian champion. His comrades, enraged by the injustice of it all, pushed into the mass of Turks, desperate to win back the corpse at least. But even as they fought forwards, John Grant among them, a colossal explosion brought them to a standstill.

Every one of them, attacker and defender alike, turned to look along the wall in time to see the Ottoman tower festooned in red and orange blossoms. A second wave of explosions erupted from it then as a cascade of barrels, each filled with gunpowder and with fuses spitting, joined those already poured at its base by the defenders on the battlements. The tower rippled and buckled like a giant tree in the grip of a gale, and then with a yawning roar it toppled backwards within a rising plume of smoke and dust.

Now John Grant did cheer, along with the rest of the defenders. Up on the battlements, the men who had dropped the scores of exploding barrels around the tower – like a deadly rain at the roots of a great tree – were dancing in jubilation.

Turning back to the job in hand once more, John Grant and his fellows pushed back against the foe, their hopes and strength renewed like a guttering flame refreshed by a wind. The feet of the warriors of both sides were slipping and sliding hideously on the blood and gore of dead men, or else stumbling over the corpses themselves. The mad and joyous horror of it held them all in its spell, and with an effort that felt like one collective out-pouring of held breath, the defenders redoubled their efforts and chopped and hewed at the weak-ening wall before them.

Where before there had been shouts and cheers from among the Turks, the sounds of excited men urging one another forward and on to greater and greater feats, now there were only groans of failing effort.

In the end, the moment of their breaking was like a turn in the air by a massed flock of birds. As though a single thought had registered in every mind, the enemy fell back – and then turned and ran. Too exhausted to pursue the rout, the de-fenders began dropping to their knees, held upright only by hands grasped around the hilts of swords thrust point downwards into the bloodied dirt.

58

Beside himself with fatigue – his every muscle screaming in protest and desiring only a soft pallet on to which to collapse and plunge beneath the waking world – John Grant made it back to the Caligaria Gate to learn of the discovery of yet another tunnel.

Will this day never end? he said, but only to himself.

Word of it had come from one of Minotto's lieutenants, and pausing only to splash his face with cold water from one of the buckets in the chain of early-warning devices, he dropped into a trot behind the messenger.

The sun, he knew, would be past its height and descending into the west once more, there to have its light extinguished by the Sea of Marmara. But the sky above was made only of murk and greyness, and he cursed the dismal weather as he spotted the familiar sight of men at work dropping a shaft into the earth – this one close by the masonry of the outer wall.

'This is a bad one,' said the lieutenant – the same that had sent the messenger to summon him.

'They're all bad,' said John Grant. 'What is different about this one?'

'There are ripples in every bowl for a distance of sixty paces along the wall.'

'Along it?'

The soldier nodded and looked down at the ground, as though expecting to see the earth itself vibrating.

John Grant considered the news. Every previous burrowing by the Turks had passed directly under the walls, perpendicular to them, in apparent hope of making it beyond the defences before striking for the surface and a clear run at the city and the citizens beyond. If the lieutenant was right in his assessment of this latest effort, the focus of the enemy's attentions had turned to the wall itself.

'If they have undermined the wall, then enough black powder would bring it down along a length too great to defend,' he said.

The lieutenant nodded and worried at his bottom lip with his top teeth.

John Grant had picked up a shovel lying by the lip of the shaft and was about to descend and join the diggers when he heard Giustiniani's voice.

'You have done enough this day,' he said.

He turned to face the commander and found the usually cheerful countenance replaced by a frown.

'You have fought hard and well,' said Giustiniani. 'Leave this one to others and get the rest you need.'

John Grant shook his head.

'I must be there,' he said. 'I could not rest knowing they are burrowing down there. It makes my skin crawl as though I had lice under my clothes.'

Giustiniani smiled, but the furrows on his forehead remained.

'If you will work on, then so will I.'

With that, the Genoan selected an iron-headed pickaxe and was first to the top of the ladder.

By the time John Grant had joined him at the bottom, the diggers had stopped their efforts and were holding up their hands for silence. Faint but unmistakable was the ping of steel upon stone, the sound of the miners at work directly beneath.

'We must make ready with our fire,' said Giustiniani.

John Grant shook his head.

'We dare not,' he said. 'If the wall is undermined, the risk is too great. At the very least, the flames would consume whatever props they have in place to support their workings. At worst, if they have black powder down there, then fire will do the job for them. Either way, we must fight them hand to hand.'

Giustiniani sighed and nodded, accepting the truth of it. By whispered commands and gestures, the message was sent topside that a force of men was urgently required. Within minutes, a little army had assembled. The vanguard was on the ladders, the rest waiting ready to follow when the first wave had gone in. When all was ready, John Grant gave the signal and the diggers hacked at the barrier of material still separating them from the foe. All at once the last of it gave way and their picks broke through into a cavity. By the dim light of the lamps inside they glimpsed the faces of many men. With a jolt of dread, John Grant realised that their own workings had been heard and an enemy force had assembled to confront them.

'With me!' he shouted, and leapt into the half-dark, followed by Giustiniani and half a dozen lightly armed men. Swords were altogether useless in the narrow confines of the tunnels and it was with knives and hammers and wooden clubs studded with iron nails that they plunged among the enemy. As always there was barely room to manoeuvre, and the only way forward was through the enemy in front. John Grant carved his way past one and then a second. He felt the press of men behind him and then, to his shocked surprise, the tunnel opened out into a chamber as wide as three men were tall. While he fought, he glimpsed timber props supporting the roof, through which lumps of masonry – the foundations of the wall – protruded like ground-down teeth. Worse still were the piled sacks between the props – surely filled with gunpowder and ready to be ignited.

Perhaps it was the fatigue of the fight at the Gate of St Romanus, or maybe the enervating toll of a sleepless night. In any case John Grant's senses finally let him down and he failed to see the assailant advancing upon him from the side while he tackled a man in front of him.

The karambit was in his hand but fell from fingers made limp from a crushing blow to the side of his head, just above the neck. He dropped poleaxed, and as he lay on his back he felt hands grabbing at his clothes and hair and hauling him clear of the fight, further into the dimly lit tunnel and beyond the reach of his comrades.

His world spun and his vision swam, and in a final moment of clarity before the darkness took him, he looked up into the face of Angus Armstrong, archer and assassin.

'Well now, lad – or should I say devil, since that's what the boys around here have taken to calling you,' he said. 'Sir Robert would like a word, if you don't mind.'

59

Michel Doukas was looking at his hands. He was perched upon a window seat in Prince Constantine's bedchamber, but he had seen enough of the city that day. He had therefore been relieved to find the shutters drawn and the room in darkness, save for the finger of light reflected on the disc of polished bronze by the prince's bed.

He was wearing fresh clothes, but his hair was still damp and the skin of his hands was puckered from the soaking. He had been by the hippodrome, close by the Church of St Sophia, at a carefully chosen vantage point overlooking the likely path of the procession.

Emperor Constantine himself had grown weary of the enervating misery of the citizens, their ceaseless appeals to this icon or that and the endless tolling of a thousand bells, the all-pervading atmosphere of defeat. He had been born into a city and an empire through which rumour and superstition were marbled like fat through meat. He understood the bottomless depth of their faith, their need for reassurance from oracles and auguries; most of all he was sensitive to – and tolerant of – their flaccid fatalism.

But enough was enough and he had told his advisers, Doukas included, what had to be done to prop them up before they dissolved entirely and sank into the dust beneath their own feet.

The time had come, the emperor had said, to call upon the Virgin herself. Constantinople was held in Mary's cupped hands, after all, and the people must see that she was with them still. Accordingly he had summoned the city's most precious icon – the likeness of the Virgin they called the Hodegetria (which meant *She who Shows the Way*) – so that it might be carried through the streets for all to see.

Doukas was immensely fat now, and his days of tramping miles through streets thronged with the grovelling faithful were definitely behind him.

Accordingly he had eschewed the march in favour of finding a location from which to watch proceedings as they passed him by. He was therefore in position beneath the eaves of the ancient and crumbling hippodrome when he heard the unmistakable sound of the procession.

It had been a decent morning – dull as usual, but still and mild. Doukas had been seated on his luxuriously upholstered bottom on a broad stone step that should have given a fine view. He heard them long before he saw them. He was hardly alone on the steps; around him were gathered hundreds of citizens, and at the sound of the Virgin's approach they set up their accustomed lament, throwing back their heads and calling out their prayers to heaven above. Finally the procession itself came into view, led by a priest in full raiment and holding aloft a golden cross heavily jewelled. Behind him came more churchmen, monks and priests, and then the common folk – men, women and children, all of them walking in time, singing or praying or a combination of both.

The Hodegetria was a sight to behold – life-size and painted, it was said, by St Luke himself. She was carried upon a wooden stage supported by the shoulders of a dozen monks, and as they approached, it was possible to believe that the Virgin was there too, inhabiting the plaster and stone.

All seemed well: the faithful swayed in time with one another and with the motion of the censers, from which cloying clouds of incense billowed and swirled; the voices swelled and rose together. Surely God himself would hear and look down

515

upon his children with loving eyes. So when the thunderclap came, rattling Doukas' teeth in their sockets and setting the hairs on his arms on end, it was as shocking and unexpected as if the Virgin had stuck out her plaster tongue and pulled aside her plaster robes to reveal a pert breast.

Women and children cried out in fright and the monks carrying the Hodegetria flinched as one so that the statue wobbled, sickeningly, and then toppled from the pallet and on to the soft ground at their feet.

If the women had cried out before, they howled now – and the men too. What worse sign could there be that the Virgin wished to be elsewhere? Doukas had risen to his feet, his mouth open and his eyes wide. The monks set down the pallet and clustered around the statue lying face down in the dirt. But before they could move it, let alone set it upright once more, a second peal of thunder rolled across the sky and sheets of hail-stones the size of peas, mixed with freezing torrents of rain, swept across the city. Within seconds the streets ran like rivers and a veritable torrent spewed around the Hodegetria until she was all but submerged.

Doukas had stood transfixed, oblivious to the drenching of the rain and the scouring of the hail. He watched in silence as men, women and children slipped and fell or were washed right off their feet by the force of the deluge. For all that the monks and others had struggled to right the fallen Virgin, calling out to her as they did so, she refused to move.

Shaken to his marrow, the cold finally penetrating his clothes and chilling his bulk, urging him to move, Doukas had turned from the scene in search of transport back to the palace.

The prince had listened without interruption to his friend's account of the morning's events. Normally it was his custom and practice to heckle and tease his erstwhile mentor, but the all-pervading citywide sense of grief and foreboding seemed to have settled upon his shoulders as well. Minutes had passed since Doukas had stopped speaking, but Constantine was content just to watch him as he studied his hands, first the backs and then the lines on his palms.

'I am growing old,' he said at last. 'I look at my hands now and see my father's. It is as though he has been within me all along and is now rising to the surface.'

'Did you love him?' asked the prince.

Doukas finished his examination of his hands and placed them on his meaty thighs before answering.

'I did.'

'Then it is no bad thing to be reminded of him,' said Constantine.

'I see his face too,' said Doukas. 'Every morning when I look in the mirror to shave.'

'Then you remember him every day,' said Constantine. 'I am sure he would be pleased – to know that he is in his son's thoughts so often, and not forgotten.'

'I remember everything,' said Doukas. 'Your father wants a record he can see, and pass onwards into the future, and so he has me write down what I have seen and what I have learned. You and I carry the truth of it in our heads; others would have it on parchment piled on shelves in darkened rooms. As long as the pages remember, they themselves are free to forget.'

'You should tell it to the bees,' said Constantine.

'The bees?' asked Doukas.

Constantine smiled. 'Something Yaminah says. She says beekeepers must tell their bees everything, or else they will feel neglected and up and fly away in search of others who will pay them more attention.'

'No one likes to be forgotten,' said Doukas. 'Overlooked.'

'Was Yaminah there?' the prince asked. 'Was she there when Our Lady took her tumble?'

The teacher was quiet for a moment, seemingly surprised by the question.

'If she was, I did not see her,' he said.

'How will you remember me?' asked the prince. 'What have you written about Prince Constantine of the house of Palaiologos?'

'It is all there,' said Doukas. He seemed happier on familiar ground. 'I am a historian, after all. If I do not write it down and keep it safe and pass it on, it will be as though it had never been. As though *you* had never been.'

'So sombre, Doukas,' said the prince.

'Are these not sombre times?'

Constantine did not answer, and looked at the backs of his own hands instead.

It was while the prince's gaze was elsewhere that Doukas felt able to begin telling him another story. Before long, Constantine was watching his old friend and teacher even more closely than before, but Doukas kept his eyes averted, anywhere but on the prince's face, as he told him what the emperor had ordered him to do.

As the story progressed, Constantine remained quiet but reached into a drawer for a handful of his shadow figures. He selected the fat Turk – the same that had always played the part of Ali Bey in the story Yaminah requested again and again – but this time he used a little pair of shears to clip off the fez. Now the shadow it cast bore a satisfactory resemblance to his old teacher, and it was joined upon the ceiling by the silhouette of a broken boy, a beautiful girl and an evil emperor.

While Doukas explained that his instructions were to go back through his pages and obliterate every reference to the empire's crippled heir, so that in years to come it would seem that he had never existed, Constantine worked his shadows with clever hands and had the boy and girl kiss, but only once and chastely, before the boy seemed to shimmer and then disappear, subsumed by the silhouette of the emperor.

'The emperor has his eyes on the future,' said Doukas. 'And he sees no future for the empire if it should pass to you.'

'To a cripple,' said Constantine, his hands and fingers busy with the play.

'He has loved you, Costa,' said Doukas.

'Not well enough,' said Constantine.

'He would see some cuttings of his tree transported to a place of safety. He might leave himself, in hopes of returning. He might send others in his stead. But whoever returns – be it him or an heir—'

'Then it must be an heir who walks on two legs – not one who is pushed around on four wheels. I see it all, Doukas. Be in no doubt. Do as you must with your pen and your pages.'

And all the while the shadow teacher had his back turned to the prince, so that for him it might be as though none of it had ever happened.

The door of the bedchamber swung wide, and while the armed men approached the bed, and Doukas kept his eyes to the wall, the young prince raised his arms in an attitude of prayer, or perhaps surrender.

60

When John Grant regained consciousness, he was seated on the floor of a tent, hard against its central pole and with his hands bound tightly behind his back.

He had a powerful headache and would have liked to rub the place between his shoulder and his neck where the weapon had come down, but the pain was of little consequence. What concerned him, when he opened his eyes and looked around, were the faces of the men watching him.

Seated in the shadows beyond a meagre fire, worn by years but hard like seasoned wood, was Sir Robert Jardine of Hawkshaw. There were three more near him and cross-legged on the floor. They were younger, but while one of them seemed vaguely familiar, he could not conjure their names.

Closest to him, on a little three-legged stool that barely raised him from the floor, was Angus Armstrong. A longbow was across his knees, an arrow nocked ready on the string. He was first to speak.

'Ah, there you are,' he said. 'How did you sleep?'

'Like a baby,' said John Grant.

'Like a baby,' said Armstrong. 'Well that is what we wanted to hear.'

'I am surprised to find myself awake and alive in your company,' said John Grant. 'Disappointed, really.'

Armstrong smiled and nodded.

'I can imagine,' he said.

He paused for emphasis and then added:

'I have been meaning to talk to you about your mother.'

John Grant studied the archer's face.

'Which one?' he asked.

Armstrong wrinkled his nose.

'Perhaps I hit you harder than I intended,' he said. 'Your mother? Jessie Grant?'

John Grant said nothing, just wondered in what direction Armstrong might be headed with his talk.

'Well, to begin with, when I first had her, she was Jessie Hunter,' said Armstrong. 'And then of course when I took her for my wife, she became an Armstrong. She was well ridden, I can assure you. Spent.'

John Grant's mind wrestled with the image of his mother lying with such a man, the one who had murdered her, murdered Badr – and who had hunted him all these years.

'We all make mistakes,' said John Grant. 'My mother included.'

'The mistake was all mine,' said Armstrong. 'The useless bitch was barren.'

He watched John Grant in hopes of a reaction, but his captive remained still, watching him impassively.

'I flung her away in the end,' said Armstrong. 'Flung her out.'

He opened his mouth and with finger and thumb freed a shred of food from between two teeth; he examined it for a moment and then tossed it towards the fire.

'And then your loving father came along, with you in his baggage, and scooped up my leavings. Helped himself to her worn-out cunt.'

'I imagine they were happy enough with all the inches beyond the worn out part,' said John Grant.

There was a snort of laughter from Sir Robert, and Armstrong blinked heavily.

'I wonder if you knew,' said Armstrong, suddenly.

'Knew what?' asked John Grant.

'About the nature of the arrangement between them.'

John Grant's face was expressionless.

'I think not,' said Armstrong. 'I think you do not know that Grant paid the bitch to take you in.'

Still John Grant remained impassive, but the archer's words had reached inside him just the same and he wondered if they were true or not, and understood too that he would never know.

'The word is, he arrived with you and with a purse of coins,' said Armstrong. 'The former was placed in her arms while the latter was squirrelled out of sight. Your mother's love was bought and paid for.'

John Grant wondered what if anything to feel while he kept his eyes, unblinking, upon his inquisitor's face.

'What did you do with her, by the way?' asked Armstrong. He had apparently grown tired of his game. 'After I skewered her properly with my arrow?'

John Grant remembered another grave, in another dark corner of his past, and wondered for a moment about the thorns; whether they had protected her all the years as Badr had said they would. For the first time in a long time he had a yearning to go home and feel soft rain on his face.

'I am more interested in your plans for me,' he said.

'Well for that you must hear from my master,' said Armstrong.

'Who's the dog now?' said John Grant.

He glanced at his mother's former landlord, heard him grunt as he stood up from his stool and stepped into the firelight.

Sir Robert folded his arms across his chest and looked at John Grant as though he were a beast in the bidding ring at a market.

'The trouble you have put me to,' he said at last. 'If I hadn't the loyalty of the finest hunter I have ever known, your trail would have gone cold long, long ago.'

'I was trained by the best,' said John Grant.

'Not quite the best, eh, given how things have turned out,' said Sir Robert. 'But never mind all that. I would much rather hear about Joan of Arc and why you are making so much trouble for the sultan.'

John Grant wriggled, trying to straighten his back against the tent pole.

'I would need my hands for that,' he said.

'I think not,' said Sir Robert. 'As it is, I am tempted to have Armstrong here cut them off at the wrists, but I have given my word you will be handed over complete and in good health. Now tell me where she is.'

'I wish I knew,' said John Grant.

Sir Robert grimaced, pulling his lips back to reveal broken teeth. He swept the stumps with his tongue and swallowed thickly before continuing.

'You see, if you would make it possible for my men to collect her, I might be minded to let you go. I will satisfy the Turk if it suits me to do so, but I would rather have the woman.'

'That won't happen,' said John Grant.

'I expected you to say as much,' said Sir Robert. 'Losing one mother might be considered an unfortunate accident, but two...'

'So you know,' said John Grant.

'Know what?' said Sir Robert. 'About your mother? Your real mother?'

John Grant met his eyes, saw the malice swimming there like a pike in deep water.

'Joan of Arc was mine,' said Sir Robert. 'Before your father got his claws and his prick into her, she was mine.'

524

'That is not quite the way she tells it,' said John Grant.

Angus Armstrong paced slowly back and forth in the shadows. Out of nowhere the thought occurred to John Grant that it was the first time he had seen the man indoors. He had the look of a hunting dog caught on the wrong side of a shut door.

'Have you any idea what she was worth back then?' said Sir Robert. 'Has it occurred to you to consider the value of a ... now how would you describe such a creature ... the value of a living saint?'

A questioning look passed across John Grant's face, and Sir Robert pounced on it like a cat upon a mouse.

'Do you not know?' he asked. 'Those Frenchmen truly believed our dear Jeannie Dark was an instrument of Lord God Almighty!'

Sir Robert raised a hand to his mouth, suddenly aware that he was shouting.

'Jeannie Dark talks to God – you know that, don't you?' he asked.

John Grant held his tongue.

'Well I tell you, lad, I don't need God or anyone else to tell me what to do. And I certainly don't need him to show me the way to the Promised Land.'

He paused then and spat thickly upon the floor of the tent, as though clearing his mouth of something rotten.

'I saw your mother for what she was,' he said. 'She was boxes filled with gold coins and fine estates in England. She was my passport – all I needed to open the doors leading to King Henry himself.'

'Are you quite *sure* you're not hearing voices?' asked John Grant.

Sir Robert eyed him coldly. He was old now, his teeth ground down to stumps and his hair gone. His joints ached and his heart along with them. He thought about what she would have done for him twenty-odd years before when he was still young, and his prick woke him in the night for more than pissing. It was one thing to live a life out of sight of dreams; quite another to have those dreams come close enough to touch and then slip past like strangers in a crowd.

'So what now?' asked John Grant.

Sir Robert was jerked back from his brooding, found himself looking into the young man's face once more.

'Long ago I needed your father,' he said. 'I would have put him on a leash and had him lead me to her.'

John Grant closed his eyes, reaching out for the peace of the fall.

'Now I have you. At long, long last I have you.'

'I won't lead you out of this tent, far less anywhere else,' he said. His eyes were still closed, the spin of the earth upon him.

'You misunderstand my intentions,' said Sir Robert. 'You will be my gift to this sultan of the Turks. I have promised you to him and he has made promises to me in return.'

'You trust him?' asked John Grant.

'God is great,' said Sir Robert Jardine.

61

Beyond the tent's flap door, in a fold of shadow, Lēna crouched and listened to the voices within. She was wearing an ill-fitting black robe, scavenged from the body of a defender, the hood up and wholly concealing her face, disguising her gender.

It had been easy enough to leave the city, and for the second time, when she heard about John Grant. Constantinople had been haemorrhaging its inhabitants, as those with the nerve and the will sought safety elsewhere. The soldiers might pay rapt attention to any attempting to enter the city, but shadowy figures making their exit were oft times overlooked as the spineless rats they were.

She listened to the voice of Sir Robert Jardine and wondered if her gift to him had worsened or improved his breath.

'If I accept for now that you do not know the precise whereabouts of Jeannie Dark, what about your father?' said Sir Robert. 'What has become of Patrick?'

'Dead,' said John Grant.

'Really?' asked Sir Robert.

'And you say your hunting dog is the best?' asked John Grant. 'I'd say you could do better.'

'Dead where?' asked Sir Robert. 'Dead how?'

'Did you hurt her?'

'Who?'

'Jeannie Dark,' said John Grant. 'Did you hurt her?'

Lẽna felt her soul shimmer like a heat haze.

'You would have to ask her if it hurt,' said Sir Robert.

John Grant watched him as he spoke, wondered at the depths he saw there.

'Sometimes ... sometimes I remember the taste of her skin,' said Sir Robert.

He paused then, as though confused by his own memories. Reminiscences and images left alone in the dark were wont to change shape after all, and now, as Sir Robert recalled his time alone with the woman, he was surprised by the thought of her eyes.

'Blue,' he said. The mean-spirited malice was briefly gone from him as the recollection held him in its thrall and he looked again at what he had once held, like a thief with a prize. 'Her eyes were blue.'

So intent was Lẽna on the conversation inside the tent, she failed to notice the arrival of the other eavesdropper until she was tapped lightly on the elbow.

She turned, knife in hand, to find a woman dressed as discreetly as herself. It had been a while since any had snuck up on her so successfully. She put the lapse down to fatigue – or perhaps age, God forbid – but she was impressed by the stealth just the same.

The woman said nothing; only raised her hands, palms outwards in a gesture of peace.

Lẽna held a finger to her own lips and motioned

the newcomer to follow as she crept away from the tent and into a pool of darkness by a heavily laden wagon parked nearby.

'*Qui êtes-vous?*' asked Lẽna. Who are you?

'*Vous êtes venus pour le diable,*' said the woman. You have come for the devil.

She was younger than Lẽna, but her face showed all the wear of hard years. '*Je peux vous aider, si vous me laissez,*' she said. I can help you, if you will let me.

Without thinking, still troubled by her failure to detect the woman's approach, Lẽna had spoken in French and the woman had replied in the same.

'How do you understand me, Muslim?' she asked.

'I was educated in the sultan's court,' she said. 'He is learned and requires the same of those likely to spend time in his presence. I speak the tongue of the Genoese as well, if you prefer, and also the Rus.'

'Why would I trust you?' asked Lẽna. 'And why would you help me – your enemy?'

'Your back was towards me as I approached you just now,' she said. 'If I meant you harm, I could have hurt you then.'

This time when she held up her hand, Lẽna caught the glint of a weapon there.

'What is your name?' she asked.

'I am Hilal,' she said. 'And the talk among the men is that Mehmet plans to skin your devil alive.'

'There is one inside the tent who is skilled with the bow,' said Lẽna. 'The rest of the men I can best easily, but not him.'

'I will help you free your friend,' said Hilal.

'He is my son,' said Lẽna.

'Then I am more determined than ever to be of assistance,' said Hilal, and her eyes flashed hot.

'Tell me why,' said Lẽna.

'This sultan is my enemy too,' said Hilal. 'He sent a man to drown my only son – a baby, but half-brother to Mehmet. I found him all but dead in his bath. I brought him back to life with my own breath – *alhamdulillah* – and we fled, little Ahmet and I.

'I am in my father's care now – he has my son. We travelled from the royal capital at Edirne, among the camp followers.

'I am sworn to strike back, to avenge my son. You tell me the one they call the devil is your son? Mehmet's men fear him like an evil spirit – and what troubles the sultan fills my own heart with happiness.

'I came to try and free him by myself, so that he might continue to torment Mehmet, and I find a mother, fighting like I fought to keep her son safe. It is the will of God that has brought us together.'

Lẽna reached out to Hilal and took her hand.

'What are you able to do for me?' she asked.

Before Hilal could answer, Lẽna looked at the ground beside them and saw her own shadow. While they had been speaking, the sun had begun to rise.

She turned back towards the tent and saw they were too late. Angus Armstrong emerged from within, leading John Grant and followed by Jardine and the rest.

Armstrong held one end of a long wooden pole

and John Grant's hands were bound to the other. He was hobbled too, by a rope around his knees, so that he could take only baby steps.

'They are taking him to Mehmet,' whispered Hilal. 'You must come with me.'

62

Prince Constantine was in total darkness. His hands were tied, but in front of him and almost as an afterthought. The men who had come for him – wheeled him away from Doukas in his contraption, with a hood over his face, and then carried him down steps and ladders before abandoning him on a rough, cold floor – evidently thought his crippled legs were fetters enough. They had removed his hood before leaving, but the blackness was so complete he could scarce tell if his eyes were open or closed.

He had thought he knew the palace well, its corridors and halls, courtyards and cloisters, but they had taken him on an endless journey, around and around, in order to confuse him utterly before depositing him in this hole. He had no idea where within (or apparently underneath) the labyrinthine complex of buildings he was presently imprisoned.

They had left him in a sitting position, his back against a roughly hewn wall of rock. It was already cool. He felt his body heat seeping out of him, into the stone, and wondered how much colder he might get. To distract himself he rested his head against the wall and willed himself to sleep, and perhaps to dream of flying.

Instead his thoughts turned inevitably to Yaminah and how she was to be married after all – though not to him. Before the soldiers took him, Doukas had talked and talked, wringing himself out like a saturated sponge until there was not a drop left. Constantine was certain his teacher had been in some reckless breach of his instructions – that it had been no one's intention for the prince to hear the emperor's plans for the future security of his line. To his credit, Doukas had not even bothered to plead with the prince to keep his indiscretion between the two of them.

When they had come for him, he found he lacked the energy, far less the spite, to think of telling tales out of school and making trouble for a man who had been his friend.

But for all that the wedding plans were going ahead, Yaminah was still missing. Having been locked for safe keeping inside the prison of Anemas, a darker hole even than the one in which he now found himself, she had escaped, Doukas said. Or rather, she had apparently been set free, by a mystery assailant who had dispatched three men-at-arms, favourites known to the emperor himself. More mysterious yet, given the circumstances and the evident skill of the lone warrior, all had been left alive.

Constantine thought about what a marvellous shadow play it would make and his slender fingers moved in the dark while he imagined the shaping of the figures he would have made dance and fight and run upon the pale blue sky painted on the ceiling above his bed.

Next he gave himself over to the sensations in his legs. The feeling was in both now, prickling and hot. If he concentrated and held his breath, and clenched his fists until the fingernails dug half-moons in his palms, he could move his toes as well. He tried to take pleasure in it, to day-dream about what it might mean, but here in the dark, somewhere deep in the ground beneath the palace, it was hard to see the pins and needles as anything more than a cruel twist of fate. There was pain too, deep and building. He might still die of thirst down here in an early grave, but on the bright side, he could move his toes.

They would come back for him, they said. He was to be kept out of sight for a little while, that was all. He closed his eyes and watched lights flash on the inside of his eyelids, and dreamed of dreaming about flying.

When he awoke, he had no idea how long he had slept. He opened his eyes into the darkness. All at once he glimpsed himself, as though in his mind's eye, and saw the hopelessness. He was helpless as a newborn baby and suddenly he was frightened too.

He had borne it all for years – years that had spanned the abyss between boyhood and man-hood. Others had vented their grief upon him or around him and always he had remained calm, seemingly untouched and untroubled. *Stoic* – that was the word they had had for him. He had heard them whisper it in a tone of admiration. Stoic – self-controlled, even in adversity.

533

He thought of walks not taken and games not played; of time trapped among the cotton sheets and silk cushions of his bed – days that turned to weeks, and then to months and then to years. He thought of shadows on a ceiling. He thought of a girl who had become a woman beneath his gaze and to whom he had given only stories of other men.

He tasted salt and realised that he was crying, and that he wanted no more of darkness.

63

'The gall of the brat,' said Emperor Constantine. 'She sends a message? To me?'

Helena had experienced her lover in all weathers. His temper was no storm, she knew – just the occasional flash of lightning. Stand still and the moment would pass.

He pursed his lips, his eyes set like dark jewels beneath his brows.

'Though I have to say, I suspect she may be the right woman for the job,' he said.

'How so?' asked Helena. She already knew, but it would serve her better to hear it from him.

They were alone in the throne room. He had come to her as soon as he had heard. He had been worshipping with some of his citizens, in the Church of the Holy Redeemer in the Fields, home to the Hodegetria. Since the storm, and her fall, the faithful had been shaken to the point of collapse. Keen to reassure them, or at least to be seen to share their pious concern, he had made the church the focus of his own worship. A runner had come, bearing word from his consort, and he had cut short his time with them so as to hasten to the palace.

'How so?' said Helena again.

'Well, if my son lacks a backbone, it seems his intended bride does not.'

He stood up from the throne and walked forward, down the two steps, until he was beside Helena on the floor of the cavernous chamber.

'Tell me her words again,' he said. 'Just as they were repeated to you.'

Helena cleared her throat.

'She said, "Leave me be now, and I will do as you command. I will attend the Church of St Sophia at the appointed time and you will see me there."'

'And that is all?' asked the emperor. 'That is all she told her messenger to say?'

Helena nodded and looked down at the floor.

'And the messenger?' asked Constantine. 'He knew nothing more?'

'It appears Yaminah sent the message through several hands,' she said, shaking her head. 'The one who brought it to me was the last in a long line. He had not seen her, and neither had the man who passed it to him.'

Constantine threw his head back and laughed aloud.

'The gall of it,' he said again. 'The little bitch has the makings of an empress, I say. And a scheming one at that.'

'What would you have us do?' asked Helena.

He stepped in close and placed both hands upon her hips. She pushed forward so that they were pressed together. She smelled of warmth and sweet spice, and he pushed too. He looked into her dark eyes as she considered his evident need with cool detachment. Her hips were saying yes but her face was only a maybe. He leaned in to kiss her but she pulled back. He paused, surprised.

'Another woman dares to make me wait,' he said.

'Would you have me here?' she said, and she smiled.

He let go of her then and turned away, but the scent of her stayed with him like a doubt.

'Tell me what must be done,' she said.

He took half a dozen paces and then turned to face her once more.

'She will come,' he said. 'Her spirit pleases me. Her nerve will serve her well. Our stand-in prince might look the part, but the ruse will work only if it has depth. I do believe Princess Yaminah will play her part better than I had imagined.'

64

John Grant hung ready on the skinner's frame, naked and tied by his wrists and ankles to wooden beams and poles set deeply into the soft ground. More than anything else, he was aware of his exposed genitals, his testicles so shrunk by anxiety his scrotum felt like half a walnut protruding from between his legs.

Before him, lined up in their hundreds (if not their thousands, it was hard to tell), were serried ranks of the soldiers of the Ottoman army. The next few minutes had clearly been set aside for the edification of the men – and it seemed he was to be the principal teaching tool.

Here at the mercy of all his foes at last was the devil who had moved among them in the tunnels like smoke, killing at will and turning them into human torches. But he was plainly not a devil. He was a man and no more, an infidel, and he had lost and they had won and now he would be made to pay.

While he had been led among the tents, on the way to the sultan's enclosure, Armstrong had taken the trouble to tell him what lay in store – that he was to be skinned in front of the Turks.

'I have seen them do it,' said Armstrong. 'It is not so much a skinning as an undressing. It is the custom of the Turks to hang the man up and make an incision right around his waist, just below the navel. It is often a woman's task, and if she knows her trade she cuts through the skin only, leaving the muscles undamaged. As the blood begins to flow, she slides both thumbs into the wound, grabs a handful of the cut skin, and tugs it down towards the fellow's knees like a pair of breeches. Then she does the same with the top half, hauling the skin of the belly and chest up towards the shoulders like a semmit. He is left then, in the sun. Death comes when it comes, but never quickly. Any minute now, John Grant – and you'll be singing.'

Between John Grant and the audience stood Sultan Mehmet II himself. He wore long white robes and his hair was wound in a turban. He was powerfully built, and tall – taller than John Grant. While the Scot was lithe and light, the Turk was all heaviness and bulk; thick-necked, broad-shouldered and barrel-chested, he was set upon the ground like a bull.

In the front row, in a clump towards the right of John Grant's field of vision, stood Angus Armstrong and Sir Robert Jardine and the rest of the Scots.

'Hear me now,' said Mehmet.

He had not needed to shout. His voice was propelled from the great chamber of his chest by all the confidence of a young god and reached the ears of every member of his audience like thoughts conjured into being inside their heads. He held them in his hands and he knew it.

Before him on the ground was a brightly coloured carpet, intricately woven with threads of gold, red, blue and green and designed and made so that it had something of the appearance of a large map. It was square, each side the length of a man, and upon it, at the centre, was a large, ripe red apple.

'The Greek citizens beyond these walls have a word, *poema*, which means something that is crafted and made,' he said. 'It is a good word. This task we have set ourselves may be accomplished only by the craft and work of our hands. The taking of the Great City, which the Prophet himself has promised us, will be our finest *poema*, which our people will know by heart and repeat for a thousand generations.

'Within the Great City, outside their greatest church, is a tall column of stone, and atop it a marble statue stands – a horseman. In his left hand he holds a globe that is the whole world. For as long as the statue remains on its plinth, the Greeks believe their emperor shall be the master of all.

'I say to you, my brothers – my hawks and my lions – that the whole world is an apple ripe for the picking. It is hanging before us, within our grasp.'

Mehmet looked down at the carpet in front of him and spread his arms wide as he considered the fruit at its centre.

'Who among you shall show us how this apple – this ripe red apple – is to be picked up without the need to tread upon the carpet?'

In spite of himself, John Grant watched the spectacle. Within the crowd, her face concealed behind a scarf and beneath the hood of her robe, Lẽna watched too.

A ripple of movement ran through the men so that for an instant they had the look of a field of corn moved by a gust of wind. There was a murmur of voices too, and a shuffling of feet, but no one spoke up and none stepped forward to face the challenge.

Mehmet shook his head as he looked out at the faces of his men. 'Do you not see?' he asked. 'Is there none among you able to seize the fruit?'

He paused.

'So I must do everything for you,' he said. 'Now turn around – all of you – until your backs are towards me.'

Mehmet had seen to it that his horde had been assembled on high ground, and when they turned from him they were faced towards the Great City and the Golden Horn – the inlet of the sea that had provided safe anchorage for imperial fleets for more than eleven millennia.

Access to the Horn from the Bosphorus was jealously controlled by the emperor, and in a time of war like this, its entrance was barred completely by a massive steel chain – each link as big as a man – that was raised across its narrow mouth from one side to the other.

The sultan's army turned, and for a few moments there was only confusion as men babbled among themselves, unsure what might befall them next.

'Watch now,' said Mehmet. 'See what I do for you – see how everything is possible if I so command it.'

As the last of his words soared over their heads – and as John Grant strained to see and Lẽna opened her eyes wide in wonder – the first of a fleet of galleys hove into view on the horizon. Each was crewed by men, and the oars moved in steady rhythm, but there was no water beneath their hulls and it was upon the land that they seemed to float. Mehmet's army watched in awe, calling out in their amazement and disbelief.

It was wondrous, and yet it was real. One by one the galleys left the waters of the Bosphorus and travelled uphill, over open ground and towards the Golden Horn. A great cheering began, building into a roar as the men realised the significance of what they were seeing. Horns began to blare and drums were beaten in a frenzy as the fleet made its steady, impossible progress over dry land towards the soft belly of their foe.

'No obstacle shall defy us,' said Mehmet.

The words were for his own hearing rather than that of his men.

He watched their incomprehension, revelled in it. Without the knowledge of his fighting men – and under the noses of the Christians – he had had his engineers build a roadway of timber logs greased with animal fat, all the way from the shore of the Bosphorus in the east to the waters of the Golden Horn in the west. Each galley was lifted from the water on a specially built cradle that could be lowered into the water on ropes and positioned beneath the hull. Teams of strong men then bent their backs and used no more than the power of their muscles to haul the vessels on to the rollers and overland until they reached the Horn.

When the first of the galleys splashed into the water – like barracuda let loose in a rock pool filled with plump goldfish – the cheers of the Turks rose to a crescendo, horns blew loudly enough to deafen those standing close by, and drums were pounded until their skins split.

'Now that I have shown you how our fleet can be made to float upon the dry ground of the infidel, if I so wish it, is there still none among you with the wit to see how this ripe apple might be picked?'

Suddenly remembering the bright carpet and the red fruit upon it, they turned to face Mehmet once more.

'Whoever solves the riddle shall carve the first cut into the devil's hide,' he said, and turned to look at John Grant as though only that moment noticing he was there at all.

He walked over to his captive and, standing to one side of him, grabbed a fistful of John Grant's hair and pulled back his head so that his face was clear for all to see.

The soldiers jeered and catcalled and John Grant was sure his testicles shrank tighter still, until it seemed they must soon be completely reabsorbed by his body.

Mehmet let go so that John Grant's head drooped forward – and while it was still on the move downwards, he landed a back-handed slap across the handsome young face with all of his strength. At the sharp sound of the blow the horde fell silent, expectant. John Grant made not a sound, but blood filled his nose and mouth and he spat it upon the ground. The glob of blood and mucus shone in the weak sunlight.

Without raising his head, still gazing at the sheen of it, he began to speak, in a voice clear and strong.

'Proclaim: in the name of thy Lord who created,' he said. 'Who created man from a blood clot.'

He spoke in the tongue of the Ottomans, which he had learned from Badr Khassan. From the soldiers who heard him came shouts of surprise, even disbelief.

Mehmet stepped close to John Grant, but did not lay a hand on him this time.

'How is it that you know the word of God, infidel?' he asked.

John Grant ignored him, remaining immobile.

'Proclaim! And thy Lord is the most generous, who teaches by the pen,' he said. 'Teaches man what he knew not.'

'Tell me, infidel!' shouted Mehmet. 'Who taught you these verses?'

There was a pause then, while John Grant spat more blood on to the dirt at the sultan's feet. Tiny droplets of it bounced upon the dust and turned into a spray that travelled unseen on to the hem of his white garments. John Grant looked at Mehmet from the corners of his hazel eyes, hazel eyes flecked with gold that sparkled like little suns.

'I learned them from my father, Badr Khassan, who is worth ten thousand of you.'

Mehmet drew back his hand to strike John Grant a second time, but before he had time to unleash the blow, a new voice rose into the sky like a bird.

'I will take the apple,' said Lẽna.

There had been a loud hubbub as the men considered the honour of running a blade across the belly of the murderous infidel while the whole army looked on. At the sound of one clear voice cutting through the chatter, like a hand through smoke, every man closed his mouth and craned his neck or rose on his toes in search of the claimant.

'I will take the apple,' said Lẽna again, and this time the sultan himself located the owner of the voice. Distracted from the impertinence of his prisoner, he pointed at her where she stood, her identity and gender still concealed by hood and scarf. With a cupping movement of one hand he indicated that it was time to stand before him, before them all, and provide the solution to the puzzle.

John Grant felt a vibration playing upon the outer edge of his senses. It was not the push – rather it was reaching his skin through the timbers of the frame to which he was bound by leather straps.

'Come, then,' said Mehmet, and Lēna began to shoulder her way through the crowd. Reaching the front rank, she emerged into full view of the silent assembled mass and stepped confidently towards the white-robed sultan.

Without a word she began slowly to circle the carpet, her eyes fixed upon the prize at its centre. Whether consciously or unconsciously, Mehmet began to circle too, at the same speed but in the opposite direction, so that his movements were as a mirror to her own. When she was closest to John Grant, and with the sultan opposite and furthest away, his face a mask of concentration as he stared at this most daring of his soldiers, she stopped.

Her face was concealed from the nose down-wards, but her eyes were clear of the scarf. She looked at the sultan, held his gaze for a second, and then dropped to her knees.

The assembled horde might have thought she was about to pray towards the east, or simply to beg forgiveness from the sultan for having made too bold a claim. There was a moment of silence then, while no one moved – and then a collective intake of breath as she took one side of the carpet with both hands and began to roll it up. She shuffled forward on her knees as she did so, and as she drew closer and closer to the red apple, understanding travelled among the men, and a sound began and then grew steadily until it was like the hum of a hundred thousand bees.

A moment later and Lẽna had rolled the carpet all the way to the apple. Swiftly she took it in one hand and stood and turned and walked lightly back to the point from which she had started. Without her weight upon it, the carpet unfurled and settled back upon the ground with a soft sound like a sigh.

Lẽna turned and held the red apple high, and sunlight glinted upon its polished skin.

For John Grant alone, blood still dripping from his nose, it was the building vibration that mattered more than the trick with the apple. With so much upon which to focus attention, no one else had noticed – not even the sultan, who was a clever man and who prided himself, among many other things, upon the acuity of his senses.

Suddenly – and to the gasping amazement of all – Lẽna insolently tossed the apple towards the sultan. It seemed her aim was bad, for the fruit sailed high and seemed certain to pass over Mehmet's head. In the heat of the moment, as surprised as the next man, he forgot himself and his status and let his instincts and reactions take over. He crouched low and then sprang upwards, arms stretched above his head as he aimed to catch the thing.

It was in that moment, while the sultan was in mid-air, his slippered feet flailing, that the vibration John Grant had been monitoring all the while became at once the roar of a descending wave. Mehmet caught the apple in both hands and landed just as the front rank of stampeding oxen burst into view, driving the Turkish tents ahead of them like white foam in front of a tidal surge. The foremost animals, the leaders of the massed herd, had flaming rags tied around their horns. Wide-eyed, maddened by fear and desperate to get away from the fires singeing their ears and cheeks, the oxen understood only that they had to run until the flames were behind them.

Only two people had known to expect their arrival – both of them women – and one of them turned from the sultan and the army and leapt towards John Grant where he hung helpless on his frame. She alone knew who it was that had tied the oil-soaked rags to the horns of a dozen of the oxen as the first light of the dawn came across the land like silvered fingers, and then set them alight and flung wide the gates of their corrals and slapped enough hindquarters to build the momentum of the herd to the point where no man could stop it.

A knife was in Lẽna's hand as she reached John Grant and with one smooth slashing movement cut the ties at his wrists. Handing him the knife (Angus Armstrong's knife) and leaving him to free his own feet, she glanced around at the melee.

Confronted by the timbers of the palisade surrounding the sultan's tents, the charging beasts had broken around it, leaving John Grant and Lẽna safely in its lee. Once past the obstruction, however, the animals came together again and ploughed towards and then into the mass of the Turkish army, scattering the soldiers left and right and crushing scores and hundreds beneath pounding hooves.

Mehmet watched, awestruck and aghast – and with all thoughts of ritual torture driven from his mind.

Lẽna had spotted the figure of Sir Robert Jardine; indeed she had sensed him while she waited in the lines and had looked around and glimpsed the back of his head.

As the beasts bore down upon the sultan's flock, she looked for him again and found his face. While the thousands fled, he stood his ground, his sword gripped tightly in his fist. But it was no warrior that challenged him now, defied his will. Instead a monstrous bull bore down on him, as tall as a man at its shoulder and its horns ablaze from root to tip. Enraged and terrified in equal measure, it sought relief from its ills in the violence of its charge.

There before it, frozen in place and with eyes wide, stood a movable object. Perhaps this two-legged creature was to blame for the pain and the terror. Perhaps its destruction would bring peace. In any event the bull came on, making the earth shake and turning the air around it into a storm of dirt and dust, flecked with white spume from its flaring nostrils.

Framed for an infinitesimal fragment of time within the flaming crescent of the beast's horns, Sir Robert Jardine, who felt himself owed so much by the world, caught sight of the woman whose death should have delivered it all to him long ago. Her face, her ageless, smiling face, was the image upon which he closed his eyes and swung his sword and felt it land between the flaming horns before he knew no more, and for ever.

Lẽna watched him fall, spread-eagled on his back. One great hoof had landed squarely in the middle of Sir Robert's face, backed by nearly two tons of beef, and she would have sworn she heard, amid the tumult, the sound of his skull cracking like an egg.

She had a momentary recall of feeling that mouth clamped upon her lips, its tongue writhing against her own like a trapped snake. She saw his arms fly upwards beneath the bull's belly and glimpsed the hands and remembered them forced inside her clothes, between her legs and grabbing at her breasts. She saw all of his bodily destruction in a blessed moment vouchsafed to her by chance, and hoped the same might happen to his everlasting soul, and then she thought of him no more.

John Grant was beside her and naked as the day he was born when both looked then into the face of the sultan. He was standing quite still, like a white rock in a river. He turned from the devastation wrought upon his army and Lẽna made sure she had his gaze before she reached up and threw back her hood. Then she unwound her scarf to let him see her face, before she smiled at him.

She turned, pulling John Grant by the shoulder and taking a path around to the rear of the enclosure. By the time they had climbed its timbers – John Grant moving gingerly, as befitted a man with no clothes, and with his scrotum and penis dangling in the breeze – Hilal was waiting for them, eyes shining with triumph and excitement.

'Your baby boy is a fine specimen,' she said, and turned to lead them both away.

65

'What have you done with the girl?' asked Lẽna.

John Grant was clothed once more, in garments gifted to him by the father of Hilal. While he had dressed he had been watched, with innocent curiosity, by a little dark-haired boy who had looked to be perhaps four or five years old. He told John Grant his name was Ahmet.

The sky was shedding the last light of the day, and now he and Lẽna were alone once more and crouched in the shadow of the Wall of Theodosius. In contrast to so many of the days they had endured so far, it had been a fine one, and bright. The sky above was clear and cold. They had crept as close as possible to the stretch of ancient masonry by the Blachernae Palace, near to the Gate of the Wooden Circus. The postern there was tucked where the wall was sharply angled around one side of the palace, and therefore out of sight of the Turks.

'She is safe,' he said. 'When we left you in the prison, she led me to some basement deep beneath the palace. She was well acquainted with the place – said it had once been part of her home.'

'What was said between you?' asked Lẽna.

'While the two of you were alone – what did she tell you?'

He shook his head as the memory came back to him. He had missed, and by a whisper, the agony of being skinned alive, but he had never felt as raw as he had when she had broken their kiss and pushed him away. He shivered and wondered if it was the memory that had goose bumps rise on his skin, or the chill of the evening.

'Something about twins,' he said.

'Twins?'

'Twins,' he said. His tone was one of disbelief, almost amusement. 'Something about souls and twins, and some being alone for all eternity and some being together. I did not understand it then and I fail to grasp her meaning still.'

Lẽna looked at him as though the madness was his.

'Oh, and she told me she was to be married,' he said.

'And what did you tell her?' asked Lẽna.

He was briefly aware that she was asking more questions than she ever had before.

'That I would help her,' he said. 'And the man she is supposed to marry.' He shook his head at the memory.

Lẽna felt her own past pulling at her, like too-thin clothes tugged by a gust of cold wind.

'What do you remember about your father?' she asked.

'Which one?' he replied. 'Patrick Grant or Badr Khassan?'

Lẽna indulged him with a tight, thin-lipped smile before continuing.

'Patrick,' she said.

He sighed and looked away, off towards the west, where the last brightness of the sun was falling away beyond the horizon, leaving a crisp sheet of darkness in its place.

'I wish that I could say I remember him bouncing me upon his knee and ruffling my hair with big hands,' he said. 'I wish I could tell you how he taught me to bait a hook and fish for trout in the big black river that flowed slow and deep beneath the weeping willow trees not far from our home.'

She watched his mouth as he spoke, achingly familiar with the shape of his lips, the set of his eyes.

'I would like to say I had a clear memory of him walking hand in hand with my mother, or hugging her so tightly her feet were lifted clean off the floor. I wish I could tell you what he looked like, but I cannot.'

He fell silent then, still watching the last of the light, or his memory of it. His face was all in shadow.

'He looked just like you,' she said. 'Or rather, you look just like him.'

She felt rather than saw him turn in the gloom to look at her once more.

'Same mouth ... same nose,' she said. 'Same hair ... and the same eyes. More than anything else it is in your eyes that I see him.'

All had been quiet while they spoke. For once, the Turkish gunners had been stood down for the night. Beyond no-man's-land, appearing one by one like stars in heaven above, little fires appeared outside those tents that had either been missed by the stampede or salvaged and re-erected in its aftermath. The Ottomans lived frugally while on campaign and made only one meal each day, always at nightfall, and around the fires were groups of men, bringing together and sharing whatever provisions they had.

A siege was hard to bear, John Grant knew. While those trapped within the walls might think they had all the troubles to bear, weeks camped outside a city's defences were wearing and disheartening too. After weeks of effort, morale among the Turks would be dipping lower each day. However hard they fought, whatever tactics they brought to bear and near broke their backs to implement, still they were denied by Constantinople's ancient walls and by the grit of those few defenders spread thin behind them.

While the stampede of oxen had caused havoc and dispatched hundreds of men, most had escaped with their hides intact. It was a distraction – no more – but still it would have served to whittle away at the Turks' resolve. Hope in the camp would be running just as short as food, and if success did not come soon, the sultan would have to call off his dogs and slink back to Edirne.

But the silence John Grant had just begun to appreciate was all at once destroyed. It was a single voice at first – a Turk's, and raised in questioning excitement. Almost at once it was joined by more of the same until a whole crescendo rose above the city of battered tents.

From where they sheltered against the wall, there was nothing for John Grant and Lẽna to see – nothing to explain the commotion. With the hairs rising on their arms and necks, they stepped away from the wall and out into open ground, looking around them all the while.

Now there was another cacophony, come to join the first but in awful discord: a wailing lament by countless voices coming from beyond the walls, within the city.

Although John Grant had felt the planet-shaking violence of the volcanic eruption that had blown an entire island to smithereens (an island thousands of miles away and in the middle of an ocean then unknown to any Scotsman), he had had no way of knowing its cause. A man blessed (or cursed) with awareness of the world's journey into the universe and all its travails, he had felt the onset of the symptoms but had had no way of understanding the malady that caused them.

So when the cloud of ash and dust, which was all that remained of that faraway island, spread around the world's skies like the shadow of the angel of death, not even John Grant understood the truth of the darkness caused by it.

Instead he looked up into the night sky above the Great City and was appalled by what he saw.

He had spent enough days and weeks among the citizen soldiers of Constantinople to know the importance they placed upon the moon and its cycle. If the people put their faith in the Virgin – *Theotokos, Mater Dei,* the Mother of God – whose image, the Hodegetria, they could reach out to and touch and kiss, then equal hope was vested in the eternal truth of the moon that was beyond their reach. It waxed and waned and the tides of the waters that surrounded their city on three sides ebbed and flowed because of it. It was a constant, unchanging rhythm and it reminded them day after day, month after month and year after year that if the light and journey of the moon was old beyond memory, then so too was their city.

Their mothers had told them, and in turn they told their own children, that the city would never fall to an enemy beneath the all-seeing eye of a full moon. Just as there had always been a moon, so there would always be Constantinople.

Tonight of all nights, when hearts and minds were breaking under the strain of the worst siege yet, and the sight of the expected full moon should have been a fixed point in a universe in flux, the sacred circle was broken.

Where there should have been a waxing moon, a solid silver coin promising that all was well, there was instead a pale grey crescent. It was the day of the full moon and yet in its place, looming over the Christian city like the most evil of omens, was the curving sword blade of the Muslim Turk.

Unbeknown to all – even to John Grant, who felt more than any other soul – the miasma of the greatest explosion in ten thousand years had slipped unseen and unsuspected between earth and moon like a cataract in a human eye.

The sky was filled with voices, the jubilant as well as the broken-hearted, and John Grant reached out for Lẽna's hand and she took it in her own and clasped it tight.

66

Constantinople, eighteen years before

We see them first from high above and far away, a man and a woman dancing together in a room as white as the buildings of the city that are visible through tall arched windows.

We spiral down towards them, like a bird of prey.

Patrick Grant holds Isabella close and they smile into each other's faces as he spins them faster and faster, around and around, until they laugh and stumble towards the bed and collapse upon it, side by side on their backs.

Badr Khassan is known then only to one of them – to Patrick. The men are friends of long standing, but these are still the days before the giant Moor has laid eyes upon his Izzi.

For these few days Patrick has been Isabella's lover, her first. He is a wonderful excitement, a secret of her own to be enjoyed and played with out of sight of her father's possessive gaze.

She is lovely, with long dark-blonde hair and a face made unforgettable by high cheekbones. He is slim and tall, fine-boned and almost feminine, with a thin face and sandy hair and hazel eyes. In perfect synch they turn their heads and look at one another.

'I should be angry with you,' Izzi says.

'But you are not,' says Patrick. 'No one stays angry with me.'

She moves as though to land a blow on his smiling face, but she is smiling too and he catches her hand and kisses the knuckles.

'It is true!' she says, and she pretends to pout but he reaches across and pinches her at the waist with strong fingers, so that she buckles and pulls her knees up to evade the tickling.

He is lovely too, but his heart belongs to another, she knew that much before the start. He was wounded when they met and she has been a dressing on the hurt, no more. She will have him for these days and then let him go for ever, surely no harm done.

'My father would have your hide anyway,' she says. 'His prize bitch ruined by a wandering stray.'

'I prefer to see myself as a lovable hound,' he says. 'And you are what you have always been – a princess.'

She is quiet then, her face made dark, as though her own private sun is briefly obscured by clouds.

'You will still come to Rome?' she asks.

'Of course,' he says. 'It is our job – to protect the delegation.'

'You say *our*,' she says. 'Who else are you taking to Rome, may I ask?'

He smiles.

'I wonder what you will make of him,' he says.

'Make of whom?' she asks.

'Of my friend,' he says. 'He is a serious fellow. And dark, very dark. I just wonder.'

Isabella frowns at him, before continuing.

'And no one will know about this, about us?' she asks.

He shakes his head, and it is his turn then to be lost for words. He is far away, remembering another woman and a baby and a little golden ring that was both given and returned.

'Nor ever will,' he says.

He sits up then and turns to look down at her.

'This could only ever be a moment,' he says. 'You and me. We could never be. A Scots mercenary and a princess of the court of Byzantium? We must remember to thank our lucky stars that we had what we had.'

'And you will remember me, Patrick?' she asks.

'Us,' he says, placing one fingertip on her lower lip. 'Trust me, Isabella, we will remember.'

And the world keeps turning and turning, spinning into the unknown, and the force of it, constant and unchanging, propels us back and away from them once more, back to where we came from. They grow smaller and smaller, the image of them contracting like a pupil in an eye opened to the sun.

67

'I loved your father, John Grant,' said Lẽna. 'He did not believe it and I gave him no cause to, but it is true.'

He kept his eyes on the crescent moon and said nothing, but felt her thoughts flooding towards him like his destiny.

'I remember his face so very clearly,' she said. 'It is twenty years and more since I last saw it, but it is before my eyes even now.'

The sound of all the voices, the happy and the sad, rose and fell, waxing and waning.

'It is your face, because he was your father,' she said. 'And it is Yaminah's face, because he was her father too.'

68

Prince Constantine was moving his feet from side to side on their heels. He could not see them, since he was enfolded in total darkness, but he could feel them. It had started with a simple desire to fight back against the chill of underground. He had begun by moving his arms, cycling them in front of himself and rolling his shoulders forwards and back.

He had bent at the waist, reaching for his knees and then his feet. He had rubbed and massaged his thighs, even drummed upon them with cupped hands – all in a bid to keep warm blood circulating, fending off the cold. And then he had realised that his feet, his long-dead feet, were moving in time with his stretches. Once he became aware of it, he had stopped all other movement and concentrated on the rocking motion that had begun all by itself. Where would it stop? he wondered. How far would the feeling rise?

While he continued with his exercises, it occurred to him that the French had the best word to describe the nature of his prison. He had heard it from Doukas. (He wondered what his old teacher was doing now. Eating, most likely, adding yet more inches to his already ample circumference, or else hovering on the edge of other people's lives, watching and remembering.)

The word was *oubliette,* a noun made out of the verb *oublier,* which meant 'to forget'. The sense of it summed up his situation perfectly, he thought. They had told him they were coming back for him, but he had his doubts. If it were best he be made to disappear, would it ever truly make sense to bring him back again? More likely they had lacked the will to finish him off. Perhaps their master – his father the emperor? Helena? – had given them the impression it did not matter either way. Kill him ... leave him to die in the dark ... the end result would be the same.

So, *oubliette* – he was to be something forgotten. His mortal remains would occupy a space on loan from the endless darkness, and old Doukas would excise the rest of the proof of his existence with the nib of his pen.

The irony of it! Just as his broken half had begun to repair itself – just as his legs had begun to awaken from their years-long slumber, to remember what they were for – his father's tolerance of his predicament had finally run out. His legs might remember, but he would be forgotten.

In his place another Prince Constantine (harvested, according to Doukas, from somewhere in the empire) would stand – and stand on his own two legs – in front of an awestruck congregation inside the Church of St Sophia and exchange rings with Yaminah. He would give the people the last ounce of hope they needed – the living proof that the Virgin had reached out her hands to fix a broken boy, just as she would restore their broken empire.

They would appear to leave the city then, on a ship bound for a place of safety where a cutting from the imperial tree might take root and thrive, ready to be replanted when the time was right and the infidel Turk had been expelled.

It was all a ruse, of course. The stand-in was no prince of the house of Palaiologos – just a cipher. Whatever they had promised him, his job was done and his life over the moment he passed out of sight of the hapless herd corralled within the church. He and Yaminah would vanish, to be slain and buried and forgotten just like Constantine himself. It was the emperor who would reap the benefit of the illusion. The people of Constantinople would have had their faith restored, and with faith for armour they might take swords and cudgels in their hands and turn back the tide of their attackers.

If anyone would flee when all was lost, aboard a ship bound for the west and the setting sun, it would not be some happy couple. It would be the emperor himself.

But there in the darkness Prince Constantine felt ... now what was it? ... a burgeoning sense of peace. He wondered first of all if he had given up hope; if it was just the calm acceptance of fate. But no – rather it was like being at the hub of a spinning wheel that was slowing down.

Beyond the dark, beyond this *oubliette,* the final pieces of a puzzle were falling gently into place. Settled peace was on its way, and someone was coming.

69

The moon, the same that had risen as a pale sickle, shook off its shroud of volcanic dust and came to full before the end of its journey across the night. Long before then, while the crescent still hung like the sword of Damocles over the citizens, Mehmet seized his moment and ordered a final assault.

Just as the defenders were close to breaking point, so too were his own men. They were an unlikely fellowship – Muslims from Mehmet's own realm, Christians pressed from far and wide – and the bindings keeping them together were frayed and split after forty days. If all was not to be lost – if the countless sacrifices made so far were not to be squandered – then the crucial moments were upon them.

On the other side of no-man's-land, Emperor Constantine stood upon an earthen rampart with his chief commander Giustiniani by his side. The relentless pressure brought to bear upon the outer wall had forced a desperate decision. Throughout the day, and on into the darkness lit only by the ill-starred crescent moon, the Genoan had had the defenders prepare a last redoubt.

It was in the Lycus valley, close by the Gate of St Romanus and with their backs to the inner wall, that they would make their stand.

'Would you bring them now?' asked the emperor.

'That I would,' answered Giustiniani. 'By the light of this accursed moon, I would bring every man and beast I had.'

Constantine was still nodding in agreement when the horns began to howl and the sound of a thousand drums began to roll towards them out of the dark.

'How many are we?' shouted the emperor above the rising din.

Giustiniani did not have to look to know the answer, but he turned his head left and right just the same, surveying the thin line of fighting men poised and ready, their fatigue pushed to the backs of their minds as they readied themselves once more.

'No more than two thousand,' he said.

He looked around again.

'The Bochiardi brothers,' he said. 'Where are they?'

'At the Gate of the Wooden Circus,' replied the emperor. 'I sent them there myself. They will sally forth and harass those Turks seeking to keep our men pinned down in defence of the palace.'

Giustiniani smiled a grim smile and looked out into the darkness. Appearing out of the void were smudges of light, burning torches spread out along the front ranks of the attacking force.

'*Azaps*,' he said.

'Lambs to the slaughter,' said Constantine.

'We shall see,' replied the Genoan, and on his last word there came the sound of bellowed commands and the attackers broke into a wild sprint across the last yards separating them from their foes.

'Now!' shouted Giustiniani, and his command was repeated up and down the line. At once a hail of arrows, javelins, crossbow bolts, and shot of lead and stone was poured down upon the attackers. They fell like wheat before the scythe but they were in such numbers it made little difference.

Cruelly pressed from behind – by janissaries under orders to cut down any man seeking to turn and flee – they continued forward into the rain of death. Once their momentum brought them to the foot of the rampart, and as they struggled for a foothold on the soft earth, the defenders turned to their Greek fire, and great gouts of flame spouted forth and deluged the foremost of the *azaps*. The fire clung to them and they were roasted alive by the dozen and by the hundred.

Still they came on, urged forward by their commanders and even by Mehmet himself, mounted upon his warhorse.

For all that they were so few in number, the defenders held firm, numb to the horror of the killing and dying they were both inflicting and suffering. After a hellish hour of constant fighting, Mehmet ordered his *azaps* to withdraw. The defenders bent forward on their weapons, gasping for breath in the moments of reprieve.

Without needing to be told, they soon cut their rest short in favour of attending to the damage to

563

their redoubt.

It was as he surveyed their desperate work with barrows and shovels, lit only by the rising moon and the light from lamps, that the Genoan turned to find himself face to face with John Grant, the woman by his side.

'Well bless my soul,' he said. 'I had thought to find you among the butchered dead.'

John Grant's face was impassive, haunted by stories too long for the telling then.

'I had my guardian angel with me,' he said.

The Genoan looked at Lẽna, but she only shook her head.

'There are no angels here, I fear,' she said. 'Or at least I have not seen them.'

Giustiniani waited for the smile that would tell him she was playing with him, but none came.

He was turning from her to peer out into the last hour of the night when a cannonball from a Turkish gun smashed into the face of the rampart beneath his feet. The force of the impact tore a massive hole, and flung the three of them through the air to land in a jumble on the level ground behind the redoubt. John Grant was first to his feet and ran forward, back into the gap, a sword in his hand. Lẽna followed, and the Genoan too.

Realising the dire peril of the situation, those defenders still able to stand dashed in behind as a howling wedge of Turks surged forward to meet them. Their momentum was too strong and the defenders were pushed back beyond their own rampart. John Grant wheeled on his heels, hacking and slashing at the foe. Out of the corners of his eyes he saw Lẽna, and Giustiniani too, locked in the dance of death with one enemy after another.

For some moments the attacking Turks were flushed with the promise of victory. Thinking they would triumph at last, they fought without fear, almost drunk on the very air they were breathing, beyond the line of the ancient walls at last.

Only once in all their thousand years had an enemy penetrated Constantinople's defences. Those Christian crusaders had come in search of plunder – treasures to take and living flesh to defile. The Muslim Turks now taking their first footsteps inside the walls promised nothing less than the ending of the world, and their arrival was greeted with an awful roar of insult and defiance by those still standing.

The intruders' ecstasy was short-lived. Rallied by Giustiniani and the rump of his Genoan force, the defenders found fresh heart and pushed back once more, butchering the Turks where they stood until the ground was slick and slippery with gore.

Cowed by the fury of it, the last of the attackers turned and ran as the first grey light of dawn sent their long shadows ahead of them.

'Hold them, Giustiniani.'

It was the emperor, mounted now upon his horse and wheeling the beast around towards the Middle Way, the broad thoroughfare leading into the heart of the city.

'Hold them, and I will return with men from the sea walls.'

He spurred his horse and the animal reared up on its hind legs before plunging forward into the fingers of light rising above the buildings beyond.

The Genoan nodded and turned at once to

address his shattered and exhausted men.

'Quickly now,' he shouted, his face a mask of exhaustion and concern. 'Make whatever repairs are possible, as quickly as you can. They will be back among us within the hour, I promise you!'

John Grant turned to Lẽna and she met his gaze. Without a word he smiled, then left her to find a horse of his own.

70

Inside the Church of St Sophia, beneath the impossible dome that seemed to hang suspended from heaven itself, a murmur of soft voices rose to mingle with the incense smoke.

At all times, but especially in the low light just before the dawn, it was like being within the crystalline heart of a dark jewel. There were shafts and sheets of brightness from windows high above, but always too there were defiant, seductive corners of scented shadow, home to all the prayers left unanswered.

Upon the vaulted ceilings, acres of gold mosaic and the details of myriad marble carvings dazzled the eye, while staring down from the cliffs of masonry that supported them, the sad surrendered eyes of painted saints and likenesses of Christ himself bore holes into the souls of all who looked upon them.

It was cold that day, unreasonably and unseasonably cold. Many of the church's windows were broken – through the neglect of years or the damage caused by fragments from countless shattered cannonballs. Some of the doorways were open to the elements as well, the doors hanging crooked on buckled hinges. The miserable weather of the outside world had seeped into the interior of the church, driven by unchecked gusts of wind. Instead of hanging like languid clouds, the smoke swirled and twisted like unhappy ghosts.

Gathered there in the perfumed chill were those hundreds of guests who had been summoned by imperial command to bear witness to a miracle. They did not know it yet, but they were to receive a gift – living proof of God's mercy and the rightness of their cause.

They had come to witness the blessing of a union, begun on earth but soon to be made everlasting by the intercession of heaven and the perfect world yet to be. For those faithful of the Great City, tested though they had been, and to the very limit of their endurance, there was no death. Since there was no death (the Son of God having conquered the end of life upon his cross), the union they were about to witness between a girl and a broken boy was eternal.

All eyes, hungry for hope, were focused on the western doorway of the church, the place where the sacred mystery and ritual of marriage would begin. But while they expected to see the bride there – Princess Yaminah, flanked by escorts bearing torches and garlands of thorns to keep her safe from evil until she could reach the sanctuary of the vestibule – it was their emperor who stepped into the space instead.

They gasped, almost as one, as he appeared from the shadows garbed as a common soldier, the two-headed eagle of the house of Palaiologos on his chest smeared with blood and filth. He had men with him, brothers in arms and similarly grimed and weary, and they strode together, without a word, into the great church and towards its centre beneath the dome.

All heads turned slowly, following their path, and saw, walking towards the emperor from a point beyond the high altar, Prince Constantine.

There was a stunned silence at first, and then shouts of astonishment. Voices were raised in praise and thanks and men and women dropped to their knees as they watched him striding confidently and with head held high. He was robed in white, with the jewelled coronet of burnished gold resting lightly upon his temples.

Among the congregation were many who had witnessed the moment six years before when the princess had dropped like an angel from heaven and into his waiting arms. They had seen him reach up and out for her, snatching her away from certain death but condemning himself to half a life in the process. In the years since, some few had glimpsed him from time to time, in his wheeled chair, as Yaminah had pushed him through the halls and courtyards of the palace. And now here he was, made whole again.

'See how our son is restored to us,' said the emperor as he reached the prince and embraced him as a father should.

'Those of you that saw the likeness of Our Lady fall to the ground by the steps of the hippodrome and thought that she had turned her back on us ... see now that she is with us still, as she always has been and always will be. This is her work.'

Taking the prince's hand in his own, he scanned the faces of the congregation in search of doubters and found none.

'Just as our son has been raised up from his sickbed – whole and hearty – so shall our Great City and our empire be raised up beyond the grasping paws of the heathens.'

Emperor Constantine's eyes flashed fire but his heart was hammering in his chest. She had promised that all was well – that if she were left in peace she would attend her wedding ceremony and play her part. Now here he was, approaching the last of his prepared lines, and still he was one bride short of a marriage.

Suddenly the moans of rapture inside the church were replaced by cries of fear. Where before all eyes had been fixed upon the emperor and the prince by his side, now every face was turned upwards, towards the dome. He craned his neck and followed their gaze, and then opened his faithless eyes wide as he beheld the cause of their concern.

All around the interior of the dome were tongues of fire – not in hues of red or orange, but violet and pink, or blue and dazzling white. They flickered and flitted, faster than the eye could track, and yet for all that they gave the appearance of an inferno, they seemed not to touch, far less to damage, the fabric of the dome itself.

As the congregation watched in horror, waiting for the flames to catch and somehow bring the whole edifice crashing down upon their sorry heads, they cried out to their God.

'Lord have mercy!' they howled. 'Do not forsake us now!'

The cries mingled with more from the city beyond, and in ones and twos, men and women ran to the doors of the church and looked outside. The dawn that had been growing like a blood-red bloom only minutes before seemed to have retreated in the face of the return of night.

It was no familiar darkness, either. Rather it seemed thick, oppressive, and it leaned down upon the city like a black hand. All around the church and by the ruins of the hippodrome and in the city beyond, people gathered in tight knots and pointed upwards. More tongues of fire, of purple and blue, lapped and curled around the topmost parts of the outside of the dome as well. Then, while the populace stared open-mouthed, the flames came together into a single shimmering tower of light and shot up, away from the church and into the blackened heaven.

'God has deserted us!' they cried, and fell upon the ground, covering their faces with their hands. 'The Holy Spirit has gone from the church, and from us, for ever!'

Nothing more – or less – than St Elmo's fire, caused by the thunder-laden weather that was yet another consequence of the volcanic eruption far away, the sight of the natural phenomenon that had wrapped itself around the dome had nonetheless been more than the faithful could bear. Born and raised in superstition and denied the science that would have explained it to them, they saw the discharge of electricity and the resultant creation of glowing plasma only as a portent of doom.

It was then, as Emperor Constantine sought to rise above the chaos and restore peace and calm, that John Grant arrived at the western doorway of the church. He jumped from his horse and moved silently into the din of frightened voices within. Along with everyone else in the city he had seen the ghostly, unearthly fire that had threatened to consume the building. For John Grant the inexplicable event had only intensified his fear for Yaminah, his need to reach her.

The bottom part of the southern wall of the church was all shadow, cast by the massive balcony suspended above, and he stepped into the darkness there and began moving further inside. Yaminah would be here – she had promised him – and he scanned the cavernous interior in search of some sign of her.

In desperation – hoping that his presence might be overlooked for as long as he needed – he stepped out from beneath the balcony, turning around and around as his eyes sought to scour every corner.

It was while he was thus distracted, giving all his attention to the search, that he found himself looking into those eyes that were almost as familiar to him as his own; not his half-sister Yaminah's, however, but Angus Armstrong's.

John Grant had been walking forwards, towards the eastern end of the church, when the push had had him turn. He was therefore walking backwards, his arms outstretched for balance, when he saw the archer. He had hoped his tormentor might be dead at last, crushed beneath the thundering hooves of the sultan's beasts of burden. Some small part of him had known, however, and with awful certainty, that he would have survived. Angus Armstrong was his fellow traveller and therefore bound to him, never for good and always for ill. His compulsion to hunt down his quarry had outlived even the death of his master. Sir Robert Jardine lay dead, destroyed upon the field of battle, and yet the trail had still called out to the archer.

He was staring at John Grant down the shaft of the arrow nocked in his bowstring. His muscles were fully tensed, vibrating with the strain of resisting the two hundred pounds of draw weight in his fully flexed bow of the good red yew. He could have dropped his quarry already with a shot to the back, but he wanted John Grant to see the arrow coming, and to know who it was that had killed him. He was especially pleased by his target's open stance, with arms outstretched and palms turned up to heaven.

Suddenly a woman's shrill cry cut through the simmering hubbub. Whether she had wanted to or not, she had captured the attention of every member of the congregation, silencing them where the emperor had failed. Every last one of them turned towards the source of the sound – including Emperor Constantine and his false prince beside him.

They saw an elderly woman standing with her arm outstretched and her hand pointing towards the balcony above. Those among them with the fastest reactions turned their heads for a second time, in the direction she was pointing, in time to see an angel fall from the sky.

Yaminah had been waiting in the balcony above, watching the proceedings and considering her options. She could see no hope, no way out. Every avenue available to her led somewhere she did not want to go. They would never let her back to Constantine; she doubted he was even still alive. Her heart dropped towards her stomach and she felt dizzy with the grief of it. Maybe it was all a punishment, dealt out by the Virgin to punish her faithless heart.

She remembered the last time she had stood on the balcony inside the Church of St Sophia. She remembered her mother, cold and dead. It was at that sad moment that she looked down over the wooden balustrade and spotted John Grant in the aisle below. He was some distance away, walking with his back to her, when he suddenly turned.

She thought he had sensed her somehow and that he was going to look into her eyes and give her strength. But his gaze had fixed on someone else and she had followed his line of sight and found that the focus of his attention was a man directly beneath her. Nearly fifty feet below the balcony upon which she stood, he had a longbow fully flexed, the arrow pointed at John Grant.

Without another thought she had climbed on to the balustrade and hopped out into space, calling out as she did so.

'Help me,' she cried.

Her hair stood straight up like fronds of weed in the clearest sea; the folds of her dress billowed with the force so that the skirt ballooned outwards. Her shapely legs, exposed for all to see, were cycling too.

Caught all unawares and focused only on his quarry, Armstrong was undone by the sound of her voice from directly above. He looked up, relaxed his bowstring and dropped the bow and arrow to the floor at his feet. He was ducking his head and holding up his arms, torn between the urge to catch and the instinct to ward off the impact, when she landed squarely on top of him, so that she broke his neck with a snapping sound heard only by him, and then he dropped beneath the weight of her, dead as a stone.

John Grant ran to them, dread flooding his chest like cold water. He reached them, a jumble of clothes and arms and legs, and was crouching down and reaching out, readying himself for yet more grief, when she rolled away from Armstrong's corpse and smiled up into his anxious face.

'I hoped I would see you again,' she said. 'And here you are, on my wedding day.'

He cocked his head to one side, his expression a mix of confusion and breathtaking relief, as he hauled her to her feet and led her by the hand towards the door and the gloomy daylight beyond.

Emperor Constantine stood like a tree in the midst of a storm, reliant as never before upon the depth of his ancient roots, and watched them go.

John Grant, the soldier who had somehow summoned and tamed the two-headed eagle, and Princess Yaminah, who should even now be standing before the priest to hear her marriage blessed.

He felt the world, his world slipping and sliding

beneath his feet. Heaven had grown dark above his head and the sky was catching fire. The eagles had flown and the Holy Spirit had abandoned the church raised by Justinian a thousand years ago. It was time.

71

Prince Constantine waited. Somewhere beyond his place of imprisonment, a noise was steadily building.

He had imagined he had been buried so deep that he was beyond all contact with the outside world. Even in the blackness it was easier to concentrate if he squeezed his eyes shut. While he watched a display of pale-coloured dots and swirls of light on the inside of his eyelids, from neurons mindlessly, happily firing in the visual cortex of his brain, he paid attention to the dim sounds of battle.

If he let his mind relax and placed the palms of both hands lightly upon the ground, he could even persuade himself he felt the vibrations of it too.

He must be close to the city walls, he thought – and since the sounds and tremors were reaching him even here, the fighting must be rising to a greater pitch than ever before.

72

With Yaminah in front of him in the saddle, John Grant kicked his horse into a full gallop. He had no wish for an encounter with the emperor and his bodyguard, far less the necessity to try and explain what had just happened in the church and why he was fleeing the scene with the bride-to-be.

He had the girl in his arms, and while he struggled to accept that she was Patrick's daughter, still he was determined to keep his promise to Badr. The Moor had died believing she was his, conceived out of love, and so that love was his still. Badr was John Grant's father too (he and she were brother and sister no matter how he twisted and turned to get away from the truth of it), and he would see her safely out of this place before his debt was paid to the Bear.

If he would keep Yaminah safe, then the city must survive, and he spurred the horse all the harder, devouring the miles that separated them from the palace and Giustiniani and hope of success.

'Thank you,' she said.

He barely heard her words above the pounding hooves and the rush of air passing his ears.

'You came for me as you said you would.'

'For all the use I was,' he replied. 'It was you who saved me.'

'I did, didn't I?' she said. 'I don't remember jumping. I only knew that I needed to stop that man hurting you.'

'I have been trying to stop that man for half my life,' he said. 'And you pulled off the trick just by sitting on him.'

He felt rather than heard her laugh.

As they drew closer to Giustiniani's redoubt, John Grant's heart began to sink towards his boots.

The fighting was a frenzy of men, just as he had left it, and as they reached as far as he dared to bring Yaminah, he saw the Genoan commander carried like a crumpled bundle between four of his men. He barely had his horse at a standstill before he leapt from the saddle and ran to him. His comrade's faces were grey masks of concern and he looked from them to Giustiniani and saw the shaft of a crossbow bolt protruding from his side.

'He lives,' said one of the men. 'But he is done. We must take him where we can tend to him.'

Giustiniani opened his eyes. They were dark, the pupils dilated to black holes.

'I will be back,' he whispered. 'I promise I will be back, once they've plucked this flower from my jacket.'

John Grant glanced at one of the men holding him and saw him shake his head and look away. Giustiniani's eyes closed once more and the men hauled him out of sight.

The sky above was black with arrows, bolts and javelins. A giant of a man, a janissary, appeared atop the rampart carrying the sultan's standard in both hands.

'*Allahu Akbar!*' he roared – God is Greater! – and he thrust the end of the shaft into the trampled earth at his feet.

There were more Turks with him, slashing at the defenders to keep them from their giant, but they were cut down, and the standard-bearer too was hacked to pieces.

The pressure from beyond the rampart was building, however, and still they came on.

Then from off to the north-west and the Gate of the Wooden Circus – the same hidden postern through which John Grant and Lẽna had returned on the night of the crescent moon – came the terrible cry the defenders had feared all their lives.

The dread was ancient, a thousand years old or more, and it had lurked within the hearts of their ancestors as well, so that the sound of their terror seemed woven through with the bitterness of the ancient dead.

'The city is taken! The city is taken!'

A desperate wailing roar came from the mouth of every defender, but greater still was the distant sound of triumph.

Even Doukas would fail to find out how it had happened – whose fault it was in the end. Suffice it to say that some or other defender, returning through the gate from yet another raid upon the relentless numbers surging around the fosse, left it unlocked and unbarred behind him.

Some would say it was treachery that was their undoing – a Judas promised Turkish coins and his pick of the womenfolk. Whatever the cause, the door was left unbarred, and through it poured the first waves of the torrent that would sweep the Christians into the sea and out of Byzantium for ever.

'The city is taken! The city is taken!'

The cry, heartbroken and terrified, was spreading like a fire and reaching all the way to the citizens cowering in their battered homes or on their bloodied knees in the churches.

John Grant ran back to his horse and hauled Yaminah from the saddle. He looked into her face, unsure for the first time what best to do.

'Come with me,' she said, and she led him away from the fighting and towards the palace gates.

73

The last moments of peace for the Great City, the Queen of Cities, were to be had in the half dark of the Church of St Sophia.

Like a rock, or perhaps a mountain, the building raised nine centuries before by the Roman Emperor Justinian waited in the light of early morning. The flames of St Elmo's fire were gone, extinguished, and it was the scent of another kind of burning that mingled with the smoke of the incense.

Three miles from the land walls, the church would be the Turks' ultimate prize, and they were coming, sweeping through the city and pausing only to slaughter and to defile. Ancient folk tales promised the invaders wealth uncountable, stored in the crypt of St Sophia as piles of gold and jewels.

The citizens' own legends promised that the infidel might come as far as the great column topped with the statue of the emperor on horseback, and no further. Any invader daring to penetrate so far would be confronted there, so the story told, by an angel bearing a flaming sword. There in the shadow of the Church of St Sophia, the infidel would be cut down and swept all the way to hell.

The faithful waited. All thoughts of a wedding for a prince and a princess were gone like dew burned off a leaf by the rising sun, and the dark jewel was filled with the heartbroken and the fearful. The priests had closed and barred the doors as best they could.

There in the shadows, or high in the dome, or coiled around the columns were the echoes of all the voices down through the centuries: voices raised in fear by those seeking sanctuary; the astonished gasps of Vikings humbled by the impossibility of the space; the mumbled prayers of Russians lost for words and knowing only that they had found the place where God lived among men.

Everything that the Church of St Sophia had ever meant was woven through the fabric of the place, or suffused the holy air.

Prayer alone remained for the thousands gathered there beneath it all, surrounded by it all – and pray they did as the beast came on. Mehmet had promised three days of pillage, and there would be barely enough blood to slake the thirst built up by the weeks of siege.

Whatever the savagery, however merciless and depraved, it could be no worse than might have been expected in other places and times from soldiers of the cross. Frankish crusaders had raped the city herself in 1204; the Byzantines had visited similar horrors on their own enemies.

But in Constantinople on the twenty-ninth day of May 1453 there came the ending of a world.

The Turks swept towards their prize and no angel came, and the great doors of the church were cleaved with axes. Few would die here – rather they would be tethered in ropes and chains and even with the fabric of their own clothes and led away to slavery. Like most of the rest of the city's folk – rich and poor, noble and base – they would be property bound for the markets of the Ottomans.

From their strange new lives elsewhere some few of them would recall – indeed would swear the truth of it upon a stack of bibles – how they had watched with their own eyes as the priests took up the holy vessels from the altar and walked towards the sanctuary. All at once a doorway opened in a wall and the priests passed through to safety before the opening vanished once more.

When all the people were gone, taken from the church, the Turks would set about tearing apart the very fabric of the place. They would search in vain for the piled gold and jewels and settle instead for taking every single item that might be moved. In the apportioning of the spoils they would fight savagely among themselves, spilling each other's blood as every man claimed his share.

By the time Mehmet entered the city in triumph, with cries of *Fatih* – Conqueror – ringing in his ears, he would confront the truth of what he once beheld. Having dreamed of Constantinople like his father and their fathers before them, he would find a shell hollowed out by the weakness and failures of men.

The great buildings, the once fine squares and courtyards, the palaces, the columns and statues – even the hippodrome and the Church of St Sophia – all of it would seem to him like the crumbling bones of a creature dead of all seven of the deadly sins.

He would dismount before the doors of St Sophia and there bow down before God. He would enter the place and gasp at a wonder laid low by greed and envy and hatred, and climb up to the dome itself and look out upon the smoking, bloodied city and know that all of it was his.

He would watch the sad procession of tens of thousands of slaves – men, women and children. He would watch the fires burn and see the smoke rise and then turn his attention to the waters of the Golden Horn and the Sea of Marmara and watch as ships laden with refugees set sail for Venice and for a West already in mourning.

He would know that all of it was his at last – that Allah had coughed up the bone and the dream was over.

74

It was as John Grant and Yaminah were making their way through a covered cloister that a figure stepped from a doorway in front of them. It was the emperor's consort, Helena.

All three halted, gauging one another.

Helena was the first to speak.

'Do you love the prince?' she asked.

Stunned by the consort's appearance in front of them like a spirit conjured from the next world, Yaminah said nothing.

'Do you love him?' she asked again.

'I do,' said Yaminah. 'Of course I do.'

'Well so do I,' said Helena. 'Now come with me.'

She turned, heading across the courtyard beside the cloister. They were following her and halfway across the open space when the sound of many booted feet thundering on flagstones had them pause and look back in the direction from which they had come.

It was the emperor, accompanied by two men of the imperial bodyguard – the Varangian Guard – of Viking descent and with fighting in their blood.

'There!' shouted Constantine. 'Take them!'

'What treachery is this?' asked Yaminah. She turned to stare at Helena and ground her teeth in sudden fury.

John Grant looked to the consort as well, but

the expression he found on her face was one of dismay.

The bodyguards had vaulted the low stone balustrade separating the cloister from the courtyard and were sprinting towards them. John Grant sighed and drew his sword.

Helena was frozen, fixed in place and momentarily wrong-footed.

She turned to look at John Grant, then at Yaminah. She was shaking her head, all but defeated, when a figure, slight and graceful, stepped into their path ten feet in front of them. They stopped – everyone stopped – and the moment stretched out like a sleepless night.

It was Lẽna, and she crouched down, slipping her hands into the loose tops of her knee-high boots. When she straightened, she had a knife grasped lightly in each.

She looked at the emperor, and as she considered his face and the expression upon it, she would have sworn he diminished before her eyes. His shoulders drooped just a fraction and his face relaxed and his lips parted as though he might say more. He was less – less distinct, as though his image had softened and receded into a past ready to receive him.

'Leave them be,' she said.

Emperor Constantine paused and shrugged, and then slowly shook his head. His guards seemed uncertain, surprised into sudden stillness by her unexpected words.

She turned then to look at John Grant and found his eyes. She nodded at him, once, and smiled.

He nodded in reply, a smile upon his own lips, and then gasped. It was a small sound, heard by none but him, but it had been coaxed from his chest by the push – though not the push as he had always known it, the forewarning of danger, but rather a blessing.

She was saying farewell, this much he knew, and as the pause ended and events returned once more to full speed, he felt for all the world like a toddler sent on his way with a pat on the behind from a loving parent.

'It was I who named you Jean,' she said. 'You are Jean – Jean Grant – like me.'

John Grant blinked on the image of her and needed suddenly to be away. He swallowed and turned to the women beside him.

'Let us go,' he said.

They ran across the flagstones and through an arched doorway and into a corridor beyond. Helena led them through the maze, turning left and right seemingly at random. When John Grant felt they had put sufficient distance between themselves and the courtyard, he had them pause for breath.

'Where is he?' asked Yaminah.

'There is a tunnel,' said Helena. 'It is as old as the city. It runs from beneath the palace to a small harbour beyond the sea wall, where a ship is kept waiting. It was a way for the emperors to flee to safety in time of need.'

'I know it,' said Yaminah.

Helena stared at her.

'I know the tunnel,' Yaminah repeated. 'I should not, but I do. There is a hatchway into it from our old apartments, where I lived with my mother. I ... I used to keep ... things dear to me down there.'

She looked at John Grant but he gave no sign that he had understood; just looked at her.

Helena had regained her composure.

'Well the Turks almost found it too – though not quite, thanks to your John Grant.'

'Thanks to me?' he asked.

'The last of their tunnels,' she said. 'The one they dug along the line of the walls and had packed with gunpowder?'

John Grant nodded, remembering the fight there and his capture.

'Their miners almost cut across the old escape route. After you were taken – after the Turks were driven out – I sent men into the old way to see how close they had come to stumbling across the city's secret.'

'And?' asked John Grant.

'And one of my men fell through the floor into the enemy workings,' she said. 'That is how close they came. The floor of the old tunnel gave way beneath the feet of my men and one of the soldiers fell through.'

'And Prince Constantine?' asked Yaminah.

'The emperor tasked me with ... getting rid of him,' she said.

'I heard you,' said Yaminah. 'I heard you plotting against him.'

Helena nodded. 'Another time I will explain it all,' she said. 'For now, just listen and hear me when I say that you were not the only one who loved him. You were not the only one who wished to see him freed from that room and that bed.'

'There is no time now,' said John Grant. 'Let me go by myself. I can find the tunnel you speak of, and the prince. Lord knows, I am as happy beneath this city as I am in its streets and palaces. If there are Turks there in the dark now, then I would rather be alone with them.'

'We will meet you there, John Grant,' said Helena. 'And we will bring help.'

75

Yaminah had protested at John Grant's decision to go alone, but Helena saw the sense of it. Even from the heart of the palace they could hear the sound of the Turks flooding into the city. The rout had begun and would not be stopped. The prince had to be reached, with all possible speed, but for now it was sanctuary they required.

Driven by instinct, Helena sought higher ground. Leading Yaminah by the hand, she made her way to the bottom of a broad staircase and they began their ascent. At the top of the second flight of stone steps there was a heavy oak door, and when Helena hauled it open, they found a timber walkway leading on to the battlements themselves.

Beyond them and for as far as they could see was the massed force of the Ottoman army. It was moving relentlessly forward, flooding through unattended gaps in the walls and pouring into the land promised to them by the Prophet long ago.

'It is over,' said Yaminah.

'Not quite,' said a voice close by.

Yaminah and Helena looked along the battlements. There, emerging from another doorway, was the false prince, sword unsheathed and in his hand.

'So here we are, together again,' he said. 'I did so enjoy your entrance at the church. What a shame you chose to leap into the arms of another.'

'A shame indeed,' said Yaminah. 'I only wish it had been your neck.'

He began walking towards them.

'You promised me a wife,' he said to Helena.

'Do you really believe that matters now?' asked the consort. 'The city is fallen. The Turks will put you to the sword and take us into slavery.'

He slowly looked her up and down, his gaze lingering first on her hips and then on her face. Yaminah felt Helena bristle at the insolence of it.

'You have had your day,' he said. 'I would say you had a beauty of a sort once upon a time, but it was the kind that is thinly spread. I see the base metal showing through the gold.'

'We have all had our day,' said Helena. 'And I suspect that beauty, thinly spread or not, will offer no advantage on this one.'

'What is your name?'

It was Yaminah who asked him, and he switched his gaze to her and looked her up and down as well.

'I am Andrew,' he said. The innocuousness of the question had taken him by surprise and he stopped his appraisal to pay attention to her words.

'The first apostle,' she said. 'Do you know the legend of the last emperor?'

The fighting raged beneath them. Men fought and cried and died. Arrows choked the sky and guns roared, and yet there on the battlement, Yaminah had his rapt attention.

He shook his head.

She stepped closer.

'They say there is a sheet of parchment kept under lock and key in one of the churches – I do not know which one, so don't ask me. On it is a gridwork of little squares. The parchment is very old, and in every square is the name of an emperor. Every time an emperor dies, his name is etched into the place allotted to it. The first square has in it the name of Constantine, our city's first. Only one square remains blank – left for the last emperor of Constantinople.'

She paused to look at him and raised her hand to her mouth, seeming to wipe her lips with her palm.

'What do you think of that, Andrew?' she asked. 'Constantine and Constantine – first and last.'

He blinked, and she leaned in towards him. His lips parted and suddenly she kissed him, and while their mouths were tight together she blew with all her might and the bone, Ama's finger bone, shot into his throat and lodged there.

She broke the kiss and stepped backwards. His look was all stunned surprise, and then he dropped the sword and his hands went to his neck and his eyes opened wide. He was silent. His airway had contracted around the obstacle and he stumbled forward. Yaminah and Helena

589

backed away from him and he fell to his knees, clawing at his throat. He looked up at Helena, and then at Yaminah, and reached out to them with pleading hands. His face was darkening, a shade between grey and purple, and his eyes bulged as though they might burst. He pitched forward. His hands, back at his throat once more, took none of the force of the fall and his face smashed hard on to the stones of the battlement.

76

Like a loved one, the darkness took John Grant in her arms. The ghost of a flame drifted in front of him, fading to yellow and then to a blue that reminded him for just an instant of the flames that had leapt from the roof of the Church of St Sophia. Uncertain who he might find below, he had chosen darkness for his ally. He waited until there was nothing before his eyes but steady blackness.

It was the silence that sometimes felt overwhelming underground. He held his breath, straining with the effort of listening. The silence pressed against him from all sides and leaned down from above. He was a threat to its dominion – likely to make a sound and tear apart the quiet. Only the darkness held him safe.

He reached out to the side with his right hand until his fingertips brushed against the cool wall of the tunnel. Crouching, bent over like a half-shut knife, he took a step forward into the cramped space, and then another and another, and then stopped.

Instead of rock, his fingers felt empty space. He had reached a corner – a twist away towards the right. He moved sideways again until his fingers regained contact with the wall and began inching silently forward once more. Sometimes his hair brushed the roughly hewn roof of the tunnel and he flinched from it like a child ducking a blow.

In his left hand, his good hand, he clutched a knife, its blade curved like a tiger's claw. Experience had taught him that a sword was unwieldy in the tunnels, an encumbrance. He made no noise as he drifted into the darkness, all but floating over the ground as he felt for each step. His breath trailed noiselessly from his open mouth. With his eyes closed he summoned his consciousness and sent it out ahead of him, further into the void.

He had covered a dozen yards beyond the corner when, on an impulse, he stopped. He trusted his impulses, however slight. The texture of the darkness had altered. Where before it had been smooth and still, now it was disturbed, ruffled. Ripples, like waves from a pebble dropped into water, pulsed against his face and chest. Beats from an anxious heart.

There was someone else there, someone else trying to be silent but disturbing the peace just the same by being alive. He smiled. With his knife held low, he reached out swiftly with his right hand, straight in front. He touched a man's face, felt stubble on the chin and cold sweat. A gasp broke the silence – split it in two.

He stepped forward into the space created there, smelt the sour gust of the exhaled breath. His knife hand moved of its own accord and he found the ties binding the man's wrists and sliced them neatly away.

Prince Constantine took a deep breath, filling his lungs, and then released it slowly, like a sigh of relief.

'I knew you'd come,' he said. There was nothing before the prince's eyes but velvet black, nothing in his thoughts but the certainty of salvation at the hands of the one who had travelled from a great distance and for many years.

For John Grant, who had always felt the spinning of the planet and its flight into infinity, the world stood still. He was at the centre at last, at the fixed, unmoving centre of it all.

'It was you,' he said.

His mind was clear and the darkness mattered not at all. There was no push any more. There at the eye of the hurricane of his life, all was still. He reached for the prince's hand and knew where it would be, and took it, and for a moment it was as though a charge coursed between them.

With certainty so bright it was blinding, he understood. It had not been for Yaminah, or for Badr, or for the woman his folk had called Jeannie Dark. He pulled on Constantine's arm and the prince stood upright on legs that trembled but held firm.

'I came for you,' he said.

77

Lẽna was wounded. She had bested the Vikings of the Varangian Guard but not without paying a price. While the second and last of them was falling away from her, his life spared but knocked senseless, he had had enough fighting instinct to plunge a short, cruel blade of his own into her left side, below the ribs.

She had turned from the encounter and the wound to see the emperor himself drawing his sword from its sheath. Looking about her, in need of some moments to assess her injury and tend to it, she saw an open door in the corner of the courtyard and ran towards it with fading strength.

The emperor ran too. The lifeblood was ebbing from his domain just as the blood was leaving the body of the woman. But while he ran full tilt behind her, he felt the presence of another.

He had called out at the sight of the trio – Helena, Yaminah and the birdman – and had stood by while his guards made to take them. All of it, all that was unfolding now throughout the tattered remnants of his realm, was madness, and he had grappled for some sense to hold on to and to pull him forward.

And then the woman had put herself in the middle of it and everyone had paused as though placed momentarily under a spell, and he had felt at his shoulder the unmistakable presence of doubt.

He was forty-eight years old. He had sat upon a threadbare throne in a crumbling palace and his empire was a field of mud and corpses. He was successor to ancestors as cruel as any of the foe; heir to men who had intrigued and betrayed, tortured, blinded and murdered to secure their sweaty grasp upon the crown.

And now at the last he had set his hardest men against a woman, and seen them bested by the purity of her calling.

He had no retinue now – no more bodyguards or advisers or servants. His lover had turned against him too, it seemed. He was a soldier and that was all. His rank and status would make no difference and so he would do what soldiers did.

Lẽna concentrated on the way ahead of her. If she was to turn and face the emperor in this condition she would need a sword. Reasoning that she would find one among the fallen, she made her way towards the wall and the Gate of the Wooden Circus. Emerging from the palace compound, she spied the stone steps between the postern and the guardroom and leapt for them, landing with a groan.

In her pain and distress she looked up towards the sky and glimpsed upon the battlements above the slender figure of Yaminah, together with the emperor's consort and the princeling from the throne room.

No sooner had she laid eyes upon them than they moved, as one, so that her view of them was blocked by the corner of a tower.

She climbed, leaning forward to use her right hand on the steps in front of her face while her left was clamped tight to her side to stem the flow of blood. She could hear the emperor behind her, and as she turned and began the second flight of steps, he was close and closing.

Reaching the top, the fighting platform wide enough for six men to march side by side, she spied a heap of slain and lunged towards it. Seizing a blood-slicked cross-hilted sword from a dead hand, she turned to face the emperor, backing away from him and weighing the threat.

Constantine took a moment to glance along the four miles of the land walls and then off towards the city. A tide of men was surging into the streets and squares, attackers and defenders together in a hellish maelstrom of fighting and fleeing. Here and there, sprouting like weeds along the wall and from the rooftops beyond, were Ottoman flags. At the sea walls the sails of cogs and carracks billowed in the breeze, preparing to depart with those carrying the coins to pay for safe passage away from the horrors to come.

Suddenly enraged once more, he turned on Lẽna as though she was to blame and passed his sword from hand to hand as he advanced upon her. Perhaps he would find the revenge he sought within her lifeless corpse.

Lẽna's left side was wet and cold with blood and she was suddenly wearied. Despite the danger, she wanted only to sit down and take a deep breath. He came for her then and her soldier's instincts took over so that she raised her own blade and parried the blow. He was off balance, and as he passed her, she turned and planted one booted foot on his rear and pushed him forward. He almost fell upon his face, but caught himself and staggered and regained his balance.

She felt a fresh punch of pain and looked down and saw blood, dark on her inner thigh. Bad luck had seen to it that the edge of his blade had caught her as he passed, slicing deeply through fabric and flesh and the vital artery within.

There were no angels now and no heavenly voices. She inhaled deeply through her nose, but there was no fresh, clean air of the sort she remembered from her father's garden long ago. She thought about the girl who had burned in the fire in her stead, and wondered what she looked like when they had cut her hair.

It was the nuns of the Great Shrine of St James who had called her Lẽna. She had brought them firewood after all, and *leña* was their word for kindling. It had made them smile then, but now it felt to her like a cruel joke. She was Jeanne – Jeanne d'Arc, daughter of Jacques and Isabelle, from the village of Domrémy. She was Jeanne Grant, mother of John.

Emperor Constantine turned towards her once more. She was down on one knee as though seeking his blessing, but he raised his sword high instead and reached way back with it. In the moment before he could begin the downward stroke that would have split her in two like a log on her chopping block, he looked into her eyes and saw there the judgement of the ages.

He nodded, once, and lowered his sword, his anger finally spent, and would have reached out a hand to her. She might have taken it then, but as she looked up into his face, and saw only sadness there, she saw too a glint of sunlight upon a sword blade as it swung towards him from his left side and parted his head from his body.

Emperor Constantine's severed head spun – long hair like a corona around the sun – and flew over the battlements and down among the Turks, where it landed unnoticed and was trampled underfoot. His corpse stayed in place for just a fraction of a second before falling sideways, to the right, on to the flagstones of the battlements.

There before her, revealed by the toppled corpse, stood the princeling, still clad in his robes of white. His face was flushed and there were gobbets of snot and saliva around his mouth.

In one hand he gripped the little bone that had all but choked him to death. He had fallen helplessly and hard on to the stone floor, and as the women fled from the sight of him, thinking him dead or dying, the impact had jogged the blockage loose. He had coughed and hacked and vomited until his airway had come clear.

Once peace had returned to his thundering chest, his blurred vision had cleared and he had seen the little cause of his pain. Reaching for it, he grasped the bone and held it in one clenched fist, determined one day to make a talisman of the thing.

It was with a shrug of mingled exasperation and disbelief then that Lẽna straightened to face this latest opponent. His face was dark with furious anger and she wondered at the heat of his rage as she passed her own sword from hand to hand.

'I wanted his head,' he said. He cleared his throat and spat, thickly. 'I wanted his head and now it is gone for ever.'

She wondered how she was seemingly to blame for the loss, and shook her own head at him as she mirrored his movements, the strength ebbing from her limbs and her vision darkening.

'With the head of the last emperor, I might have stood before the sultan himself.'

Lẽna felt his words wash over her. She could see that he was talking but she was not listening. She paid attention to the tumult of the battle still raging below and wondered if she might hear another's voice above it.

Instead it was her own that she heard. She had not thought to speak but the words came fresh and clear, like water bubbling bell-like from a spring.

'Greater than the cup – though a gift of gold – in honour of what to me is given,' she said.

At the sudden sound of her voice, the false prince fell silent.

'He received my love as payment,' she said, and she smiled – not at the princeling, but for her father and for herself.

And it was in his silence and sudden confusion, briefly captured as in a net by the calm of her words, and blindly raising his sword to land a fatal blow, that he was undone. With no more strength to fight, yet certain of her path and determined to remain upon it, she thrust straight forward with her own blade and punctured his throat clean through.

She pulled the point free and the blade made a

rasping, sucking sound as she did so, and he fell lifeless to the floor.

She looked around then and saw the slick, dark trail of her own blood. She knew that she was dying, and it was with trembling hands that were hard to control that she stripped the fine robes from his body.

With what little strength remained to her, she struggled to pull the garments over her own head. She was smoothing them down and attending to her hair, black and cut short like a boy's and threaded now with silver, when she glimpsed the unmistakable glint of gold. Tucked into his belt was the coronet the colour of butter, studded with jewels polished *en cabochon*. On an impulse she stooped and plucked it free and placed it on her own head.

There was a flight of three stone steps beside her, and when she climbed to the top of them she was able to stand between two crenellations. She gazed out and saw that of the Byzantine Empire that had lasted for a thousand years, nothing at all remained. Upon the trampled field below, men fought their last with swords and knives and with teeth bared and fingernails torn.

She listened for a voice and heard none. She was Jeanne d'Arc and her death was long overdue, and she was happy now, happy to pay it.

She heard a shout from below, and then a rising roar, and when she looked down again, ten thousand faces were gazing up at her. The fighting stalled and for a moment they stared and saw a figure clad in shining raiment and wearing a circlet of gold upon its head.

For those with sharp eyes, there was too the sight of blood, red as claret and seeping into the fabric between the figure's legs.

The sun was casting the vision into silhouette so that it was hard to look at it and be certain, but surely here was Constantine Palaiologos, they thought, in Christ true emperor and autocrat of the Romans, come to face eternity with a sword in his hand and a crown upon his head.

At the end, only Jeanne d'Arc knew the truth of it. She stood upon the walls of the Great City and remembered how she had been shown her fate in the middle of a storm of thunder and lightning with her hands tied behind her back.

The Christian defenders would remember an angel come among them, mortally wounded and promising salvation in death, but Jeanne d'Arc knew that the angels came for her, and for her alone.

She leapt high, out into the sky and down, down, down among them, and the Turks fell upon her body even as it touched the earth, and hacked and sliced at it until she was utterly destroyed.

When later the head was brought before Mehmet as proof of the emperor's death, he wept, for his prey had eluded him at the last.

They had thought to bring him the head of Constantine, and believed it was the grimace of final defeat they saw frozen upon its features.

But their sultan knew different.

In their bloodlust and haste they had failed to see it was the head of a woman; a beautiful woman with her hair cut short like a boy's, and smiling.

600

78

When Yaminah reached them, they were standing side by side in the dark.

They had heard her anxious footsteps and known it was her – noticed too the approach of a pale glow before she turned the final corner.

Constantine had wanted her to see him standing by himself. He held his arms straight out by his sides for balance, but John Grant was close by, in a similar posture and ready to catch him if he should fall.

She had a flaming torch in her hand, and as she came closer, its light cast their shadows on to the wall of the tunnel behind them. Prince Constantine and John Grant looked into one another's faces then, for the first time. Like two leaves blown from a tree they had come together for just one moment of the fall.

For an instant the shadow had the look of two birds mantling their wings, or one bird with two heads. Twins, she thought, and gasped. Two souls entwined. With her free hand she fumbled in her pocket, feeling for Ama's finger bone – and then she remembered what Ama had done for her, and withdrew her empty hand, and promised herself she would remember to tell her.

And by then Yaminah was too close to her prince and to John Grant, and the image was transformed into a simple circle of black.

She dropped the torch and ran into Constantine's arms, and he held her tight. She squeezed too, and she heard him groan and relaxed her arms and leaned back until she could look into his face and see that she had not hurt him.

'All is well,' he said, and he stroked her chestnut-brown hair with the fingers of one hand. 'I will not be winning any races for a while, but...'

'But you are standing here before me,' she said. 'I love you, Costa. I always have and I always will.'

She kissed him and he kissed her back, and then she broke from him and looked into his face again.

'How can this be?' she asked. 'How can this be?'

'I owe it to this man, this birdman of yours,' he said. 'I drew strength from him and he draws his own, or some of it at least, from me. What else can I say? What say you, birdman?'

John Grant said nothing, but stepped close to Yaminah and took her right hand and slipped a little gold ring on to the middle finger.

He was about to speak, but the sound of footsteps in the darkness beyond them had him bridle and pick up the still flaming torch Yaminah had dropped.

It was Helena who led them – soldiers – each with a naked sword in one hand and a torch in the other.

Constantine turned to Yaminah, a question in his eyes.

'I was wrong about some people,' she said. 'But I was never wrong about you.'

Helena led the way once more, confident of her

path. Prince Constantine walked slowly, supported at all times between two soldiers. When they reached a small, heavily barred wooden door, Helena opened it with a long key from within the pockets of her skirt. Beyond was the Sea of Marmara, and a ship safely moored.

In single file the little company poured from the darkness, ducking beneath the low lintel and into the light of the harbour. Yaminah was last. She halted, still in the shadows, and looked at the ring. The gold shone with a soft light, and for the first time she noticed it was fashioned in the shape of a little belt, the buckle undone.

She looked out of the tunnel and into the light, searching for the man who was Constantine's soul twin, but John Grant had disappeared, as was his intention.

The publishers hope that this book has given you enjoyable reading. Large Print Books are especially designed to be as easy to see and hold as possible. If you wish a complete list of our books please ask at your local library or write directly to:

Magna Large Print Books
Magna House, Long Preston,
Skipton, North Yorkshire.
BD23 4ND

This Large Print Book for the partially sighted, who cannot read normal print, is published under the auspices of

THE ULVERSCROFT FOUNDATION

THE ULVERSCROFT FOUNDATION

... we hope that you have enjoyed this Large Print Book. Please think for a moment about those people who have worse eyesight problems than you ... and are unable to even read or enjoy Large Print, without great difficulty.

You can help them by sending a donation, large or small to:

**The Ulverscroft Foundation,
1, The Green, Bradgate Road,
Anstey, Leicestershire, LE7 7FU,
England.**
or request a copy of our brochure for more details.

The Foundation will use all your help to assist those people who are handicapped by various sight problems and need special attention.

Thank you very much for your help.